MW00714493

Taylor's best frien
vacation. Checking into an all male resort, he and
Sergio discover a dead body, which disappears. As
Taylor stumbles over it again, the probelms have
only started in this tropical paradise.

Taylor befriends the hottest male porn star,
an angry drag queen, and a mystery novelist,
whose new novel is paralleling Taylor's trip. Men
ar dropping at his feet, dead, and Taylor needs to
escape this trip to hell.

Mother Nature has other plans. Now, Taylor
must blend in and with the hindrance of Sergio,
he'll be in the spotlight for sure. This duo is turning
Club Fred into Club Dead.

MLR Press Authors

Featuring a roll call of some of the best writers of gay erotica and mysteries today!

M. Jules Aedin	Maura Anderson	Victor J. Banis
Jeanne Barrack	Laura Baumbach	Alex Beecroft
Sarah Black	Ally Blue	J.P. Bowie
Michael Breyette	P.A. Brown	Brenda Bryce
Jade Buchanan	James Buchanan	Charlie Cochrane
Jamie Craig	Kirby Crow	Dick D.
Ethan Day	Diana DeRicci	Jason Edding
Angela Fiddler	Dakota Flint	S.J. Frost
Kimberly Gardner	Roland Graeme	Storm Grant
Amber Green	LB Gregg	Drewey Wayne Gunn
David Juhren	Samantha Kane	Kiernan Kelly
M. King	Matthew Lang	J.L. Langley
Josh Lanyon	Clare London	William Maltese
Gary Martine	Z.A. Maxfield	Timothy McGivney
Patric Michael	AKM Miles	Reiko Morgan
Jet Mykles	William Neale	Willa Okati
L. Picaro	Neil S. Plakcy	Jordan Castillo Price
Luisa Prieto	Rick R. Reed	A.M. Riley
George Seaton	Jardonn Smith	Caro Soles
JoAnne Soper-Cook	Richard Stevenson	Marshall Thornton
Lex Valentine	Haley Walsh	Missy Welsh
Stevie Woods	Lance Zarimba	

Check out titles, both available and forthcoming, at
www.mlrpress.com

VACATION
THERAPY

LANCE ZARIMBA

mlrpress
www.mlrpress.com

Copyright 2011 by Lance Zarimba

All rights reserved, including the right of reproduction in whole or in part in any form.
Published by
MLR Press, LLC
3052 Gaines Waterport Rd.
Albion, NY 14411
Visit ManLoveRomance Press, LLC on the Internet:
www.mlrpress.com

Cover Art by Deana C. Jamroz
Editing by Neil Plakcy
ISBN# 978-1-60820-226-3
Issued 2011

Trademarks Acknowledgment

The author acknowledges the trademark status and trademark owners of the following wordmarks mentioned in this work of fiction:
Speedo: Speedo Holdings
Nike: Nike, Inc.
American Tourister: Samsonite IP Holdings
7-Up: Dr. Pepper/Seven Up Inc.
Tecate: Cerveceria Mexicana
Bud Light: Anheuser–Busch, Inc.
Jose Cuervo: Tequila Cuervo La Rojena
Pepsi: Pepsico, Inc.
Nerf: Hasbro, Inc.

This book is dedicated to my Grandpa, Steve Zarimba Sr. and Grandma, Jean Zarimba. Thanks for buying me so many books as I grew up and giving me the gift of reading.

Vacation Therapy has been a long time in coming, and many people have helped along the way.

My Stacey (Quade) this one is for you. You have always been my number one fan and thank you for all the faith you have in me.

Thank you Laura Baumbach for seeing the fun in this book and giving Taylor and Sergio a chance to run wild in Mexico. Next Neil Plakcy, editor and friend, thanks for keeping me honest and making this book even better.

In Sioux Falls, the "Writers Without a Clause", Georgia Totten, Thea Miller Ryan, Nancy Steedle, and Amy Holm, thanks for listening to this book one chapter a week for over a year.

This book all started from a trip Dennis Peterson and I took to St. Martin in the middle of hurricane season, when the co-pilot's window blew out, we should have known better.

Thanks to Pat Dennis, Marilyn Victor, Wendy Nelson, Chris Everheart, and Gary Bush for helping with the Minneapolis version of this book. Pat and Gary at Once Upon A Time for making me feel like an author, even with only one short story.

Gary Johnson for all the fun at Bouchercon and Mayhem in the Midlands conferences.

Marilyn Meredith for the great critique that started the ball rolling.

Doris Ann Norris for supporting this book the first time around.

Paul McKenzie for all the support and love I could ever want or need. Thanks for your faith in my skills.

Ripley, I know you've listened to this book over and over again, thanks for taking me out for a ride, a walk, and a run around the house with your cape. Riley, I miss you.

I heard the sound of the shower running as I knocked on the bathroom door.

No answer.

Entering, I said, "I'm sorry. Can you forgive me?" The forceful spray drowned out my quiet apology.

No response.

I spoke louder. "Are you okay?" I didn't see anything move behind the curtain. Stepping closer, I strained to hear. Only the sound of running water echoed in the small space.

A part of the shower curtain hung over the edge of the tub. A rivulet of water splattered on the tile, pooling into a rusty puddle.

"Is that water clean?"

Still no response.

Had he slipped and hit his head?

Panicked, I ripped the curtain open.

No one stood in the tub, but a big man lay in there on his back. His chin rested on his hairy chest as the water ran over him. Blood poured from his neck, ran along the opening of his black leather vest, and soaked into his denim shorts.

Bending over, I checked to see if he was breathing. As I reached down to feel for a pulse, a hand grabbed my shoulder.

I let out an unmanly shriek and turned…

CHAPTER 1 - BLIND FAITH

A week in Mexico sounded like the perfect vacation; hot sun baking down on a sea of tan skin, while ocean waves gently broke on the white, sandy beaches. A soft breeze would caress the sweat from my brow as I read book after book and drank tall drinks with umbrellas in them. The ideal vacation spot; no phones, no patients, and no responsibilities. All alone. Just food, drinks, sun, and sleep. What more could I want?

Beads of perspiration ran down my brow as I finally found the right gate for the special charter flight to the all-inclusive resort. Everything I needed was jammed into one large carry-on. With the tropical temperatures, shorts and T-shirts didn't take up much room. My books took up more space than my clothing.

Was I finally in the right place? Everyone in the waiting area was male, and they all had deep, dark tans. They all looked like they had just come back from vacation, not like they were going *on* vacation.

I rubbed my arm, pale from the lack of sun. I looked like Casper, the friendly ghost; living in South Dakota and working full time didn't allow for much sun tanning. I plopped my luggage on the empty seat next to me and sat. I dug out my boarding pass and checked the flight numbers. They matched. Yeah, the right place.

I put the ticket back into my carry-on, pulled out a book and tried to read. The feeling of being observed came from all directions. I glanced up and noticed a few guys staring at me. I nodded and smiled.

Several smiled back, while others nodded. A few others' eyes darted away. I returned to my book, but I couldn't concentrate. I was picking up a vibe.

I glanced around the waiting area. The men around me wore brightly colored shirts and shorts in waves of red, orange, and yellow. Maybe there was going to be a fashion shoot for a catalog at this resort.

"Flight 1069 to Guaymas Sonora, Mexico will be boarding in a few minutes. Anyone traveling with small children may pre-board at this time," a woman's voice announced.

A low rumble of laughter came from the crowd at this announcement. I glanced at the woman standing at the podium and watched her face redden. Her shoulders rose in apology and she mouthed, "Sorry."

I smiled. They must be laughing because there wouldn't be any children on this flight due to the Club Med atmosphere. But the announcer was the only woman I saw. Then a thought struck me. Like a light bulb in a cartoon, a joke started to form in my mind, but it didn't make me laugh. I grabbed my carry-on, moved down the walkway, and pulled out my cell phone.

If you can't trust your friends, who can you trust in this world? I've trusted my best friend Molly with my life, several times. I've even trusted her with my dog's life, and that means *extreme* trust in my book.

Flipping it open, I scrolled through my contact list and pressed the number for Look Book, Sioux Falls' only used bookstore. Molly had better be there.

"I have one question for you," I said as soon as she picked up the phone. "Where did you get your information for my trip?"

"Taylor, aren't you supposed to be on vacation?" Molly asked.

"I'm waiting for my flight, but I need to know how you came up with Club Fred."

"From the travel agent."

"He recommended this place?"

"I didn't say that. When I went to Sergio's salon to get my hair done, he talked—"

"Crap."

"What's wrong, Taylor? You sound stressed."

"Last call for Flight 1069. All passengers must board at this time," the overhead intercom boomed.

"Isn't that your flight?" Molly asked.

"Yes, but I don't think…"

"You don't have to think. You're on vacation. Vacation therapy for the therapist. You need to go and have fun, let it loose, that's all. Bon voyage." The phone clicked in my ear.

"Last call…" the voice announced as the gate agent waved me to hurry.

Molly's words hadn't put my mind at ease. I had to decide and quick. I didn't think I should go on this trip, but my feet led me forward.

I stepped up to the gate attendant and opened my mouth to speak. "I think… Is this…?"

She gave me a shy grin. "We don't want you to miss your flight." She reached into my carry-on and took the boarding pass from the pocket. She scanned it, returned it, and waved me through.

As I walked onto the plane, I looked right and left. All I could see were men, in all shapes and sizes. I connected the dots in my head. Molly's gay friend Sergio had recommended this club to her. Everyone on the plane seemed to be male and from the profusion of tans and colognes, I had a feeling they were all members of the same club Sergio belonged to.

It looked like I was headed for a gay old time.

CHAPTER 2 - FLY THE FRIENDLY SKIES

The flight attendants readied the cabin for take-off as I hurried to find my aisle seat. The overhead storage was full, so I crammed my luggage underneath the seat in front, avoiding eye contact with the person sitting next to me. I detected movement from my peripheral vision.

I bolted forward and snatched my Ian Rankin out of the carry-on. Maybe, if I got involved in my book, I'd be safe. Avoid looking left, and maybe avoid a conversation, one that could last until we landed in Mexico. I always got stuck next to a chatty traveler. Flipping the book open, making sure it was the right way up, I tried to shake the feeling of being stuck next to the only psycho on the plane. So far, no eye contact. I was safe.

Besides, reading helped distract me from my fear of flying.

As I found my place, I used my peripheral vision to scope out my neighbor. The words blurred as the image of a tan man swam into focus next to me. Brown hair with blond streaks, a sheer T-shirt sculpted to his torso. Very short shorts revealed long, deeply tanned legs. They were perfectly formed with great muscle definition and not a hair in sight.

This guy must be a body builder, no doubt. In the hospital's rehab unit where I worked as an occupational therapist, all I saw were flabby or flaccid muscles on the patients who had suffered from a stroke or a head injury.

I turned a page and almost jumped out of my seat when the man moved and reached for his carry-on. My knees slammed together as he removed a bottle of lotion. He flipped open the lid, squeezed a blob into his hands, and started to rub the cream onto his long legs. He slipped his feet out of his leather woven sandals, his toes as deeply tanned as the rest of his body.

I jerked back to my book when I felt his gaze on me. *Don't make eye contact.*

A light fruity aroma wafted around me.

I inhaled. Kind of a feminine lotion to be rubbing over your body, I thought. I knew Molly only used 100% natural lotions, so I guessed he must be health conscious also. With all the time he spent working on his muscles and tan, I was sure he was very aware of what he applied to his skin.

I sniffed again, deeply.

Watermelon?

That's what it smelled like, watermelon. Great. Just what I needed. A good smelling scent to make my mouth water. I prayed my stomach wouldn't start rumbling. If only I'd asked someone sooner… If only I had eaten something… If only I would've found out more about this trip… If only…

I was being ridiculous. All men on this flight, yeah right. There were women here, somewhere, I knew that. I just missed them when I was talking to Molly.

Maybe you'll wake up from this dream.

Stop it.

Nightmare?

I'm on vacation.

Relax.

Breathe.

I inhaled deeply again and stopped in mid-sniff. Would he think…?

Glancing up from my book, I wasn't able to take my mind off the concerns that were threatening to overtake me. I was sure I was picking up on old stereotypes. Television and the media planted all the wrong ideas in people's heads.

But why weren't there *any* women on this flight?

The flight was rough, and turbulence shook the plane. I peeked out the window once at the end of the flight and watched as we landed on a much too short runway. The airline was going to send me a bill for the removal of my fingernails from the padded armrest. Grabbing my carry-on, I joined the men heading down the plane's aisle, ignoring the melee of excited chatter and tossing of beach balls and carry-ons that surrounded me.

Nearing the plane's door, a blinding light welcomed us. Had I died and gone to heaven? As I approached the hatch, a blast of hot, humid air greeted me. This wasn't going to be heaven. Waves of heat rose from the asphalt and melted my shirt to my skin.

This was hell.

Two burly men pushed a wheeled staircase up to the plane from the runway. It felt like stepping into a movie from the seventies. It was probably still the seventies down here.

As I descended the stairs, the airport looked like a revolution was underway. Uniformed militia lined the runway, machine guns slung over their shoulders, and bandoleers of bullets crisscrossed each chest.

Had war broken out while we were in flight?

Welcome to Mexico.

I didn't have a chance to relax. After customs, signs and security guards herded us to a tour bus, which hopefully was our last leg of the journey.

The bus lurched to an abrupt stop, and I awoke. The bus's door opened and Madonna's "Holiday" welcomed us. Everyone stood and pushed down the aisle to get out the door. I shook my head and waited for the crowd to clear.

A row of staff lined each side of the long canopy that lead to the lobby. As I descended from the bus, and my feet hit the tiled walkway, someone thrust a margarita into my hand from the left.

"Greetings! And welcome to Club Fred. I'm Mike, and this is John and Gary," a short man with closely cut hair said, as he pointed to a slim blond with long hair and a bald bodybuilder. "We'll be your hosts for your week here in Mexico. If there are any problems, please don't hesitate to speak to one of us. We'll try and help you as much as we can." His infomercial voice was infused with enthusiasm. "Unlike the *other* resorts, which use international staffing to blend cultures, we at Club Fred bring our own *special* staff to meet your own *special* needs, and we use the locals for the rest."

I knew I'd be talking to these guys a lot sooner than they thought.

"Those travelers who already have a roommate, please follow John and Gary to the pool area. They'll be handing out your room assignments and keys. Those of you who are seeking a roommate, please line up in the lobby area. Try and find a partner to share a room with before I get back." Mike motioned for John and Gary to lead the way to the pool.

The herd of men followed, and Mike brought up the rear.

I watched the crowd thin and disappear. Tentatively, I glanced around the nearly vacant lobby. Two guys with multiple piercings stood close together talking animatedly. A willowy man stood in the center of a mound of suitcases, hatboxes, and steamer trunks. He turned and stared at me.

I avoided eye contact, but involuntarily turned toward him, since he was the only one left. I swallowed hard and almost took a small step forward, when a hand ran up my back and stroked my shoulder. It circled over my deltoid.

"I see you're looking for a roomie. How about me, big boy?" A husky voice came from behind me.

I cringed.

Don't turn around. Pretend you didn't hear that. Don't turn around, my mind screamed, but against my will, I turned around to see who had caressed my shoulder.

"Surprise!" Sergio spread his arms out to the side, almost spilling his drink. His spiked blond hair contrasted against his deep tan. A flowered lei hung around his neck, clashing with the Hawaiian shirt and white shorts that covered his slender body.

The lungful of air that I'd been holding burst forth. "You scared the hell out of me."

"What? Moi?" He pointed to his chest and tried to look innocent. Then a puzzled look crossed his face. "What the hell are you doing here? You're not…"

But he didn't wait for my response, he figured out my problem.

"Molly. She asked me about male vacations." His animated speech came to an abrupt stop. "I thought she was asking for someone else. She didn't want a… Oops. She didn't know this was gay?" His confusion turned into gales of laughter.

"I don't see what's so funny," I said. "What are you doing here?"

"I'm on vacation. Well, kinda. I was hired to cut hair in exchange for a discount." Sergio leaned forward. "I get to keep the tips, so I may even make some money while I'm here." His eyebrows rose and fell with excitement.

"Are you looking for a roomie?"

"Sure. Aren't you?" He scanned the dwindling crowd. Leaning forward as he took a sip from his drink, he whispered, "Slim pickings around here."

"I was kind of hoping to be the last one picked, or not picked, so I could get a room all to myself," I confessed.

"No such luck, babe. They overbooked the resort. I heard that they were hoping some of the guys wouldn't show. There aren't any single rooms left. Believe me, I've already asked."

Sergio saw the disappointment in my face. He reached

forward and put his hand on my shoulder. "Come on, Taylor, you can bunk with me."

"What?"

"Whoa! Chill out. I didn't mean it *that* way. I meant, I guess, I'd be willing to share a room with you. Jeez, I didn't think *you* were homophobic?" He lowered his voice, "And this isn't the place to let that show, if you know what I mean."

"I'm not homophobic..."

Sergio cocked his head. His expression plainly revealed his doubt. "Now you can see what it's like on the other side of the fence. You'll be the minority here, just like I am back in South Dakota. Gays don't exist there, except for me." He gave me a wistful smile.

"Sorry, Sergio. I didn't mean anything by it. I'm just a little stressed right now, and I don't want to ruin your holiday." I looked over at the only other option for a roommate.

The willowy man waited, sitting on top of a steamer trunk with various colored feathers and other clothing items sticking out of the side. The other two guys, who didn't look old enough to shave, but had all available body parts pierced, several times, looked like they had paired up. Or were they stuck together by the magnetic field their piercings were generating?

I looked back at Sergio. "Are you sure? I don't know what you were looking for in a roommate, but I doubt that I'm the man of your dreams."

"If only you knew," Sergio said, under his breath.

That remark didn't calm my nerves.

"So do you want to share with me, or do you have another preference?" Sergio pointed to Leona Helmsley and her luggage.

The magnetic brothers were gravitating to the pool. I hoped they wouldn't fall in and rust. I stuck out my hand. "Hi, I'm Taylor Kozlowski. I'm from South Dakota. Sioux Falls to be exact. Are you looking for a roommate?"

"I'd thought you'd never ask." Sergio grabbed my hand and

kissed it, batting his eyes at me.

I pulled my hand out of his grasp and mumbled, "Thanks a lot."

"He's mine, all mine," Sergio said to the only person within earshot. "So don't any of you girls get any ideas. Keep your claws to yourself."

I felt my face burn, but I couldn't think of anything nice to say.

A hand slipped into my back pocket. "Hey, blondie. You can room with me," a husky voice said from behind me. He squeezed my butt once before he removed his offending appendage from my pocket.

Sergio and I spun and stared. My mouth dropped open. The man who had goosed me was half human and half…bear. Maybe Bigfoot, I wasn't sure. He wore a black leather vest that barely covered his big, hairy chest. His Levi cut-offs were short, way too short, but I think they were cut that way on purpose.

It didn't appear that there would be any reasoning with this guy.

Sergio grabbed my arm, concern in his eyes.

Bigfoot ran his fingers through his beard and then down his chest. Was this his come on? His body looked like he would have to comb his entire torso, even more frequently than I brushed Regan, my schnauzer.

I swallowed hard.

"Do something," Sergio hissed.

My head shook slightly.

"What would Molly do?" he asked.

And with those magic words, the idea came. "I think he was talking to you," I said, and bent over to retrieve my carry-on.

"What? Oh." He paused for a second, almost dropping his drink. "No, I think he's talking to you." Sergio poked me, and my bag fell back to the ground.

I pushed his hand away and faced the man. "Were you talking to me?" I pointed to my head. "I'm not blond."

The hairy man stepped forward, raising one hand at us.

Sergio's eyes widened. "That's a laugh. Are you calling me a blond? This comes from a bottle, honey." He motioned to his bleached, spiked hair standing straight up on top of his head.

"If you weren't blind," I pulled on a lock of my hair and held it for Sergio. "You'd know that this is brown. You'd better get your eyes checked."

Bigfoot moved closer, but Sergio flashed him his palm.

Sergio reached over and tugged on the tuft of my hair. "That shade of *blond* must have come from somewhere. Hmm. Your mother's a hairdresser, isn't she? Maybe she taught you a few of her tricks."

"You leave my mother out of this. If the sun didn't highlight my hair so much, it wouldn't look so... so... blond!"

"Ha! See. You admit it. You are blond." Sergio poked me in the chest.

"At least mine is natural, not from a bottle...of Clorox."

"Why..." Sergio expelled the air nosily.

"Or is it Hy-lex? I keep forgetting which one is cheaper."

"Excuse me," the hairy man interrupted.

"Stay out of this," Sergio and I said in unison, but didn't look in his direction.

I felt Bigfoot's hand pat and squeeze my butt. "All I'm looking for is a roommate here." He squeezed me one more time on the word here.

I jumped from his touch, he pulled his hand back.

Sergio saw what Bigfoot had done and jumped between us. "Did you just touch him? Who said you could touch him?" He pushed the yeti back. "I can't believe you grabbed his ass." Then he turned to me. "I bet you liked that."

"What?"

"You heard me. You just wanted to pair up with somebody else on this vacation." Sergio grabbed my arm. "Well, it's not going to happen. We're going to *our* room, right now."

"But…" The hairy man took a step forward, hand extended, concern in his eyes.

"But nothing." Sergio spun around, stopping the bear in his tracks. "Come on dear, let's go find our room."

I bent, picked up my carry-on, and tossed the strap over my shoulder.

Sergio linked elbows with me. He set his drink down on a table and escorted me to the pool to get another key for his room. Under his breath he said, "Good thinking. Sparring with Molly really pays off."

"You're telling me," I agreed.

"I know. Where do you think I get some of my best insults?"

CHAPTER 4 - UNPACKING THE BAGGAGE

"What's this?" Sergio pulled something from the side pocket of my carry-on. "Some kinky sex toy?"

"That's just my folding reacher." I continued putting my clothes into the dresser. The dresser was over eight feet long and dominated the whole wall. "Could they have found a bigger dresser?"

"What's it doing in your suitcase? I thought you were off duty. Vacation, remember?"

"I must've forgotten to take it out of my bag. The last workshop I went to, the Smith and Nephew rep gave everyone a new reacher. She wanted us to try them out and order a bunch to sell to our patients."

"So what did they think about them?" Sergio unfolded the reacher and flipped it open. He held it like a gun and pulled the trigger. The grabber end opened and closed like a lobster's claw with each pull.

"I forgot to take it out of my bag, so no one has tried it yet." I walked between the double beds and put the last of my underwear away. In the mirror above the dresser, I watched Sergio. He extended his arm and twisted his wrist in an attempt to make a grab for my backside with the reacher. "It's supposed to help you get dressed, but you're twisting your wrist too much," I warned. "You'll get carpal tunnel."

"I have weak wrists." Sergio pantomimed a classic limp wrist. "Remember?"

"How can I forget? You keep reminding me. Are you questioning my memory?"

"No, just your judgment." Sergio tossed the reacher on top of the dresser and flopped down on his bed.

"And what do you mean by that?"

Sergio opened his mouth and then closed it.

"Well?" I waited.

"I can't believe that you trusted Molly, of all people, to plan your vacation."

"I've been so busy at work, I didn't even have a chance to pack."

Sergio pushed himself up from his bed, headed over to my drawer and pulled it open. "You let Molly pack for you, too? I have to see this." He reached in and started rifling through my clothes.

"Hey! Get out of my stuff." I sidestepped in front of the drawer, trying to block his access. Too late. "Molly packed as I washed clothes and…"

"Wha-hoo!" Sergio pulled out a bright blue Speedo and held it up. "What's this? Is this yours?"

I felt my face flush and I grabbed for the suit. "I had to buy that for PE class in college."

Sergio raised the Speedo over my head and dangled it out of my reach. "Are you going to wear it?" His face lit up with excitement. "Here?"

"No!" I jumped and ripped it out of his hands. "I can't believe she packed that thing."

"Oh, I think it's cute."

"You would. Knock it off." I tossed the Speedo back into the drawer and slammed it shut. Sitting down quickly on top of the dresser, I glared at him, daring him to try again.

"Testy," Sergio said.

"Please stay out of my drawers."

Sergio smiled.

Not seeing any reaction from me, he continued. "Oh, come on, Taylor. I've always wanted a brother so I could share his clothes. Alas, I had three sisters, and you can see how I turned out. I raided the wrong closet." He flopped down on his bed.

"Don't put yourself down like that," I said.

Avoiding his gaze, I walked to the bathroom and unpacked my toiletries.

As I put my bag into the closet, Sergio laughed. "I was wondering something."

"What?" I asked, warily.

"Did that guy's mother mate with a gorilla, or was he a genetic experiment gone way wrong?"

The image of the Bigfoot who had tried to pick us up in the lobby lumbered back into my mind. Innocently, I said, "I thought you liked big, hairy guys."

"Not *that* big, and definitely not *that* hairy." Sergio scrunched up his face. "Didn't you just want to…shave him?"

"No." I smiled. "I thought he needed a flea dip."

"Good one. You're learning. You'll fit in just fine around here."

My smile died. "And what did you mean by that?"

"Whoa!" Sergio held up his hands in surrender. "You don't have to get so defensive. I didn't mean anything by it. I wasn't insulting your manhood or anything."

"I think you were. I think you think that I'm gay, and this is a way you came up with to spend some time with me."

"What? Now wait a minute. I never—" he began.

"You didn't have to," I shot back. My blood pressure was rising.

"Fine." Sergio stood up. "You're going to believe whatever you want to no matter what I say. Maybe I should've left you to fend for yourself in the lobby." He walked across the room. "And guess what, I'm doing that right now."

"What?"

He walked to the door and turned the doorknob. "I'm letting you have supper all by yourself, and I hope you find a nice date.

Maybe Bigfoot will be waiting for you." With that Sergio slammed the door to punctuate his point.

I looked at the back of the door. What a stupid idiot I was. I was taking my disappointment out on Sergio. I should be mad at Molly. She was the one who got me into this. It wasn't Sergio's fault. Taking a step toward the door, I stopped. No, I should be mad at myself. I'm the one who got myself into this situation in the first place. And yes, some homophobia was rising.

I grabbed my room key from the dresser and headed out the door. I needed to find Sergio and apologize, but more desperately, I needed something to eat.

There weren't any Sergio or Bigfoot sightings at supper. I found a small open table in the corner. Most of the guests milled around in pairs, wearing shorts and bright shirts, which seemed to be the evening's dress code. Everyone spoke with animation and excitement. The noise level rose and echoed in the dining room.

"Did you see the brochure about the wildlife to avoid at this resort?" a blond surfer type asked his dinner companion.

"I haven't seen one yet." The bald man smiled.

"No, I'm serious. It shows what snakes, spiders…"

"I'm on a manhunt. The animals can fend for themselves."

And the chatter went on and on.

By the time supper was over, my head was pounding from all the noise and excitement of over six hundred men. All I needed was some down time.

So much for my relaxing week in the sun. I was starting to think I wasn't going to find any relaxation. It's only a resort, I told myself.

Yeah, a gay resort.

Stop.

Breathe.

I was the one in control here. I could make or break my vacation. Since this was the only time I'd have off for months, I had better make the most of it.

And the first item on my agenda was to apologize to Sergio.

My footsteps echoed along the dimly lit fourth floor hallway as I neared our room. Hotels always seemed like a maze to me. All the rooms looked alike. When I finally found room 417, I took a deep breath and slipped the key in.

I was wrong, and I wanted Sergio to know it. The lock released, and I pushed the room door open. "Sergio?"

As the door swung wider, the sound of the shower running greeted me.

Darn it. With this headache, I really needed to get into the bathroom and take something. My pocket vial of Excedrin was at home in Sioux Falls. I had been afraid of carrying tablets through customs. I'd heard too many horror stories about drugs and foreign countries.

I knocked on the bathroom door. "Sergio? I need to get some Excedrin."

No answer.

"Sergio? I'm sorry. I was a big fat idiot. I was wrong. Can you forgive me?"

I turned my ear toward the door to hear better. The shower continued, but no response came from Sergio.

Why wasn't he answering me? Was he still mad? I pounded on the door again, louder this time. "Sergio."

I had apologized. What more could I do? I waited for another minute.

My head pounded, and I needed Excedrin. There was a shower curtain, I reasoned. I knocked on the door again. "I'm coming in," I said, and opened the door. I headed straight to my shaving kit. Quickly, I found the bottle of Excedrin and shook out two caplets. I poured some bottled water into the glass and swallowed.

Darn it. With the water running, now I realized my bladder was full.

"Sergio?"

No reply.

"Are you okay?" There didn't appear to be any movement behind the curtain. I stepped closer, straining to hear better through the plastic. Only the sound of running water. Looking down at the floor, a part of the shower curtain had pulled outside of the tub. A small pool of water had splattered on the tile. On closer inspection, the water looked kind of rusty.

"Is that water even clean?" I asked.

Still no response.

Something was wrong. An image flashed in my mind. Maybe Sergio had slipped and hit his head. I yanked the curtain back.

No one was standing, but Bigfoot lay in a big hairy heap. Our lobby friend, who only hours earlier had wanted to room with us, was slumped in the tub. His chin lay on his chest as the water sprayed over his body. A stream of blood and red water ran down his neck and through the hair on his chest. His exposed skin appeared pale through the opening of his black leather vest.

Bending over, I tried to see if he was still breathing.

"What are you…?" Sergio said, tapping me on the shoulder.

I let out an unmanly shriek and turned, standing bolt upright to face him.

"What's wrong?" he asked.

I opened my mouth to speak, but nothing came out. So I moved to the side and pointed.

Sergio peered around me. "Jesus Christ! What did you do?"

"What did I do? I found him that way." The Excedrin threatened to come back up. "What did you do?"

"I didn't do anything." He was indignant. "I just got back from supper."

"So did I. I needed something for my headache, and I thought you were in the shower. When you didn't answer…" I pointed to the tub. "We need to find help." I pushed past Sergio.

"I think he's beyond help. Don't you?" Sergio followed me into the bedroom.

"Fine. You stay here, and I'll go." I touched the room's doorknob.

"I'm not staying here alone with him." He glanced into the bathroom. "I'm coming with you."

I opened the door and stepped out into the hallway. "Who's going to stay with…?"

"I'm sure he'll be just fine all by himself," Sergio said, and he pushed me out of the room.

The door slammed shut and locked behind us as we ran down the hall.

It took us twenty minutes to find Geoff the GO (Gentil Organisateur—or, freely translated, Gracious Organizer). He said he worked security at the resort as he unlocked the door to our room with his passkey. His dark Jamaican complexion contrasted greatly with his white shorts and shirt. His six-foot frame loomed ahead of us as he carefully pushed our room door open and motioned for us to follow. He was one of the international employees Club Fred kept.

Sergio and I tentatively stepped across the threshold and peered at the closed bathroom door.

Silence greeted us.

"Did you shut off the water?" I asked, turning to Sergio.

"I didn't close that door." Sergio's eyebrows shot up, innocently.

"Don't look at me. I didn't do it," I said.

"But you were behind me."

I knew that the water had been running when we fled the room, and that door had been open. "I didn't touch anything, not even the body." Despite how much I had wanted to search for a pulse, I hadn't. Something was wrong. I knew Sergio hadn't turned off the water or closed that door.

Geoff pushed the bathroom door open, and we all stared into the empty room. He turned to look at us, "This some kinda joke, mon?" his Jamaican whiskey-soaked voice demanded.

"No. He was right there." I said, pointing to the clean and empty bathtub. "There's no way that he could've moved. He was dead."

Sergio shook his head and repeated, "Dead."

"I think you boys had too much sun." Geoff scratched his curly head.

"Why would we lie about...?" I stopped. There was no way he was going to believe us without a body.

My eyes scanned the bathroom. "Wait a minute," I said, and grabbed a white hand towel from the counter to wipe the damp floor. Sand and grit clung to the nap, but nothing stained the white cloth. I reached into the tub and wiped around the drain. It was wet, but no discoloration appeared on the towel.

Geoff looked at the cloth, doubt plainly written across his face.

"He was right there, with blood running down his chest." I shook the towel. "The floor and the tub are still wet. That should prove something. Right?" The conviction was quickly draining from my voice. "I don't understand how they could've gotten him out of here so fast, and still had a chance to clean up." My eyes left Geoff and turned to Sergio. "Help me," I mouthed.

"He was there. I saw him too. Honest." Sergio said.

"Ya, you two had your laugh, now leave me be." Geoff shook his head and stormed out of the room.

"So much for being a gracious organizer," I said to the place where Geoff had stood, then turned to Sergio. "Where do you think he went?" I walked over between the beds and searched underneath. Nothing.

Sergio opened the closet door and looked in. "Maybe whoever killed him came back and took the body."

"You think so?" I snapped.

Sergio's face fell.

Oops. "Sorry, Sergio. I didn't mean to snap at you. This just can't be happening. I'm on vacation."

"That's okay, I understand," Sergio said, rolling his eyes. "I just meant that they didn't have very much time to move the body."

"That's right," I said, and jumped to my feet. "So, it can't be too far away from our room." As I passed Sergio, I motioned for him to follow.

"No way. I'm not going hunting for a dead body. I want a nice warm one…"

"Fine. Then stay here. I'll go look for it by myself." I opened the door and stepped into the hallway. Looking right and left, there were no telltale wet drag marks across the tiled floor. Whoever cleaned up did a great job. Yellow lights illuminated the pink stucco walls, but barely cast enough light to see much of anything. As I continued down the hall, I read 418, Laundry, 419, 420. "Aha!"

"Aha, what?" Sergio said, from behind me.

"Yikes." I spun around, arms ready to fight. "What the hell are you doing sneaking up on me like that? I could've killed you," I said, unclenching my fists.

"Like you did to your new buddy?" he smirked.

"You're the one that disappeared at supper, not me. Maybe you…" I squinted at him. Seeing this had no effect on him, I continued, "So, are you going to help me or not?"

"All right. I'll help you," he whined.

I didn't respond.

"It's not like I have anything better to do," he said. "I'm only on vacation."

"Where's Molly when you really need her?"

"Isn't she the one who got you into this in the first place?"

"You're not helping," I warned from between tight lips.

"Just tell me what you want me to do, Nancy Drew." Sergio clapped his hands and rubbed them together with forced excitement.

I ignored his comment. "I figure, whoever moved the body didn't have a lot of time to hide it, so…"

"So it's probably still around here. Close by." Sergio pointed to the door. "Like in the laundry room."

"Exactly."

Sergio rubbed his nails on his chest and looked down at them. "My mama didn't raise no idiots," he said with a cowboy twang.

"Mine did," I said flatly.

"What?"

"Never mind." I reached forward and tried the knob. Locked.

"Here, let me do that." Sergio bumped me out of the way with his hip. He rattled the knob, pulled out his room key and inserted it halfway, jiggled it, pushed it in a little further, jiggled some more, and pushed.

Click. The door swung open in his hand.

He smiled proudly and held his hands in a "Price is Right" motion, both hands framing the open door. But as suddenly as his smile had appeared, he grimaced. "We don't really have to look in there, do we?"

The door swung completely open and hit the wall. Darkness greeted us.

I reached into the room, searching for the light switch. My fingers brushed against a warm, wet, sticky dampness inside the door. "Yuck." I pulled my hand back, reflexively, as a wet mop flopped out and landed at our feet.

"Let me." Sergio pulled out a lighter and flicked it. The flame revealed a pull cord. He pulled the string and a twenty-watt bulb barely illuminated the closet. Rows of neatly folded sheets, towels, and pillowcases lined the room. But no body.

"Damn it!"

"What? Were you actually hoping we'd find that body?" Sergio placed his hands on his hips and gave me attitude with head movements.

"Yes. Well, no. I don't know. I guess I just wanted to make sure they believed us."

"Believe us? If we found that body, I think it would cause us more problems. Don't you?" Sergio bent and picked up the mop. "Feel this," he said, and touched the mop's head. The strands were warm. A faint, metallic smell tainted the air. The strands appeared dirty, but the light wasn't bright enough to see what color they were.

"Do you see any blood?" Sergio asked.

"I'm night blind. I detached my retina, and with this poor light, I can't see much. But even without my night vision, I'm sure there's some blood here. I can smell it. Can't you? That copper penny smell. It's been diluted by the water, but it's there."

"Maybe we should take a sample," Sergio suggested.

"Where would we get it analyzed?" I saw his disappointed expression. "Besides, they don't believe us anyway. Why would they test a wet mop? We still don't have a body. They could say the blood came from anywhere, from anyone for that matter."

Sergio propped the mop back in the closet and closed the door. "Let's check the rest of the floor, and see if we can find anything else."

We canvassed the entire fourth floor, searching every nook and cranny for any wet drag marks or a dead body, but our search revealed nothing.

We stopped outside of our room. Sergio glanced at his watch. "It's almost 11:00. Disco time. I gotta go. I'll catch you later." He slapped me on the shoulder and headed down the stairs to the lobby.

"Wait," I called after him, not wanting him to leave me alone.

He paused on the steps. "Are you going to come with me?"

"No. I don't need any more commotion tonight. I think I'm going to take a nice long walk on the beach. Look at the moon and the stars, and try to unwind. Then I'll probably head back to the room and read. Today hasn't been all that relaxing for the first day of my vacation."

Sergio shrugged. "Suit yourself. Ciao."

How could he go dancing after finding a dead body in our shower? How was I going to shower in that tub? I shuddered. I pulled the room key out of my pocket and paused. Did I really want to go back in there? Alone?

You never know what you're going to find in that room, my mind warned.

A gentle cool breeze blew salty air over my sweaty body. "The beach is calling," I said to the night. "And it looks like it's going to be a peaceful evening after all."

As if on cue, a low thundering bass beat reverberated throughout the night air.

So much for sleep tonight.

"It's Raining Men" throbbed and echoed throughout the tiled courtyard. Ripples in the huge figure-eight swimming pool pulsated in time with the music. I walked past rows of chaise lounges, but the ocean's surf drew me to the beach. The force of the music pushed me faster to get away from the disco and find some peace and quiet.

Flashes of lights danced across the water's surface and I wondered—why would an oceanside resort need such a big pool? Why would they need a pool, period? This concept was beyond me, but then this whole trip was beyond me. I hoped the walk would help clear my head.

The heavy smell of chlorine hung around the pool, but a trace of fresh air filtered through, dissipated with the night's breeze. I followed the salty scent around the cabana and a wave of marine brine greeted me. I inhaled deeply; this was more like it.

I scanned along the guardrail, which surrounded the pool's deck, and spotted an opening. Rounding the building's corner, I saw the thunderous waves crash against the beach, drowning out the disco's thumping beat. Three wooden steps led down to the sand.

As soon as my feet hit the sand, I knew I'd be waking up early to stake my claim on the beach. Palm fronds rustled with the wind as the salty tang tingled my sinuses. I breathed freely for the first time in months and prayed that my allergies wouldn't act up in paradise. Another deep breath entered and exited my lungs, and despite the day's events, my muscles started to relax. The tension headache was gone, and I doubted it was the Excedrin. It was the magic of water.

Moving to South Dakota had changed my life. It kept me a safe distance from my dysfunctional family, but growing up near Lake Superior had definitely shaped me. The effects of being so close to such a large body of water seemed to calm and center my spirit. It always had. Maybe that's what caused my restlessness in Sioux Falls.

Or was it Molly?

That was a toss-up.

The day's heat still radiated off the white sand, which reflected the full moon's glow. The trade winds blew across the water and picked up moisture along the way. The spray felt good against my face, but as I closed my eyes, images of the shower and a bleeding body threatened to re-emerge in my mind. I opened my eyes and tried to push those thoughts aside.

Two tall, lean men in their thirties held hands as they strolled along the beach, greeting me as they walked past. Hurrying up the steps, the couple headed in the direction of the music. Why did I feel like I was going in the wrong direction? Nothing new there.

More chaise lounges and umbrellas made from palm fronds ran along the shore, and the wind rustled the dry leaves. White waves crashed on the beach as the foam hissed and dissolved into the sand. Kicking off my tennis shoes, I stepped into the surf, and my bare feet splashed in the cool water.

A volleyball net whistled in the wind, and off to the right stood several vacant tennis courts. In the distance, a row of wind boards waited for the next day's events. The moonlight muted their bright colors, and with my limited night vision they looked black and indigo.

The disco's music tingled faintly in the distance above the surf. I continued on my walk, passing the wind boards, and wondered how anyone could stand on them in the rolling water.

The waves continued to intensify and forced me to move farther from the waterline. A row of palm trees sprouted up from a mound of sand to my right. Each tree appeared like a waiting skeleton, glowing white in the dark from the lime painted up their trunks to prevent insects from invading their foliage. As I neared the tree line, it was amazing to see how high they had to paint the lime. It looked like eight feet or the tree wouldn't survive the insects' invasion. What kinds of bugs were that persistent?

I glanced back at the resort. A warm glow flickered in the horizon's blackness, outlining the hotel, and the full moon added a cold, bluish illumination. That's when I realized how far I had walked on the beach.

As I turned to head back, the hair on the back of my neck prickled. I felt as if someone were watching me. Turning, I scanned the darkness, but no one was visible. I felt eyes following me as I walked along the surf. The tide had calmed into a soft lap on the sand. I hadn't noticed when the thunderous pounding or hissing foam disappeared.

I couldn't ignore the feeling of being watched. Unsettled, I started my return trip. After two steps, the moon slipped behind a cloud and plunged the beach into blackness. What night vision I had was gone. I blinked hard, trying to force my eyes to adjust and pierce the blackness. Only a warm glow burned from the resort's lights at the far end of the beach.

I took a tentative step, feeling the way with my feet.

A soft rustling in a pile of palm fronds made me stop. Despite the darkness, it looked like a palm frond had lifted up off the ground a few inches, and then slowly sank back down. The pile of leaves wasn't large enough to hide a person; at least I didn't think so. Maybe something wild was nesting in them.

In the earlier conversation at supper, the men had mentioned a pamphlet telling about the wildlife at the resort, but I hadn't read it yet. Images of lizards and alligators, along with many Hollywood monsters, flooded my mind.

I sidestepped closer to the water, but my eyes never left the heap. My hands clenched my shoes like a weapon, ready to use them in case anything sprang from it.

More rustling shook the pile.

My eyes slowly adjusted to the dark. I took a deep breath and saw something dart out from underneath the fronds. I didn't wait to find out what it was. I leapt forward and ran. I bolted down the beach, the moon remaining behind the only cloud in the night sky. I hadn't noticed when my shadow disappeared, and I wasn't going to stop and worry about that. I veered closer to the water's edge. My feet splashed in the surf as I picked up speed on the sand where it was firmer.

Blindly, I pressed forward. Panic urged me to run faster, but somewhere in my mind, I wondered how stupid I looked.

I passed the wind boards. The volleyball net whistled a warning, and I swerved to avoid it.

And then, thump.

My body hit the damp beach.

I landed hard on my chest and forearms. My shoes flew from my hands, and the force drove the breath out of my lungs. Sand sprayed into my face, and my chest burned when I tried to inhale. Did I break a rib? Puncture a lung? A gasp slowly allowed oxygen to re-enter my body. I lay there for a while as my respiration returned.

When I tried to get up, I realized that my feet were tangled up with whatever I had tripped over. What had washed ashore with the tide?

"Ta-y-lor? Are you out there?" Sergio called in a singsong voice.

Great. As if I didn't feel foolish enough already, he was the last person I needed. And now he was going to see how easily I had scared myself. Hurrying, I pushed up onto my knees. Reaching down to my feet, my fingers found something wet.

"Taylor!" Sergio called again.

"Over here." I called as my fingers explored, trying to identify what had tripped me.

Then I felt wet leather. My hand moved down and brushed denim, then veered over to touch hairy skin.

A body.

A wet, hairy body.

A cold, dead, wet, hairy body, clad in leather and denim.

I knew this body, and I pulled my hand away in horror.

As if summoned from the night, Sergio stepped off the path and headed directly toward me. "Taylor? Is that you?"

"Yeah, it's me."

Sergio neared, just as the moon escaped from behind the cloud. "What are you do…? Oh no. Not again." Sergio started to back up.

"Sergio."

But he wasn't listening. He was running.

He ran as fast as he could back to the resort, yelling all the way.

"Sergio!" I shouted after him. "Get back here!"

Sergio's flight through the resort had alerted Mike and Geoff. All three of them stared down at the hairy corpse lying at my feet. At least this time, we had a body to show them.

Mike still clung to Sergio's arm. The same one he had used to drag him back to the beach, despite all of his protests. "I really have to get going. I'm late. I didn't even find the body. I just... Well, never mind what I just did..." Sergio said.

"Explain this to me one more time," Mike said, trying to pry the details out of his reluctant captive. "Calmly, this time." His hand tugged on Sergio, forcing him to make eye contact as they moved closer to me. Despite all of the protests and fidgeting, Mike didn't let go.

In the dark, I stood with my back to the body and had a few minutes to slip on my shoes and compose myself as I waited for them to approach Bigfoot and me. What was I going to say? How could I explain this one?

Geoff's maglight flashed to life and scanned the beach, finally coming to illuminate the body. "So, you boys done found the body." Reaching into his hip holster, he pulled out the walkie-talkie's mouthpiece. He depressed the side button and spoke. "We got a floater."

Static replied.

With Mike's attention drawn to Geoff, Sergio finally broke free from his grasp. He turned his back to me and avoided looking at the body.

Mike gave up trying to corral Sergio and stepped over to Geoff to hear what came across the radio. Seeing his chance, Sergio started to slink away.

"Stop right there. You need to answer a few more questions," Mike told him in no uncertain terms. He looked to Geoff, who motioned toward me. Mike turned and asked, "Are you all right?"

"As well as can be expected," I said.

"Can you tell me what happened?" Mike asked.

"I really don't know. All I did was go for a walk on the beach." I pointed down the shoreline. "The moon went behind a cloud, something sprang out of the bushes, and I guess I kind of panicked." I felt my face begin to burn. "I ran down the beach. It was so dark. I couldn't see anything. The next thing I knew, I was sprawled out across the sand. I reached down and felt..." I said, pointing to the body. "That's when I heard Sergio calling me. Just as he arrived, the moon came out from behind the cloud, and you can see what we found."

"Did you know the man?" Mike asked.

Sergio blurted out, "No!"

Both Mike and Geoff looked at me.

"No," I shook my head. "He wanted to room with us earlier." As I heard the words come out of my mouth, I realized how stupid that sounded. "I mean, no, I've never met him before."

"But you just said that he wanted to room with you," Mike pressed.

"Well, it wasn't just me," I motioned toward Sergio.

"Don't get me involved in this little charade," Sergio retorted. "I had nothing to do with this. He was grabbing your ass, not mine."

Geoff clipped the mouthpiece back onto its holster and said, "So mon, is this the body from your room?"

"Yes," I said.

"No," Sergio said, at the same time.

"Which is it?" Mike demanded.

"We don't know," I said.

Sergio agreed.

"But I think it's the body from our room," I added.

"But I don't," Sergio said.

I glared at him.

"Well, I don't. It could be another body that just happened to…" he stopped. "I don't spy on men in the shower…" He waved his hand at Mike. "Never mind."

Two resort workers approached carrying a stretcher with a pile of blankets.

I took a step back.

Geoff held up his hand. "I'm security, don't nobody move till we search the place." He pulled a pair of rubber gloves out of his back pocket and prepared to examine the body.

I looked down at the sand. My sprawl mark and footprints were everywhere. So much for not disturbing the scene of the crime or destroying evidence. Could I have set myself up any better as a suspect?

The body's feet were bare, and no other footprints were visible around him, except mine. The surf must have washed everything else away. Everything, except for my floundering.

Geoff shined his light across the body and stopped on its jeans' back pocket. The beam played across a thick rectangular bulge. A wallet. He handed me the flashlight and bent to retrieve the wallet. His gloved fingers quickly removed it, opened it, and pulled out a driver's license. "Shine the light here."

I shined the light into his eyes.

"The card," he said, and waved it at me.

"Sorry." I aimed the beam so he could read it.

"Duane Wayne," he said.

I started to snicker. The flashlight's beam jiggled. His Jamaican accent made him sound like Elmer Fudd. I looked at his expression and bit the inside of my cheek. This wasn't the time or place for my sick sense of humor to escape.

Sergio's eyes flashed me a warning.

I pursed my lips tighter, and shrugged my shoulders while I tried not to laugh, hoping my hysteria wouldn't show.

Geoff searched the rest of the wallet. He pulled out a few wet bills and a condom.

"Doesn't that boy know anything?" Sergio said. "Latex'll break down in his pock…"

We all stared at him.

"Well, it will. Body heat and all."

"I don't think he has to worry about that right now," I said, tightly.

"As if. That guy never stood a chance. That look is so 80's. It's so over. It's so dead." Sergio grimaced as soon as he said it.

"You're not helping," I said.

"That man wasn't robbed. There's a lot a money here."

"Did he drown?" Mike asked.

"I don't know, mon. I gotta turn 'im over."

"Shouldn't we wait for the police?" I asked.

"I am he."

Great, the cavalry had arrived. But why didn't I feel any better? "Don't you have to take photos of the crime scene first?"

"With all your footprints?" Geoff pointed around the body.

I felt my face burn again.

Geoff searched around the body one more time. After finding nothing, he carefully reached over and pulled on the man's shoulders. He log-rolled the body over onto his back. Rigor was starting to set in. "Shine the light on 'im."

The security guard and I shone the lights on his face.

Duane's eyes were partially open. They stared vacantly up, glazed and cloudy. His mouth gaped open like a fish.

Mike grabbed one of the security officer's arms and trained his maglight on the body. "What's that?" The beam passed over his neck, and a flash of silver glinted in the light.

"What?" Geoff asked, and focused on what we were pointing at on the body's neck.

"It looks like there's a piece of metal tangled in his beard," Mike said.

Gently, Geoff combed his fingers through the long wiry hair. Untangling the long strands, he removed a small pair of barber shears from the corpse's throat. The blades slipped out of their recesses, the tips emerging coated with a thin layer of clotted blood.

Sergio had moved next to me to get a better view. When the scissors slid out, his body stiffened next to me.

"What's wrong? Can't stand the sight of blood?" I asked.

"No, it's not that," he whispered.

"Then what?"

"Those are mine."

"What? The scissors?"

"Yes."

"Are you sure?"

Sergio nodded his head slowly.

"How?" I asked, but didn't wait for a response. "But Geoff won't know that."

Sergio's eyes told me differently.

I continued in a whisper. "Besides, I doubt they'll be able to tell that they are yours." I looked into his haunted eyes. "They won't be able to figure that out, will they?"

But before Sergio could answer, Geoff said, "What's dis? Shine the light 'ere." He wiped the blood away from the small blades with his index finger. "There's writing on it."

I knew what the engraved letters spelled out before he read, "Sergio."

Chapter 8 - Sweet Dreams

Geoff asked question upon question, repeatedly, trying to get every detail down. What did he think? That I was going to forget the details? As if I had seen anything in the dark anyway. After what seemed like hours, he finally allowed me to go back to my room.

My body felt like it had been given the rubber hose and hot light bulb treatment. I unlocked the door and was welcomed by the bedside lamps, along with the blue, muted glow of the television.

Mike had taken Sergio to his room at the resort to question him, while Geoff interviewed me in his office. Now, Sergio sat, propped up at the head of his bed, snoring. An open book lay splayed next to him. How had he gotten back to the room before I did? His scissors were the murder weapon.

I tiptoed across the room and retrieved a pair of sleeping shorts from the dresser. I crept to the bathroom and swallowed hard, taking a deep breath as I entered. My eyes avoided the shower, and I worked quickly, brushing my teeth and taking out my contacts. The foggy image in the mirror peered at me. I was ready for bed, or so I thought.

Since I wasn't familiar with my environment, I retrieved my glasses from my shaving kit. I rarely wore them. Their thick lenses dug into my nose, and I hated to admit that my vanity would prefer a stubbed toe to being caught wearing them. I saw better with my contacts, so I didn't waste the money updating the prescription lenses or frames. I was legally blind without them.

I snuck across the room with my Coke bottles on. As I stepped between the beds, my foot kicked one of Sergio's sandals and sent it sliding across the tiled floor and under my bed.

Sergio sat bolt upright. "Who's there?" His pupils were dilated, and his hands flapped around in the covers.

"It's just me. Were you waiting up for me?" I said in a singsong tone.

"No," Sergio said as he rubbed his eyes and scrambled to pick up his book. "No, I wasn't sleeping." He flipped the book open. "I was reading. I just closed my eyes to…" he blinked a few times, trying to get the sleep out of them, "…to rest them."

The blanket was pulled tightly across his body, so only his arms were exposed, and he held a copy of *A Body to Dye For* upside-down in his hands.

"Good book?" I asked, slipping into bed. I sat with my back against the headboard, which wasn't attached to the frame but mounted to the wall.

"Yeah," he settled back into his mound of pillows. "It's about this hairdresser who finds a dead body with a ribbon wrapped around his…" He paused as realization dawned on him. "Geoff sure kept you a long time. What did he ask?" He closed his book and set it aside.

"I'm sure the same things he asked you. He just kept asking me them over and over again. Did you know the guy? What did you see? How did you find the body? Did you touch anything? Was he the same body we found in our shower?" I yawned.

"He asked you all that?"

"No, but he should've. Obviously, he's forgotten our first encounter."

"That's fine by me." Sergio yawned. "Geoff said I was seen cutting a guy's hair after supper, so I had an alibi, but I was getting pretty upset with him. And he wouldn't give me my scissors back. It's a matched set. Who does he think he is? The way he was treating me, he acted like I killed the guy. Can you believe that?"

I closed my eyes and shook my head. Trying to change the subject, I pointed to his book. "Should you be reading something like that before you go to bed?"

"I don't know if I'll be able to sleep again." His mouth opened wide into another big yawn.

"You look pretty tired. Maybe you should turn off the light and try."

"I'm not tired." His head bobbed up and down as he struggled to keep his eyes open.

Yeah right. "Maybe you're afraid to fall asleep?" An evil grin played across my face.

"No," he said, quickly.

"Are you sure?" I raised my eyebrows at him.

"I just want to finish this chapter, then I'll turn off the light." He quickly picked up his book and opened it up. It was still upside-down.

"Suit yourself. At least, you're not afraid of me." I looked at him. "Are you?"

"No," he said, even quicker than his first time. "Whatever gave you that idea?"

"I wouldn't blame you, you know. You don't know me all that well, and you don't think that I could...?" I left the sentence hang in the air. My eyes narrowed at him. "Do you?"

"I know you couldn't...wouldn't..."

I smiled and nodded. "Good," I said with a soothing quality in my voice. "I mean, I don't know you that well either, but I'm sure that you didn't kill him. Did you?" I took a deep breath. "But I trust you. You trust me, right?"

"Yeah, I guess so," but Sergio's voice wasn't convincing.

"So, I guess we'll both have to trust each other, now won't we? It's not like I've stumbled across *that* many dead bodies."

Sergio gave me a nervous look. "Yeah?"

"Besides, you don't have another pair of scissors in your case that I would be able to slip out when you're sleeping and..." I made a stabbing motion in the air, and then grasped my throat with both hands. My tongue stuck out and gurgling noises came out of my throat. I smiled. "Well, I'm beat." I snuggled under the blanket and rolled over onto my side, and then rolled back to face him. "Oh, by the way, when did you learn to read upside down?"

"What? Why are you asking me that?" Sergio asked, as a puzzled expression worried his brow.

"I noticed that you were holding that book upside down." My hand slipped out from under the covers and pointed to it. I took off my glasses and placed them on the nightstand. "Good night," I said, and reached up and turned off the light next to my bed.

As I rolled over on to my side and pulled the covers over my shoulders, I smiled to myself. "We'll see how well you sleep tonight, Sergio. You're not the only one that can tease around here."

CHAPTER 9 - BREAKFAST

Sergio had trouble getting up. Something about not sleeping well emanated from underneath his sheets. I reminded him about his choice of bedtime reading material, and I barely escaped in one piece.

I carried my breakfast tray through the dining area, looking for a place to sit. All the tables were full and not a single chair was vacant. It surprised me that so many were up this early in the morning. I continued walking around scanning the room. In the far back corner, one small table had an open seat. A guy sat alone. His back was to the crowded room. I looked around one more time, but didn't see anything else open.

Oh well, I had to make the most of this trip, and I did need a place to sit. As I approached the table, a dark-haired guy with blond highlights looked up. Great, another bronzed model. "Do you mind if I join you?" I asked, motioning toward the empty chair.

"Sure." He shrugged.

The low rumble of conversation stopped in the room.

I looked around as I set my tray down and pulled out the chair. My face flushed. Had everyone heard about the commotion on the beach last night? I felt a roomful of eyes focusing on me. What was going on? I sat down, ignoring their glares, and took a sip of my orange juice. I wiped my hand on my shorts and extended it. "Hi, I'm Taylor."

The man wiped his hand on his napkin and shook mine. "I'm Tom."

"Nice to meet you, Tom." I released his hand and picked up my fork, starting on my scrambled eggs. The room was still silent.

"Where are you from?" Tom asked.

"Sioux Falls, South Dakota," I said, through a mouthful of eggs. I turned to the side, looking for Sergio. Instead, the entire dining room stared back at us. Correction. Stared at me.

Did everyone know that I had found a dead body on the beach?

I shifted uncomfortably in my seat, smiled, and turned back to my food. "I seem to be the center of attention again. I just don't understand it." I felt my face burn.

Tom smirked, took a piece of pineapple and popped it into his mouth, but didn't say anything.

"So where are you from?" I asked.

"LA."

Not a big conversationalist. I looked around the room. The majority of the diners had slowly returned to eating and talking, but a few continued staring at me. Some had pinched expressions on their faces. One even stuck his pierced tongue out at me.

"Are you waiting for someone?" he asked.

"No," I said, quickly.

"Are you sure? I'm almost done and…" Tom pushed his chair back slightly from the table.

"Don't go." I fought the urge to look around again. "I think I've made a big mistake coming here."

"To this table?"

"No, to this resort."

"Why do you think that?"

"Don't ask."

"Okay," he said slowly. "What do you do in South Dakota?"

"I'm an occupational therapist. I work with people after a stroke, head injury, and spinal cord injury. What about yourself?"

"I do some modeling and a little bit of acting," he said smugly.

"Sorry, I don't recognize you. I usually wear Levis and T-shirts. I don't get any men's fashion magazines, and I don't think I've seen you in any movies."

Tom smiled at me. "I don't think my movies have made their

way to South Dakota, at least not yet."

"Independent films?"

"You could say that."

"Don't feel bad. Not many get there. We have an alternative film series that plays some art and foreign movies, but that's only twice a year."

Tom just nodded his head and smiled.

I obviously wasn't getting the joke.

"Ah hum," sounded from behind Tom's back.

I looked up into Sergio's eyes. They gleamed like I had never seen before, glowing from deep within.

"Pull up a chair," I said, motioning to the one sitting next to the wall. I turned back to Tom. "You don't mind, do you?"

Tom smiled and shook his head. "Sure. Join us," he said simply, extending his hand in greeting.

Sergio didn't move. He just stood there, frozen, with a stupid expression on his face.

I stood up, walked over, and pulled the chair over for Sergio. I patted it. "Sit," I said, just as I did for my terrier, Regan.

Sergio sat blindly, almost missing his seat, but he kept staring at Tom with his mouth gaping open.

Tom smiled at him and then turned back to me. "I'm done with breakfast," he said and pushed his plate away. "I'll let you two be alone."

"You don't have to go. He's usually more talkative than I am." I nudged Sergio with my elbow. "Once he's had a cup of coffee in him."

Tom motioned to stand up. "I need to stake out a spot to work on my tan. Where were you planning on laying out today?"

"Well, I came to Mexico. I'm hitting the beach. I can always lie around a pool at home."

"That's how I feel. Well, if you're looking for a place to set up on the beach, come find me. I'll save you a spot."

"Cool. I'd like that. I'll finish here, and get my stuff. I'd like to hear more about LA and your movies, okay?"

"That'd be great. If you haven't noticed, not too many people have talked to me, until you." Tom pushed his chair back and stood up.

I rose with him. "I'll catch you later." I extended my hand again. "It was nice meeting you, Tom."

He looked at my hand for a few seconds and then took it and shook it firmly. "It was really nice meeting you, Taylor. I'll save you a place." He let go and waved a two-fingered salute to Sergio.

Sergio waved a floppy hand back at him.

Tom grabbed his towel and beach bag. Slowly, he strolled through the maze of tables and headed for the beach, his sandals flip-flopping as he went.

Sergio grabbed my arm. His fingers dug into my flesh, hard.

"Ouch. You're hurting me."

"Do...do...do..." he started.

I pulled his fingers from my arm. Red marks rose up on my pale skin. I rubbed them away. "What is your problem?" I sat back down and picked up a cold piece of bacon.

"Do...do you know who that was?" Sergio finally got out of his mouth.

"Yes," I smiled and said, "Tom." Then I realized that was all I knew.

Sergio smiled smugly. "Well, *Tom*, as you put it, is only the hottest male actor around. And you talked to him. You of all people talked to him and you even touched him, and he touched you." Sergio looked at my hand, grabbed it, and rubbed it all over his.

I yanked my hand back.

"He even asked you to sit with him on the beach." He burst out into a gale of laughter, which made everyone in the dining area stare at us, again. "Taylor's got a boyfriend."

"He seems like a nice guy, kind of a loner, but nice. I'm sure he's just looking for a friend."

"He could have anyone here," Sergio waved his arm around to the crowd, "to be his friend, and he picks you. You of all people."

"What? Am I such an awful person, that he wouldn't want to get to know me?" Anger rose in my voice. "Or do you think I'm the harbinger of death here?"

Sergio looked at me.

"Let me rephrase that."

"Taylor. You still don't get it, do you? Think of where you are." He paused for a moment. "Tom is the sexiest male actor in movies. *Gay* movies. He's *the* biggest, and I mean the biggest, porn star in the business today, and you have a date with him." Sergio grabbed at his chest and pounded down hard on it. "I can't breathe, I can't breathe," he gasped.

"Well, stop hitting yourself on the chest and maybe you could." I ate the last bite of scrambled eggs on my plate. They were cold and congealed at this point. I stood. "You can join us if you want. I'm sure Tom won't mind."

"You're such an idiot," Sergio shook his head.

I startled at his anger. "What did I do?"

"What did I do? What did I do?" Sergio said, mockingly in my voice. "You only scored with the hottest guy at the resort and you ask, 'What did I do?' Look out Club Fred, Taylor's on a roll. Wait until Molly hears this one."

"Stop it," I said and started to leave. "I'll let you calm down, and if you want, you can join us on the beach. That is if *you* want. It's up to you." I left Sergio sitting at the table, alone.

As I worked my way across the dining room, I saw several guys point at me and whisper something behind their hands. I tried not to let them rattle me. Sergio was exaggerating, as he always did. I avoided all eye contact and headed to pick up a piece of fruit. As I reached for a banana on the buffet, I heard the person standing next to me say, "Bitch."

Looking over, I saw a guy in a black Speedo. He glared at me, daring me to say something. He knew I had heard his comment.

I reached over, picked up two apples and two extra oranges. "One's for Tom." I waved them in his face, and raced out of the dining room for my life.

CHAPTER 10 - MEETING THE AUTHOR

As I headed back to my room, my mind was spinning. This couldn't be happening to me. A date with a gay porn star? I had to get out of there. I was in way over my head, out of my league. Who was I trying to kid? I wasn't going to make it another…

Bang. I slammed into a guest. Head on. We both stumbled backward, trying to regain our balance. The apples and oranges I carried dropped out of my hands and rolled down the hallway. "Excuse me." I began rubbing my forehead and looked up. This time it was my mouth that fell open, and my eyes that bulged out of their sockets. I recognized this guy. "Aren't you…?"

"Shhh," he looked around the hallway. Not seeing anyone within earshot, he continued. "Yeah, I'm Logan Zachary, in the flesh."

Logan's picture had graced the back covers of all his books. His full black beard was peppered with gray. His five foot eight stature surprised me. He looked a lot taller in print than he did in person. "I know, sorry I ran into you. Literally," I smiled at my bad joke. I bent down and retrieved my fallen fruit.

Logan picked up the apple at his feet and handed it to me.

I stepped forward and accepted it. "I love your books. I've read them all, but I think *Knowing Me, Killing You* is your best. Not to say that the award-winning *Wring Wring* wasn't bordering on genius." I stopped gushing. "What are you doing here?" I paused. "Oh, I'm sorry. You must be on vacation, too."

"Shh, well, yes and no. I've always wanted to go to Mexico, but I've never had the chance. Well, here's my chance." Logan smiled.

My eyebrows shot up.

"Oh, I'm not gay, if that's what you're thinking." His gaze darted around looking to see who could hear us. "Not that there's anything wrong with that. It's just that I… I mean my… my agent wanted me to set my next mystery at a gay resort, so here I am. Researching."

I nodded, but wasn't able to figure out how his characters Axel Bolton and Bruce Abel would fit into a gay resort.

"What do you do for a living…?" Logan asked, quickly before I could ask him anything else.

"Oh, sorry, I'm Taylor," I said, extending my hand. "I'm an occupational therapist."

"Like physical therapy?" Logan asked.

"In a way. PT's work on the legs and mobility, while OT's work on self care and hand function. We teach everything from dressing to bathing, from brushing your teeth to combing your hair. We assess arm strength, coordination, vision, memory, and problem solving, and we make sure the patients are safe in the kitchen and the bathroom." What the heck was I babbling about? I sounded like a college catalogue.

"It must be an interesting job. Working with people, making life and death decisions every day." He paused, pondering something for a moment. He lowered his voice. "Have you come across any dead people?"

Shock must have registered on my face.

He quickly continued. "I mean in the hospital? You know, one that passed away mysteriously or had been murdered?"

I swallowed hard. How was I going to explain that one? I had a few stories to tell, but I didn't want to bring up those memories right now, at least not after last night. Then I thought, maybe, it would take my mind off everything that had happened so far.

My mother's voice came to mind. She always said it was easier to tell the truth than to lie. That way you didn't have to remember all the lies you had told. So I answered him, truthfully. "No."

"Too bad," he scratched his head. "Maybe we could talk later on. I have a few medical questions that you might be able to help me with. I have an idea for another book…"

"Sure, that would be great. Just let me know what works for

you, and I'll try to answer any questions you may have. At least, I can tell you what I know."

"Great, I'd really appreciate that."

"Is your new book going to be part of the regular series, or are you starting a new one? I can't see Axel Bolton ending up here." I looked around.

"That's exactly what I told my agent, but he suggested sending Bruce Abel, Axel's sidekick, to the gay resort, by accident, of course." He smiled. "I'm calling it *Kill Me! Kill Me! Kill Me! (A Man After Midnight)*."

"What a great idea." I leaned closer. "Is there anything else you can tell me about it?"

"I really don't like talking about my books while I'm plotting them, but I can tell you this. Bruce comes back from a late supper at the resort and finds a dead body in his bed. While he goes for help, the body disappears."

Goosebumps rose across my body.

But Logan continued. "Later on, he falls into the pool and the body is floating, and you can guess the rest. There'll be a few attempts on his life, and all the people he meets at the resort will make him pretty paranoid. They're all suspects. Are they trying to kiss him or kill him? Needless to say, this one should be great fun. Poor Bruce, he'll really have to confront his homophobic feelings in a big way."

My face must have revealed my thoughts.

"What's wrong?" A look of concern came across Logan's face. "Don't you like the premise?"

"Oh no. It's a great premise," I said.

That is, if you're not living it.

CHAPTER 11 - BACK ON THE BEACH

After making me promise to get in touch with him later in the day and help him to come up with a few ideas for murders that could take place in a hospital, Logan went off in search of breakfast. I wished him better luck than I had had.

I ran up to our room and found my beach towel and bag. A pile of books sat on top of the dresser. I grabbed one, took a few steps, went back, grabbed an extra book, just in case, and threw everything into my tote bag.

I picked up my camera lying on the dresser, and looked at myself in the mirror. Should I or shouldn't I? I'm sure Molly expected me to record all the things that happened at the resort this week. Well, almost everything. I ignored the bathroom.

I put the camera in my underwear drawer. I didn't want to make Tom feel uncomfortable. After all, he was on vacation too, just like me, and he'd probably want to stay away from cameras.

I opened the drawer. But Molly would like a picture of the hottest porn star in the business. I closed the drawer. Maybe later. I'd get to know him better before I started acting like a tourist. Or like Sergio.

I shook my head. Sergio. Where did he come up with these stories?

The sunscreen was in the bathroom. I glanced at the open door. A chill ran down my spine. When Sergio had been in the room, I was able to take a shower, but now… I entered it quickly and avoided looking in the shower. I grabbed the bottle of sunscreen and hurried out of the room.

The beach was alive with color and early morning excitement. Red, yellow, and blue towels littered the beach, while tan-skinned bathers lounged around in skimpy swimwear. I felt overdressed in my boxer short swim trunks.

Nervously, I pulled up my waistband, wishing they were a

little longer. When I saw more of my thigh, I pulled them lower, wishing they covered more of my white legs. I closed my eyes and prayed. "Let me blend in, just a little."

I retraced my trek from the night before. The ocean waves calmed me again, but my blood pressure rose slightly as I stepped over the spot where… My eyes scanned the area in the daylight. Was anyone watching? No trace of the body remained. Had everything been washed clean with the morning tide? Or had Geoff and his cohorts cleaned up?

How many people knew about the murder? Looking around the beach, the vacationers seemed to be enjoying the sun. It didn't look like the news was too well known, if at all. Maybe all that talk in the dining room *was* about Tom. Could Sergio have been right? Not that I was going to tell him that.

Ducking past a game of volleyball, I spotted Tom in the last set of chaise lounges under a palm frond umbrella. He was crouching on the side of a chaise, sunglasses pulled low on his face, ready to pounce on a skinny guy with red spiked hair.

I slowed my pace, not wanting to intrude, unsure if I should approach.

The skinny man waved his arms around wildly. Angry words were shouted back and forth between the men. The redhead turned and pointed at the guests, the ocean, and the sun. "You need to get out there and mingle. What am I paying you for…?" He pulled out his wallet and waved it under Tom's nose.

Tom's face turned red. He bolted to his feet and pushed the man backward. "Don't make me angry!"

As the redhead stepped back to maintain his balance, he dropped his wallet in the sand. Red bent to retrieve it, and Tom spotted and waved me over. He pushed his sunglasses up on top of his head, and forced a huge smile. "Taylor. Over here."

He actually wanted me to join him.

The gangly man turned, squinting into the sun, trying to see who was distracting the focus of his rage.

Over the redhead's shoulder, Tom caught my eye. He motioned to the guy with his eyes and waved his hands to shoo him away. "Where have you been?" he called. "I was getting worried."

"Sorry. Sergio wanted to talk and I couldn't get away." I turned to face the guy. "Some people never know when they've overstayed their welcome." I smiled and closed in on the vacant chair. "Thanks for saving me a seat."

The redhead stepped to the side, slowly, uncertainty playing across his face. "No problem," Tom said, standing his ground. "You invited Sergio to join us, right?"

"Yes, and I also ran into Logan. You know how it is when you run into him. He can never stop talking." I rolled my eyes to Tom. I pulled my beach blanket out of my bag, shook it, and spread it across the vacant plastic lounger.

"It was nice seeing you again, Sean. I hope you have a great vacation too," Tom said. He reached over, grabbed my tote bag, and pulled out a book, Elizabeth George's *In the Presence of the Enemy*. He held it up to me. "You remembered to bring it. Thanks."

I could feel my brows wrinkling with confusion.

Sean turned to stare at me.

I unfurrowed my brow.

His anger was easy to read. His eyes ran me up one side and down the other. He sized up my scrawny body and lack of tan.

I could hear his thoughts, loud and clear. Glancing over at Tom, I saw his expression as he pleaded with me. "Oh. Don't mention it," I replied, playing along.

Sean turned, rage still burning behind his eyes. He glared at me one more time and forced a smile. "I'll let you two enjoy the sun. Glad to see you're not hiding in your room, Tom." He nodded and stormed off down the beach.

"Another adoring fan?" I asked.

"He's my agent, and he got Club Fred to pay me to be here. Sorry about that, and thanks for bailing me out. Sean thought that he was going to be my date for the week." He paused as his face flushed.

"I'm getting pretty good at going with the flow. Sergio's teaching me well. Being a movie star must be a rough business, never a free moment. Your life must be so exposed." My face burned red.

Tom face fell. "He told you, didn't he?"

"Sergio said something, but…" I paused. "I never know what to believe, and I don't believe half of the stories he tells me."

"You don't have to hang out with me, if you don't want. I'd understand if…" and his voice trailed off.

"Are you trying to get rid of me?" I interrupted and sat down on the chaise.

"No. I just meant…"

"I know what you meant. I don't mind. Your job is your job, but it isn't all you are."

"You really didn't recognize me, did you?" Then the realization came into his eyes. "You're not…"

"I'm not what?" I asked. "Gay?"

"Never mind. That's not a fair question to ask." He sat down on the lounger. "So, how the hell did you get all the way down here from South Dakota?"

"It's a long story." I pulled out the bottle of sunscreen and started applying a thick coating on my legs.

"I think I have the time." Tom rolled over onto his side, propping his torso up with his left arm.

The white cream matted the hair on my legs into big clumps. The more I tried to massage it in, the more sand it gathered, and the chunkier it appeared.

"Is that the waterproof kind?" he asked.

I read the label. "It says it is."

"Once you have enough on, wait a few minutes, and then go

rinse the extra off in the ocean. The sand should go with it."

"Thanks." It took five minutes to finish applying the lotion. "I'll be right back."

"I'll be here. I can't wait to hear how *you* got here."

After rinsing off and returning clump free, I told him about Molly and how blind faith planned my vacation. "So, don't mind me. I haven't had a very relaxing trip so far."

"Here's your book back. I hope you didn't mind me rifling through your bag." He straightened out the canvas. "Mayhem in the Midlands? What's that?"

"It's an annual mystery convention. It's held in Omaha over Memorial Day weekend. The conference is a great chance to meet your favorite authors and get your books signed."

"I hope I didn't get any suntan lotion on your book."

"Don't worry. I brought used books I wanted to read on vacation. I didn't want to ruin any of my signed copies on the beach. Read it if you want. I started this other one." I held up my Ian Rankin.

Tom said, "So, you're a man of mystery. I don't get to read very much, but have you read a book called *Slaughterloo*? Now that was one of my favorites."

"Really? I loved that one too." I paused for a second before continuing. "It's funny that you said that, because Logan Zachary is here, at this resort. That was *the* Logan that I ran into, literally."

"Cool. I think I have his new book in my room." He held up my paperback. "You don't mind if I read this then?" he asked, shaking it at me.

"No, not at all. I have more back in the room."

Tom set the book down next to him. He had visibly relaxed. He leaned back, stretched out on his chair, and closed his eyes. "How did you sleep last night?"

"Let's just say that I didn't get as much sleep as I wanted."

Tom opened one eye and smirked at me.

"And not for that reason."

"I was just kidding. When I was getting ready for bed, I thought I saw some kind of commotion on the beach, just down there a little way." Tom pointed exactly to the stop where I had tripped.

A cold shiver ran down my back. "Did you see anything?"

"I thought I overheard something about a body washing up on the beach."

"Really?" I tried to act surprised.

"Do you think it was one of the guests?"

I didn't answer.

Tom sat up and rested his arms on his knees. His eyes narrowed. "What do you know?"

"Nothing."

"You know something, don't you? You have a very expressive face. I doubt that you can hide very much." Tom pointed at me.

Lady Gaga wouldn't think I had a poker face. I tried so hard for my feelings not to show.

"Come on, tell me," Tom encouraged.

"All right, I'll tell you. I was the one who found the body."

"What? No way. That was you? Tell me what happened."

But before I began my story, I had the distinct impression that Tom had known I was the one who had found the body. Or was I just being paranoid?

CHAPTER 12 - STRANGE COMPANY

Sergio appeared with his towel and my camera in hand. His eyes were still glazed.

"Did you want to join us?" I asked, glancing up from my book.

"Come on. Pull up a chair," Tom said, pointing to a vacant one a few feet away. He stood up and moved his chair over to make more room for another lounger.

"Are you sure?" he asked, a questioning but excited look playing across his hopeful face.

I rolled my eyes. "Yes."

Sergio threw his towel and the camera at me and ran to pull the chair over. He picked it up and carried it between Tom's and my chairs. "Just kidding." He smiled and moved his chair on the other side of me.

Tom looked over at me when Sergio had his back to us. I shrugged my shoulders in question. Tom smiled and relaxed back, closing his eyes against the sun's intensifying rays.

Sergio retrieved and spread his towel over his chair and motioned for my camera.

I shook my head.

"What's wrong?" he asked.

"I don't think this is the time for pictures."

"I wasn't going to take *your* picture," Sergio said. "I just wanted to remember this trip and *all* the beautiful people I see."

I eyed him suspiciously.

"Honest. Scout's honor." Sergio held up three fingers and crossed his heart.

"Like you were ever a scout."

"I don't mind, Taylor," Tom's voice came from behind us

before Sergio could respond.

"Thank you, Tom." Sergio grabbed the camera from my hand and aimed it out to the shoreline and snapped a picture. "I wasn't going to just take your picture without your permission, you know." He said to Tom, but looked directly at me. "Taylor, check that out." He pointed down the beach.

Geoff waded in the surf with a camera taking pictures. He stood near the spot I had tripped last night, but instead of the crime scene, he was snapping photos of an older man with a very young male companion, barely eighteen.

"Sergio, you can take my picture. I'm used to it. It does get a bit old sometimes. I just don't want a crowd to mob us. Do you?" Tom asked, rolling over to face us.

"No. I just want to get some sun." Sergio lowered his camera and his voice. "At least, I don't need as much as Taylor does." He turned back to me. "You do have sunscreen on, don't you? Molly would kill me if I let you come back as a French fry."

"Yes, Mom." I turned away from Geoff and smiled at Sergio.

Tom sat up. "You know this Molly too?"

"Don't we all?" Sergio said. "She's a mutual friend back in Sioux Falls."

Tom smiled, settled back, and closed his eyes.

Sergio pulled off his T-shirt and applied a smooth even coating of sunscreen before settling back into his seat. His lotion absorbed right in, no clumps or anything.

I opened my book and started reading, but the sand and surf and sun kept pulling my attention away from the story. My eyes grew heavy, and my body slowly melted into the chaise. After five minutes of trying to read the same page and retaining nothing, I closed the book and decided to relax and enjoy the sun.

Just as I closed my eyes, Sergio asked in a hushed tone. "Did you hear that there were a few celebrities running around at this resort?"

My eyes met his from under his sunglasses, and I glanced over at Tom, who didn't look up. His breathing had become even and rhythmic. Playing along with Sergio's game, I asked. "So, who's supposed to be here? Mel Gibson? Tom Cruise?"

"Don't I wish." He waved his hand at me. "No. There is a famous porn star here."

I wrinkled my brow, shaking my head. "Really. Tell me something new." I glanced over at Tom, feeling uncomfortable talking about him while he slept.

"He's sleeping, and I doubt he heard a word I said." Sergio reached over and twisted open his bottle of water. The day's humidity had condensed on the outside. A trail of drops crossed his towel and chest. He took a drink, recapped, and set it back down in the sand. He savored the water in his mouth and finally swallowed. "There's supposed to be a famous author here too." Sergio's eyes lit up with excitement. "A famous mystery author."

"Logan Zachary." I said.

"How did you know?" Sergio looked crestfallen. "Did Tom tell you?"

"No, I ran into Logan after breakfast."

"Yeah right." But Sergio paused. "Like you've met him already? You sure work fast for a straight boy." He pushed his sunglasses up onto his head. "So you've actually talked to Logan Zachary?"

"Well, yes. I had to apologize for hitting him."

"You hit him? Was he getting fresh with you?"

"No. I told you, I ran into him. Bang. Who else is here at the resort? You said there were *celebrities* staying here."

"Well there are, Logan and him." Sergio nodded toward Tom.

"But that's only two."

"How many do you want? Two is all you need to put the 's' on celebrities."

"Out of all these people…"

"I'm sure there could be more, but they're on vacation, just like us, so let's let it drop."

"Let it drop? Now wait a minute, I wasn't the one who was all…" I opened my mouth and closed it, searching for the right words, "…all, I've got a secret. You started this."

"I just thought that you'd like to know that a famous mystery author was here. That's all. I'm sure you're a fan of his. I'm not like some groupie, clinging to the shirttails of some celebrity, like…" Sergio nodded back to Tom again.

"Why would Tom be hanging onto my…" Then the realization hit me. "Are you jealous?"

"Hey, Taylor," a voice called from the left.

Sergio and I turned to see who was calling. Logan approached with a towel, a bottle of water, sunscreen, and a notebook. A white cap, like Gilligan's, was perched low on his head.

"Do you mind if I join you guys?" he asked.

"No, not at all." A sinking feeling started to settle over me. I doubted that I was going to get to spend the week reading on the beach, after all. I wanted a vacation away from people, and here, I had my own little crowd of *all* the celebrities at Club Fred. So much for my reading and relaxing. At least I was blending in and getting to work on my tan.

Logan dropped his things on my chair. His eyes swept over me and went to Tom, who had just awoken from the commotion.

"You're… You're…" Logan said pointing at Tom, and stopped suddenly, "no, my mistake."

"I'm Tom," he said, smiling as he sat up and extended his hand. "Nice to meet you, Logan. I'm a big fan of your series. I have your new book in my room."

"Really?" Logan's weathered face flushed.

"Yeah. I'll have to get it later and have you sign it for me."

"Really?" Logan asked. He rocked back and forth, uncertain what else to say.

"Really," Tom said.

Logan smiled with pride as he walked off to find a lounger.

Wasn't it funny that Logan had recognized Tom? And Tom had recognized Logan?

Logan had finally found a lounger and was busy writing in his spiral-bound notebook. My curiosity was piqued, but I resisted. My exhaustion, added to the wonderful effects of sun, surf, and heat, washed over my whole body. My eyes grew as heavy as the Ian Rankin book in my hand.

I inserted my bookmark, closed the book, and placed it back into the tote bag. I closed my eyes and settled back. Sleep welcomed me.

Blasts of a horn Gabriel himself must have blown jolted me to an upright position. Calypso music blared out of the cabana and radiated across the beach.

"What the hell?" I asked.

Mike's voice echoed through the speakers, barely drowning out the music's backbeat. "Greetings, everyone! And welcome to Club Fred! I'm Mike, and I want to welcome you all to a week of fun and excitement."

"I can vouch for that," I mumbled to myself.

"Check out these two guys over here. The guy with the long brown hair is John, and the bald bodybuilder's name is Gary. And we're your Club Fred crew. If you have any problems throughout your stay, we'll be at the Club Fred table, right next to the pool. We'll have the answers to any questions you may have, along with daily schedules of the planned events and entertainment."

The horns blew again, and the song started over.

"Right on cue. This is the song to listen for. It'll signal the start of a new event. So when you hear it, you'll know fun is close behind. Now, everyone should gather around and get the basic information you'll need. Find out how this resort works, and what you can expect in the upcoming week."

"What?" Sergio demanded. "We have to go through orientation to survive here? What do they think we're doing?

Going to college?" He rolled over onto his stomach and pulled his beach towel over his head.

"Don't we have to attend this thing?" I asked.

Logan continued writing in his notebook, and Tom appeared to be sleeping through the commotion.

Shrugging my shoulders and not expecting any answers, I swung my legs over the side of my chair and stood up.

Sergio peered out from under his towel. "If you're going to go and play freshman, can you bring me back a cold water?"

"Sure."

"And don't forget your sandals." He pulled the towel back over his head and settled down into his lounger.

"Yes, Mother," I said with a wrinkled nose.

"Suit yourself," Sergio said from under his haven.

Ignoring him, I passed under the umbrella and took two steps onto the sand. The white, hot, burning sand. The shock didn't register at first. I took a few more steps and then it felt like I had stepped into a scalding bathtub. But here, there wasn't any bathmat to escape to, just more hot sand, yards and yards of it. The cabana seemed to pull away from me, and from where I stood, it was too far away to go forward, but I'd be damned if I'd go back and let Sergio know he was right.

Glancing ahead, I jumped onto a vacant towel laid out by a sun worshiper. I leap-frogged across towels to the small pool at the base of the steps that entered the cabana.

A sign read, "Wash your feet before entering Cabana." Steam came off my feet as I soaked. Just what I needed, a third-degree burn on the soles of my feet.

"Hot one, isn't it?" an elderly man in sandals and a gaudy shirt asked as he ascended the stairs.

I smiled tightly and just nodded. "Hot."

"You should really wear your sandals, or you're going to burn your feet."

I saluted him. "Thanks for the tip, I'll remember that for my return trip." You had better believe it.

I tested the temperature of the wooden stairs. They were warm to my wet feet, but not hot enough to burn the remaining skin off.

Mike's voice continued to call everyone over. "Don't be shy, you're on vacation. Hopefully, you'll all get to meet each other and have a wonderful time."

I rounded the corner of the building and entered the pool area, just as Mike held up a beach towel. "This is our official Club Fred beach towel. This is a wonderful souvenir to remember your trip." The towel had a picture of a male model emerging from the surf in a wet T-shirt and a Speedo, tossing his long hair back out of his face in a graceful arc.

I could just see my redneck neighbor's look with *that* beach towel hanging on my clothesline.

"We have T-shirts, sun visors, sunglasses, sunscreen, anything that you may have forgotten at home. You can purchase any of these items here, and for your convenience, all you need to do is tell us your room number, and we'll charge it to your room. This will save you having to carry your wallet and worrying about losing your money or credit card on the beach."

Mike handed the microphone over to John, who flipped his long hair back, just like he did on the towel. "Hi, I'm John, and I'm in charge of *all* the excursions. We have a few trips planned. There is a jungle cruise right here at the resort. All you have to do is take the shuttle to the dock and a boat will take you through a mangrove swamp. You'll be able to see the lush vegetation of the tropical jungle, just like on the Discovery channel, but live." He held up a pamphlet. "And the best thing about it is, it's free!"

The crowd cheered.

"We also have a whole range of great trips lined up for you for just a small extra charge."

Boos emanated from the crowd.

"The other trips are cheap. Trust me. We have a trip scheduled to the flea market and mall. There is one to a banana plantation, and there will be a sunset cruise also. Very romantic, if that's what you're looking for." He paused for effect. "And best for last, a snorkeling trip to Seal Island. This is a daylong event, so plan ahead. I heard it has some great places to take underwater photos, so sign up soon. Only a limited amount of people can go on each of these trips. So come and visit me at the Club Fred table and sign up today."

John handed the microphone back to Gary.

"Hi, I'm Gary." He flexed his muscles. "And I'm in charge of the resort's activities. I'll help you set up volleyball games, horseback riding, wind surfing, boogie boarding. Anything you can think of doing at the resort."

A bunch of catcalls, hootings, and laughter burst from the crowd.

"Aw, come on guys! Get your minds out of the gutter." He smiled. "Unless you take me along with you."

More hoots and hollering followed, along with some suggestions. I could feel my face beginning to turn red, and not due to the heat.

Gary tried to talk, but the crowd continued its uproar. Realizing that he was unable to regain control, he gave the microphone back to Mike.

"Hey guys, listen up. We're almost done here, and then you can go back to your fun." He took a deep breath. "Meals are served in blocks of time, make sure you eat then, because the cooks aren't able to make you anything special. Also, in this heat, we can't leave the food out all day."

Boos came again.

"As you may have noticed on the bus ride here, there aren't any restaurants within walking distance. There isn't anything within walking distance. So you'd better eat when you have the chance." He raised his arms up in apology. "And you need to eat if you plan on drinking. You can dehydrate in this heat if you don't drink enough water and if you drink too much alcohol. Before you 'boo' me, you are all adults here, and I'm not your mother, so be responsible, but have fun. You're on vacation!"

Mike glanced at his watch. "I don't want to waste any more of your time, but there are pre- and post-supper shows every night, and a disco and piano bar after the shows. The daily schedule will have all that information. You can read that for yourselves. Go enjoy and have fun. Don't forget to come see one of us if there is a problem, or if you'd like to buy a Club Fred souvenir. Thanks for listening." Gabriel's horn blasted again as the crowd dispersed, and I headed over to the bar.

Geoff the GO was bartending. "What can I get you for, mon?"

"Two bottled waters."

"You hittin' the hard stuff too early, mon. Take it easy." He gave me a toothy grin. "No more bodies on the beach, huh?"

"Oh, there are bodies on the beach, but all alive and well." Burnt, but alive.

He handed me two Agua Pure bottles and turned to the next customer.

I walked away and stopped in my tracks. I hadn't paid for the drinks.

Mike was walking by and stopped at my puzzled look. "Something wrong?"

"I didn't pay for these drinks," I said, sheepishly showing him the bottles.

"You did already. They're included in the resort price, so help yourself." He looked at the two bottles. "Let me know if I can do anything for you, and..." his voice dipped down to a whisper, "can you keep last night under wraps? I don't want to spoil anyone's vacation with a...a drowning so early in the week. Okay?"

"Yeah, sure."

"Thanks, bud. See you around and watch out for the sun."

"Thanks," I said and walked off. My pallor must be a novelty to him.

I retraced my path and as soon as my feet hit the sand, I jumped back into the rinsing pool. In the short time I had been at the meeting and the bar, the beach had gotten even hotter, if that was possible. I looked down the long stretch to my chair. Guys were lying on the towels that I had hop-scotched across earlier. So much for my return trip.

I walked back to the Club Fred table. John with the long hair was manning the booth. His tan body glistened with oil as he lay back, stretching out in his chair soaking up the sun. "Can I help you?"

"I would like a…" I looked at the piles of towels and T-shirts. "Do you have any sandals?"

"Nope."

"Do you have…a plain beach towel?"

John picked up the Club Fred towel and unrolled it. "Don't you like the design?"

"I'd really like just a plain one." I didn't want to hurt his feelings.

"Sorry, but it's all we have. But I can sign this one for you if you want."

"What?" I said, almost taking a step back from him.

He held the towel up next to his face. "That's me."

There he was, bigger than life. How could I refuse? "Sure, sign one for me."

"Cool. My first sale of the day. Whom should I make it out to?"

"Tay…" I stopped. "Make it out to Sergio."

He grabbed a Sharpie marker and wrote something and then signed his name to the towel. "So what's your room number?" he asked.

"What?" Was he hitting on me?

He gave me a surprised looked and said, "I need your room number so I can charge it to the right one."

"Oh, yeah. Sorry. I'm in room 417."

"Thanks, Sergio. See you around."

"Yeah, right."

I hurried around the cabana and looked back at John. He had watched me leave and waved. I waved back and peered at the ocean. A few minutes passed, and a guy approached the Club Fred table. As soon as he stepped in front of John, blocking his view of me, I threw the towel down on the beach and stepped onto John's face. As fast as I could with the bottled water tucked under my arms, I hopped across the hot sand, back to my chair, moving the towel with me.

Sergio peered up. "Told you the beach was hot."

I sat down quickly, fanning my feet. I threw him a bottle of water, and then I threw him the towel.

Sergio unfolded it and looked at me. "What's this?"

"A souvenir."

"Okay, but I'd like to know one thing."

"And what's that?"

"Are you going to meet John tonight, or am I?"

"What?"

Sergio held up the towel, so I could see what John had written.

"He's all yours," I said quickly, picking up my book. I began to read, trying to ignore Sergio's laughter.

CHAPTER 14 - JUNGLE CRUISE

Even with 30 SPF sun block, I could feel the sun cooking me. Using Sergio's sunglasses as a mirror, I saw that my face glowed pink. I should've tanned before I went on vacation. Like I'd had time to do that. If there had been time to work on my base tan, then I would've planned my own trip, and I wouldn't be here at Club Fred.

Logan continued working in his notebook, Sergio had run off to do a few haircuts, and Tom was still sleeping, but my stomach wasn't. It growled, letting me know breakfast was long gone. Since no one seemed interested in lunch, and I needed to get some shade, I went in search of food, but this time with my sandals on.

Lunch was being served poolside at the cabana. The walls around the pool were doors made from full length Venetian blinds, like along the streets of New Orleans. I walked past the bar and buffet tables and veered toward the pool.

My heart raced for a few seconds as I neared the Club Fred table. I was ready to bolt back to the beach at the first sight of John, but luckily he was nowhere to be seen. The other guy, the bodybuilder, manned the table. "Gary" was written in big block letters on a peel-and-stick nametag glued to his bare chest.

Muscles bulged in all directions. It looked like he had been sucking on an air hose, instead of the bottle of water in his hand. My gaze trailed from the nametag across his chest and down his abdomen. So that's what a washboard stomach looked like. I could see his six-pack. No, there were eight.

"Did you see something you wanted?"

"What? No. I don't…" I startled and blushed when I saw his expression.

"Hot." Gary raised his arm over his head and poured the water over his head. It trickled down his tan torso and he shook his head, spraying water everywhere.

I stepped back, trying to avoid the shower.

"Come on and look, it won't cost you anything, unless you stare at me. That will cost you." He waved me closer. "Just kidding, one of these trips will get you out of the sun for a couple of hours, and it looks like you could use a break from it."

I wiped my brow and felt my skin tingle with the sweat. Maybe a look at the clipboard was in order. The sheet for the jungle cruise only had two guys signed up for this afternoon.

Gary noticed my gaze. "Good choice, the jungle cruise. It takes off at two o'clock. Probably the best time to be out of the sun." His eyebrows raised in anticipation. "Come on, it'll be fun."

"Why not?" I picked up the pen and bent over to sign up for the trip. Quickly, I wrote my name down and then asked, "I thought this trip was free."

"It is."

"If it's free, why do I have to put my room number down?"

Gary took a deep breath and exhaled. "It just keeps track of how many people use the services. It's not our rule, it's the resort's."

I wrote my room number in the blank, but for some reason, it bothered me.

"Good. All you have to do is be in the parking lot in front of the hotel fifteen minutes before the trip, and the shuttle will take you to the boat."

"Thanks." I smiled and went in search of lunch.

A banquet of chicken, hot dogs, fish, spaghetti, mashed potatoes, rice, corn, salad, and fruit lined the buffet table. Several swimsuit-clad men trickled through the line, picked at the serving dishes, and placed small blobs of food on their plates.

I flipped a chicken breast and scooped a pile of mashed potatoes on my plate, but nothing else looked appetizing. Trying to avoid the sun for a few minutes, I chose a table inside the cabana. All the doors and windows were closed on the seaside in an attempt to prevent the wind from blowing the food across the room.

A minute after I sat down, sweat dripped along my brow, down my nose, and landed in my mashed potatoes. My temperature perception had been fooled by the ocean's breeze. It had cooled the air, making the beach's temperature comfortable, but in this enclosed space, it had little effect. The thick humidity threatened to drown me.

Sitting in the shade and out of the breeze, I felt the real temperature. Sweat broke out over my body, and the hot, humid air clung to my skin. No wonder the sand had been so hot to walk on barefoot. It must be over a hundred degrees in the shade. What would it be like in the sun without the breeze?

Looking around the pool area and hoping John had gone to take a nap or something, I watched the men mill around the pool. A long line stood at the bar, waiting for a cool drink. Geoff still bartended. He nodded in my direction when he noticed me looking.

I picked at the chicken with my fork, but it refused to pull apart. I stabbed the entire piece and took a bite out of it. The chicken was overcooked, tough, and dry. I chewed and chewed, and forced it down with a hard swallow. Maybe the mashed potatoes. After one bite, I knew this meal was going to be dry and tasteless. Hopefully, supper would be better. It couldn't get any worse, could it?

Before running back to the room, I found Sergio, still cutting hair, and took my camera back. Our room was hot and humid, so I turned on the air conditioner. The fan clicked and hummed and, eventually, cool air started to blow, cold enough to send shivers across my tender skin. I stood there for a minute, bathing in the refreshing breeze. This room was going to feel great after the afternoon in the sun.

The digital clock read one-thirty. I turned on the television. Flipping through the channels, I found four stations, two with Mexican soap operas, and HBO and CNN in Spanish. Not much to choose from. My high school had only offered French, so these channels did nothing for me. CNN's storm watch bulletin flashed on the screen, but I clicked the remote back to HBO. The movie *Death Becomes Her* was playing. Goldie Hawn, not in her own voice, rattled off something in Spanish, and I didn't understand a single word. I turned off the set, picked up my camera, and looked into the mirror. My beet red face was slowly turning pink, but it seemed to glow in contrast to my yellow shirt. I quickly applied another layer of sunscreen, just to be safe, and walked down to the front desk to await my ride.

My footsteps echoed in the open tiled corridor. Despite the hollow expanse, I got the distinct feeling that someone was watching me. I turned around, poised, ready for I don't know what.

No one was in sight.

Was someone following me? I scanned the lobby and alcoves, along with all the little nooks and crannies, but no one was visible behind the plants, pillars, or furniture.

Continuing on to the parking lot, I could see the resort had spared no expense for their guests. The transportation to the Jungle Cruise looked like a retired migrant worker truck. The wooden sides appeared to have been green years ago, or was that mold? My allergies would answer that question soon enough.

The bench seats were worn smooth from overuse. Three guys turned to watch my approach. The two magnetic boys with all their earrings or whatever you called the decorations when they weren't in their ears, and an overweight gentleman, who appeared to be in his late fifties. The elderly gentleman wore a Panama hat pulled down low over his eyes, which were hidden by mirrored sunglasses.

Footsteps echoed behind me. I peered over my shoulder as Gary approached. "All aboard," he called, waving his clipboard.

Had he been the one I felt watching me?

Gary walked past me without a second glance and motioned for us to get in the back of the truck.

With his body builder physique, he wasn't going to be sneaking around this place spying on people. Someone else had been watching me. I knew it.

The magnetic boys scampered into the back of the truck, giggling as the older gentleman struggled to get up. Gary stepped up from behind and finally gave him a gentle boost. The bed of the truck dropped a few inches with his weight.

Great shock absorbers.

Gary motioned for me to go next. After I had climbed in, he hurdled into the back in a single bound. He walked to the cab of the truck and pounded on the roof twice. The engine roared, and the muffler expelled a cloud of black exhaust, followed by a gunshot-sounding backfire.

"We're probably going to be sold off into indentured servitude on this trip," I said under my breath, trying to joke with no one in particular.

Gary was the only one to laugh. "Wouldn't you be surprised." His stare held a menace I didn't understand.

"Thanks, I really needed that." I shifted uncomfortably on the wooden bench. The feeling of eyes burrowing into the back of my neck returned, forcing me to turn and look around the parking lot.

Nothing.

I strained to detect something; a shadow, a flicker, anything.

Gary's voice startled me. "Relax. I'm trying to make your vacation memorable." He ran his fingers over his bald head.

"Oh, that it is. Believe me." Slowly, the hair on my neck bristled, and goosebumps rose across my arms against the tropical heat. I rubbed at the tingle in my arms. That uneasy feeling intensified.

Before Gary could say anything else, the truck lurched forward, bottomed out in a rut, and threw everyone off balance. We all slid back and forth, up and down, the truck threatening to tip over as it rolled through the grooves in the gravel road. Palm trees coated with lime whizzed by like a picket fence. How could this antique achieve this speed?

The unease that had settled over me continued along the truck's path. Was someone following me or would this truck explode? Maybe that's what was bothering me. Maybe I should have asked Sergio to go with me. Or what about Logan or even Tom? Anyone for that matter? Then the thought struck me. I hadn't left a note for Sergio telling him where I had gone.

No one knew where I was going. I didn't even know where I was going.

Now was a fine time to start worrying about that.

Gary started talking to the older gentleman, asking him where he was from and what he did for a living. The magnetic boys were too busy with each other's company to notice the ride or anyone else around them.

The truck drove along the beach's edge. We watched as the terrain sloped down and the underbrush began to thicken. The road veered left, and vegetation appeared on both sides of the truck. Cacti, aloe vera plants, and sagebrush loomed closer as the road narrowed, and then suddenly parted to a small clearing. A yellow fiberglass boat with an outboard motor sat next to a floating dock. Was there room enough for all of us on that thing? And would the boat even stay afloat?

The truck turned around and backed up to the dock. It backfired and died. I doubted it would ever start again. Jumping down, we headed toward the dock. As we neared the boat, it appeared to grow bigger than I had originally thought. The bright yellow fiberglass was deeply scratched. In some places, if I looked hard enough, I could see right through it.

I walked across the pontoons as they bobbed on the water. Choosing the only single seat, I sat down on the front bench and got my camera ready as the other travelers found places to sit.

The magnetic boys sat behind me. The heavyset guy and Gary sat behind them. One seat remained open, in front of the guy who was manning the motor. Our captain, for lack of a better term, had no front teeth, dusty clothes, and what looked like a child's captain's hat perched on the top of his greasy black hair. Toni Tennille would pass out if she saw this captain.

I checked my camera. Then all of a sudden, that piercing sensation returned, this time at the base of my neck. It sent a cold shiver up and down my spine. More goosebumps broke out, and the hair on the back of my neck stood straight up on end.

I turned around and scanned the jungle, but couldn't see anyone. Trying to ignore my prickling skin, I went back to fumbling with the settings on my camera and tried to settle back, waiting for the ride to begin.

A few minutes passed, and then Tom emerged from the brush. He wore denim shorts and his white shirt blew in the breeze, revealing his chest. He started toward the boat. As he approached, he scanned the passengers and smiled when he saw me.

I waved him over.

"So, you're going cruising too?" Tom asked, standing on the dock. He looked down at me sitting in the boat.

"I guess so, otherwise I've been sitting here for nothing." I glanced over at Gary. "I was coerced into this."

Gary smiled when we made eye contact, but kept talking, ignoring my comment.

Tom started, "I was walking on the beach, and Mike said if I went through that grove, I could take a boat ride through the swamp. I was thinking of going, but…"

"But what?"

"I…" he shrugged his shoulders, "…thought it looked lame." He avoided eye contact, but didn't continue.

"I'm sure there's still room." The ice-cold prickles still lingered, but they seemed to be lessening.

He glanced at the back of the boat and appeared to be disappointed, but he said nothing.

I looked at where he had been staring, and the last bench was still open. "I can move to the back of the boat if you wanted company," I offered.

"No," Tom held up his hands, "you're in the front seat…"

I stood.

"Sit down," Gary shouted.

I stopped, with one foot in the boat and one foot on the bobbing dock. "What?" I asked.

All eyes turned to stare at Gary.

"I don't want you to…" his face flushed, as he seemed to search for the right word, "…tip us over." He smiled, pleased at what he had said.

"I'll be careful," I said, in Sergio's tone of voice. I stepped out on to the dock. "See."

Tom stood in my way. "I didn't ask you to move."

"I know, I volunteered."

"What about your pictures?" Tom protested.

"I can see the jungle just as well from the back of the boat as from the front." I pushed past him. "I hear it's all around us."

"But your camera…"

"I took it just in case." Without waiting for any further argument, I continued around him to the back of the boat and climbed onto the open bench. I motioned for him to follow.

"Thanks," he said, sitting down next to me, "but I think you should really stay up in front."

Gary turned around and glared at us.

"I'm glad you came. I'll enjoy the company." I motioned for Gary to turn around and face forward. "I was feeling a little uncomfortable going on this trip alone." I nodded toward the front seat that I had just vacated and lowered my voice. "I didn't really want to be up front, but it was the only single seat on the boat, so I just…"

"I know how you feel. No one at this resort seems to want to talk to me, except you." Tom paused for a moment. "Being a star, I get all kinds of responses, but to be avoided like this at Club Fred is very strange. I wonder why?"

"I don't know," I looked around at the people on the boat. Well, maybe I did.

Tom shook his head, puzzlement still played across his face.

"Don't worry about it, I'm sure it's nothing."

"All aboard," the captain said in a heavy Spanish accent. His face was deeply creased from exposure to the sun. He pulled the cord on the outboard. The motor coughed and choked, sputtered a few times.

Tom and I turned around.

The old man winked as us. "She's a bit temperamental at times, just like a woman." He pulled the cord again; this time the motor caught and revved.

"Wait! Wait!" A skinny guy with knobby knees and a bright yellow shirt bounced across the dock. "Is there room for one more?"

Gary said, "Not really, if you didn't sign up at the resort with your room number..."

But the guy said, "Yeah, sure, there's an open seat up front." The guy crawled on board and settled into his seat.

Gary turned to the back of the boat and called over the motor. "I think we're ready."

The Captain nodded, tossed the rope onto the dock and eased the boat out into the waterway.

"I never thought of Mexico as having a jungle. Did you?" I asked Tom.

"I knew it had a tropical climate, but I guess I always thought of it being more desert-like."

The boat entered a canopy of overgrown trees and plant life. The mangrove closed in and slowly darkened. Branches interwove into a low ceiling of green and brown. The temperature decreased a few degrees, but the humidity increased as the tunnel of trees moved in closer. The brackish water smelled of decaying plants and animal life. Even in the full sunlight, the water appeared black, unlike the ocean's bright blue transparencies. Here, the sun didn't penetrate the brine.

"I wonder what's underneath the water's surface. It's so dark. You can't see anything."

A flash of silver splashed out of the water next to me. I jumped in my seat, and almost landed in Tom's lap. My heart throbbed in my chest.

Tom laughed. "I know there are supposed to be piranha in these waters." He moved closer to me and pressed me closer to the side of the boat.

I pushed back against him. "I was wondering what could live in there, but I doubt there are piranha."

"It's true. They have piranha. I read it in the resort's pamphlet."

I stared at him, not believing a word.

"You know the pamphlet that told us all about the things to beware of while outside of the hotel." His eyebrows rose up, questioning.

"Next thing you'll be telling me that we're right in the middle of Jurassic Park. Hurry folks, come to Club Fred. It's better than Disneyland. The lines are shorter because our attractions eat the visitors."

"You got it." Tom laughed.

"But I don't want it, remember? A friend of mine signed me up for this."

"And you're telling me you're not having fun?"

"Don't get me started."

"Duck!" Gary shouted.

I ducked as the canopy closed in on us.

Tom didn't duck in time, and a low branch slapped him in the side of the head. "Oww!" he said, rubbing the area.

"Did it hit you in the eye?"

"I don't think so." Tom pulled his hand away and turned to face me. "Any blood?" His eye was tearing and a scratch ran along side of his cheek, along with a red spot where the branch hit him.

"Your eye looks fine. There's a little scratch with a few drops of blood…"

"Blood. Won't that attract sharks?" Tom asked.

Gary turned around and scowled at us.

"I hope it does. Maybe I'll get to use my camera after all." I brought it to my eye and peered through the lens. "Go ahead, stick your head in the water, and we'll see what finds you."

The older traveler looked around the jungle and snapped a few pictures, and the magnetic boys held a lip lock that made me wonder if their pierced tongues were stuck together.

The boat changed directions sharply and scraped up against another tree branch. A shower of dead leaves cascaded down into the boat. The river continued to twist and turn, sending us deeper into the swamp. More fish—at least I hoped they were fish—jumped in the water alongside. A heron flew overhead with a crab dangling from its beak.

For the next forty-five minutes, we dodged and ducked tree limbs, enjoying the various shades of green and the variety of exotic foliage as it floated by.

Our boat rounded a bend, and the bow of another yellow boat, just like the one we rode in, poked out of the water to our left. The paint was faded, and the hull was covered with mud and vegetation. How long had that been there, I wondered, and what had happened to its passengers?

Everyone else on board must have been thinking the same thing, because we all leaned forward, trying to see if a skeleton was inside, floating just below the water's surface.

The feeling someone was watching me returned. Before I could turn around, I thought I heard a low grunt and a sharp *snap*.

Glancing up, a flash of gray-white contrasted against the dark green canopy. Something came sailing through the air. It looked like a tree limb falling, but this wood was moving, wiggling. Another shower of leaves cascaded around us in all directions as the large brown and gray object coiled and uncoiled. It almost caught hold of a branch. It hung there for a second and then landed right in the lap of the skinny guy in the bright yellow shirt.

My mind flashed. *Snake.*

The man shrieked in panic. "Black Mamba! Black Mamba!" he cried, beating at his lap.

The confused snake rolled around, trying to right itself. Its light underbelly flashed with each turn.

The skinny guy thrashed around in his seat, rocking the whole boat wildly from side to side, threatening to tip us over.

Everyone grabbed on to the sides of the boat, trying to stabilize it. I glanced to the right where I thought the snake had come from and thought I saw a shadow dash off into the jungle.

The magnetic boys jumped into action. One of them spun the panicked guy around and slapped him in the face, trying to calm him down. After he was stunned into silence, the other magnetic guy reached into his lap and snatched the snake up. He grasped it by the neck and turned it around to look into its black eyes. He growled at it once, and then tossed it into the water.

The snake swam off into the grove.

"Everything all right up there?" the captain called from behind us.

"Yeah," the magnetic boys answered in unison.

"Okay," the captain said, and continued grumbling in Spanish as he made on our way, as if nothing had happened.

Had someone just thrown that snake into our boat?

"Are you all right?" Tom asked. "You look pale."

I whispered. "I don't do snakes and I think someone threw that snake into the boat."

"What?"

"I think I saw someone on shore run into the jungle right after the snake landed in that guy's lap."

"Are you sure?" Tom looked into the foliage.

"I don't know, but on the way to the jungle cruise, I had this strange feeling that someone was following me, but it disappeared once I got into the boat."

"Was that before or after I arrived?" Tom asked.

"It disappeared right after you showed up."

Chapter 15 - The Tide is High

Once our boat docked, everyone huddled around Gary as he checked over the snake-shocked skinny guy. He continued mumbling about Black Mambas and wiping at his pants. Gary pulled the guy's yellow shirt off and inspected his quivering body for any visible bite marks. Each rib stuck out under his pale skin, but no red spots marked his torso.

Stepping forward, I asked Gary, "Are his pupils the same size?"

He tipped the guy's head back and examined his eyes. "Yeah, they're about the same." He turned the guy's head to the side and revealed an angry red spot, which had risen up on the cheek where the magnetic boy slapped him.

"Sorry man," the magnetic boy apologized, his tongue clicking a stud against his teeth.

"I panicked," the skinny guy said. "I needed it." His eyes still held a blank stare and tremors racked his slender frame.

"Is there a blanket on the truck?" I asked Gary. "It may help prevent him from going into shock."

The group helped move him toward the truck as Gary ran ahead and returned with a serape. He wrapped it around the guy and pulled him next to his broad body.

Seeing that everything was under control, I veered away from the truck and turned to Tom. "How did you get here?"

Tom motioned to a path that cut through the trees. A white arrow reading "Beach" pointed in the same direction. "I came through there," he said. The crash of the surf rolled through the foliage.

"Gary," I called over my shoulder. "I'm walking back to the resort. I need some fresh air." Before Gary could respond, I headed into the narrow opening in the scrub trees and pushed my way through. I wasn't waiting for Gary to take a head count for our return trip.

"I'll keep you company." Tom scrambled to keep up.

Great. All I wanted was to be left alone for just a few minutes to process what had just happened. But how could I tactfully refuse Tom without hurting his feelings? For all I knew, he was the one who had followed me to the jungle cruise.

Pushing through the brushwood, my mind raced. Was Tom stalking me? Why would he do that? The feeling of being watched had disappeared as soon as he appeared. Maybe he had been watching me from the trees, but why?

And why had he tried to get me to stay in that front seat of the boat? Did he know that the snake was going to land there? Had he somehow signaled someone to drop that snake on the guy sitting in the front seat? But how could he have done that? Cell phone?

Now I was starting to sound like one of my patients with a head injury.

As the undergrowth scratched at my legs, the thought struck me: Tom wasn't the only one who had wanted me to stay in the front seat. Gary had yelled at me when I stood up and moved to the back of the boat. He said he was worried that I would tip the boat over, but I don't think that I could have with him and that heavyset guy sitting there. The boat had seemed pretty stable when I got in and out.

Could they both have tried to drop that snake on me? But they didn't know that I was afraid of snakes. Or did they? But what would their motive have been? Well, I hadn't listened to either one of them, and moved to the back of the boat.

But if Tom hadn't shown up, I probably would've stayed in the front seat. My body shuddered at that thought. So in a way, Tom had saved me from that snake. A branch snagged my yellow T-shirt and refused to untangle. I jerked my shoulder hard and heard my shirt rip. The twig cracked and broke off as I stormed through the brush. It dangled from the tear and I reached up and pulled it free. Throwing it down onto the ground, I grumbled under my breath. "Molly, I'm going to kill you when I get home."

"Maybe I should call and warn her," Tom said from behind me.

The vegetation thinned and pulled back, opening out onto the beach. The sun hung low in the sky and turned it a greenish pink. Thick heavy clouds clumped at the horizon. Stepping out onto the sand, I was invigorated by the ocean's cool breeze over my sweating body. The roar of the surf calmed my senses, but an electric buzz tingled over me, making all the hair on my body stand up on end. Now what was brewing? Or was I slowly bleeding to death from all the tiny cuts I received walking through the jungle?

Tom stepped into stride next to me. "So do I need to warn Molly or..."

"I'm sorry Tom, but I'm really not in the mood for company right now." Looking down the beach toward the resort, I saw that only a few guys littered the beach. "Where did everyone go?"

A smirk played across Tom mouth. "I'm sure they're cleaning up for supper. Some *men* can be even more prissy than women, especially when they're on the hunt."

My forehead wrinkled in confusion, and then the light came on. "I see. So supper is going to be an event?"

"Of course. Everyone has to show off how much color they got today. They'll be comparing tans and darkening their tan lines in a big way, all week long."

My face itched from the sun, and prickles ran down my neck and across my whole body. A shower was going to feel great when I got back to the room, despite what had been in there last night. I looked down at my pink, scraped arms. The sunscreen hadn't blocked enough ultraviolet rays. I'd need my Benadryl to prevent an awful allergic reaction.

I grabbed my shirt and pulled it away from my chest. Yellow. Just like the yellow shirt the guy had on when the snake dropped on him.

"What?" Tom asked when we stopped in our tracks.

"My shirt... it's the same color as the one..."

"The guy was wearing on the boat," Tom finished. "Do you think the snake was meant for you?"

I tried to read Tom's face, but because he was an actor, it made me question what was real and what was for show. Could I trust him? Maybe he was the one who had followed me to the boat? Why else had he shown up on the jungle cruise?

He must have read my expression, because he said, "You don't think that I had anything to do with that, do you?"

"I really don't know what to think anymore. It just seems like too much of a coincidence for a snake to be dropped in the same place I was sitting only a short time before." I swallowed hard.

"But why would anyone do that?"

"To scare me off of the resort?" I asked.

"But why?" And the obvious answer came to him. "The body!"

"I was just starting to think that myself." I ran my fingers through my hair.

"Do you think whoever killed him is after you?"

"What else can I think? If I hadn't moved to the back of the boat with you..."

Tom scratched his head. "I tried to make you stay in the front seat. I probably look pretty suspicious to you right about now, don't I?"

Nodding my head, we started walking toward the resort again.

Tom hit the side of his head with his palm. "Idiot! No wonder you look like you were going to jump out of your skin. I'm sorry." He held up his hands in surrender. "You had a great seat, and I didn't want you giving it up to sit with me. I could've sat alone."

I looked into his eyes. Could he have planned to drop a snake on me during the cruise? But if he had, why did he get on the boat? To make sure I went? To make sure the snake fell on the right person? To scare the hell out of me? Throw me overboard?

But why? Nothing seemed to be making sense.

The volleyball net whistled in the breeze. Ducking underneath, I tentatively glanced over at the spot where I tripped over Duane's body the night before.

Tom followed my gaze. "Is that where you found him? Then why the hell were we sitting so close to that spot?" Then he answered the question for himself. "Because that's where I chose to sit today, right?"

Before I could respond, he continued. "We can sit somewhere else tomorrow." A pained look fell across his face when he saw my facial expression. "That is, if you don't suspect me of…"

Passing our chaise lounges and palm frond umbrella, I paused and glanced around. "It sure was a great place to lie out. Away from the pool and most of the commotion of the resort," I said.

"But we can go wherever you want." Tom waved his hand across the beach.

"Maybe I should stay in my room for the rest of this trip."

"You can't do that. You're on vacation. You've paid too much money to come here and not have any fun."

I knew doubt was written all over my face.

"What did you work all year for, if not to relax and have fun?"

If he was the one trying to scare me off this resort, this didn't sound like what he should be saying. Especially if he plotted to drop a snake on me in the middle of the jungle cruise. I smiled. "I'll try, but I'm not promising anything."

We walked up the stairway to the resort. I paused at the stairwell leading to my room.

"Do you have plans for dinner?" Tom asked.

"No," I said, putting my foot up one step.

"Good. Then meet me for supper," Tom said. "Feel free to invite your friends."

"I don't think…"

"I don't want you to eat alone, and I doubt you do either. Especially after this afternoon, right?"

I took a deep breath and exhaled. "Sure, why not?" What could possibly go wrong at supper?

CHAPTER 16 - A CALL HOME

"And you'll never guess who Taylor's been hanging around with…" Sergio laughed into my cell phone. He sprawled across my bed, his sandals still on his feet.

"Who are you talking to?" I demanded.

Sergio looked directly into my eyes and said into the phone. "The hottest male porn star in the world." He nodded and burst into laughter. "You got it, babe." He pulled the phone away from his ear and covered the mouthpiece with his other hand. "Even Molly knows who Tom is."

"Why does Molly know who Tom is? Is that Molly?" I took a step forward. I wanted to ask her if she knew what kind of place this was.

"Maybe," he said, bringing the phone back to his ear. "What was that, dear?"

"Stop messing with me." Turning my back to him, I tossed the camera bag on the dresser. It hit the folding reacher, sending both across the dresser. They bounced off the lamp and slid to a stop. I spun around. "Give me that phone. I want to talk to her." I held my hand out for the phone.

"I'm not done yet," he said, pressing the phone against his skinny chest.

"Oh, yes, you are."

The phone flew up to his ear. "Sorry, Moll, I gotta go. Bye." Sergio sat up on the edge of my bed, extending his arm to the bedside table in an attempt to hang it up.

I dove across the bed and grabbed for Sergio's shoulders. "Give me that phone," I said, pulling him back onto the bed.

Sergio tried to roll himself into a ball, but was only able to hunch over onto his lap.

I pulled him back, and his legs curled up to his chest. As he rolled over onto his side, he pulled the phone away from me. "No, no, you can't talk to her. She's mine, all mine."

He tried to roll over onto his stomach to further protect the phone, but my body prevented it. Pinning one arm behind him with a wrestler's hold, I struggled to retrieve the phone. "I need to talk to her. Give me that phone."

My hand tried to dig underneath his arm, but Sergio held it glued to his side. My fingers slid down along his arm, and I started to tickle his side.

"Molly!" Sergio yelled. "He's attacking me. Help!" He squirmed harder under my assault, twisting his torso from side to side, trying to avoid my fingers. He tried not to laugh and still hang on to the phone for dear life, but he was lost.

A hard knocking came from the door. "Is everything all right in there?" a man's voice asked.

The distraction caused Sergio to let his guard down. His body relaxed just enough for me to reach in and snatch the phone. I rolled off him and sat down hard on the floor.

"Give it back." Sergio untangled himself from the bedspread.

"I'm calling security," the voice warned.

"Molly? Is that you?" I asked, breathlessly into the phone.

"Who do you think it is?" Molly demanded. "You're not beating up Sergio, are you?"

"No, I just needed to talk to you, and he wouldn't give me the phone."

"I need to talk to you, too. I can see why the K-9 Kennel Klub wouldn't take Regan back."

"Why? What did she do now? She didn't flood my house like she did the kennel, did she?"

"No. Your house is fine. Stevie and I ran to the Dairy Queen to get supper and…"

"You didn't take her with, did you?"

"No."

"Mistake number one."

"So I learned. I just wanted to make it a fast trip," Molly whined.

"Did you at least get her a hamburger?"

"No."

"Mistake number two." I shook my head.

"Taking care of *your* dog was mistake number one."

"You volunteered…"

"Yeah, well, after what she did, she doesn't deserve a hamburger. Do you have any idea what she did?" Molly's voice rose on the phone.

"No, but I'm sure you're going to tell me."

"She jumped up *on your bed* and peed all the way around it."

"Around my bed?" I asked.

"No, sweetheart. *On your bed.* All around *your* brand new down comforter."

"What?"

"Don't worry. I washed it," Molly said. "You don't think that I'd let that thing sit around until you got home, do you?"

"No, but you could've taken it to the dry cleaners."

"Why would I do that? It was already wet. Dry cleaning wouldn't have…" Molly's voice died off. "Ah, I see. Well, you can do that when you get home. I'm sure that will help fluff it up a bit. It looks kinda…" static sparked across the line, "…flat."

I swallowed hard. I could just see it. "Thanks for taking care of that for me." I forced happy into my voice. My brand new comforter. I closed my eyes and shook my head.

"No prob. What are friends for? Oh yeah, she also…"

I interrupted. "Don't tell me. I'll find out when I get home." *If* I got home.

"Oh. Okay, by the way, did you get me anything yet? Not that I'm expecting anything, but…"

Sergio rolled across my bed, laughing to himself.

"I have an idea." I glared at Sergio. "Would you like a shrunken head?"

"Would it be anyone I know?"

"Oh, it might be."

Sergio stopped laughing.

"So are you boys having fun? Sergio said that you've stumbled across a dead body, twice, hooked up with the hottest porn star and a best-selling mystery author, and you have several of the staff members writing marriage proposals to you on beach towels. Not bad for your first day at the resort."

"Did you know that this place was…?"

"Gay? No. I thought it was odd when I didn't see any women in the brochure, but I figured, it was one of those Iron John, he-man places, you know where you get to do all that macho shit."

"Oh, yeah, this is really macho. I'm sure the Village People are here somewhere pumping iron."

"Cool, can you get me their autograph? Well, at least the cowboy. He was the cutest one, but so was the construction worker."

"Yeah, he was my favorite too." Anger burned my words.

"So, who's the author? Sergio wouldn't say. Anyone I'd know?"

"I don't think you've read anything by…Logan Zachary? Have you?" I smiled at that one.

"Logan Zachary! That's not fair. I'd give anything to meet Logan." The phone line crackled again. "Take lots of pictures, especially on the nude beach. Woo baby. You could get one heck of a Christmas card out of those pictures." More crackles echoed on the line. "Check out these candy canes for Christmas!" Molly hooted, "Who needs Santy Claus, when you can get Sandy Buns." More laughter was interspersed with static.

"I'm glad you're having this much fun at my expense."

"Just think of all the stories you can tell them back at work."

Molly laughed.

There wasn't anything I could tell anyone about this trip.

"Before I forget. Did you hear about the hurr—" more static broke out across the line, drowning out Molly's voice.

"What?" I said into the phone.

A click shot into my ear, and then the hum of an open line resonated. Molly was gone. Turning back to Sergio. "We were cut off."

"I didn't see you or Tom all afternoon. Where have you two been?"

I said nothing.

"What were you two doing?" Sergio leaned forward.

"You don't want to know." I stood and hung up the phone. Maybe she'd try and call back.

Sergio noticed my wild hair, ripped and dirty shirt, along with the scratches on my face and arms. "You look a little... disheveled. Did you get lucky? Tell me, tell me." He licked his lips and waited.

"I need a shower, first," I said, quickly gathering a change of clothes. "I'll tell you at supper. We've been invited to eat with Tom." Then I escaped to the bathroom and locked the door before Sergio could ask any further questions.

Supper was served poolside. More tables had been moved down from the main dining hall and filled the afternoon's sunbathing deck. Long buffet tables surrounded the dining area with "Mediterranean Night" signs, even though Caribbean music played gently from tinny sounding speakers scattered around the pool. A small stage walled the far side of the pool.

I hadn't noticed the stage this afternoon, with all the "other" things running through my mind. "Maybe we're going to have some entertainment at dinner tonight," I said to the back of Sergio's head, as he continued to pull me through the maze of tables. His grip never relaxed on my shirt. Was he afraid I'd bolt?

Then the thought struck me, and I prayed, please God, don't let it be a murder mystery dinner. Not tonight. That's all I needed, another body dropping dead at my feet.

Sergio scanned the crowd as he continued to pull me to the tables in the back corner, farthest from the stage. He smiled and waved at a few guys in the crowd, but paid extra attention to one in particular. "Doesn't he have the most fabulous hair?" he asked.

"He must've given you a big tip," I teased.

"Better than that," Sergio smiled.

"What's better...?" I realized what Sergio meant and said, "I don't want to know." My eyes tried to scan the tables as Sergio's breakneck speed increased.

Tom sat alone in the corner near the first buffet table, watching the bright orange liquid swirl around in his glass. As he looked up, he smiled and waved us over. His body seemed to relax. He took a long sip from his drink and settled back in his chair.

"Mind if we join you?" Sergio asked, pulling out the chair next to Tom before he could answer.

He shrugged his shoulders. "Sure, I thought Taylor invited you..."

"Oh, he did, or he was going to, but he just needed to take a shower after he got back to our room." Sergio winked at him, "Must have gotten pretty *hot* in the sun this afternoon."

Before Tom could respond, Logan walked up to our table and asked, "Do you mind if I join you guys?"

"No, not at all." I pulled out my chair and sat down. Sergio and Tom motioned for Logan to take the empty seat.

Logan pulled out his chair as Sergio scooted closer to Tom's. "Taylor, where's your camera?" Sergio put his arm around Tom's shoulder and pulled him closer.

Tom gave me a questioning smile.

"I left it in the room. I didn't think…"

Tom interrupted, "You'll have to wait until the end of the week to take pictures. That's when our tans will be the darkest."

"If we last that long," I mumbled, under my breath.

"What was that?" Sergio asked.

"I really like this song," I said as the trumpets started to blast, announcing another event was about to begin. "Can't we just eat supper in peace. This is like summer camp where they have things planned for us every second of the day. I just want to relax."

"So, therapist, aren't you healing yourself?" Sergio said, snidely. He glanced from me over to Tom. "Didn't you do any *therapy* this afternoon?" His eyes went wide.

"That's right," Logan began. "You're a therapist. My fingers tingle after I've been writing for a while…"

"How much did you write today?" I asked.

"Only twelve pages."

"Did you warm up first? Stretch between pages? And are you using proper body mechanics?"

"In this climate I figured the temperature was warm enough, I wouldn't have to…" Logan balled his fingers into a fist and straightened them out, wiggling them as if he was typing on a keyboard.

"Just because it's warm down here, doesn't mean your body won't hurt if you overdo or work in a bad position."

"Enough shop talk," Sergio interrupted. "Let's discuss something more interesting." He turned to Tom. "So. What did *you* do all afternoon?"

Tom turned to Sergio. "We can talk about that later, I'd like to hear more about what Logan's working on. I must've missed it this morning when I was napping."

Sergio scrunched up his face, but said nothing.

"I'm working on a new mystery," Logan began. "Have you heard of the Axel Bolton and Bruce Abel mysteries? They're my detectives."

"I hate stereotypes. Are they gay?" Sergio asked, quickly. "Are you?"

Subtle Sergio, real subtle, I mused.

"Oh, no," Logan's face flushed a bright red, "we're not, I mean, I'm not." He took a breath. "Not that there's anything wrong with being gay, but…"

"What about your characters? Aren't they gay? I love Grant Michaels. He writes about a hairdresser, who just happens to be gay," Sergio pressed.

"I've read him. He has a fun series, a bit stereotypical of the profession." Logan looked at Sergio. "Don't you think?"

"Well, if the shoe fits…" Sergio said.

"I guess, but in my new book, I'm sending my character Bruce on vacation."

"And he's the gay one, right?" Sergio burst out into laughter. "Well, that's a stupid question. Aren't all Bruces gay?"

We all stared at him. Talk about stereotyping, Sergio.

Becoming defensive, Sergio huffed. "Well, they are, aren't they?"

Tom and Logan broke out into laughter at Sergio's perceived joke. I smiled to myself and shook my head. I bet Sergio really believed it.

Logan continued, "Bruce is very straight. He's going on vacation, away from his partner, Axel." Logan looked at Sergio, "They're partners in a detective agency, but that's it. Anyway, I'm calling this book, *Kill Me! Kill Me! Kill Me! (A Man After Midnight).* Bruce's vacation plans get mixed up somehow, and he finds himself at a gay resort in Mexico. As luck would have it, he finds a body in his bed, and then it disappears. Later on, he'll stumble across it again."

Sergio coughed, spitting a mouthful of water that he had been drinking across the table. Embarrassed, he wiped his mouth. "I'm so sorry."

Sergio glanced over at me, but I refused to make eye contact. I knew what he was thinking. I prayed, "Please don't say anything." I felt with all the prayers I'd been saying on this trip, it was quickly becoming a religious retreat.

Tom stared at me, and I read the same question in his mind.

Logan glanced from me to Tom to Sergio. "What's going on here with you three? You all look like you've just seen a ghost."

"It's difficult to explain," I said, trying hard to decide if I should tell him the truth.

But before I could say another word, I heard, "There, they're over here. Come on. I'm sure they won't mind if two more join them at their table."

All eyes watched as a couple wove their way through the tables. The skinny guy from the jungle cruise wore a red and yellow Hawaiian shirt. His friend, a portly balding man with a red face, which may have been from sun or exertion, followed close behind.

"Hi. Do you remember me?" the skinny guy said to me.

Oh crap. I looked at him, shaking my head no, hoping to prevent them from joining us if I seemed not to remember him.

"I was on that boat this afternoon. You two were there, right?" He pointed from Tom to me.

Before I could answer, he continued. "I'm David, and this is David. Most people call us David and David."

"These two saved my life today," Skinny David said to Chubby David, pointing from Tom to me. "Not that they were the two that actually removed the snake from around my neck. Two other guys did that. No, actually one did. The other one slapped me when I kept screaming about the Black Mamba. I was sure I was going to tip the whole boat over, but these two guys saved us all." He pointed at Tom and me.

Maybe you should go find the other guys who really saved your life and join them, I thought.

Tom rolled his eyes and avoided the Davids' stares.

"I can't believe that big old snake fell right into my lap. If I didn't know any better, I would've sworn someone threw it at me. But who'd do a thing like that?"

I could think of a few, my mind screamed, but just then an image flashed in my mind. The silhouette.

Tuning out what Skinny David was saying, I strained to remember. The scene replayed in my mind, but this time in slow motion. I heard a low grunt and a snap of something hitting branches. That was when the twisting, withering mass flew through the air. Two hands had launched it. I could see the arms tossing the snake and the shadow of a man hitting the dirt. Definitely, someone had thrown that snake into the boat.

Skinny David stood up. "I'd like to make a toast." He paused with his glass in hand. "Hey you," he shouted to the magnetic boys, sitting a few tables away.

"Those are the two who really saved your life," Tom said.

"That's right," I piped in, "You should really go and thank them."

"Personally," Sergio said, quickly adding, "like in person." He stood, trying to shoo them in the magnetic boys' direction.

Chubby David stood up and took Skinny David's hand and headed over to the magnetic boys' table.

A sigh of relief escaped from all of us.

Sergio broke the silence. "Well, you two must've had one wild afternoon."

Tom glanced from me to Sergio. He opened his mouth to begin, but the trumpet music blasted from the speakers, cutting him off. This time Mike stepped out onto the stage with Gary close behind. "Tonight, we have a special treat. All the food that you would find in the Mediterranean is here tonight. But don't leave after you've stuffed yourself, because tonight, after supper, we have a very special show for you. A local group of dancers, singers, and musicians will show the history and heritage of Mexico in native song and dance."

"When did Mexico get moved to the Mediterranean? Great, just what we want to see after dinner, *Dysentery, The Musical,*" Sergio said to our table.

Mike waved his hand into the air, and metallic clinks sounded around the perimeter of the dining area as the waiters lifted the lids off the serving trays. Tom pushed his chair back and headed to the buffet tables. I stood up and followed his lead. At the first table, Tom picked up two plates and handed one to me. The table was covered with lettuce, veggies, and every salad topping imaginable. I waited as Tom piled a heap of lettuce on his plate and covered it with French dressing. He looked at mine. "Aren't you hungry?"

"Starved, but I'm not a salad eater, lettuce isn't..."

"Sure," Tom interrupted. "You're just saving room for all the other exotic dishes."

I leaned forward. "I can't wait to see what they have."

"Cut in front of me." Tom stepped to the side. "I may be a while." He motioned to the salad bar.

The next table was covered with metal pans held in heating racks with cans of Sterno flaming underneath. Frog legs, fried in a light batter, were piled high in the first pan. I looked closely at them. Small pointed toes were still visible through the batter.

I thought I could see a tinge of green under the light coating. Skin? Frog skin? Weren't they supposed to peel that off before battering? A flash of biology lab and formaldehyde stabbed into my nose.

I swallowed hard and continued to the next pan. A dark liquid bubbled from the heat. I picked up the large serving spoon and dug into the depths. Small squids or octopi rose to the surface. Their tentacles were still attached, and they quivered and squirmed in the liquid. Were they still alive?

I dropped the spoon into the pan and peered over to the next one. This one was labeled: Boiled Fish. I didn't look. Next.

The Red Snapper had slices of limes sticking out of its belly and gill slits. One even protruded from the mouth of its triangular head. Flying fish were fried crisp with their wings fanned out to each side. A pan of shrimp with their shells and heads still intact looked back at me. Grill lines transversed more fish, crisscrossing their scales and skulls, as their milky white eyes stared off into the night sky. My stomach began to roll.

Saliva production increased, and not due to the delicacies set before me, but what threatened to come back up. I forced a hard swallow. My skin crawled. This wasn't a buffet. This was a science experiment.

The next table was covered in bowls and dishes of things I've never seen before. The only thing that I recognized, or thought I recognized, was mashed potatoes. And with my luck, they were probably left over from lunch. I scooped two big clumps onto my plate. At the end of the buffet stood a wicker basket full of rolls. I quickly snatched up three.

Tom watched as I walked by, glancing down at my food. "Is that all you're going to eat?"

"That's all I can eat. I bet they'll put out some fruit and desserts later. I'll get something then."

Sergio bounded back to the table with his plate covered with a little of everything. He smiled and dug into his heap.

I pushed my mashed potatoes away and started on my rolls.

The crust was too hard for my fingers to break. My knife sawed the bread like wood. Dunking it into my water glass made it chewable. I watched as Sergio shoveled food into his mouth.

He must have felt me watching him, because suddenly the tentacles began to slip out of his mouth, like a wave of spaghetti. They slid in and back out. Then he sucked them back in. He grinned at me. "I think it's still alive. I can feel it swimming around in my stomach." Sergio grabbed his stomach like the guy in *Alien*. "It's alive, it's alive," he said as he clutched his belly.

"You think you're so cute."

"I am," Sergio said, and stroked the side of his neck with his hand. "I wish they had taken the suction cups off these tentacles before they cooked them." A funny expression played across his face. "I think one of them is stuck in my throat."

"Don't expect me to do the Heimlich on you," I stated. I tried to clear the image of the suction cup from my mind.

"Fine. I'll behave, but only if you tell me what happened this afternoon."

Great. Now, he was resorting to blackmail to get what he wanted. Tom and I told him about our adventure on the Jungle Cruise. Logan hung on every word, as if taking mental notes on the details of our trip. I wondered if this story was going to end up in his novel.

Tom turned to me and asked, "What was that expression that came over your face when David and David were here?"

I told them what I had remembered.

Sergio broke the silence. "Do you think that someone threw that snake into your boat?"

I nodded my head, slowly. "Skinny David had on a yellow T-shirt, just like the one I was wearing. The strange thing is, I had sat in the same seat that Skinny David took over after I moved back to keep Tom company." I glanced over at Tom. "Both Gary and Tom tried to keep me in my seat, but I didn't listen, and now I'm glad I didn't."

Tom opened his mouth to say something, but closed it.

"I'll be the first to admit that I don't like snakes, but now, I'm starting to think that someone wanted to drop that snake on *me*."

"Wow," Sergio said. "This is sooo cool."

"But why would someone want to drop a snake on you?" Logan asked.

I glanced from Tom to Sergio, and they both nodded their heads in agreement.

Logan still looked puzzled.

"Last night, I came back to my room, and the shower was running. I thought Sergio was in there, but it turned out to be a body. A dead body."

"A hairy one," Sergio added.

"We ran to get help, but when we got back to the room…"

Logan finished, "The body was gone."

Sergio and I nodded.

"Did you stumble across…?" Logan began.

"I tripped over him on the beach later that night."

"Just like in my book." Logan rubbed his forehead. "You must think…" He paused. "That's why all of you gave me such a strange look earlier."

"It makes you look suspicious," Sergio accused.

"It's just a coincidence," Logan explained.

I had my doubts.

"So what do we do now?" Tom asked.

"I think we should go out into the jungle tomorrow and look for clues," Sergio suggested. "If we verify what Taylor saw, maybe we can find who threw the snake at him, and prove that the killer was trying to tie up the loose ends."

"I don't really want to go back on that boat," I said, turning to Tom, "Do you?"

"I didn't mean back on the boat," Sergio said.

My body cringed at what was coming next.

"We can walk through the jungle." Sergio rubbed his hands together in excitement.

"Just like Tarzan?" I asked.

"Exactly." Sergio smiled.

In the next few minutes, we discussed plans for our investigation. Sergio finally said, "Then it's settled, we'll set off into the jungle tomorrow morning after breakfast and see if we can find anything that proves someone threw that snake at Taylor and hopefully find the killer."

Logan nodded his head in agreement.

"But if we find something that proves that Taylor is the target, then what?" Sergio asked.

"Then," Tom sighed, "we'll have to protect Taylor. Wherever he goes and whatever he does, we'll go with him."

Sergio's eyes lit up with Tom's offer, but my heart sank. So much for my relaxing week alone in the sun, just me and my books.

CHAPTER 19 - A WALK IN THE JUNGLE

"You can't be serious," I said, stepping out of the bathroom.

Sergio stood waiting by the door. "What?" He held his hands out, questioning.

"You have to ask?" I pointed to his outfit.

Sergio stood by the door with a safari helmet on his head, high-top hiking boots, wool socks, khaki shorts and shirt. Two thick utility belts crisscrossed his skinny chest, while a huge machete hung from his slender hip and pulled his pelvis cockeyed. "They have a prop and costume room with everything you could ever want to play dress up with. And I mean everything." He swung his machete. "It's real."

"Indiana Jones you're not," I said.

"What about Lara Croft?"

"You'll need to be digitally enhanced and in more ways than one."

"Well, I doubt that your black shirt and jeans are the appropriate attire for this little adventure," Sergio eyed me. "Maybe if you were stalking someone at midnight or playing Ninja warrior, but you'll die of heat exhaustion out there in that get-up."

I glanced at the reflection in the bathroom mirror. Maybe he was right. Even this early in the morning, the black would absorb the humidity and heat. "Fine. I'll put on a light colored shirt, but I'm not changing my jeans. I can just imagine what else is living in that foliage." Images of the slides from my microbiology, parasitology, and mycology classes came to mind, followed by the diseases they caused.

Sergio pulled a string from the side of his helmet and a net sprang free and surrounded his head.

I smiled and started to laugh.

Sergio looked at himself in the mirror and burst out, "I look like Mrs. Howell."

I laughed even harder, and tears formed at the corners of my eyes. "I need to change, and I think you do too." I rifled through my clothes and found a tan long-sleeved shirt. I quickly changed my shirt. With all of my allergies, I wasn't taking any chances, and with the threat of snakes, there was no way I was going to wear shorts, no matter how hot it got.

Sergio removed his bandoleers and helmet, changed his boots for white tennis shoes, but kept his khaki shirt and shorts. "Do I meet your approval?"

"Yes. At least, I can be seen with you in public."

"Well, don't wait for Tarzan to be picking up your sorry ass in that get-up." Sergio opened the door and headed down for breakfast. The machete bounced with each step.

"And that's just fine with me," I called after him. Following him, I scratched my head. "Can I ask you something?"

"Sure."

"Where did you get that machete?"

"Wouldn't you like to know?" he said, looking over his shoulder. "The costume closet has everything. Trust me."

After breakfast, Logan, Tom, Sergio and I headed through the front door of the resort and across the parking lot. The shuttle stood ready to take the next group of unsuspecting tourists to their fate. We ignored the driver's calls and headed down the dirt road toward the jungle cruise.

"So what exactly are we looking for?" Sergio asked.

"First, I think we need to find the place were the snake fell and look around there," I said.

"I thought you said the snake was thrown," Logan remarked, with a small notepad and pen in hand.

"I said I thought I saw hands throw the snake, but I want to make sure."

"Do you even remember where this happened?" Sergio asked.

"There was a sunken boat in the clearing close to where it happened," Tom replied. "We need to find that boat and look around there. I'm sure we'll find something."

As we neared the grove of trees where the boat departed, I pointed to a worn trail that wound into the foliage. "This looks like a path."

"That?" Sergio's voice raised a few octaves.

"It's all we have," Tom said. "Unless we go by boat."

"We can see where it takes us," Logan offered.

I removed my camera from the fanny pack and opened its shutter.

"Who wants to lead the way?" Sergio asked.

"You're the one with the machete. I think you should take lead," Tom said.

Sergio unsheathed the blade and passed the handle to Tom. "It's all yours."

I smiled to myself; he did look more like Mrs. Howell than Indiana Jones, and Lara Croft would have taken charge.

Tom grasped the handle and swung the machete from side to side. The blade cut through the air with a swooshing sound.

I wondered how sharp the blade was. "Did you bring this with you from Sioux Falls?" Tom asked.

"I have my connections." Sergio smiled, but refused to say more.

Tom sliced a small branch off the tree and pushed into the underbrush. The blade cut the wood without any effort.

I followed Tom with Sergio behind me, and Logan brought up the rear. I felt a slight tap on my backside. I turned and glared at Sergio.

"Sorry," he said, his face flushed. "I thought I saw…"

I held up my hand, turned around, and followed Tom.

Branches that Tom didn't cut slapped me and clawed at my shirt. The wet shirt clung to my back and chest like a second skin. Another shower waited for me when we got back to the resort. If we got back. Why was I such an optimist?

The foliage thickened and the branches became larger.

"This reminds me of *Romancing the Stone*," Sergio said. "All we need to find is an airplane with a skeleton in it and…" Sergio paused when I turned around and glared at him. "Never mind."

We walked a little further, and he started up again. "You know, this reminds me of that movie *Anaconda*. Did you see it? Jennifer Lopez was in it, but that was before she exposed her bazoobees to the whole world. Anyway, there was this huge snake that swallowed Jon Voight whole, and after it digested him a little bit, it spit him out."

"Thanks. That's just the wonderful image I was searching for." I didn't want to be out there to begin with, but I needed to know if I was going crazy. "I'm freaked out enough about snakes, especially ones being thrown at me, and all this talk about snakes isn't helping."

"You really need to rent the movie," he continued.

Logan humphed behind us.

"Okay. Run Toto, Run," Sergio said, and then began singing, "Lions and tigers and bears, oh my."

"Lions and tigers and…"

On the second chorus, I let a branch snap back. *Whack.*

"Ouch!" Sergio swore under his breath.

"Watch out for that flying monkey," I called.

"Thanks," Sergio grumbled.

"I'll separate you two if you don't knock it off," Tom said in a fatherly tone. "Don't make me come back there."

We fell into silence for the next twenty minutes. Our eyes scanned the trees for any sign that someone had been through there in the last day or so.

Small things skirted across the trail, while insects buzzed and swarmed us. Birds squawked and who knows what else followed our trek.

Internally, I wished I had put on the pair of high-top boots that Sergio took off and left in the room. My Reeboks weren't giving me all the protection I needed.

A glimmer of yellow shone between the leaves to our left.

Tom stopped and pointed in the same direction. "I think we found the boat. Now, before we trample any evidence, I think we should look around for any broken branches."

The small clearing had a few patches that appeared a little trampled down, but nothing distinct. Had it been the weather? Wildlife? Or someone else?

"Taylor, why don't you take a few pictures? Maybe the film will pick up something we miss." Sergio looked around the area. "I hope the resort has a computer so we can blow up and really examine the pictures, otherwise you'll have some pretty dull photos to show your friends at home. Molly will get a kick out of it."

"I think my sanity is worth a bunch of bad pictures," I said, and I snapped a few shots of the ground and the surrounding trees and brush.

Once the photos were taken, Tom divided the search area into four quadrants and sent us to explore our sections.

The ground was sun baked and cracked, and no footprints were visible.

Something splashed in the water next to the sunken boat. I waited for something to slither out of the swamp, but nothing appeared. It was probably a fish, maybe piranhas, at least, according to Tom.

"Hey! Over here," Sergio called a few minutes later.

Tom, Logan, and I headed toward Sergio and slowed as we neared. He pointed to a dark blue object stuck in a lower branch of a small tree.

I snapped a picture of it.

Sergio reached to touch it, but Tom stepped forward, machete blade blocking his reach. "Here, let me get that."

"Should we touch that?" Logan asked.

"How many police officers have you seen around here?" I asked.

"I'll use the blade, so I won't smudge any fingerprints," Tom said. He worked the blade underneath the object and pried it loose. A Nike gym bag fell to the ground at our feet. The top was unzipped and gaped open. Tom slipped the blade into the bag's mouth and waited for something to jump out. Nothing did.

Tom pushed one of the sides back, and we all peered inside.

"What's that smell?" Sergio asked, covering his nose. "Whoa, did someone forget to wash out their jocks and socks?"

"That smells like urine," Logan said.

Tom moved the blade and pulled back on the other side of the gym bag. Sergio pulled back the other side with a stick he had found on the ground.

The bag was empty. Well, almost empty.

"What's that?" Sergio dug into the bag with his stick. He pulled out a small tattered piece of transparent paper-like material. It appeared to have a honeycomb texture. As it exited the bag, it fluttered in the breeze and threatened to blow off the tip of the stick.

"It looks like skin," Logan said.

"Skin?" Sergio scrunched up his eyes as he brought the tip closer. A sudden gust of wind caught it and blew it into his face, sticking it to his lips.

"Snake skin," Logan corrected him at the moment of contact.

"Aaack." Sergio spat the skin onto the ground and wiped his mouth with the back of his hand. "I need mouthwash!" He spat again and rubbed his mouth harder, his lips darkening from the force. "I think I'm going to be sick." He moved away from us as gagging noises rose from his throat.

Logan pulled a handkerchief out of his back pocket and handed it to Sergio.

"Thanks," Sergio said, grabbing the cloth from his hand and rubbing his lips even harder. "Is it coming off?"

"Your lips?" I asked.

Sergio spat again. "No. The skin!" His voice took on a panicked tone.

I bit the inside of my cheek so I wouldn't laugh. "No. It's gone," I said through tight lips.

Sergio looked from me to Tom, and then Logan, his eyes pleading with us.

"It's gone," Tom said.

"Completely," Logan agreed.

"Really?" tears pooled in Sergio's eyes and threatened to fall.

I stepped forward and rubbed his shoulder. "It's gone, really."

Sergio's breathing started to slow. His chest's heaving decreased, and he took several deep breaths in an attempt to calm his heart rate.

"Anything else in there?" Logan picked up the stick from where Sergio had dropped it. He pulled the opening wider and peered in.

The inside appeared as stained and well used as the outside. The zipper looked like it was getting ready to pull away from the vinyl. Otherwise, nothing. No writing, no names, no addresses.

"Nothing but some white crusty splatters that covered the bottom of the bag," I said.

"That's the snake's urine," Logan added. "Snakes have solid urates, just like birds."

We all looked at him in amazement.

"I used it in a book once."

"That's right, in *Wring, Wring.*" I took a deep breath. "Maybe we'll find something else in there when we get back to the resort. I'm sure Geoff will want to fingerprint it or something. That is, after we search it further. We might be destroying evidence."

"Like the snake skin?" Sergio asked. "It's gone. It must've blown away when I panicked and spat."

"I'm sure it's around here someplace," I said.

We looked for ten minutes and found nothing.

Tom and Logan finally gave up looking. "Even without the piece of skin, I'm sure the urine in the bag should be proof enough that a snake was inside. Maybe there are a few more smaller pieces inside that we can't see?" Logan said. "But I'm not sure they will be able to tell what kind of snake it was."

"Is that important?" Tom asked.

"It could be," Logan said.

"Why?" Sergio asked.

"If the snake was poisonous or not," I said. "It makes a difference if it was meant to scare or…" I swallowed hard and didn't finish the sentence.

Sergio broke the silence. "Well, at least now we know someone threw that snake."

"Yeah, but that still leaves three big questions unanswered." I said, more to myself than to anyone in particular. "Who killed Duane, who threw the snake, and who was it intended for?"

Geoff was less than excited with our evidence. "Mon, get that smelly bag out of here," he said, pushing it across the desktop away from him.

"But it proves that someone tried to kill Taylor with a snake yesterday." Sergio used the machete to push the gym bag back in front of him.

Gary stood beside Geoff, but said nothing.

Logan, Tom, Sergio, and I stood our ground. "We're not leaving until you do something," Sergio said. He crossed his arms over his chest, machete still in hand. We ducked when he tapped the flat edge of the blade against his shoulder.

I cringed and waited for the blood to flow.

Gary reached across the desk and picked up the bag by the handle.

"Fingerprints!" everyone shouted at him at the same time.

Gary's hand released the handles and let it drop. "Sorry," he said and wiped his hand on his pants.

"Do you realize what you just did? You just contaminated the evidence," Sergio sprang forward and waved the machete at Gary. Good thing the desk was between them.

"Yeah," Logan said.

"I said I was sorry," Gary said, and stepped behind Geoff for protection.

Geoff rolled his eyes. "What do you want me to do? Fingerprint the whole resort?"

"Well, of course," Sergio said. "Isn't that your job?" He poked Geoff in the chest with the tip of the machete.

"I don't got the mon power to do that." Geoff pushed the blade away from his chest and then poked at the Nike bag with a pencil. "There's too many to check, and there's no way to be sure with the fingerprints here. I can send this to the lab, but..."

"But nothing. What are you going to do? Now! We had a dead body in our shower. Someone tried to kill Taylor with a snake. Isn't that enough?" Sergio's arm flapped to his side with a whoosh of the machete and almost cut off his leg.

Gary put his hand on Geoff's shoulder and leaned forward. "What can we do to make you feel that we are trying to solve this problem?"

No one said anything.

"See. That's where we are at too." Gary stepped to Geoff's side. "You said there was snake skin in there. Where is it? We can smell the urine, but you guys could have peed in the bag."

"Are you calling us liars?" Sergio demanded. The blade swung back toward Geoff and Gary.

"Boys. Boys," Geoff said and pushed the blade aside. "This isn't helpin'."

"Well, neither are you," Sergio retorted.

"I doubt we're going to get much analyzed from that bag down here," Logan said. "I don't think they have the testing facilities in Mexico like we have back in the States. Unless there is something else left in the bag, which can link it to the owner, I don't think the fingerprints or urine will help us."

"Why not?" I asked.

"Do you know how long it would take to try and match the fingerprints from the resort's guests? And I don't think this place's computer has a database or the speed to complete that task. Do you?" Logan scratched his head.

My heart sank. So much for finding our snake thrower. "I think we've wasted enough of your time," I said, and walked out of the small office.

Tom, Logan, and Sergio followed me.

Sergio grabbed my shoulder and spun me around. "What did

you mean by that?"

"If we want to find out who threw that snake, I think we're going to have to do it ourselves, without their help."

"So now what?" Tom asked.

"I guess we can hit the beach and relax for now," I said. "Maybe we'll come up with something else. The killer is going to have to wait until I change out of these hot black jeans and shower the jungle off of me."

Our chaise lounges still held our towels, folded neatly on each seat. Spreading my towel out across the white plastic, I noticed that the ocean breeze had picked up. The surf crashed on the sand in larger waves than yesterday. The bright blue water appeared to be darker and debris floated in the once clear waves. White caps rolled and hissed as they dissolved into the sand. Maybe it was high tide.

Sergio rubbed sunscreen over his legs and arms. I lay back on my lounge chair, and an ice cold prickling started at the base of my neck.

At first, I thought it was the sunburn acting up, but then it bore deeply into me.

Eyes.

I could feel someone watching me, just like on the way to the jungle cruise. I scanned the beach, avoiding the nude flesh.

Tom was gone.

Logan was gone.

The chill sent goose bumps across my skin, despite the heat.

Someone was watching me.

"What's wrong?" Sergio pushed his sunglasses up onto his forehead.

I rolled over. "I think someone's watching me," I whispered.

"I know, isn't it great?" Sergio smiled at me, and then he frowned, finally understanding what I meant. "Where?" He sat up and scanned the beach and surf for the observer.

"I don't know." My eyes continued to search the area. "All I can tell you is that someone is watching. I had this feeling right before the jungle cruise, and you know how that turned out."

A drop of ice water dripped on my back and drove me up into a sitting position.

"Sorry, I didn't mean to scare you," Tom apologized, handing me a bottle of water. "Want one?" he asked Sergio, who nodded. Tom tossed him a bottle and put one on Logan's chair. He leaned over the notebook and squinted at the pages. "Should we take a look and see what he's been working on?"

"Don't you dare," a voice commanded.

Tom stood up and spun around. Sergio and I turned to find Logan standing there.

"I can't even run to the bathroom without you guys trying to sneak a peek at my work." Logan frowned at each one of us separately, but focused on Tom, who was standing closest to his notebook.

"You shouldn't leave it lying around," Sergio said, "tempting us. Personally, I don't see what the big deal of reading a mystery is all about. All you have to do is look at the last chapter, and you'll know who did it."

Logan looked like Sergio had punched him. He opened his mouth, but before he could reply, Gary walked across the volleyball court and headed in our direction. "Good, I found you.

Do you want some company for lunch today?"

Logan returned to writing in the notebook, oblivious to us. Tom looked like he had fallen asleep.

I glanced at Sergio, who was looking over the top of his sunglasses.

Gary turned his back to Sergio and stared at me.

I started to say no when Sergio began nodding his head and mouthed, "Yes."

I followed his nod and said, "Sure, why not?"

"Twelve-thirty?" he asked.

"Fine, I'll meet you in the cabana," I said.

Sergio made an okay sign with his fingers.

"Good, see you then," Gary said and turned toward Sergio, who quickly ran his "okay" signed fingers through his spiky blond hair. "Are you going to join us?" Gary asked.

Sergio nodded curtly. "Why not?"

Gary bowed his bald head and then followed the path John had taken to the cabana.

"Aren't you just turning out to be the belle of the ball?" Sergio smirked.

I rolled over onto my side, turning my back to him. His laughter burned in my ears, so I sat up and turned to him. "Why do you want us to have lunch with him?" I demanded.

"So we could pump him for information, why else?" Sergio shook his head. "Duh."

"Good thinking," I said.

"And you're the mystery reader. Ha."

When we entered the cabana, Gary was nowhere in sight. A table for eight sat empty in the back corner. "Why don't we use that table and see who he picks," Sergio suggested. Each one of us chose a spot with one open chair between us. I faced the pool.

Sergio sat to my right, while Tom had the pool to his back, and Logan sat to my left.

No sooner than we had settled into our chairs, Gary appeared by the pool. He glanced around the dining area. He waved when he recognized us and headed in our direction.

Gary walked over to Sergio and laid his hands on his shoulders. "Two guys signed up for haircuts this afternoon. Okay?"

Sergio swallowed hard. "Ah, sure."

"Good, I know they're big tippers," Gary said.

"No problem," Sergio said.

Gary looked over at Tom and Logan and nodded. He then pulled out the chair between Sergio and me. He sat down with his back to me and still looked at Sergio.

I smiled to myself. He picked Sergio. He picked Sergio. Ha, ha, ha.

Gary turned around and smiled at me. "So, are you having fun?"

"Oh shit," I said under my breath.

"I hope you're still not upset about the fingerprints." Gary scooted his chair closer to me. "You have to understand we don't have the manpower for such a large task here." He waved his hand over the crowd.

"Let's forget all of that for a while. I'm hungry," Sergio said, "let's eat." He made a break for the buffet tables.

Logan and Tom followed close behind.

Watching them leave, I thought, *You guys are rats fleeing from a sinking ship. I wish I was running with you.* I turned back to Gary and smiled. At least he wasn't the one who threw that snake at me.

But a voice echoed in my mind. *He could have been involved.*

I ignored it and plunged forward. "Gary, can I ask you a question?"

"Sure."

"Why didn't you want me to change seats on the jungle cruise?"

A shadow crossed his eyes and then disappeared as suddenly as it had appeared. He scratched his head, thinking. "What do you mean?"

"Do you remember when Tom walked up to the boat, and I offered to move to the back with him? You told me to stay in my seat. Why?"

Gary took a deep breath and exhaled. "I didn't want you to tip the boat over when you got up. It was almost full, and we were ready to leave. It wouldn't have been good if you tipped us over just before we even took off. Would it?"

"But you didn't seem to be that concerned when I got in. Why all the concern when I was going to move back? You practically yelled at me."

Gary hesitated before blurted out, "Liability. You know

how many people are suing resorts for accidents with faulty equipment. It happens all the time. And the cost for insurance is going up and up, like I need to tell you that." He folded his hands and rested them on his lap. "I just wanted to make sure that our trip was fun and safe."

"Oh." I eyed him carefully, not completely believing him.

Reading something in my face, he changed the subject. "Aren't you hungry?" he shoved his chair back and stood up before I could respond.

I pushed away from the table and stood. "I hope they have something better for lunch than they had yesterday or last night." My stomach began to rumble in response.

Gary moved his chair out of the way and motioned me to go first. "After you," he said.

Such a gentleman.

I wove my way through the maze of tables to the food with Gary close behind. Too close behind. As I neared the table, Sergio approached with a plate heaping of food, balancing it in one hand. "Can you grab a Diet Coke for me? I forgot." He batted his eyes at me.

What did he mean by that? "Sure," I said.

Before I could ask, Sergio cut between Gary and me. He bumped into Gary hard and pushed him back with his free hand. "Oh, I'm sorry. I forgot to get some silverware too," he apologized.

When Gary stepped back, Sergio fisted his free hand and slipped it into his pocket. Quickly, he pulled it out and reached for a set of utensils. "Thanks," he smiled at Gary. "I hate to be such a bother."

I turned and grabbed a plate. Whatever.

Lettuce and salad fixings covered the first table. I passed. The next table was covered with large silver serving pans. Whole shrimp with the heads still on were piled high in the first pan. Slabs of fish, dressed with slices of lemon not big enough to hide its skin, swam in oil.

Leftovers from last night? I kept going.

The next table had Spanish rice and mashed potatoes. Good thing I had breakfast this morning. I scooped a clump of potatoes, hoping that they had gotten it right this time, and then tossed on a few dinner rolls, just in case.

After grabbing a Diet Coke for Sergio and a Coke for me, I headed back to the table, not bothering to wait for Gary.

Sergio leaned forward as soon as I sat down, but stopped at seeing Gary rapidly approaching. He whispered, "I'll tell you later."

As Gary neared, Logan asked, "So, how long have you been working for Club Fred?"

Gary set his plate down. "I've been with them for about nine months." He glanced at my plate. "Aren't you hungry?"

"I don't seem to be having very good luck with the food around here." I saw what he carried. A thick, juicy cheeseburger sat on a toasted bun with crisp French fries. "Where did you get that?" I asked.

Gary turned around and pointed to the grill. "Over there."

Now, why hadn't I seen that?

"Did you want me to get you one?" he offered.

"I'll get one when I finish this," I said, scooping up a spoonful of cold mashed potatoes. It was almost to my mouth when a black bug buzzed my hand. It sounded like a hornet, so I swiped my hand away, trying to avoid a sting and an allergic reaction. The clump of potatoes flew through the air and landed on Gary's lap.

Before I realized what I was doing, I reached over and plucked the blob off Gary's shorts. When patients dropped food on themselves in dining group at the hospital, I'd just wiped it up automatically.

The surprised look on Gary's face made my face turn red, white, and then red again.

"Not at the table, Taylor," Sergio scolded. "There's other places for that."

"I'm so sorry." I apologized and reached for the napkin and wiped Gary's lap again, trying to remove the last of the potatoes, and stopped when I realized what I was doing and felt his response.

"No problem." Gary smiled at me and winked.

Sergio laughed behind me.

The clump of potatoes was still between my fingers in one hand, and the napkin in the other. I turned away from him and dropped them onto my plate and picked up a roll. I ripped the hard crust easily between my fingers, glancing at Sergio.

Sergio swallowed hard, forcing his laugher down. "So Gary, do you work for Club Fred full-time, or do you have another job?"

Gary took a bite out of his burger. Mayo and burger juice ran down his chin. He wiped it away with the back of his hand. He chewed quickly and swallowed. "I have a bunch of odd jobs back in California. That way I don't get bored so fast."

"This must be an exciting job, getting to travel and meet a lot of interesting people," Sergio pressed.

Gary smiled as he picked up a French fry and dipped it into the ketchup. "You wouldn't believe the things I've picked up on these trips."

"I can just imagine." Sergio smirked.

"It's not like that. You have to be careful, you know. I mean, all the things that I've learned about people and how they operate. You'd be surprised at what I've seen."

"You should talk to Logan," I suggested. "He may be able to use some of your ideas in one of his books. Maybe you could come up with a motive or two."

"A motive for what?" Gary asked.

"Murder," I said, just as he took another bite of his burger.

A violent coughing spell hit him.

Sergio jumped to his feet and started pounding on his back. "Breathe, breathe!" he yelled at Gary.

Gary spat out his chunk of burger and coughed. "I'm trying to, if you'd stop knocking it out of my chest." Gary gasped for breath.

"Sorry." Sergio scanned the dining area at everyone staring at him. "I thought he was choking," he said to his audience and sat down in his chair.

"Are you okay?" I asked Gary.

"I must have tried to swallow without chewing." He tentatively picked up his burger and took another bite, smaller this time. After he chewed and swallowed, he asked Logan, "So you write mysteries?"

Logan nodded. "I'm doing some research and working on my new novel right now. It's set in a gay resort."

"Well, you've come to the right place." He leaned forward toward Logan. "If you want, I could tell you about a few things that go on behind the scenes." He raised his eyebrows.

"That would be great. Have there been any murders at this resort?" Logan asked.

Gary opened his mouth to say something and then closed it again. He took a long sip from his can of pop. "Not that I know of." He set his can down. "But I'm sure you could ask someone on the local staff. This place has been open for ten years."

"Is that all?" Sergio blurted out and shrugged his shoulders. "It looks a lot older than that. The heat must have beaten the hell out of this place."

Gary paused before taking another bite. "I don't know about that, but the tropical storms can get pretty fierce."

"I can believe that," Logan agreed. "Well, if you find someone willing to talk to me about any murders that took place at this resort, I'd greatly appreciate it. I know I will have some questions for you, but we can talk later. I have them saved on my computer."

"No problem." Gary put down his burger. "I'm here to make sure you have a safe and memorable vacation."

Gary droned on and on about Club Fred and all the events they had planned for the rest of the week. While he spoke, everyone else ate. Logan and Tom quickly finished their meals and made their escape. My rolls were gone, but the potatoes remained on the plate.

"Well, Taylor." Gary pushed his chair away from the table. "I hope I get to see a lot more of you over the rest of the week. Maybe we could have supper…?"

The word "alone" hung unspoken in the air, and I was glad when Sergio said, "That would be nice. Thanks for inviting us."

Gary frowned. "Well, I have to head back to work. It's my turn to man the Club Fred table. Stop by later on and sign up for a snorkeling trip." He leaned forward. "I'll even give you guys a discount. How about that?"

"Great, we'll stop by," I promised.

"See you then." With that Gary went back to work.

"So what do you think of Gary?" Sergio asked.

"What am I supposed to think? He sure knows how to push Club Fred. He's like a walking infomercial."

"I know." Sergio slid over into the chair next to me. "So, do you think he knows anything?"

"I think lunch was a complete waste of time. The only thing I almost got out of him was a date." I set my pop can down with a bang.

"Really?" Sergio's eyebrows went up. "Well, I got a lot out of Gary."

"Oh yeah. What?" I demanded.

Sergio held up a resort room key. "This."

"How did you get that?" I asked, amazed by the key dangling from Sergio's fingers.

"I get around," Sergio smiled. "More than you think." He took the last sip from his Diet Coke and shook his empty can. "Actually, I was the designated driver in Cosmo School. So, I had to learn how to pick pockets to get the keys from my inebriated friends. Friends don't let friends drive drunk."

"I'm glad you're such a humanitarian, but it seems that misdemeanors run in your bloodstream." I pushed my chair back and stood up.

Sergio touched my arm. "Let's go check out his room."

"Now? You want to add breaking and entering to your list?"

"I have the key." Sergio shook it in his hand as he rose. "It's hardly breaking. I'm sure Gary is more than willing to show you his room, so there goes our entry. We're almost invited."

"I'm not listening," I put my fingers in my ears.

"You can search his room with me, or you can search his room with him." Sergio smiled as he pulled my arms down and gazed into my eyes. "The choice is yours."

"I'm not going to hear the end of this until we check this out, right?"

"You got it." He smiled.

"Should we tell Logan and Tom?" I motioned to the beach.

"In this case, I don't think the more is the merrier."

"All right. I'll go along with you, just this one time. But first, we need to find out how long Gary is going to be working at the table."

"Fine, we can sign up for tomorrow's snorkeling trip." Sergio headed toward the Club Fred table.

Gary sat oiled and shirtless behind the table. His "Gary" nametag stuck to his chest.

"Let's go." Sergio waved for me to follow.

Sergio walked over to Gary and picked up the clipboard. "Seal Island. No one will be throwing snakes on this excursion, will they?" Sergio smiled a toothy grin.

Gray's face flushed. "No. I don't think you have to worry about that on this trip." He quickly changed the focus. "So, just the two of you?" He waved his fingers between us. "How about your friends?"

Why was he getting so testy about the trip, especially since he was the one who had suggested it? "I'm sure they'll want to go too." I reached over, picked up the pen lying on the table, and handed it to Sergio.

Sergio looked at the pen and turned it tip up. "Look," he said showing me the pen. The pen had a man with a disappearing swimsuit.

I tapped the sign-up sheet.

He quickly flipped the pen over and wrote our four names down, along with our room number.

I smiled at him. "Do you have a long shift this afternoon, or do you get to enjoy some more of the surf and sun?"

"Oh, I'm here until supper." He stretched back in his chair, flexing his muscles. "No fun for me this afternoon."

Good, I thought. "Too bad. At least you'll get to work on your tan."

Sergio pulled on my shirtsleeve. "Stop flirting."

"Well, we're off to get some more sun." Sergio pulled me back to the beach.

Gary called after us. "Don't forget about your haircuts, Sergio. I'm sure the first one is waiting there right now."

"Crap."

"Hey, Taylor," Sergio called as he walked across the beach. "I'm done with my haircuts, and you told me to tell you when it was four o'clock. It's four."

"Thanks, Sergio." I swung my legs over the side of the chaise. "I think I've had enough sun. I'm going to hit the shower."

"I'll join you," Sergio said quickly.

I glared over at him as I threw my things into my tote. My eyes bore into his.

"After you're done." Sergio picked up his beach towel and motioned me to hurry.

Tom called after us. "Want to meet up for supper tonight?"

"Sure," I called over my shoulder. "Save us a place." We scrambled across the beach and raced through the cabana.

"So, what's his room number?" I asked as we ran up the stairway.

Sergio read the plastic diamond. "420."

"That's just down the hall from us."

"I know," Sergio's voice went up. "Isn't *that* convenient?"

"For who?" I asked.

Sergio opened our room door and tossed our towels and my bag on the bed. "Let's go."

There was no one in the hallway. We pressed our backs along the wall and made our way toward Gary's room.

Sergio pulled the key out of his pocket and causally inserted it into the lock.

Leaning forward, I whispered, "Do you think he has a roommate?"

Sergio froze. "Now is a fine time to think of that," he muttered from between clenched teeth.

"Well, he could," I answered, defensively.

"What should we do?" Sergio held the key in place.

"We've come this far, we might as well see it through to the end."

Sergio's eyebrows shot up. "Here goes nothing." He pushed the door open and peered into the room. "Empty."

"Well, hurry up and get in." I pushed him through the door and followed close behind.

Scanning the room, everything was neatly set out. Except for a wet towel hanging on the bathroom doorknob, nothing seemed suspicious or out of place.

Sergio walked over to the dresser and slid open the top drawer. He reached in and pulled out a skimpy pair of red bikini underwear and held them up for me to see.

I shuddered at the image it brought to my mind. I frowned at Sergio. "We're supposed to be looking for clues, not underwear."

"I am looking for clues." He placed the underwear back in the drawer. "If I had anything to hide, this wouldn't be where I'd hide it at the resort." He shook his head. "But I'd hide it in my underwear drawer at home. I'm not just getting my kicks out of this you know."

"Whatever." I walked into the bathroom. A shaving kit was spread out on the marble countertop, a damp pair of swimming trunks hung from the curtain rod. I lifted the toilet tank lid with both hands and peered inside. Just water.

Walking back into the room, I scanned the area. Sergio was gone. "Sergio?" I whispered. "Sergio?" I repeated, louder.

"What?" a voice said from under the bed.

"I thought you had abandoned me," I said.

Sergio's head popped up from the far side of the bed by the patio door. "Why would I do that?" He pushed himself up into a standing position and wiped his hands together. "There's nothing under that bed but dust bunnies."

"I still don't know what we're looking for."

Sergio pointed to the closet. "Look in there."

I opened the door and felt my eyebrows wrinkle. What was

that smell? I sniffed the air, but the scent avoided my detection. It was faint and familiar, but I couldn't quiet place it. A heap of clothes was tossed in one corner. An image of a locker room only earthier formed in my mind. I kicked at the pile with the toe of my sandal; T-shirts, underwear, socks, and shorts. Digging a little deeper, I found a small black notebook poking out of a pair of jeans. I reached over and carefully pulled it out.

"Did you find something?"

"Yikes." I jerked upright and my back slammed into Sergio's body. "Don't do that."

He stepped back and rubbed his chest. "Sorry, but I didn't find anything over there, so I came over here to help. Did you find something?" He peered at the book in my hand.

Before I could answer him, heavy footsteps echoed down the hallway.

"Gary!" Sergio and I said at the same time.

Panic struck. I slipped the notebook into my back pocket and edged away from the door.

The footsteps stopped outside in the hallway.

I held my breath and watched. In the space under the door, the shadow moved closer and then continued down the hallway.

I let out the breath I had been holding.

I turned and saw Sergio pull the patio's sliding door open.

"What are you doing?"

"I was going to jump over to the next balcony," he said.

"Who do you think you are? Tarzan?"

"At least I didn't freeze and do nothing, unlike some people."

"At least I wasn't going to kill myself, trying to play Spiderman on the balcony."

Sergio closed the door and stormed across the room. He snatched the doorknob and twisted hard. "I'm leaving." He jerked the door open and continued down the hallway to our room.

"Wait," I called after him. "I haven't finish searching the closet." I ran after him. A few seconds later, our room door flung open and slammed into the wall with a bang.

Gary's room door closed behind me as I ran down the hall. I rounded the curve in the hallway just in time to see our door close. I dug into my pocket to retrieve the room key, then I remembered. The notebook.

Without thinking, I turned and headed back to Gary's room. I had to put the notebook back. At the door, I reached forward and turned the knob. Locked.

What was I thinking? The door had locked automatically when it closed, and Sergio had the key. I spun around and walked right into Gary. I bounced off of his massive oiled chest.

"What are you doing here?" he asked.

"I... I..." I stuttered and tried to regain my balance before I toppled over.

Gary stepped forward and caught me, stabilizing me on my feet. "I got off early." He smiled and took another step. Before I could say anything, his grasp increased on my arms and pinned them down next to my side. He moved in closer.

"Wait a minute," I said, pushing hard against Gary's chest. My hands slid across his oiled torso. He released my arms, and I stepped back. "I think you're confused."

"No, Taylor, I think you're the one who's confused, confused about your feelings." As he exhaled, I could smell alcohol on his breath.

I stared at him in shock. "What?"

"You keep telling everyone your friend Molly booked your trip to Club Fred, when we all know that's a lie. You wanted her to send you here. Why else would she do it?" His eyes narrowed. "She knows you better than you know yourself."

I looked at him with my mouth open. Had I stepped into a parallel universe? Why wasn't I waking up from this nightmare?

Gary grabbed my arms again and held them securely down by my sides. I bent my elbows and grabbed onto his forearms, rock solid forearms. I didn't need to manual muscle test him to know his strength was five out of five. Twisting my shoulders from side to side, I tried to break his hold. My feet dug into the tile floor, seeking traction to force my body away from his.

Gary smiled an evil grin. "You're getting excited, aren't you?"

That stopped my struggle. "What?"

"I'm getting hard." He licked his lips. "Aren't you?"

I closed my eyes and clenched my fists. Sweat erupted from the pores on my palms as my nails dug into them.

This was not happening. This was not happening, my mind screamed.

I opened my eyes, oh, but it was.

Gary's eyes twinkled and a lecherous smile curled on his lips. His tongue snaked out of his mouth and traced his lips slowly, while his eyebrows raised and dropped. An image of Groucho

Marx came to mind, but instead of saying, "Guess the secret word," he said, "Give me a little kiss."

Instantly, my fight or flight reflexes kicked in. My hands pushed against his forearms and I pulled away from him with all my weight. My mind was whirling with too many thoughts. Was he the one who had stalked me on the beach? Was he involved in throwing the snake? He was in the boat with me. How could he have thrown it? What did he really want? Mashed potatoes on his lap? As soon as that question crossed my mind, an image flashed across my mind. "No way!"

I took a deep breath and exhaled. "Let go of me now." I said each word slowly and distinctly, so there could be no misunderstanding.

"I like it when you play hard to get." Gary's hands still held me in place. He puckered his lips and came in for the kill, or should I say kiss.

"I'm not playing," I said, helplessly, wrenching my neck from side to side. I could taste the whiskey on his breath when I opened my mouth to holler. Just before the scream could erupt, out of the corner of my eye, I saw a flash behind Gary. My mouth closed and my eyes focused on the metallic object that rose above his head.

Suddenly, I recognized it. Sergio's machete. As it shook above his head, "No, Sergio!" exploded from my mouth.

The blade lowered behind Gary's towering form.

From between puckered lips, he breathed into my mouth. "Don't think you can fool me…" and then a dull thud sounded behind him. His eyes focused on me. His head and lips pushed against mine, and as our mouths met, his eyes rolled back into his head and went blank. His hands released my arms; his body crumbled forward and knocked me to the floor.

I landed hard on my butt, Gary's dead weight flattened and trapped me under his body.

"What were you two boys doing?" Sergio smirked, standing over us with the machete hiked up to his shoulder like a soldier standing at attention. "I'm telling Molly."

Gary lay on top of me with his nose sticking in my ear. I pushed up onto my elbows and slowly slid out from beneath him. As my legs escaped from under his body, I ignored all my years of therapy training. Instead of cradling his head, I let it hit the floor with a hollow thud.

"I can't believe you hit him with the machete. You could've given him a head injury," I scolded him as I struggled to my feet.

Sergio puckered his mouth and then started. "Is that all the thanks I get? I just saved your virtue. Or did I prevent…" He tapped the back of the blade on his palm. "Besides, I hit him with the handle, I could've used the other end." He gently ran his finger along the cutting edge, and jerked it away suddenly. "Ouch." He stuck his bleeding finger into his mouth.

Ignoring Sergio's finger, I knelt next to Gary and placed my fingers on his neck to check his pulse. His breathing was even, and a strong heartbeat throbbed in his neck. My fingers explored the back of his head. I felt a huge lump rising, but no blood seemed to be oozing out of him. Pulling open one of his eyelids, I watched his pupil constrict as the light hit it. The other eye did the same, symmetrically. No sign of head injury. I turned to face Sergio. "You could've killed him." The panic still shrilled in my voice. I took a deep, calming breath.

"Oh, I'm sure. I doubt I could even crack that concrete between his ears," he retorted.

Standing up, I grabbed under Gary's arms and tried to lift him. His limp body hardly budged. Glancing at Sergio I asked, "Are you going to help me?"

"Do what? Take advantage of him?" Sergio's eyebrows rose up and down, just like Gary's had. "Haven't you done enough?"

"Do you see where he is? We need to hide him." I peeked down the hallway at the utility closet. "Maybe we should bring him into his room, because I don't want to be around when he wakes up."

Sergio opened his mouth to say something.

"We can't leave him here," I said, before he could respond.

"Why not? It'll look like he had too much to drink and knocked himself out," Sergio sniffed the air, "and from the smell of it, we wouldn't be too far off."

"Well, I'm not taking any chances. He could've been the one who followed me the first night on the beach, remember? And he could've been involved with that thrown snake on the jungle cruise."

Sergio shook his head while he set down his machete. He bent forward and grabbed Gary's legs. As we struggled to pick him up, he asked, "How much does he weigh?" With a heavy grunt, we lifted him off the ground. Sergio pulled one way and I the other; Gary's body slipped out of our hands. This time, I caught his head before it bounced off the tile, but Sergio let his half fall. Gary's bottom hit with full force. "Why didn't you try to catch him?" I demanded.

Sergio put his hands on his hips. "It looks like he has enough padding," he said, glancing down at Gary's butt. "More than enough, and how much oil does he have covering his body?"

I exhaled hard. "Can we at least go in the same direction?"

"Well, where are we going with him?" Sergio asked.

"To his closet," I said.

"Too late. I think he came out a long time ago, and he ain't going back."

"In his room." I rolled my eyes, grabbed under Gary's arms again, and pulled him up. Sergio followed with his legs, holding onto him higher this time. We moved him across the hall and closer to his room.

We heard footsteps echoing up the stairwell. Sergio mouthed, "Hurry."

We shuffled Gary's body to his door, where Sergio dropped his legs without warning. Gary's sandals clattered on the tile. Sergio reached into his pocket, fished out the room key, and slipped it into the lock. The footsteps paused at the top of the stairs and then headed in our direction.

Sergio swung the door open, and I spun Gary's unconscious form around and dragged him into his room. Sergio waited behind the door. When Gary's feet cleared the door, Sergio slammed it shut, just before the guest walked by the door.

"Whew. That was close."

"Too close," I agreed.

"So, now what do we do? Take off his clothes?" Sergio nodded his head in short rapid jerks.

"That'll help a lot," I said.

"It wouldn't hurt," Sergio grinned.

I scanned the room and motioned toward the bed. "Why don't we just put him on the bed and make it look like he fell asleep? Maybe he won't remember seeing me in the hallway and that you clobbered him."

"I didn't clobber him, I rescued you."

"Whatever."

We picked Gary up again and placed him on the bed. We straightened out his arms and legs and took off his sandals.

"Shouldn't we get an icepack for his head?" Sergio asked.

"Then he'll know someone *nice* knocked him out?"

"Oh, I didn't think of that." He scratched his head.

Before we could do anything else, Gary's phone rang. Sergio and I jumped.

"Let's get the hell out of here." Sergio made a break for the door.

I glanced at the phone, wondering who was calling Gary. My hand reached to answer it, but as soon as my fingertips touched, I heard the room door open. I turned. Sergio was gone, and I bolted.

"I can't believe you hit him with the machete," I said, emptying my tote bag on the dresser.

"Taylor?"

"What were you thinking?"

"Taylor!" Urgency filled his tone.

"What?" I said, but didn't turn around. I shook the sand out of my paperback and placed it on the dresser. Looking into the mirror, I saw my sunburned face. I really should've started tanning before I left Sioux Falls.

"You know that snake that was thrown at you? Was it poisonous?"

"I don't know, maybe." I leaned forward and ran my fingers through my hair. I could see my brilliant pink scalp underneath. No wonder my head itched. "Why?"

"Because one just came out from under your bed. It must've followed you home." Sergio bumped into me as he backed up and pressed his body against the dresser.

"Ha. Ha…" I started, but looking into the mirror I saw what Sergio was talking about. A large, dark brown, almost black, snake with yellow crossbars slithered out from under the dust ruffle. Its diamond-shaped head rose slightly, and its tongue flicked in and out, scanning the environment. Sensing our presence, it headed in our direction.

We scrambled over each other to get on top of the dresser. Once on top, we wondered how we had gotten there.

The snake side-wound around itself, uncoiling to over six feet in length, as it crossed the tiled floor. It raised its head again, sticking out its forked tongue, searching for us. Its cold black eyes bore down on us, unblinking, as it continued crawling closer.

My mind raced back to the Discovery channel shows that I

had turned off when the snakes came on. Did motion or heat attract them? Weren't they afraid of things bigger than them?

Sergio nudged me forward, bringing me back to the problem at hand. "Do something," he hissed.

My body tensed, and I pushed back against him. "I don't do snakes."

"Well, neither do I. Marlin Perkins I ain't." He edged away from me, and the dresser swayed with the weight shift.

I took a step back. "Then be Jim. He did all the dirty work on that show anyway."

"I'm not Jim either." He motioned to the snake. "All you have to do is just grab it right behind its head and take it out of the room."

"That's all?"

"Yes."

"That's easy for you to say, but I'm not touching that thing." I moved closer to Sergio, the dresser rocking back and forth under our weight.

"Well, neither am I." He wrung his hands together. "Careful! You're gonna tip us over."

"So how do we get rid of it?"

"Call room service?" Sergio suggested.

We stared at the nightstand between the beds; the phone mocked us.

"Why don't you go and call for help, and I'll keep its attention." He waved his hands in the air.

"No way. You go call." I nudged him toward the phone.

The snake slid closer to the foot of the dresser and stopped where we were standing. It reared its head up off the floor, searching.

I grabbed Sergio's hands and stopped his waving. "Let's not get its attention right now."

"How high can one of those things reach?" Sergio asked.

Pressing my back up against the wall I said, "I don't know, and I don't want to find out." I nudged Sergio. "Reach? Reacher. Grab the reacher."

"What?" he looked at me confused.

"The reacher," I nodded to his right. "Grab the reacher. We can use that to catch the snake and get rid of it." I pointed to the aluminum device, lying at the end of the dresser.

Sergio slowly made his way to the edge and picked it up. "Here, catch." He wound his arm back, getting ready to toss it to me.

"No!" I shouted.

"Why not? Do you think I'll throw like a girl?" Sergio shot back, his hand holding the reacher at his cocked hip.

"No. I can't catch."

"Why not?"

"You know, my detached retina. I don't have any depth perception. I couldn't catch anything to save my life. And for that matter, I don't think I can trust myself to grab the snake with the reacher."

"You've got to be kidding. You use them everyday, don't you?"

"I don't, my patients do."

"Oh great," he said and sidestepped back to me.

"I can teach you how to use it. I'm sure you'll be able to catch it."

"Forget that, think of another plan." He handed the reacher to me.

"All you have to do is pull the trigger," I said, pulling it with my index finger and the plastic claw opened and closed.

"You're the expert. You do it." He folded his hands under his arms and refused to take it from me. "I'll open the door so you can throw it off the balcony."

"I can't throw it off the balcony. The fall might kill it."

Sergio glared at me. "I don't care. I just don't want *it* to kill *us*. Every man for himself."

"What if it falls on someone or lands on someone else's balcony?"

"Who cares? Then that's their problem, not ours." Sergio snapped.

"Aren't you the humanitarian of the year."

"I don't care. I just want that snake out of here. Don't you?"

The snake rose higher, flicking its tongue toward us. Its head extended halfway up the dresser.

"Fine. I'll do it. Just stand back and give me room." I spread my arms out to the side, almost dropping the reacher in the process of making eye contact with Sergio. "As soon as I grab the snake, you jump down and open the patio door. Okay?"

Sergio stared down at the snake, and he didn't say anything.

"Okay?" I raised my voice and tapped him with the reacher.

"Okay. Just do it."

I took a deep breath and exhaled loudly. "Find something to throw to distract it, and then I'll jump down and grab it."

Sergio bent over and picked up my paperback.

"No! Not that!" I cried.

"Then what?" he asked, setting my book down.

"I don't care, you can use anything you want, just not my book."

Sergio knelt down, reached over the edge of the dresser, and slowly opened my top drawer.

The snake reared its head back, hissing as its forked tongue sensed the movement of air. It rocked its body side to side, following Sergio's movements like a mirror.

Blindly, Sergio grabbed something and stood up. "Will this do?" He shook a scrap of bright blue cloth in his knuckled fist.

My Speedo.

"I don't care, just do it," I said through pursed lips.

Sergio threw the Speedo to the right of the snake.

It lurched forward, following the swimwear's arc of descent. Its head shot through a leg opening and landed on the floor.

I jumped down, extending my arm with the reacher's claw wide open, ready to grab. The Speedo wrapped around the snake's neck, slowing it down just long enough for the claw to find its hold. My index finger pulled the trigger. The snake reared its head up and back against the aluminum and plastic, trying to escape. I squeezed down harder, praying the plastic wouldn't break. I glanced back at the dresser.

Sergio still stood on top of it with his hands over his eyes.

"Sergio!" I shouted as the snake started to coil its body around the shaft of the reacher. I tensed and extended my arm straight out in front of me, turning to face him.

He brought his hands down, and as he opened his eyes, he let out a blood-curdling scream. The reacher with the trapped snake's head was eye level with him.

His scream scared me so much that I almost lost my grip and dropped the snake. Squeezing tighter on the trigger, I pointed the snake's black eyes into Sergio's face and then pointed it at the balcony. "The door!"

Sergio bolted from the dresser and scrambled across the room. With his eyes glued to the snake, he fumbled in blind panic with the latch. It snapped, and he threw the door wide open.

I rushed across the room and into the welcoming sea breeze. My pelvis hit the balcony wall, and I bent over the railing with the reacher. Seeing no one below, I released the trigger.

As soon as the pressure released from its neck, the snake clung to the reacher for dear life. Its body started pulsating, coiling back up and around the shaft, moving closer to my hand. I shook the reacher, but the snake wouldn't let go.

"Drop it!" Sergio yelled, as he stood next to my side.

"I can't! It won't let go!"

Sergio bumped into my side as he reached over the railing to help.

The snake's tail slapped his forearm. Sergio screamed again and backed up. From behind me, he grabbed me by the shoulders and shook my whole body. "*You* have to let go, it won't."

This time, the snake's tail brushed against my fingers on the handle. Instantly, my hand released the reacher. It and the snake tumbled through the air, plummeting toward the ground.

We watched as the snake and the reacher rolled end over end, all the way to the courtyard. The reacher clattered when it struck the tiles below. The snake flopped once and then lay motionless, still partially wrapped around the reacher.

"Thanks," I said as my legs collapsed, bringing me down to the balcony floor.

"Tell that vendor they make one hell of a reacher," Sergio said, sliding down the balcony wall and joining me on the floor.

The phone began to ring. "Now what?" I asked, pushing myself up to my feet and answering it.

"This is the front desk. Is there a problem in your room?"

"No. Why? *Is* there a problem?" My hand shook at my ear.

"We've had complaints about yelling and screaming. Are you in trouble?"

"We had a problem, but now it's gone."

"Can you answer that or are you danger? Is someone listening? We can send someone up if you need help."

"We're fine now."

Sergio stood at the foot of the bed. "What's wrong?"

Putting my hand over the receiver, I said, "Someone called the front desk about all the screaming coming out of our room."

"I'd like to see what they would've done with a snake that size in *their* room," he huffed.

The voice on the phone was talking again. "Are you still there?"

I uncovered the phone. "I'm still here." I took a deep breath and exhaled. When in doubt, tell the truth. "You see, there was a snake in our room, and we just threw it off the balcony. So, that's what all the screaming was about."

"Oh." The voice said sounding confused, and then paused. "Uh, sir? Did you know that there are no pets allowed in the hotel?"

My eyes rolled. "This snake wasn't a pet," I began, but Sergio grabbed the phone out of my hand.

"Listen," he said. "We didn't come to this resort to be chased by snakes. We came for peace and quiet. We came to work on our tans, read cheap trashy novels in the sun, and relax! Get it! Not fight snakes!" Sergio took a deep breath and started up again. "So, if you guys ever cleaned these rooms, and maybe, just maybe, called an exterminator once in a while, we wouldn't be fighting for our lives against huge poisonous reptiles that crawl out from under our beds."

"But sir…"

"Don't 'but sir' me. I'm paying good money here. I want service, not snakes. Better yet, I just want to be left the hell alone." And with that Sergio slammed the phone down, making the bells ring. He turned to face me, calm as could be. "So, now what?"

I smiled. "I think that about covers it."

"So how do you think that thing got in here?" Sergio walked over to the bathroom door. "Could it have crawled up the sewer pipe? I don't think I'll be able to take a shower again."

He disappeared into the bathroom, and I heard the shower curtain rings ride along the metal bar. I walked over to the door that connected our room to the next one. Turning the knob, it didn't budge. The deadbolt was set. I looked at the bottom edge of the door. The gap underneath didn't appear big enough for the snake. No heating or air vents were visible in the room, only the wall air-conditioner.

"I don't think it could have fit in the drain," he said, emerging from the bathroom. He turned around suddenly, and looked back at me. "You don't think it came up from the toilet? Didn't you see *Porky's Two*? A huge snake came up through the commode in that movie." A look of horror crossed his face and he covered his groin. "I'm not going to be using that one again. No way, no how."

"Do you think it could have crawled up four stories?"

"It could," he said, eyeing the bathroom suspiciously, "couldn't it?"

I shook my head. Just then an idea struck. "Wait a minute, I need to check something out." I knelt down on the floor and climbed under my bed. Sergio's sandal lay on its side with a small damp spot nearby. Inhaling, an earthly scent hung in the musty air underneath the bed. It was a familiar smell, one I had just recently encountered.

I breathed in again as Sergio's face appeared under the dust ruff on the opposite side. "Whoa. Who peed under your bed?"

That's it. The image came into clear focus: The Nike bag.

We both pushed up from the floor and sat on the bed.

I ran my fingers through my hair. "I think it was the snake. At least, that was the same smell that came from the Nike bag we found." Suddenly, the smell from Gary's closet came back to me. It was the same one from the gym bag. "And do you know what? It was the same smell that was in Gary's closet."

"What?" Sergio's brow wrinkled as he thought, then it slowly unfurrowed. "You mean Gary was keeping the snake in his room?"

"It sure seems that way to me."

"Let's go have a talk with him." Sergio bounced up from my bed and headed to the door. He turned around to hurry me along. "Aren't you com…?" A second later, he slapped the side of his head. "We just knocked him out."

I nodded.

"We can't ask him anything right now, can we?"

I shook my head. "I think we should just go down to supper and act like nothing happened."

"What about the snake?" Sergio asked as he headed to the balcony. "Won't we need that as evidence?"

I stood up from the bed and walked over to the patio. Cautiously, we peered over the railing. My reacher lay on the tiled courtyard, but the snake was gone.

"Where is it?" I asked. "The fall should've killed it."

"Are you sure?" Sergio asked.

"It fell four stories and landed on terra cotta tile. It should be dead. I can't believe that fall only stunned it."

"What about your Speedo?" He pointed to the reacher. "Where is it?"

"It's gone too? Who would want that thing?"

"Maybe someone used it to pick up the dead snake?" Sergio curled his hands into fists and cringed. "I wouldn't wear that suit once you find it."

"It's not like I'm going to wear that thing again anyway, especially now, you know, after that snake touched it."

"I don't blame you. I don't think I'll be able to wear my sandals again." He turned to me. "Could I use yours?" Sergio knelt down and looked under my bed, retrieving his sandal.

"I doubt the snake touched it."

"Oh, that's good," he said and slipped it on his bare foot.

"It probably just peed on it when you scared it out from under my bed. So I'd worry about the urine instead of the..."

"Ahhh," Sergio yelled and kicked at me. The sandal flew off his foot. I ducked to the side, and it flew over the balcony railing, down to join my reacher below.

"Why are you two so quiet?" Tom asked. "Having too much excitement on your vacation?"

Sergio's head rested on his hand as he picked at his food. "If you only knew," he muttered under his breath.

My hard rolls and bland mashed potatoes were untouched.

"Maybe you should ask Gary to pull a few strings in the kitchen," Tom offered. "I'm sure he could get you something you'd like."

"I'm hungry, but not that desperate." I had been wondering when Gary was going to wake up and how bad his headache would to be. I felt bad about his head, but I was glad Sergio hit him. That was better than the other option.

John walked up to the table and turned to me. "Have you guys seen Gary?"

"No, not since this afternoon," I lied.

"Mike's been calling his room, and no one's seen him since he left the Club Fred table. We're worried about him."

"Has anyone checked his room?" Sergio asked.

"No," John said.

"Maybe he fell asleep or was in the shower when Mike called," I suggested.

"He could have slipped in the shower," Tom added.

Sergio and I turned and glared at him, and he said, "Sorry, it was just a thought."

"I hope not," John scratched his head. "Maybe I should go check his room."

"Did you want some help?" I offered.

"You don't have to come. You're on vacation. Relax." John turned and started to leave.

"Wait," I called. "Now you've got us worried. We'd like to go with you. Okay?"

"Sure, I'd appreciate the company." John waved for us to follow.

As we walked through the dining area and up to Gary's room, guilt played heavily upon me. Sergio kept giving me worried looks as Tom rattled on and on, about what I don't know.

John knocked on the door. "Gary? Are you in there?"

No answer.

John reached into his pocket and searched for his passkey.

Sergio plunged his hand into his pocket and almost pulled out Gary's key. I shook my head sharply and slapped his hand back into his pocket.

John finally found the key and inserted it into the lock. The tumblers clicked and the door swung in.

A faint scent greeted us as John reached inside, searching for the light switch. Nothing happened.

He continued walking into the room and headed for the light next to the bed. His foot kicked something. "There's something all over the floor," he said, shuffling his feet across the tiles. "Whoa. It's really slippery over here by the bed." His shadow reached over toward the nightstand.

Tom, Sergio, and I stepped into the room and waited by the bathroom door.

John found the switch and flipped on the lamp. As the room flooded with light, we gasped.

The room had been tossed. All of Gary's furniture and things had been thrown around. A spray of blood covered the headboard and wall above. A dark, crimson wave ran across the pillow, down the side, and pooled on the floor. John stood in the center of the pool.

Gary's body lay on the bed in the same position we had left him, but his bruised head was covered in clotted blood. A huge, gaping hole with fragments of white glistened in the light. Gary's sightless eyes stared at the ceiling.

Sergio and Tom backed away to the door. John and I headed to the bed.

John's eyes bore into mine, seeming to wait for a reaction. When I didn't do anything, he turned back, reached over, and felt for Gary's pulse.

I knew he wouldn't find one.

"He's dead," John said, covered his mouth, and started to gag.

"But I only…" Sergio began.

I moved back and bumped into his side, stopping him from saying any more, just as John turned to look at him.

"I mean, I…" he looked at me and then turned back to John, "…I only really met him this morning. We had lunch with him. All of us." He waved his hands in a circle in front of us to include Tom and me. Then his whole body began to shiver.

I wrapped my arm around his shoulders and hugged his quaking body next to mine. Sergio glanced at Gary one more time and quickly looked away. I gave him another gentle squeeze to try and calm him down.

"Did he act…strange?" John walked around the foot of the bed and faced us.

Tom shrugged his shoulders, but said nothing.

"When didn't he?" Sergio asked.

Squeezing him a little harder, I began, "He seemed to be trying to get something from us, but I don't know what."

"I do," Sergio whispered. His body trembled.

"Maybe he was feeling guilty about the snake being thrown on the jungle cruise and was worried that one of us would sue," I interjected before John could ask him what he meant. "We had lunch with him and then he signed us up for a snorkeling trip, but that was the last time we saw him. Right, Sergio?"

He nodded his head slowly.

John stared at us, then turned to Tom, who asked him, "Shouldn't you call security…?" Tom motioned toward the bed.

"I will," he said, heading back toward the phone, and then turned around. "I don't think I should use that phone. Can I use yours?"

"Sure," Sergio responded, before I could answer.

I couldn't believe he just offered our phone in our room.

"What?" he asked.

John didn't wait for our answer. He pushed between Tom, Sergio, and me and headed down the hallway to our room. Tom followed close behind.

Sergio turned to me as we stepped through the door. "What's your problem? We have to cooperate or they'll start to suspect us," he whispered.

"I know, but we have the machete in our room. Remember?" I made a clubbing motion. "I don't think it's a good idea to invite them in, do you?"

"I didn't think about that." His body began shaking even more violently.

"Maybe he won't notice it," I said, and hurried Sergio to our door before John used his passkey. "Are you going to be all right?" I asked, worried that Sergio was starting to go into shock.

"I'm fine. I'm just a little cold," he said, and I released him. He hugged himself and rubbed his hands over his arms, trying to warm up.

I reached into my pocket and pulled out my room key, hoping I could get Sergio to lie down before he passed out. But just as I inserted the key into the lock, a strange thought came to me. I turned to stare at John this time. "How did you know which room was ours?"

John hesitated for a moment. "You wrote it on the sheet when you asked me to charge the beach towel to your room." He motioned toward the door, encouraging me to open it faster.

The key turned, the lock clicked, and I swung the door open.

John pushed past me and headed straight for our phone.

Before we could follow, footsteps echoed up the hall. Tom stepped back and watched as a guest's head bobbed up the stairs, "I should go make sure Gary's door is closed." He motioned down the hall.

I didn't have a chance to respond before Tom hurried back to Gary's room.

"Let him go. I'm glad I'm not the one standing guard," Sergio said. He looked down at his hands and started rubbing them together. "I touched a dead man." His face blanched. "I should go wash my hands, right now." He grabbed at his stomach and rushed into the bathroom.

Gary hadn't been dead when we carried him to his room. I wanted to call after Sergio, but I couldn't with John there. Standing in the threshold, I wasn't quite sure which way to go, or who to follow. Finally deciding, I entered our room.

John flipped his long hair away from his face as he looked up from the phone. His eyes went to the bathroom. "Is he gonna to be okay?" he asked me.

"I hope so." I looked around our room. Where had Sergio put the machete? I couldn't remember if he picked it up from the hallway after we had dragged Gary into his room, or had he left it in there?

Before I could search any further, Sergio emerged from the bathroom, wiping his hands on his pant legs. His face still looked pale and his eyes hollow.

"Are you all right?" I asked.

Sergio held up a finger as John spoke into the phone. "Geoff? Can you come up to 417? We have a little problem up here." There was a pause, and he started again, "We have another body." Another pause and he nodded. "I'll do that right away." He hung up the phone and walked over to me. "I have to stand guard by the…" He swallowed hard. "…by Gary. Can you take care of him?" He motioned to Sergio.

"Sure," I said, and John left.

Sergio stood staring at the floor, body trembling uncontrollably.

I walked into the closet, pulled a light blanket off of the shelf, and wrapped it around his shoulders. Gently, I guided him to his bed and encouraged him to sit. "Maybe you should lie down."

"I'm fine. Could you get me a drink?"

"Alcohol isn't—"

"Water's fine."

I walked into the bathroom and poured him a glass of water. "It's not cold, but I could get you some ice," I said, but didn't think he should be left alone.

He reached up and took the glass. "That's fine," he said, sipping from it.

"Are you dizzy?" I asked.

"What blond isn't?"

"You know what I mean. Are you nauseous or having any chest pains?" I reached over and picked up his wrist. His skin was cool to the touch, but not clammy. My index and middle finger searched for a pulse and found one, a bit rapid, but strong. Conflicting symptoms, but that could be shock.

"I'm fine," he said, "just a little shook up. I've never seen a dead body before, that is, until I met you."

"Gee, thanks." His wit was coming back, so I started to relax a bit. Now, maybe I could look for the machete. I walked around the room, looked under the beds, under the dresser and in the closet.

"What are you looking for? Another snake?" Sergio asked, with his head between his knees and the blanket pulled over his head. The tremors looked like they were lessening.

"Do you remember where you put your machete?"

Nothing came from under the blanket.

I watched as it rose and fell, so I knew he was breathing. Finally, he asked, "Did you pick it up from the hallway? I don't remember bringing it back from Gary's room. Did you take it?"

"What machete?" Geoff asked from behind me.

"Shit," I said, spinning around to face him. "You scared me."

"John called. Is he dead?" Geoff pointed to Sergio's form underneath the blanket.

"No. Not him. That's just Sergio. He's alive, more or less." He probably wished he was dead right now, I mused. "Gary's down the hall in his room. John's standing watch."

Just as Geoff turned around, John approached. "I heard your voice, so I thought I'd better come and bring you to the right room. I told you the wrong one on the phone."

"Don't you know where you're at?" Geoff shook his head and followed John down the hall. He turned to me. "Don't you be leaving, mon. I may be needing to talk to you later."

"I'll be here." Where else could I go?

After John and Geoff disappeared down the hallway, I finished searching our room.

We sat facing each other on our beds. Neither one of us could recall seeing the machete after Sergio hit Gary with it. The machete was gone. Someone at this resort had taken and used it on Gary, and our fingerprints were all over it.

"I think someone is trying to set us up for Gary's murder," Sergio said. He sat up in bed and emerged from under the blanket. Before I could respond, he continued, "Think about it. The machete I used on Gary, when he was grabbing you, disappeared. Do you think that was a coincidence?" He took a deep breath. "I don't. My fingerprints were all over that thing." His eyes squinted. "And if a speck of Gary's blood or hair is found on it." His eyes widened. "Then what? I'll be sent to the electric chair. BZZZT! BZZZT!" His arms extended as his body convulsed under the blanket. "And Duane was killed with my scissors."

"Geoff said they didn't have the capabilities to match fingerprints, so I doubt he can find yours, let alone match Gary's hair and blood samples. We're in Mexico. He said they couldn't do anything with the Nike bag we found, so we'll be home months before they get any of the evidence back."

"So, are you counting on your luck or mine?" Sergio looked around our room. "If this is one of their deluxe hotels, can you imagine what their jails are like?"

"Don't even think about that. We need to figure out why these things are happening to us. Do we know something, or did we see something that we shouldn't have? That's the only thing I can figure out to explain what's been going on. Unless you have another idea?"

"Maybe we have something they want," he offered.

Then I remembered. "The notebook."

"What notebook?" John asked from the doorway.

"I think I lost my notebook on the beach today. You didn't find one, did you?" I stood up, pushing Gary's book deeper into my back pocket. I walked over to the dresser and searched my tote bag. "Nope, it's not in there."

John remained silent, but flipped his long hair back.

"Is there a lost and found here at the resort?" Sergio asked.

John looked from Sergio to me and back again before answering. "It's down at the front desk."

"Thanks." Sergio turned to me. "Taylor, maybe we should go check it out. Now." He threw off the blanket and stood up, coming to stand next to me.

"Wait," John ordered.

We're in for it now, I thought.

"Before you guys go anywhere, we need to talk." John stepped into our room and closed the door.

I checked to make sure the notebook was still in my pocket. What about his towel? Did Sergio put it away carefully or was it discarded in a heap?

John leaned his back against the door. He motioned with his head down the hall. "It's about Gary."

"Yes," we said, in unison, waiting for the other shoe to drop.

"Geoff asked me to tell you to keep Gary's death under wraps. I know Mike talked to you before about Duane Wayne's murder. So please don't say anything to the other guests. I don't want to start a panic. We really don't know very much, so for right now, don't mention it. Don't even talk about it to each other, okay?"

"I guess that'll be all right." I turned to Sergio.

He nodded. "It's nothing I want to brag about. It sure gives me the creeps. I don't want to be walking around here alone at night. That's for sure."

"I think that's a good idea, for you guys to use the buddy system and stick together."

"We'll be joined at the hips." Sergio said.

Sergio led the way back to our room. My mind raced in many directions as we walked around the pool. Too many strange events had happened since we arrived at this place. If Molly had only known what she was sending me into. So much for rest and relaxation. In two days, there had been two murders, two snakes, and two days of mashed potatoes and hard rolls. What did they say about things happening in threes?

The four Pepsis I drank at the bar had worked their way through my system. The cool night breeze, along with the soft, constant sound of water flowing from the pool made my walking very uncomfortable. As we neared the men's restroom, I paused. "Sergio, I need to make a quick pit stop."

I entered the restroom. My face was wind blown and pink from the sun, or so the mirrors above the sinks reflected. My feet echoed across the tile floor as water dripped in the urinals. Great plumbing. At least they were beyond the outhouse. Three empty urinals stood in a row. I headed for the first one, the one closest to the door.

I stood facing the wall at the urinal, when a soft rustling entered the restroom. I heard footsteps tapping into the room, and they stopped at the urinal right next to me. Was Sergio trying to be funny? Didn't he know the rules of the urinals? Never use the one next to a guy, unless there is a line and no other choice. Then an uncomfortable feeling of being watched came over me, like a pair of eyes boring into my neck. Didn't he know rule number two? Eyes straight ahead? I glanced to the side, breaking rule two and saw a red, yellow, and green Carmen Miranda standing next to me.

Had I walked into the wrong bathroom? I thought it said "Men" on the door. Had I missed the "W-O"? I swallowed hard and looked at my reflection in the pipes of the urinal.

A urinal.

She was using a urinal. I closed my eyes. Why was I here?

I zipped quickly and turned the other way to avoid eye contact.

"What we women don't do to make ourselves look wonderful for men," she said.

I continued to the sink and looked into its depths, not the mirrors. A rustling of fabric told me I was being followed. He was following me, or should I say she? The water splashed over my hands. Why had I stopped to wash my hands? Why didn't I just bolt for our room? Habits from the hospital were so hard to break. I looked into the mirror and tried to maintain eye contact with my reflection, but the vibrant colors of the dress drew my eyes to her.

"Am I straight?" she asked.

"Excuse me?"

She grabbed her bodice and pulled it away from her chest, jiggling her bosom up and down. "There. How's that?" She pressed out her chest for my inspection.

My eyes went to her cleavage and noticed the right one was a tad bit higher. Pointing to it, I said, "That one's a little higher."

She glanced into the mirror and pushed it down. "How's that?" She rocked them from side to side.

"Perfect." I turned off the water, gave her the thumbs up, and reached over to wipe my hands on a paper towel.

"Thanks, sweetheart." She followed me, black wig towering over her head.

Sergio stood outside waiting. He peered around and blanched when he saw whom I had in tow. "Now who did you pick up? I can't leave you alone for a minute."

She pushed past me and extended her hand like royalty in a PBS mini-series. "Let me introduce myself. I'm Cha-Cha." Her sculpted nails glistened red in the light.

Sergio took her hand and tried to shake it.

Cha-Cha firmly kept her hand palm down. "You're supposed

to kiss the hand of aristocracy, dear."

Sergio was tired and not in the mood to play along. "When I meet one, then I will." He pulled his hand away from hers.

A cold sneer sliced across her mouth. "You will bow in my presence and call me Queen Bee."

"And we all know what the 'B' stands for." Sergio turned and headed toward the stairs, not waiting to see if I followed.

Cha-Cha's eyes narrowed at his back.

"Sorry. He's had a rough day. We've both had a bad day, and we're tired. Don't take it personally." I nodded down low, almost bowing to her, and hurried after Sergio.

"Not as sorry as he's going to be," she said, and stamped her foot, punctuating the point. "I will not be ignored."

"Great. Just what we need, a drag queen on the rampage," I mumbled to myself. Rounding the second flight of stairs, I rubbed my forehead and almost bumped into Sergio.

"Do you have a headache?" he asked, but he didn't sound concerned.

"Nah, I'm just tired."

"Well, if you would stop talking to everyone at this resort, you may find some time to rest." And he continued up the stairs.

"But… but…" Now what had I done? I hurried to catch up.

Sergio stood by our room door and looked off into the night sky. "Don't those clouds look like something's brewing?"

Looking into the black night, I saw nothing. "It must be all the humidity in the air." As I reached into my pocket, Sergio pulled out his room key and inserted it into the lock.

When the door shut, Sergio turned and asked, "What do you think we'll find in Gary's notebook?"

With all the excitement, I had forgotten about it. Sitting down on Sergio's bed, I pulled out the slim black book. It looked like a leather-bound checkbook. Opening it, I saw it needed to be turned on its side like a regular book. A calendar's week covered each sheet, two weeks printed side by side.

The last pages were lined and blank. Neatly inserted in the back cover's plastic pocket were computer printouts. They appeared to be lists of the room numbers and guests. Flipping to the fourth floor list, I saw:

415 John Dahl

416 Logan Zachary

417 Taylor Kozlowski

Sergio Wyzlic

418 Duane Wayne

419 David Ferron

David Campbell

420 Gary Morgan

"Isn't that strange?" I turned the book so Sergio could see. "Everyone that we've been running around with has a room on the same floor."

He took the list from me and scanned it. "Where's Tom's room?"

Flipping to the previous sheet, I found his name next to room number 413 and pointed to it.

"So why are all the guys we're hanging out with all on the same floor? Do you think that's a coincidence?" Sergio asked.

"I was wondering the same thing myself."

"Did someone set up these room assignments for a special purpose, or did they just happen to fall that way? Is there a date on the room assignments?" Sergio scanned the lists for a date, but found none. "No date. That would've shown us if they had planned our rooms before we arrived or typed them in afterward."

"I didn't know you were going to be here, so I didn't put your name down as my roommate." My eyes narrowed. "Did you know I was going to be here? Did Molly and you plan…?"

"I didn't know you were coming, honest. I was hoping to hang back and get stuck in a room by myself. I couldn't afford the single supplement to guarantee a private room."

"Neither could I, but then I didn't know I was going to be staying at Club Fred."

"You say that with disgust. Is there a problem with this resort?" He flopped back on his bed and stared at the ceiling. Suddenly, he sat bolt upright and pointed to the top of the dresser.

My eyes scanned the surface. My tote bag sat neatly folded next to the television. Two paperbacks and a key. A resort room key. Turning to Sergio, I asked. "Whose key is that?" I could feel mine digging into my leg, and I distinctly remembered him pulling out his key and putting it back into his pocket.

"That's my key on the dresser," he said, digging into his pocket. "This key is…"

"Gary's," we said together.

"But why did it open our door?" He looked at the number 420.

I fished out my key and handed it to Sergio. He lined them up and held them to the light. A perfect match. "Why did Gary have a key to our room?" I asked.

"But I opened Gary's room with this one." Sergio jumped up and raced to our door. Pulling it open, he tried the key in our lock, and it worked. Hurrying down the hallway to 416, Logan's room, Sergio inserted it again.

"He might be in there," I said.

But there was no stopping Sergio. The lock's tumblers clicked open. We could get into Logan's room if we wanted.

We went to room 415. The key opened John's door. Slipping past the top of the stairs, we approached Tom's room. The key opened 413. The key opened all of the doors we tried.

"What the heck is going on?" I asked.

"Do you think we were given a passkey? By mistake?" Sergio turned the key over and examined it carefully.

"Gary might've had one, but I doubt our keys should be able to open all the other doors." We re-entered our room and stood next to the door. "Could all of the locks have the same key?" I looked at the one in my hand and then to the door's lock.

"You mean," Sergio swallowed hard, "we could get into any room on the resort?" A smile crossed his face. "Like Tom's?"

I nodded. "Yeah, but think about it."

"What?" he asked, wrinkling his brow.

"If we can get into anyone else's room…"

We stood there, staring at each other, the rest of my sentence hanging in the air unsaid. At the same time, we reached over and set the dead bolt firmly into our door.

While Sergio showered, I picked up the notebook and continued flipping through it. What was I missing? As I re-read the room lists, I paused on Duane's room, number 418. That was right next door.

Had someone searched Duane's room? My room key poked into my leg and urged me into action before reason could talk me out of it. I set the book down and snuck across the room, pausing by the bathroom door. The thunk of a dropped shampoo bottle echoed in the shower as I unlocked the deadbolt and slipped out the door.

I looked around the hallway; no one was in sight. I causally strolled to my left and stood in front of 418. My ears strained to hear if anyone was coming up the stairs or moving around inside. The room's door looked exactly like ours. The doorknob was even on the same side, unlike most hotels that staggered their rooms' entries. Scanning up and down the hall, I slipped the key into the slot and pushed the door open. What was I doing? I couldn't do this. This was something Sergio would be doing if he weren't in the shower.

My eyes adjusted to the dark and the light from the hallway helped reveal Duane's room. It was an exact duplicate of ours. Two double beds stood to the right, while the wall length dresser lined up to the left. Closet to the immediate left and bathroom opposite.

Could Duane have entered the wrong room? This room was a carbon copy of ours. If he was being followed and he ran into our room by mistake, his key would have opened the door; he had probably thought he was in his own room.

So, whoever killed him might have thought the same. My mind jumped again. Maybe whatever the killer was looking for hadn't been found yet. It could still be in here.

Hurrying across the room, I closed the drapes before the

door clicked shut. I turned on the lamp on the dresser. Where to begin? I should be a pro by now. This wasn't the first room I'd rifled through on this trip. I hoped this wasn't becoming a habit. Scanning the room, I thought the closet looked like the obvious place to start. At least, that's where Gary had kept his smelly secrets.

Opening the white wooden doors, I saw a row of black leather vests, chaps, and blue Levis carefully lined up on hangers. Each hanger was an inch apart. Nothing touched on the rack. "A little compulsive, Duane?" I asked.

Not anymore, Sergio's voice responded in my mind.

Duane's suitcase lay open on the floor, empty, as was the shelf above the hanging clothes.

The bathroom door stood open. Tentatively, I flipped on the light switch. Neatly piled towels and a shaving kit were lined up on the vanity. Nothing looked out of place. Stepping in front of the stool, I removed the tank's lid. Only water and the toilet tank's insides stared back at me. Maybe I had seen too many movies or read too many books, or maybe this wasn't such a good idea after all.

His dresser held underwear, T-shirts, and socks. No books or magazines. What was wrong with this guy? Didn't he read? What was he going to be doing all week? Closing the last drawer, I heard the shower stop next door. Sergio must be done, so I had better hurry. I glanced around the room; only the beds were left.

The one by the bathroom didn't have anything underneath it. Crawling over to the other bed, I tensed and pulled up the dust ruffle. Nothing.

Sitting on the floor, I scanned the room one more time. There was something different in this room, but I couldn't quite place it. Then the bed next to the bathroom drew my attention, but what was it? I scanned the bedspread from the foot of the bed to the pillow. Then my eyes darted back a few feet from the pillow. A small depression dimpled the smooth covering. Two depressions. It looked like someone had sat on the edge of the bed, but the dents appeared to be too far apart. Unless the person had a really big butt. And Duane didn't. He was big, like a body builder, one of those who concentrated on his arms, and ignored his legs. That's it. Feet. Someone had stood on the bed.

Looking up, I saw what the difference was in this room. Our room had a vaulted ceiling, and this one had a drop-tiled ceiling. One tile had a slight sag in it, and it was directly above the bed's indentations. I hurried over to that spot and stared at the tile. A faint smudge ran along one side, and it looked like a fingerprint. Another one, fainter than the first, was directly across from it.

Stepping up onto the bed, I strained to push the tile up. There was something heavy on it. The bed sagged underneath my feet. Bouncing, I bumped the tile up and over. Next, I punched the tile's sag, and a leather briefcase slipped into sight.

I pulled on the handle, and the heavy case dropped from the ceiling and almost pulled me off the bed. Laying it on its side, I reached over and flipped the latches open. I raised the lid and saw a pile of manila folders resting neatly inside. Each tab had a precisely printed name in big block letters. Flipping through, I recognized a few of the names: David Campbell, John Dahl, and David Ferron. Searching further, it looked like there was a file for each man staying and working at the resort.

My fingers flipped through the tabs. A few more familiar names flew by; Tom, Logan, Cha-Cha. I paused on the next one.

Sergio Wyzlic? I slipped his folder out. What was going on? I swallowed hard as I glanced at the next file. "Taylor" was neatly printed in black letters. This was getting way too strange. Had I stepped into an old *Mission: Impossible* episode?

Why did Duane have files on everyone staying at the resort? Why did he have a file on me? And better yet, what was in it?

My palms started to sweat and my heart raced inside my ribcage.

Running through the files again, I pulled out the familiar names, and even found one on Mike and Geoff. I wanted to take all of the files, but I didn't think I should take the briefcase. What if someone knew it should be in here and found it missing? I didn't want him searching and finding it in our room. I figured it was better to take a few files and return to get more later on than get caught with the whole bundle.

I placed the pile of pulled files at the foot of the bed and quickly jumped up to replace the briefcase into its hiding place. After bouncing the tile back into place, I remembered to wipe the smudges off the tile. Only the slight sag could be seen. But before grabbing the files, I puffed up the mattress and smoothed out the bedspread, removing all evidence that I or someone had stood on the bed. I wasn't going to make it easy for someone else to find it.

I picked up the files and headed for the door. As I neared it, I saw a shadow move by the crack under the threshold. I backed away from the door, and strained to hear what was going on outside. I heard a key slide into the lock. My back pressed against the closet door. My arms hugged the files against my chest, trying to stop the rise and fall of my lungs.

Before the key could turn, Skinny David's voice echoed down the hallway. "I can't believe that they are so low on lime juice. This is a resort after all. Isn't it?"

The key slipped out of the lock, and I heard footsteps dash down the hallway away from the stairway. The shadow followed the footsteps.

Skinny David's voice grew louder. "Good thing we took extra traveler's checks on this trip. The brochure said that everything was included in the price, but they didn't say it would be so primitive…" and his voice trailed off.

My heart pounded in my chest. Nearing the door, I pressed my ear against the wood. The next door slammed, and David's voice finally disappeared. I counted to ten and bolted back to my room.

"Where the hell have you been?" Sergio demanded when I stepped back into the room. His eyes focused on what I carried. "And what do you have there?"

"Wait until you see this." I hurried over and sat on the bed. Flipping through the pile, I pulled out his folder, turned it around, and flashed him his name.

He read Sergio Wyzlic and snatched it from my hands. "Where did you get this?" he asked, sitting down on the bed next to me.

"I searched Duane's room and found a briefcase full of files. It looks like he had files on everyone at the resort. Let me tell you, it was pretty creepy, but I really flipped out when I saw your name on a file." I motioned to the one in his hands.

Tentatively, he opened the manila folder. The top sheet contained a Xeroxed copy of his South Dakota driver's license.

"How did they get that?" he asked.

"When's your birthday? And what year were you born?" I asked, trying to peer over his shoulder to see how old he really was.

Sergio quickly flipped the sheet over. "Let's see what else is in here."

Copies of his cosmetology license, birth certificate, credit card bills, and bank statement came next. The last sheet had "Arrest Record" written in fine black print. "What's this?" I pulled the sheet out.

"Nothing," Sergio said, grabbing it out of my hands. He quickly crumpled it into a ball and shoved it between his legs.

"You were arrested?" My eyebrows wrinkled. "For what?"

"It was all a mistake." He shifted on the bed, trying hard to protect the crumpled paper.

"You're kidding, right? You were never arrested."

"That's right. The sheet is wrong. The case was thrown out of court. Dismissed."

"Dismissed?" I was confused. "So, you were arrested? Really?"

"I don't want to talk about it." He closed his file and set it down on the other side of him. He folded his arms across his chest and hugged himself tightly.

With his defensive posturing, I had to approach this carefully. "Maybe it would help us understand what Duane had on everyone, that is, if we knew whether the information was true or not."

Suddenly, a new idea struck. "Could he have been blackmailing people?" I lifted the pile of folders off my lap and shook them. "Maybe there's something in these files that someone would kill to keep under wraps?"

Sergio's skinny legs gently tremored up and down, and he avoided making eye contact.

"How bad could it be?" I nudged him in the shoulder. "You didn't kill anyone, did you?"

He stopped tapping his leg, and his body tensed visibly.

"Come on, you can trust me." I placed my hand on his folder.

He flinched, but didn't pull away. He took a deep breath and exhaled. "When I was in cosmo school…" He swallowed hard. "I can't."

"I've done a lot of stupid things in my life. Things I'm not proud of, but I've learned from them, and they made me who I am today. For better or for worse."

He struggled with himself for a while and then finally started. "It's so stupid really. These two guys jumped me after class one night." His tone resounded with disgust. "I think they wanted to show me how tough they were." He stared straight ahead and ignored my eye contact.

Great. I was going to make him cry. That's just what I needed.

Trying to help, I offered, "They wouldn't have arrested you

for that. It wasn't your fault. Those guys were jerks. You didn't provoke them, did you?"

"You don't understand," he said, turning to face me. "I hurt one. Really bad."

"What?" I looked at his bony frame. How could Sergio hurt anyone? Let alone badly. He didn't seem like the threatening type to me. This story just wasn't making any sense. "What happened?" I pressed.

"I was getting into my car and these two guys jumped me. They pulled me out of my car and threw me to the ground. I thought they were going to steal my car or take my wallet, but they started throwing all of my stuff around." He took a deep breath.

"One guy was pulling out all of my things, rollers, curling irons, and throwing them around the parking lot and calling me all kinds of names. The other one came after me. Luckily, my curling rods were scattered across the lot and as he grabbed for me, he slipped."

I thought he was going to burst into tears, when he suddenly erupted into laughter. I waited for him to explain.

"While he was on the ground, Suzy Q beat him up."

"Who beat him up?" I asked, not following his story.

"Not who, what. Suzy Q was my mannequin head that I practiced on. The other guy pulled her out of my car and dropkicked her to my feet. The next thing I knew, I had her by the hair, covered in blood, and was chasing the other guy down the street." He shook his head. "That was until the policeman arrested me for assault and battery with a head."

"So, what happened?"

"The case was thrown out of court. The guys dropped their charges once they found out they would have to testify about what happened." He smiled. "I doubt their fragile egos would have been able to handle that."

"You were lucky they didn't hurt you."

"I think I would've rather they had. It would've been easier to live with than knowing how much violence can be bottled up inside of me."

"You were only defending yourself. Surely, they could see…"

"I think that was part of why they dropped the charges." Sergio pointed to his chest. "Afraid of how it would look if someone like me had beaten one of them senseless."

Gently, taking the folder from his lap, I looked over its contents again. "Wow! That's what you owe on your credit card," I said, pointing to the grand total. "And I thought my student loan total looked overwhelming."

Sergio ran his fingers through his damp hair, causing it to spike on top. Then he re-filed everything into his folder, and curtly nodded. "Well, let's see what he has on you." He reached across me and rummaged through the stack for my folder. Finding it, he smiled as he opened it. "Now, we get to expose Taylor for what he really is." His hands flung the folder open, and a single sheet of paper floated out and landed on the floor.

I bent forward and picked it up. It was a copy of my driver's license. "That's it?" I said, flipping the piece of paper over.

Sergio shook the manila folder. Nothing else fell out.

There wasn't anything else in my file. No South Dakota OT license, no bank statements, no credit card bills. Nothing. Just my horrible driver's license picture. "You would have thought that he could have gathered something else on me, wouldn't you?"

"You sound so disappointed," he said. "What skeletons do you have in your closet?"

"I… I… don't have any."

"My, aren't you just so perfect." Sergio shook his head.

Ignoring him as I placed my one sheet back into the folder, I said, "I bet since Molly signed me up so late, he didn't have time to find anything on me."

"Oh yeah. Like they could find anything on Mr. Perfect."

"You would be surprised."

"Oh yeah, tell me." Sergio leaned forward and waited.

"I almost got kicked out of grad school for unprofessional behavior."

"What?" The surprised look on Sergio's face was priceless.

"It's a long story, but in short, I wrote a petition against an instructor, uncovered that the chair of our department was falsifying students' record, sought out legal counsel from the ombudsman, and made an instructor cry."

"Bad boy. Is that all?" Disappointment played across his face.

"Isn't that enough?"

"I was hoping for some sordid sex scandal to improve your grade point average."

"I know that happened with our fieldwork coordinator to get preferential internship placements."

"Did you…?" His eyes brightened.

"No."

Sergio slumped down on the bed.

"I got a speeding ticket, once," I offered.

"Oh, you're so bad." Sergio exhaled loudly. "I guess that's why Duane didn't waste any time on you. You weren't worth the bother."

I looked at him, confused.

"He must've looked at my bank book and credit card bills and figured he wouldn't get a cent out of me. And you, ha."

"Thanks a lot." I picked up the rest of the folders and placed them on my lap.

"You know what I mean." He elbowed me in the side. "You wouldn't hurt anyone. Not intentionally."

"If I was pushed or someone I cared about was being threatened." My voice trailed off as I looked down at the pile of folders. Glancing at the clock, I saw it was after midnight. But I was too wide-awake to think of sleep. "Shouldn't we look at the others?" I tipped the first folder open. "I mean, see what they have to hide?"

Sergio leaped forward and picked up the top file. "I can't wait."

"Isn't this an invasion of privacy?"

Pausing for a second with the folder half-open, Sergio shook his head. "This is a fine time to get a conscience." He looked at the folder and flipped it open the rest of the way. "But Duane did all of this invasion before we did."

"So…" I started.

"So what? You're the one who stole them in the first place. If you didn't plan on reading them, then why did you take them?" He didn't wait for an answer. "Besides, I don't want them to go to waste. I'm reading them."

Looking over his shoulder, I asked, "Whose file do you have?"

"Tom's." He turned the file so I could read the tab.

Inside, we found Tom's driver's license, a small credit card debt, comfortable savings and checking account balances, reviews and publicity photos of his movies, and a marriage license.

"Whoa! What is this?" Sergio handed me the sheet. "Do you think he filed for this when he was young and confused?"

Scanning the license, I pointed to the date. "Maybe, if he was confused eight months ago."

"What?" He grabbed it back. "Let me see that. Do you think they mistyped the bride's name, like backward? Maybe it should be James Stephanie, instead of Stephanie James."

"I guess we'll have to ask him about it. But it does look like a real license."

"That would make Tom 'Gay for Pay,' you know, straight but willing to do gay movies for the money, and that could hurt his career."

"I didn't think many people stayed in the porn business very long."

"No. That would be gross."

"Right. So the important thing is do you think Tom would kill to keep his marriage a secret?"

"Tom's studio would, if they thought it would hurt sales." Sergio scratched his head. "And probably his agent would, if he thought that he would lose his percentage."

"I met Tom's agent yesterday, and he didn't look very happy with Tom then. Maybe he found out?"

"Maybe we can weasel that out of him tomorrow on the snorkeling trip." Sergio's eyebrows rose, "So, who's next?"

Logan's name was on the next tab. After the usual financial information, the file was filled with copies of book covers and reviews. Following the critiques was a copy of an e-mail from Logan's agent.

"Check this out," I said and read the letter out loud.

"Dear Logan,

We regret to inform you that your new book, Kill Me! Kill Me! Kill Me! (A Man After Midnight) is the last book your publisher will be producing at this time. Due to declining sales, they are no longer able to keep a slot open for your series in their annual release schedule.

However, if this new book opens with a bang, they will reconsider signing you to a new three-book contract. After careful consideration, I'm suggesting that you use a possible publicity stunt, which could parallel your novel to draw attention to its release. Remember, sex and scandal sells!

Yours truly,

Sean Harris"

"That's cold," Sergio said.

"From what I've read about publishing, if the book isn't a blockbuster like Grafton, Grisham, or King, its shelf life is about thirty days."

"Look at this." Sergio pulled a stapled packet of paper out of the folder. Photos of the same man separated copies of each book's dedication sheet. The man's name was the same for each book's dedication. "Are you thinking what I'm thinking?" he asked.

I rolled my eyes. "You think everyone is gay."

"Until proven otherwise." He smiled.

"Whatever. Who's next?"

Sergio grabbed Geoff's folder off the top of the pile. Inside, he found a newspaper article. "Listen to this." He read from the article, *"Florida's Finest Fired!"*

"Detective Geoff de la Vega was indicted for the shooting of his partner, Fernando Kingston. After a surveillance team had set up a sting for a local smuggling ring, de la Vega and Kingston entered the premises of Tabago Shipping Company. Both men were caught in cross fire, resulting in Kingston's death. Ballistics revealed that the bullet that killed Kingston was fired from de la Vega's gun. Suspicion to de la Vega's involvement in the smuggling operation had been an ongoing investigation in the Miami police department. Along with repeated reprimands for intoxication during work hours, de la Vega has been suspended from the police force without pay."

"Do you think he should be bartending?" Sergio asked.

I shook my head and looked at the folder. "That explains how he got here and possibly why he hates this job."

"I think he needs to re-evaluate his life and choose a different profession."

"Could you do anything else besides being a hairdresser?" I asked.

"What else would you do?" he countered.

I shook my head. No matter how frustrated I became at work some days, I hadn't been able to find a different field. "I haven't found one yet."

"Neither have I. It must be in the genes." He reached over and picked up the next two folders that were stuck together. Nothing too revealing was discovered about David and David, who ran an import/export business in New York. A few bank letters revealed that the business was having some financial troubles due to lost shipments of pieces of art. Their insurance company was still investigating these losses, but reimbursement was pending.

Gary's file revealed an overdrawn and over-extended man. His credit report made Sergio look like a millionaire. No clear record of steady employment could help explain his money flow, but odd deposits peppered his statements. He had an arrest for steroid use and sales, but it wasn't enough to do any jail time. Why was he working here?

John's folder was fat with photos of him and copies of the ads he modeled in. All of them showed a lot more of him than I wanted to see. His finances and investments looked profitable.

Cha-Cha, born Charles Champion, had worked in Las Vegas, New York, and Hollywood. Her talents ranged from stripper to escort, showgirl to bartender, and massage therapist to movie star. She had done it all and had the rap sheet to prove it. Many of her arrests and job changes appeared due to violent outbursts when she was ignored.

"Way to go." I turned to Sergio. "She wasn't the best person to upset on this trip."

"No drag queen is going to scare me."

"She's starting to scare me," I said, flipping through the rap sheet. "I wouldn't want her to do anything in that file to me." I pointed at assault with a vibrator, and then to a hairy man shaved with an Epilady, which made Sergio cringe. After that, I put the sheets back together and closed the folder.

"Don't worry, I'll protect you from her."

"But who's going to protect you?"

Ignoring my comment, he opened the last file. Mike owned

and operated Club Fred. Four times a year, he would rent an entire resort, and open it up to gay visitors. He had yet to return to the same resort. "I doubt they'll let him come back here," I mused.

"It looks like Mike hires travelers, like me, ones who can't afford the trip, but can offer a service to his guests to make their vacation complete."

"So, who else is on Mike's payroll, besides the guys running the Club Fred table?"

"Now, that's an interesting question. I'll see if I can find out from Mike, in a roundabout way." Sergio yawned and stretched his arms over his head.

"Well, I can wait for that," I said, handing the stack of folders to Sergio. "I'm beat, and my eyes are killing me." I stood up and walked to the bathroom. "I need to take these contacts out and get to bed. Besides, we really need to get some sleep. We have a big day ahead of us tomorrow. We're going snorkeling in the morning, remember?"

Before going down to breakfast, Sergio used his remaining pair of scissors to unravel the stitching on one of the box springs. I wrapped the stolen folders in a towel and inserted the whole package inside. Sergio carefully folded the fabric to match the seam and quickly sewed a running stitch, or so he told me, to conceal his handiwork. We scanned the room one more time and made sure our hiding spot appeared secure.

An hour later, our tour boat headed out, right on time. Guys filled the deck and Mariachi music blared out of the tinny speakers. White water bubbled and turned underneath the hull. Tom, Logan, Sergio, and I sat in the white plastic deck chairs and watched the horizon swallow the resort.

As the boat pulled away from the dock, I noticed Geoff taking photos of our departure. Before I could comment, the horns blasted the event music and drowned out anything I would have said.

When the music ended, Mike stepped into the middle of the deck. "Seal Island is two hours straight ahead," he spoke into the intercom of the boat, before the regular music returned. "A fog bank is hiding it right now, but we'll be able to see it clearly as we sail closer and the sun burns off the humidity." He droned on in his well-rehearsed tour guide speech.

Sergio's face appeared pale in the morning sun. "Are you feeling all right?" I asked. Sergio hadn't told me if he had snorkeled before, so I assumed he had. But come to think of it, he hadn't said much on this outing.

"I must've had too much to drink last night," Sergio said, rubbing his temples and then his stomach. "Or stayed up too late reading."

"Do you need an aspirin?" I asked, patting my left pocket, which wasn't there. I looked down. Swimming shorts with no pockets. "Sorry, I left them…" I said, pointing back to the resort.

Sergio's pallor slowly turned green. Aquamarine to be exact. The boat rolled over a swell as we veered slightly to the right. Sergio clutched his belly and closed his eyes, trying to ride out the waves of nausea.

This was going to be a very long trip.

Two hours later, we reached our location, but Sergio still sat in his chair with his head hanging down between his knees. He moaned in a low voice.

"Are you going to be all right?" I called.

"Yeah, go ahead and enjoy." Sergio waved us away with his hand. "Let me die in peace."

"Suit yourself," Tom called, stepping off the boat and into the brine.

The back of Logan's head bobbed in the ocean as he swam toward the island.

Slipping my facemask into place, it fogged over immediately after forming a tight seal around my eyes and nose. My mouthpiece tasted of rubber and salt. I bit down on the teeth-guard, took a deep breath, and pushed my body off the boat. Once submerged, the fog thickened.

Tom said, "You have to spit on the lens in the water and then put it on wet. Otherwise, it'll fog up." He dove under the surface and was gone.

Treading water, I followed his directions and suddenly found that the water was crystal clear, warm, but refreshing against the tropical sun. Huge clouds filled the blue-green sky as the wind blew harder.

Dog-paddling away from the boat, I attempted to submerge my face, now that I could see. Tom arched his back and dove deep into the water. I dog-paddled at the surface; my breathing still wasn't under control.

Gradually, stroke by stroke, my face slowly entered the water, and the underwater world came into clear focus. I smiled to myself; Molly would be so amazed at this adventurous side of me. My disposable underwater camera slapped against my wrist. With all the trouble controlling my breath, I had forgotten it was there. This was so cool. I could say that I took this picture of swimming seals, an underwater picture. And the impressive part was that I took it *myself.*

Three seals dove off the rock and swam in synchronized movements. Deeper and deeper they dove, fanning out underneath me. I followed their movements, deeper into the surf. Suddenly, I realized they were directly underneath me. Forgetting the picture I was trying to take, I covered my groin protectively, dunking my head completely underneath the water's surface.

Water rushed down the snorkel tube, flooding my mouth.

Coughing and choking, I struggled to right myself at the surface. Spitting seawater out, I tried to catch my breath from all the excitement. A minute later, I had regained my composure and looked around to see if any of the other snorkelers had noticed.

No one had. They were all too busy enjoying the underwater sights.

Smiling, I swam forward, my face in the water, watching the texture of the ocean bottom change.

Three hours later, the boat was heading back to the resort. In all of the excitement of the trip, not one of the staff members seemed too concerned about leaving anyone behind. I did a quick head count. Thirty-one. Shouldn't there have been thirty-two? Everything on this trip seemed to be so pair oriented, so why would the resort have sent out an odd number of swimmers? Weren't we supposed to be using the buddy system or was I the only one?

Tom and Logan were pointing at the pelicans circling overhead. At least I thought they were pelicans. Sergio was still clutching his stomach with one hand and hanging onto my camera with the other. The three I came with were here. So who was missing?

I scanned the water's surface. What was I looking for? Was I hoping to see a floating body? But if someone had drowned, the body wouldn't float right away. It would sink for a while, until decomposition gas formed and caused it to float, days, maybe weeks later.

"Shouldn't someone do a head count?" I asked, to no one in particular.

Mike and John were reaching into a red cooler and brought out several bottles of tequila and 7-Up. Mike held up the Cuervo and shouted, "Tequila Slammers!"

"Great," I said, "just what we need, alcohol." At least they were using it after the snorkeling, and not before.

I stopped myself. I didn't want to be a prude, especially on vacation, but I had seen the effects of booze on way too many people's lives at the hospital.

But these people would drink wisely. They were on vacation.

Yeah right. I sat down next to Sergio. He tipped his head to the side and looked at me. "Why so serious?"

"Just thinking."

"Well, stop that. You're on vacation." And with that, he put his head back down on his lap.

So, after such a wonderful adventure, what was really bothering me? The alcohol or the odd head count?

All the way back to the resort, I stewed. What kind of place was this? Didn't these guys take *any* responsibility for their guests' safety? Didn't they care?

Mike and John should've been more aware of the risks they were putting their vacationers in. One of them should've been paying attention to the guests while they were drinking, instead of encouraging them to drink more tequila.

Well, I'd had enough of this. If these guys weren't going to do their jobs, then I wasn't sticking around. I was getting out before something bad happened. I couldn't stand by and watch people being put into harm's way. And nothing was being done about finding the killer at the resort. So, that was it. I was going home.

I peered around the boat. The waves appeared to have increased, and the sky had gained a haze. The cloud masses were building, but the strange thing was the colors, green, pink, and lavender in the once blue sky. At home, the only time the sky turned that color was when conditions were right for a tornado.

A cool breeze blew across the side of the boat. Goosebumps rose across my arms.

"Ahh. A cool breeze. Finally," Sergio sighed.

A little too cool for my liking. Looking off into the horizon, I tried to remember what my dad said, red sky at night… "The ocean does seem to be more turbulent, but high tide must be coming in."

The crests of the waves turned white, sharp-edged, and moving faster toward the shore. Good thing we had the tail wind to hasten our trip. The resort was rapidly approaching. Rubbing my hands together, I smiled. I was going home. Now I only had to convince Sergio to go with me.

Mike sat with his feet up on his desk, both arms crossed and lying on his chest. "I can't give you a refund if you go home now."

Shaking my head, I said, "I don't want a refund. I just want to leave the resort and go home. When is the next plane leaving?"

Mike's arms reached forward. He straightened and picked up the clipboard on the desk and rifled through a few pages. "It looks like the next flight leaves tomorrow morning at ten o'clock."

"Fine. I'll take it. Can you call and see if there is a seat available for me?" When he didn't respond, I continued, "And I'll need a taxi to take me to the airport. I doubt the hotel shuttle will make it that far."

"The resort has a shuttle?" Mike looked up at me, puzzled. Then his eyes focused on me, and he grinned. "Oh, you mean the plantation truck. It does look like it has seen better days."

"I don't want to be rude, but can you set this up for me?" I pressed, trying to push Mike into action.

"I will, but besides the two deaths, is there any other reason why you want to leave?"

Why did I have to explain this to him? All I wanted was to go home. And why was I starting to feel so defensive? I didn't need to explain this to him at all. I unclenched my fists and began carefully, trying hard not to complain or accuse. "I'm just tired of how lax the safety has been around here, especially on today's excursion. No one did a head count before we headed back to the resort."

"So?"

"So. There was an odd number on the boat. Is someone missing?"

"What do you mean by that? Did we leave someone behind?"

Now was a fine time to ask. "Isn't that something you should know?" Pausing for a moment of therapeutic silence, I continued. "So, how many people were supposed to be on this morning's trip?"

Mike flipped a few more pages. "Thirty-two were signed up…"

"But I only counted thirty-one on the return."

He ran his finger down the row of names. Each one had a check by it. A frown worried his brow. He counted again and scratched his head. "Why do you think we're missing someone? Were there thirty-two guys on the boat when it left?"

"Isn't that something you should know?" wanted to come out of my mouth, but I took a deep breath. "Sergio didn't go into the water. He got seasick, so there must have been a lone swimmer."

My mind flashed back to the snorkeling trip, and my breath caught in my throat. They don't care about anyone. All Mike wanted is to make money and have a good time. Safety wasn't a concern. I stood up from my chair. "I really should go and pack."

"Taylor, sit down for a second. You're not making any sense," Mike soothed. "Who do you think we left behind?"

"I don't know who. I just know that we only had thirty-one people on board for the trip back to the resort, when we should've had thirty-two."

"Did you count thirty-two when you got on board?"

I looked at him. His eyes seemed genuinely concerned. "Well, no…" I began.

"So, how can you say for sure that we left someone behind? Did you see a body floating? Or do you know of anyone who is missing?"

"I don't know." I exhaled hard and tried expressing myself in a different way. "Everything that goes on at this place is so pair-oriented, that I thought there shouldn't have been a single person swimming. We were supposed to use the buddy system when we went snorkeling…"

"So, who lost his partner?"

"Sergio did," I said simply.

"And who was his partner? I thought you signed up with him. Oh, that's right. You've been off flirting with Tom." He tossed his head back, dramatically. "I thought he signed up with that writer guy. Whatever his name is." Mike's finger ran up and down the list of names.

"Logan."

"Yeah, that's it."So, Logan and Tom were both on the boat coming back, right?"

"Yes."

"And Sergio didn't go into the water?"

"No."

"So, there must have been an odd number on the boat when it left."

"But are you sure?" My voice sounded whiny, even to my ears.

Mike's finger stopped on a name in the list. "Gary was supposed to help on the excursion, and his name has been checked off. He wasn't on board, now was he?" Mike cocked his head to the side and waited for my answer.

"Well, no."

"So there's your missing person, Gary. He was signed up to go, but he died last night. That explains why there were only thirty-one on the tour."

"But…" I started.

"But nothing. Are you trying to start a panic? Someone has been starting all kinds of rumors. There's even one about a hurricane moving in our direction." Mike slammed down the clipboard. "And I want them to stop."

"There's a hurricane coming?" I asked.

"No. The locals are saying that since there are so many homosexuals here, we've angered the gods or something, and this is their punishment on us." Mike took a deep breath and started again, slowly and calmer this time. "There isn't a hurricane coming. The weather is going to be beautiful all week long. There. Is. No. Hurricane. Coming," he said, each word like a bullet piercing my eardrum. "Okay?"

I rolled my eyes. "What about Gary?"

"What about him? He died. That's it."

"He was murdered, wasn't he? And no one is doing anything to find out who killed him."

"Geoff has been…" Mike began.

"Geoff has been what? Drinking? Partying? What has he done so far? It sure hasn't been his job, now has it?"

"Gary had an unfortunate accident."

"An accident. His head was bashed in. Do you call that an accident? I suppose Duane was trimming his beard, when his hand slipped on Sergio's scissors and plunged them into his neck?"

"See! There's another rumor," he shouted. Pushing himself up, he flew around the desk and towered over me. "Are you the one starting them?" He poked his index finger into my chest. "Maybe you're trying to sabotage my business."

"Mike, all I want is to go home, and as soon as possible. Today."

"Well, you can't. You've missed the last plane out of here today. You'll have to wait until tomorrow."

"Fine. Then set things up, and I won't cause any more problems." I walked to the office door and turned around. "I'll be ready and waiting in the lobby at seven o'clock tomorrow morning."

"Fine. I'll call and have a taxi ready and waiting for you." He reached across his desk and picked up the phone. "Just stop spreading the rumors around here." His fingers pounded out the numbers. "Club Fred isn't bankrupt. I'm not losing my job. A hurricane isn't coming. A murderer isn't loose…"

I turned and walked out of his office, shaking my head. All I knew was that I was going home tomorrow.

After supper that night, everywhere I turned, I heard the same conversation over and over again. Sergio even put several guys up to it. "CNN Storm Report says there's a hurricane heading straight for our resort. Go ask Mike if it's coming." He'd elbow me in the side as he sent the next unsuspecting person off with an innocent grin.

"Is there a hurricane coming?" The guest would ask Mike.

"There's no hurricane coming." Mike would snap.

"But CNN's Storm Report said…"

He would then interrupt them. "Wouldn't *I* know if there was a hurricane coming?"

Well, he should have.

My alarm went off, and I swung my legs over the side of the bed. I was going home and nothing was going to stop me. Nothing.

Looking over at Sergio's sleeping form, I felt guilty, because I still hadn't asked him to leave with me. Would he even consider it? Or would he try to convince me to stay and see the week out, or worse, make me feel guilty about leaving before these murders were solved? Ever since he and Molly teamed up in Sioux Falls, they both seemed to have the same skill for dragging me into their problems.

My bare feet shuffled across the cool tile floor and picked up a coating of sandy grit. Didn't the maids mop in here? As I neared the bathroom, I saw a red sheet of paper on the floor. Mike must have gotten my early checkout receipt ready and slipped it under our door. As I bent over to pick up the sheet, I squinted hard, trying to read the print, but I knew without my contacts I wouldn't be able to read it.

"Whaawho! Now, that's a sight I like to wake up to…" Sergio said from under his covers.

Resisting the urge to flip him off, which would only encourage him, I stood up quickly, ignoring the impulse to cover my boxer-clad butt. I brought the paper to my face.

"Warning! Hurricane Alert!" stood out in giant black letters on the top of the page. My eyes struggled to focus and read the rest of the print as it got smaller: "A hurricane is rapidly approaching our resort. Please Do Not Panic!"

"What are you reading?" Sergio asked.

I pulled the paper away from my face and turned to his bed. "According to this piece of paper, a hurricane is heading straight for the resort."

"But last night Mike said…"

"I know. He lied." I handed the sheet to Sergio and went into the bathroom to put in my contact lenses and brush my teeth.

A few minutes later, Sergio sat crossed-legged in his bed. "Did you read this? Number twenty-four. Do not drink alcohol during the hurricane. It may impair your judgment. Number twenty-five. Do not have sexual intercourse." He put the paper down in his lap. "What can we do? Sit around in the bathroom with our heads between our knees?"

"I think that's about it." I opened the dresser drawer and pulled out a pair of shorts and a white T-shirt. The rest of my clothes were already packed in my suitcase, waiting for me in the closet.

"Well, that's boring. I want to see what a *real* hurricane looks like." Sergio jumped out of bed and headed for the bathroom. He paused at the door and turned to me, "I wonder if it's like what you see on television. You know, all the rain blowing sideways and people getting sucked out to sea."

"Sounds like where I want to be, right at ground zero for that storm."

"Hurry up. You're going to miss all of the fun." Sergio ran a comb through his hair, making it stand straight up on end. He slipped on his sandals and opened the door.

I finished changing into a clean pair of Levi shorts and T-shirt.

"What are you waiting for? All the food will be gone, besides, I want to be *there*, when the storm hits."

Walking into my sandals, I followed, grabbing my tote bag and camera. "I need to be down in the lobby by seven a.m. sharp anyway, or I'll miss my taxi to the airport."

"What?" Sergio said, stopping in his tracks.

"I'm leaving the resort. Mike called and set up a ride for me to the airport, along with a flight home."

"But why?" Sergio whined.

"Do I need to explain this to you? Where have you been? Haven't you seen what's been going on around here?" I waited for him to say something.

He didn't.

"Besides, I don't belong here, and you know it."

"But you'll miss all of the fun. Besides, you can't leave me here alone with the killer. Molly would never forgive you if anything happened to me." He stomped his foot like a two-year-old and pouted.

"A hurricane's fun? I think I can live without that excitement, and I want you to come with me, so you'll be safe."

"I don't want to go, and I'm staying to weather out the storm and find the killer, with or without you." A smile broke out across Sergio's mouth. "I doubt you're leaving," he laughed. "I'll bet Mike didn't even call for the flight or the taxi." He shrugged his shoulders. "It's not like a cab would venture out here if a hurricane was coming, anyway. Right?" Sergio closed the door to the bathroom.

Truer words were never spoken.

The sky was gray with tints of pink and green. The ocean breeze had intensified overnight. A constant gust blew and blew. Usually, the wind would let up at times, but now instead of slowing, there were surges of harder wind. The lowering atmospheric pressure pushed on my eardrums while an electric hum seemed to fill the air. The hair on my arms and legs stood straight up. I caught sight of my reflection in a hallway mirror. The hair on my head was even standing on end. I had never seen wind like this before.

As we entered the dining room, it buzzed with excitement. Nervous energy propelled people around like ionized particles, everyone picked up speed with each encounter. The bar was open with the longest line I've seen so far. No waiting for coffee or tea. I guessed caffeine wasn't needed today.

We walked down the buffet line and picked up a plate. At the end, all I had was a scorched pancake and two slices of slimy bacon. On the last table stood a wooden bowl of hard rolls. I tossed two in my bag, but before I moved on, I stepped back and threw a dozen more in. It didn't look like there was a run on buns, at least not when the bar was open.

Bottled water lined up on another table. Picking up two bottles, I added them to my tote bag. Sergio might need these when the storm hit, and I doubted he'd think to stock up, not in this frenzy. My bag was starting to dig into my shoulder, so I turned to scan for Sergio.

He waved me over to a table, and I walked through the maze to join him. Two men who I hadn't seen before sat with him; both were speaking in excited French. They smiled as I pulled my chair out but continued with their conversation.

I looked up from my bacon and my pancake, which was black on the outside and soggy on the inside. I eyed the candle sitting in the center of the table. Glancing at the guys, I slipped it into the tote bag while neither one noticed. A lighter lay on its side next to the guy with a crew cut and the Euro-chic glasses. As I stood up to leave, I slipped the lighter into my pocket and nodded "goodbye" to them.

Sergio followed me, and the French men quickly returned to their rapid speech, all the time motioning toward the ocean with their hands.

Sergio poked me in the back. "I saw that," he said. "Smooth."

"Must be all the fine motor coordination exercises I do with my patients at work."

"You could easily live a life of crime." He raised his eyebrows and smirked.

"Gee, thanks. I'm glad you think so highly of me." We walked back to our room and I unloaded my tote bag in the bathroom.

"What did you take all of this stuff for?" He picked up a hard roll and a bottle of water.

"I figured you may need them, once the storm hits." I finished emptying my bag.

"What about you?" He set the bottle back down on the counter.

"I'm going home, remember?"

"Do you really think that cab is going to pick you up?"

I hated to admit it, but that same sinking feeling had been plaguing me all morning. I thought I might have waited too long to go home. I tried to push that thought out of my mind, but knowing my luck, a hurricane was heading straight for this resort.

The same resort with a snake-throwing killer running around loose. A resort filled with gay men and horrible, inedible food. And I was trapped in the middle of it.

I sat in the lobby on my suitcase for two hours, but no taxi came. As my butt became numb, I watched the traffic in the parking lot. No one arrived, only left, like rats from a sinking ship, but that seemed like an exaggeration. I'm sure they were only the night crew going home. But it looked like the *entire* night shift and day shift, every shift. But why wasn't anyone coming *in* for the day shift? Did they know something we didn't?

As each staff member loaded up in his or her car, I wished my Spanish was good enough to hitch a ride to the airport or at least into town. But no. Luther L. Wright High School had only offered French, and this wasn't Gay Paree. Well, at least part of that was correct.

As the time went by, the sky grew a deeper and darker gray. The morning was completely overcast. No rays of sun broke through the dense cloud cover. What was really amazing was the intensity of the wind. It kept increasing with each passing minute.

As someone departed, they would walk into the wall of wind, which was starting to shake the whole resort. And the wind never let up. Where was all of the wind coming from? In Sioux Falls, the wind would blow and let up, but this was a constant gust. In my mind, I pictured a huge fan far out at sea, blowing and blowing. And someone had forgotten to turn it off.

The lobby's clock rattled and tried to chime off nine, but the hammer seemed to keep missing the chime.

While contemplating going back to my room, I turned to look over my shoulder. Sergio approached, shaking his head. "That's the same place I left you hours ago. Haven't you gone yet?" He stretched his hand out and pulled me to my feet.

"I think they forgot me."

"It's their loss. Just be thankful I'm still here with you." Sergio said and patted me on the shoulder.

"Oh yeah, I feel so much better already."

"The cab isn't coming, but the hurricane is. So much for believing Mike; you were an idiot to have trusted him. Did he even call for a cab or your plane ticket? I'm sure it's too late to find out. You missed your flight, and we're here for the duration of the building storm."

I picked up my carry-on.

"Come on. This will be fun." He reached over, picked up my suitcase and hoisted the strap over his shoulder. He grabbed my wrist and pulled me back to our room. "Just think of the stories we're going to be able to tell Molly and all of our friends back at home. It's not every vacation that you get caught in a hurricane."

And what were the odds of that? I didn't even want to think about it.

As we left the lobby, the wind whipped down the stairway, howled, and blew us backward. We took a step back, regained our footing, and then leaned forward and pressed into the tempest. We braced ourselves by squatting and spreading our legs as we used the handrails to pull ourselves to the fourth floor.

Standing on our landing, I wondered. Was the top level the safest place to be? Wouldn't the roof be blown off first? Or would the foundation crumble from the waves that pelted the beach? Maybe I should've been a civil engineer, instead of an occupational therapist. Then I would've known the answer.

Sergio smiled as we approached our room's door and inserted his key.

Then the thought struck me. He was really enjoying this. Maybe it was a good thing the cab never came. Someone had to keep an eye on him and keep him safe. And I doubted that anyone at the resort would.

Besides, Molly would kill me if anything happened to Sergio.

CHAPTER 36 - PARTY ON THE BEACH

An hour later, Sergio and I leaned against the railing of our balcony, watching hundreds of men surround the beach bar to watch the storm approach. The sky had darkened to a steel gray, and the wind had picked up, even more than I thought it could. The palm trees swayed at sharp angles, threatening to snap. Low clouds raced overhead. Every once in a while, a gust would rattle the whole building.

I looked over at Sergio. He pleaded with me.

"I know you want you to go down there and join them, but…"

"But what?" he whined. "It's not like this storm is a tornado. Well, it is, but we have time. Look," he said, pointing down to the beach. "It's open down there. It's not like we can't see it coming."

He was right. Since we had received the storm warning, the sky had darkened and the wind had intensified, but that's about it. No rain or anything else. Besides, once the storm hit the resort, we would be confined to our rooms. And with all of the covered walkways connecting the buildings, we should be safe getting back to our room…if we'd leave as soon as the weather took a turn.

"I guess we could…"

And Sergio had me down on the beach in the center of everything. He walked to the side of the bar and opened up the cooler. He held up a Tecate and a Bud Light.

I shook my head.

He reached in again and held up a 7-Up.

I nodded. Why not be responsible and social at the same time?

He pulled out two for me and took two Tecate for himself.

"I thought we weren't supposed to drink alcohol during a hurricane," I said as he approached. "Wasn't that on our list of things…"

A man in a Club Fred shirt with a picture of the model John flipping his wet hair back from his face glared at me. He took a long drag on his beer and turned his back to us deliberately.

Sergio handed me the cans of 7-Up and popped open one of his beers. He took a big sip. "Try and stop them." He motioned toward the crowd, bellying up to the bar.

A hush descended on the crowd as Mike walked through the melee. He held up his hands and motioned for everyone to be quiet. "Listen up! A hurricane is coming, and everyone needs to be back in their rooms in thirty minutes."

A chorus of "Ah's" arose from the crowd.

"You don't have to be in your *own* room. I don't care *whose* room you pick to be in, but you need to be in *a room* in thirty minutes."

A few catcalls and suggestions responded to his announcement.

"No, seriously. It's for your own safety. You all need to be back in your rooms in thirty minutes."

"All right, all right, thirty minutes, just pass me another beer," someone yelled.

"Beer! Beer! Beer!" rose as a chant against the gale.

I walked away from the shelter alongside the bar, and a wall of wind pushed me back. "Wow. That wind is getting stronger."

Sergio followed and stepped back to maintain his balance. "I see what you mean. I wonder how many miles an hour it's blowing?"

On the beach, white-capped waves beat the shore. The storm loomed in the distance. Wind whipped at my clothes and hair. Living in Sioux Falls, we saw many days of wind, but nothing had prepared me for this. I was having a difficult time comprehending the wind's force. I spread my arms out to the side. The pressure felt like I'd stuck my arm outside my car window going sixty-five miles an hour on the interstate.

"Twenty minutes!" Mike yelled into the wind, but no one seemed to pay any attention to him. Another wave of bottles appeared on the bar as soon as the other ones emptied. The stream of drinkers strolled by. The supply of bottles amazed me just as much as the wind.

Suddenly, a thundering gust struck me. Sergio grabbed me before I fell off the deck. The entire beach bar rumbled underneath our feet. The melee paused for a second and everyone was quiet. The rattling stopped, and the party resumed as if nothing had happened.

Sergio downed his first beer and opened the next one.

"Take it easy on those," I shouted.

"That's why I brought you along, you're the designated walker." His voice battled against the wind.

"I don't mind if you have a drink or two, just don't overdo it."

"I won't, Mother!"

Another hour passed and the wind continued to blow. The endless supply of bottles had slowed a little, but they kept coming, just like a magician's handkerchief. Mike was still yelling "ten minutes," but no one was paying any attention to him. And Sergio wouldn't listen to my pleas to get to our room.

"Look at that." Sergio pointed directly above us. A flock of gray pelicans hovered overhead in a long line that strung out along the beach. No wing movement could be detected. They just faced into the wind and hung there, overhead, waiting, watching.

The pulsating vibe seemed to be growing around us. I could almost see the static electricity building between each man. It forced all the hair on my arms and legs to stand and seem to extend out to whoever was next to me. It was hard to tell if it was from the wind or the storm's electricity.

"Cool," Sergio said, as the swarm of birds moved closer. They hovered above; their black eyes vacant and unblinking, boring into us.

"What are they waiting for?" I asked.

"Supper," he said. "I wonder which one of us is on the menu tonight?"

Mike's voice fought the wind's roar. "Five minutes, guys, five minutes."

A group of guys ventured out on the beach and waded into the crashing surf. Even without the sun, they were enjoying the day.

"See, Taylor, you just have to make the best of things," Sergio shouted at me.

"I'm trying," I yelled back.

The sky was twilight gray. The wind had started to irritate my skin and eardrums. Maybe it was the sand from the beach blasting my body, but I was exhausted. "Are you ready to head back to the room, yet? I'm tired, and I'm hungry," I shouted.

"Mike said they were going to be bringing cold lunches around to the rooms." Sergio tossed his empty beer can into the bin.

"I can just imagine what they'll come up with."

"I heard the day shift didn't even come in. They boarded up their homes and stayed there. They're all nice, safe and secure, while we're out partying like there's no tomorrow."

"Maybe they know something we don't." The unknown was starting to unsettle me.

"Don't worry. This is fun," he shouted in the tempest and opened another beer.

An hour later, Mike was still yelling, "One more minute! Come on you guys. Go back to your rooms. Food will be served there. The storm has stalled at sea, but now it's almost here."

The crowd had thinned a little, but many still milled around the beach and the bar. Empty bottles littered the bar area where the wind wasn't whipping. Sergio grabbed a bottle of wine and finally said, "Let's go up to the dining hall and see if we can find something to eat."

We walked up the stairs to the main building of the resort. Halfway up, the wind turned freezing cold. The temperature must have dropped twenty degrees in just a few seconds.

"I think something's getting close," I said and showed Sergio my arm. Goosebumps stood out on my arms and legs.

"Nah," Sergio said. He motioned me on into the dining room.

The lights were off and no one was in the hall. As we walked between the empty tables and chairs, we scanned them for food. In the gloom, we found one banana and an apple. I picked them up and tossed the apple to Sergio.

"Thanks," he said, and took a big bite. "I don't think we're going to find anything else, do you?"

"It appears everything has been pretty well picked over. Maybe Mike brought something to our room."

"Yeah, right," Sergio said and took another bite of his apple.

As the wind hit, the goosebumps broke out across my entire body. "Well, I think it's here." I shouted against the gale.

Before Sergio could respond, huge cold drops of rain fell from the sky and splattered across the walkway. "Do you think…" was all that he got out of his mouth when the sky opened up. A wall of cold water dropped from above and blew horizontally into our faces. We peered at each other, nodded, and ran for our room.

"Are we done with our scavenger hunt?" Sergio demanded, his hands on his hips.

"What?"

He pointed to the paper in my hand. "Did we do everything on that hurricane list?"

The drapes billowed away from the patio doors as the storm raged outside. They were drawn tightly over the glass covered with large "X's" of tape. All our furniture was off the patio and pushed up against the walls, along with the rest of the room's furniture.

We walked to the bathroom. My books, wallet, checkbook, and passport were in my shaving kit in the bathroom. An extra pair of disposable contact lenses was safely tucked inside the pocket of my jeans, just in case. I patted the pocket to double check.

Sergio's important things were jammed in his essential hair valise. It rested along side the bottles of water, candles, and the stolen dinner rolls. Everything was neatly lined up on the countertop. I made one last check of the list, and we were ready for the hurricane.

Sergio clapped his hands and rubbed them together, briskly. "All we need now is our supper."

"Mike promised…" I began.

"Don't get me started on his promises. I doubt we're going to see any food tonight, except for those hard buns you pinched from the dining room."

"Don't say that too loud. Someone may get the wrong idea."

"You can't still be worried about what people think. This is a gay resort. Big deal. No one can hear us," he motioned to the patio door. "I doubt anyone could hear someone screaming for their life tonight with that gale-force wind blowing out there."

A pocket of air puffed the entire curtain out into the room. As it escaped, the bottom edge flapped violently. It was going to be a wild night. Luckily, no rain had been driven in. Yet.

As if reading my mind, Sergio asked, "Shouldn't we put a few towels along the patio door to prevent any water from soaking in?"

I grabbed the damp towels from this morning, since the maids hadn't given us dry ones, and decided to use the wet ones we used after our drenching run across the resort instead. "Use the soaked ones." I headed to the patio door.

Sergio knelt down next to me and tucked the bottom edge of the drapes into the row of damp towels to help secure them all to the floor. "The food can come anytime now," he said, as he pushed up to his feet.

Nine o'clock came and went, but no Mike and no supper.

"I doubt Mike even called for a taxi or the airline for you." Sergio rolled over onto his back and stared at the ceiling. "If he lied about supper, he'd lie about that."

"But why would he lie?" I asked, glancing up from my book. Actually, it was Sergio's book, *A Body to Dye For* by Grant Michaels.

"Well, it's not like this resort has been all it was supposed to be. I should've listened to you earlier. Well, my faith in Club Fred is finally over." Sergio held up his palm to the door and turned his head away. "Anything Mike says from now on, is not going to be believed, no matter how good he makes it sound." He pointed to the crumbs on his bed. "After eating those hard rolls, I think he owes us a meal. A good one, right?"

"I think he owes us a lot more than that." My finger held my place in the trade paperback, but before I could return to reading, the phone rang, making me jump. I dropped the book and reached to answer the phone. "Hello?"

"Hey guys, how's it going? This is Mike," he said in his party voice. "I just wanted to check on how you two are doing."

"We're still waiting for our supper," I said.

"Oh, yeah, that." He paused. "We had a little problem with the staff, and we didn't have enough time to make up any snack boxes before the storm hit."

You were too busy drinking on the beach to worry about our lunch or supper, I thought, but I bit my tongue. I replied simply, "Oh."

Silence.

Finally, Mike said, "We'll have something for you to eat as soon as the storm breaks, whenever that is. But…" he paused again. "I've heard that the hurricane has stalled over us and…"

"And what?" I pressed.

"…And that… you may not get anything to eat tonight. But we're hopeful that there'll be breakfast first thing tomorrow morning."

I didn't say a word. Therapeutic silence forced people to explain further and kept them on the spot.

Mike exhaled forcefully. "I wish I could do more, but…"

"But we're stuck here, aren't we?" So much for therapeutic silence. Before he could respond, I said, "What happened to my taxi, Mike?"

"What…?" His voice died out, and he was silent. "Oh that."

"Yeah, that."

"I called, and they promised that they'd be here. I guess the storm prevented them from getting in. Sorry."

Yeah right, I thought.

"Anyway, hang tight, and I'm sure you guys will be all right. Did you get everything done on the list?"

Just then, a violent wind gust struck the resort. The entire building rumbled and shook. The ceiling threatened to rip off and split the room wide open. The floor shook, and the furniture shifted away from the walls. The lights flashed off, plunging the room into blackness, and then flickered back on. The phone clicked in my ear and died.

"So much for that." I said, setting the receiver down.

"What did he say about supper?" Sergio swung his legs over the edge of the bed and sat up. His eyes scanned the corners of the room, looking for any cracks or damage to the walls.

"They'll feed us as soon as the storm blows over."

"That shouldn't take too long. Should it?"

"I think the hurricane has stalled out, right on top of us. We probably won't be fed tonight. If we're lucky, we'll get breakfast tomorrow."

"Good thing you took those rolls. I know it's only bread and water, but we are prisoners here, aren't we?"

It sure felt that way.

The wind continued to howl and whip as rain blasted against the window. The drapes remained closed, but as each gust rocked the building, they billowed out into the room. Their rhythmic sway hypnotized us. *CNN en Espanol* warned of Hurricane Brian. The reports predicted a category two hurricane with winds up to one hundred and ten miles an hour. At least, that was all I could gather from the few words of Spanish I understood, the interrupted satellite signal, and the flickering electricity.

Unable to resist the temptation of the wind, I crept to the patio door and peered around the drapes. With my face pressed against the cold glass, my breath fogged it. Just then, a gust of wind rattled the thick glass, making it bend and flex like a piece of paper. I pulled my head back and examined the door's frame.

Air whistled around the plastic and aluminum frame, as rain was driven through and around the edges. The drapes were damp and heavy, but they didn't appear strong enough to stop even the smallest shard of glass if the window broke.

Another gust hit the door at full force. My curiosity was looking like it could kill the cat and the idiot from the Midwest who had never seen a hurricane before.

I slid the curtain back, leaving a slit just big enough for one eye to peer out into the tempest. The emergency lights that lit the walkways flickered, but I wasn't able to see if it was from debris or power failure. So far, the generator seemed to be still working.

As that thought crossed my mind, I noticed a light bobbing along the side of the building across the walkway. Had one of the emergency lights broke lose?

No. This light moved along the tiled hallway slowly, methodically, not like the melee of wind and rain. It looked like it was searching for something. Then the realization struck me: Someone was out there, walking around in that storm.

A hand grabbed my shoulder, causing my heart to stop. My entire body went rigid as a flash of white light blinded me, and my hand flew up to cover my mouth, preventing the scream that threatened to erupt.

"What are you looking at?" Sergio asked, butting me out of the way with his bony hip. "Move over so I can see, too."

Swallowing hard and gasping to catch my breath, I croaked, "I think someone's out there."

"What? Are you crazy?" He turned away from peeking out and faced me. "No one would be out in that storm. There's no way that they could walk around out there. They'd blow away with all that wind and rain."

"I know what I saw."

"In the dark? You're as blind as a bat. What are you talking about?"

I moved next to him and pulled the curtain back. "Look over there," I said, pointing toward the edge of the courtyard below. "See that light? The one moving over there?"

"No," he said, with his hands cupped against the glass and his face pressed into them.

"Remember where the snake and reacher fell?"

"Yeah."

"Veer over to the right, where the retaining wall is." I looked back into our room. The lights were on. Whoever was out there could see us looking out into the storm.

"Maybe it's just the branches blowing in front of one of the emergency lights."

I tried to decide what to do next; pull him away from the window or show him the danger. I decided on the latter. "It's moving too smoothly and controlled."

As if the light heard me, it went out, and the shadow seemed to look up straight into my eyes. A surge of lightning flashed cold and blue, illuminating the single figure, dressed in black, silhouetted against the short stucco wall. Its hand rose over its head, and then nothing.

The world returned to blackness, but the shadow burned into my retina.

Another thundering rumble shook the building, rattling the pane of glass that separated us from the tempest. We both stepped back, instinctively.

"I saw him. Close the curtains!" Sergio said, jumping up and down and pointing to where the silhouette had been standing. He pulled the curtain closed and pressed it against the glass. "It looked like he was going to throw something."

"Like closing the curtains is going to stop that." I grabbed Sergio and spun him with me so our backs were to the patio, and we covered our heads.

A second later, shattering glass exploded from the room beneath us. Amidst the rain, thunder, and wind, I heard what sounded like a blood-curdling scream. It lasted for only a few seconds, rose up against the tempest, and then was cut off, severed into silence.

"Was that...?" Sergio asked, his eyes wide in shock. He pulled the drapes back to look out into the storm, but thought twice and ripped them back to cover the glass.

"I don't know. It sounded like a scream to me." I ran for the door. "We have to go and see if we can help him."

"Help him what? Die?" Sergio grabbed me and swung me

around to face him. "No way. I'm not going out there, and neither are you. No way, no how. We'd never make it down there, let alone get back in one piece."

"We could stay there…"

"With no windows?" He pointed to the door. "Besides, there's nothing we can do. Nothing." Panic dilated his pupils.

A sick, helpless feeling settled over me. He was right. There wasn't anything we could do now. We weren't even sure if it was a scream. It could have been the wind, a television set. Anything.

Another gust of wind struck our entire building, thundering the structure to its core. The roar of thunder rattled the glass door, as if someone wanted in. Another flash blazed outside. The lights flickered once and went out, plunging us into darkness for good this time.

Sergio and I dove for our beds, but we landed in Sergio's. Wrestling for position and the blankets, we ripped the covers off and tried to get underneath them. Something slammed against our patio window. Our arms came up, our heads turned away, and we waited for the glass to implode into our room.

When nothing happened, Sergio pushed me out of his bed and propelled me into mine. "The bathroom. Grab your pillow and blankets and run," he shouted.

I bounced on my bed and ripped them from their places. Spinning on my heels, I heard the bathroom door slam shut. "Wait for me." I dove across Sergio's bed and pushed against the bathroom door. "Open up, open…"

The door gave way, and I flew into darkness.

CHAPTER 38 - BATHROOM BUDDIES

"Holy shit! Can you believe that?" Sergio picked me up from the bathroom floor, spun me around, and slammed the door shut. His nimble fingers twisted the lock on the doorknob.

"Do you think locking the door's going to help?" I nodded toward the lock. Slowly, I backed away and sat down on the edge of the tub. My blanket was wrapped around my body like a shroud.

Ignoring my comment, he lit the candles and joined me on the tub's lip. With his blanket pulled over his head and the flickering candlelight, he looked like he was wearing a nun's habit. Turning to face me he asked, "Who do you think was out there?"

Thunder pounded in my ears, and it took me several seconds to realize that it was my heartbeat drowning out the storm. My breathing came in gasping bursts, just like Sergio's.

Before I could answer, a crash echoed through the room next to us. Our arms reflexively rose up and covered our heads, expecting the ceiling to be ripped off and the tempest to enter.

When nothing happened, we tentatively peeked out from under our covers and up at the ceiling. Half expecting it to be gone, we saw the exhaust fan vent cover flapping with the gusting storm.

Sergio tossed off his blanket, grabbed a hand towel, and stepped onto the stool. As he jammed the cloth into the opening, he said, "That should prevent anything from blowing in." He stepped down to re-gather his blanket around him. Joining me on the tub, he pressed his body up alongside me.

Usually, if anyone came this close to me, I moved away. My tactile defensiveness increased in times of stress, and after all of this, my reaction should have been homicidal. After all we'd been through, the closeness seemed to help calm me. Surprised by my body's response, I fumbled. "Who… who do you think was out there?"

"I don't know. It happened so fast. I…" His words were drowned out as the whole building shuddered hard, rocking the foundation. The candles bounced across the countertop and dimmed. Threatening to extinguish themselves, they sputtered a few times and returned with small flames. Sergio exhaled the breath he had been holding. "I have this strange feeling. Didn't you think his body looked familiar?"

"I didn't see a body, all I saw was a silhouette." I pulled the blanket tighter. The candles flickered in the mirror, driving shadows around the room and across the shower curtain. The image of Duane's body in our shower came back in full detail, followed by another image, the one of him washed up on the beach with Sergio's scissors sticking out of his throat.

Suddenly, the wind slowed, the howling died, and the building stopped rumbling. Eeriness settled over the small room. It lasted only a few seconds and started up again with a vengeance.

Sergio shuddered. "I know, but it looked like Tom to me."

I closed my eyes, trying to push Duane's image out and the silhouette back into my mind. As it flashed across the back of my eye, Mike's form superimposed itself there. "It looked more like Mike than Tom."

"No way. Did you see those shoulders? They were huge. Just like Tom's. Besides, Mike wouldn't have thrown that rock overhand, he's an underhanded thrower if I ever saw one."

"What?" I said, pushing even more unwanted images from my mind. "Never mind. What about his legs? Tom has really long and muscular legs. The thrower seemed to have short squat legs, more like Mike's."

"I did notice the frog-like legs," Sergio nodded in agreement. "Maybe he was crouching down." He shrugged. "Anyway, his upper body was powerful." He paused, eyes staring straight ahead. "Kinda like Geoff's."

"Now that you mention it, it did look a little boxy like Sean."

"Sean? Who's Sean?" Sergio turned to face me.

"That's right, you haven't met him. He's Tom's crabby agent, the one he was fighting with on the beach."

"They were fighting?" Sergio leaned forward.

"Not fist fighting, but arguing about something. I walked in on the last part and missed what it was all about. All I know is that Sean wasn't happy with Tom's lack of participation at the resort."

"Lack of participation? What did he want him to do? Perform a strip tease on the beach? Or better yet, bang someone during supper?"

"I don't think he meant that. But you know, it's weird."

"What is?" he pressed.

"I feel like I'm protecting Tom from something."

"Here? At the resort?" Sergio screwed up his face, questioning me.

"I think Sean is forcing him to be here, or at least do some publicity here that he doesn't want to do."

"But it keeps his paycheck coming in, right?" he asked.

"I know, but I keep getting the feeling that he's holding something back."

"He is. Himself. He wants to jump your bones." Sergio elbowed me lightly in the ribs.

"He's married. Will you get serious." I pushed him back.

"You're the one who said that he was after something. He's not after me, he wants you." He batted his eyes at me innocently.

I rolled my eyes. "I feel like I'm acting as a buffer for him here at the resort."

A metallic ripping cut through the air, and a loud bang sounded. We jumped and looked at the thin wood, praying it would hold.

Bang. Bang. Bang. Metal slammed against the side of the

building a few more times, squealing loud enough to hurt my ears. It thumped and slid along the hallway with the wind.

"It must've been the rain gutter ripped from the eaves," I suggested.

Sergio nodded in agreement and smiled. "I know, you're Tom's beard."

"I'm a what?"

"A beard," he motioned with his hand for me to understand him. "A gay man's cover."

My confused look forced him to explain.

"Some gay men use women in public to prove they're not gay."

Finally realizing that he wasn't talking about the metal noises outside, I made the connection. "I...what?" My voice went up a few octaves.

"He's using you to keep the other guys away from him. Duh." Sergio slapped the side of his head.

"But I invited *him* to spend time some with us. I think."

"He would make you feel that way. He's an *actor*, remember?"

"I guess."

"Come on, admit it. You're his little buddy, right?" Sergio teased.

Playing along, I nudged him. "No. I'm your little buddy, not his."

"I wish," he said, or at least that's what I thought he said, as he threw his hands up and flipped his head back.

"Yeah, right." I pulled the blankets tightly around my shoulders. The wind continued to howl outside as sheets of rain beat down on our building. "Cute, but let's get serious. Could that silhouette have been Logan? He has that square build."

"Like centuries ago." Sergio scoffed.

"He could've been the one out there throwing rocks at us."

"But why?"

"Well. His file said he was going to be dropped by his publisher if his next book wasn't a blockbuster."

"How many books do you have to sell to have a blockbuster? A million?"

"You know, they have to hit the *New York Times* best seller list. They need to sell like Grisham, King, or Collins."

"Oh, I just love Jackie Collins. She always has so much dirt on her characters, and you know she bases them on real people in Hollywood. I bet Tom is in one of her books."

Closing my eyes, I counted to ten. "Getting back to Logan, he's won a few critical awards for his earlier novels, but the new ones haven't sold as well as his first ones did."

"But why not? Aren't they any good?"

"Molly and I love them, but we tend to like something different, something new, and not the same old story over and over again." I ran my hand through my hair. "Other writers are more violent, and not as beautifully written or character-driven. Vile crimes seem to sell more than great characters."

He nodded in agreement. "Molly's said the same thing, but what about that guy? The one the books are dedicated to?"

"I almost forgot about him. He did seem to be in a lot of the same places as Logan. Hey." I stood up and flipped through my pile of books.

"You brought your books in here?" Sergio asked.

"I wasn't going to let them get damaged in the storm." *Slaughterloo* rested on the bottom of the pile. Flipping it open, I read the dedication page, "And to John, who is always there."

"Who's John?" Sergio asked.

"My guess is that he's the guy in all those pictures in the file."

"Have you seen him running around the resort? He isn't the model John as..." he nodded toward the autographed towel hanging from the rack, "as in that John? Do you think?" he squinted hard to see the resemblance.

"I doubt they're the same one." I squinted hard in the gloom. "But there is a similarity, maybe." I slipped the book back into the pile.

"So is Logan gay?" Sergio pulled his blanket up to his neck.

"You don't know? What does your gaydar say?"

"Closet case, just like you."

The whole building shook again. My eyes narrowed at him.

"Just kidding." He held up his hands in surrender. "Can't you take a joke? So, what are his books like?"

"There aren't any gay characters in them."

"Oh, men's books," Sergio's voice lowered as he flexed his arm muscles.

"Not the kind you're thinking of."

"What kind are *you* talking about? You're reading one of *my* books, right? Maybe I'm trying to recruit you." His eyes widened. "Look into my eyes. You are in my power."

"Yeah, right. My dad couldn't get me signed up for the Marines, so I doubt you'll get me to join 'the Club.'"

"Your loss," he shrugged. "Like we'd even invite *you* to join. Do you think Logan would kill to keep being gay a secret?"

"It would make more sense for him to use this vacation as a publicity stunt to sell his new novel than resort to murder."

"Homophobia isn't pretty."

"Well, his crimes aren't pretty in the novels. They're very explicit and violent, but he doesn't seem dangerous to me."

"He's an author you like. You wouldn't suspect him anyway, now would you?"

"His body looked nothing like the silhouette out there."

"How do you know? You can't see in the dark, and besides the wind was whipping a zillion miles an hour. Do you really think you saw it clearly?"

"And you did?" I countered, licking my dry, sunburned lips.

"Well, I have a plan." Sergio smiled at me. He stood up and crawled underneath the sink's counter. "I'm going to bed and I'm sleeping here tonight."

"And where am I going to sleep?"

Sergio rolled onto his side, lifted his blanket, and motioned to the space he had just made.

"Great. Why was I afraid you'd say that?"

"Do you have any better ideas?"

Something blew down the open hallway outside of our room, scratching along the wall as it went.

Standing up, I placed the blanket down inside the bathtub. Stepping inside, I felt the cool porcelain supporting my body. "I guess I'm trapped here…" My voice echoed in the hollow.

"You can always come over here," he offered again.

"I'll take my chances here. Thanks." I settled my head down on the pillow.

"So, do we have a plan for tomorrow?" he asked.

"You're not going to suggest that we split up and question our list of suspects, are you?"

"You are good. Molly said you were slow to catch on to most things, but I think she underestimates you." Sergio shook his head.

"Thanks. I think."

"Fine then, we have a plan." Sergio ticked off the list. "Tomorrow, you pump Logan about his John, ask Mike if he was running around in the storm throwing rocks at us, and see if Tom is engaged and using you as his beard. I'll go check on the Davids, see if John is looking for a writer husband, and see if Geoff ventured out into the storm. And we'll see what we get."

"What about Cha-Cha? She could have been the one out there throwing rocks."

"I've read all about what happened at Stonewall. Drag queens and bricks, she's all yours," he said, rolling over, turning his back to me, thus ending our conversation.

My feet fought the blanket for room within the tight quarters, and my back chilled from the porcelain of the tub. In my cramped space, I wondered why he got to hide under the counter. Rolling over onto my side, peeking over the edge of the tub I asked, "Who do you think we can trust here?"

I closed my eyes and images flooded in of Skinny David's panic from the thrown snake. Gary's blood-covered head and bed. The snake that slithered out from under my bed. What lay bleeding beneath us.

"No one." He rolled over and faced me from under his blanket.

"Exactly. We sound like Mulder and Scully. Trust No One."

"Can I be Scully? She's smarter," Sergio asked, with a serious expression on his face, but then it brightened into a big grin, "but Mulder is soo…"

"Whatever." I rolled over, turning my back to him. My mind re-read the files; everyone had a secret, but whose was big enough to kill for?

CHAPTER 39 - THE MORNING AFTER

The hurricane stalled over the resort throughout the night, and my sleep was restless and fitful. Between Sergio's snoring and his constant waking and asking, "What was that?" each time something bumped or banged in the night, I got little sleep.

Maybe I was expecting someone or something to come bursting in through the bathroom door or the storm to rip the ceiling off. Either way, my adrenaline was high, and sleep eluded me.

Finally, giving up on sleep, I put my contacts back in, kicked Sergio out of the bathroom, and jumped into the shower to use what was left of the hot water.

Sergio followed suit, and we sat looking at each other. What should we do next? The two hard rolls sat on the bathroom counter, but they weren't calling to us. The cafeteria was. Well, correction: Sergio was. He was cranky and demanding to be fed.

I opened our door, and the rain started to fall harder. "If you would've been faster in the shower," Sergio said, motioning toward the rain, "we could've made it to the dining hall before it started up again."

"You were in there twice as long as I was."

He held up his hand to me and headed down the stairwell. Stopping at the courtyard, we watched the heavy drops of rain splatter across the tile. Taking a deep breath, we stepped out into the courtyard and were instantly soaked. My T-shirt became a second skin. The stairwells and the tiled walkways were mined with puddles. My sandals splashed and slid with each step.

Sergio turned around to look back at me and inhaled sharply. I spun around with my arms up in a defensive stance. He shook his head and pointed to the room below ours.

The patio door was gone. Glass, frame, drapes and all. A gaping, jagged hole stood where it should have been. My eyes strayed to see into the depths of the room. A dark stain covered the back wall, and if I used my imagination, the streaks looked like a man's body had been thrown against it, and a firing squad had opened fire.

It was five o'clock, and the dining hall was empty. No other guests wandered around. Not even the morning crew had arrived. As if they were going to be in today, anyway. So much for our food being set up in the buffet line. The kitchen door was closed, and no sounds emanated from behind. I'm sure before the hurricane hit, the staff had no trouble getting into work and would have already busy creating all that inedible food that I had so far refused to eat. Except those hard rolls, which were probably brought in from town.

Mike and Geoff were nowhere to be found. Maybe they washed away with the storm after throwing rocks at us last night, but more probably they were still in bed. It's not like we needed them anyway. What did they really do? I didn't really expect them to be up this early, cooking or providing food for their guests.

"Hey, where's all the food?" Sergio asked from behind me.

I called over my shoulder. "The locals haven't arrived yet. Maybe they can't get back to the resort."

"So, we're going to starve to death while they wait for the weather to clear? Wait a minute. If they can't get in…" he paused for dramatic tension, "we can't get out. We're trapped."

I rolled my eyes. "Let's not start a panic. We still have two rolls left back in the room. I'm sure they'll have this problem corrected by lunch."

"What are they going to serve? Those who didn't survive the hurricane?" Sergio smiled at his clever wit.

"I'm sure they have a storeroom full of food," I began.

Sergio grabbed my wet T-shirt. "So? What are *we* waiting for? You teach people to cook everyday at the hospital, right? I'm sure you can scramble us a few eggs." He dragged my protesting feet after him.

He let go of me as we passed the coffee and hot water dispensers. He reached over to check if the hot water was on.

A cup of tea with extra sugar would hold off my stomach's growling and maybe warm me up just a little bit.

Finding it empty, Sergio proceeded to the kitchen door and peered into the round window. He waved me over and tried to push the swinging doors open. They wouldn't budge. "It's locked." He ran his fingers through his damp hair. Even it refused to stand up on end.

"I'm sure after the drunken party on the beach, Mike locked the doors to prevent himself from being eaten out of house and home. Or maybe he joined in and drank himself into the poor house and now he's passed out…"

"Aren't you being a bit snotty? We took a few cans of beer and pop, too. Actually, you took them and gave them to me."

His eyes gleamed with mischief.

I hated when the devil took him. There was just no reasoning with him when he was this way. "That was all I had. No food. No booze. Nothing else. Someone had to be responsible." Echoes of my mother's voice rolled through my ears. Great. Now I was starting to sound like my mother.

"And you did it so well, now didn't you?" he said coolly.

"Does your key work on this door too?" I asked, trying to distract him.

He patted his pant pocket and fished out his key chain. Slipping it into the lock, he turned it. Nothing.

"So much for that idea. The keys open every other door in this place, but not the kitchen." I exhaled deeply.

"You give up way too easily." He tried a few more keys on his ring, but quickly gave up on them. He then pulled a long, thin piece of metal from his key chain and inserted that into the slot. In a few quick twists, an audible click echoed through the air. "Bingo!" He smiled brightly and motioned me to open the door.

I looked around the dining room to make sure no one was

watching. No one had joined us, so I hurried, pushed the door open, and snuck into the kitchen with Sergio close behind.

The kitchen was dark, and long shadows emerged from every corner. A few windows were set high up on the walls, but the overcast day, rain, and coating of grease allowed little light to come through.

"Do you see a light switch?" Sergio asked.

While I waited for my eyes to adjust to the gloom, he expelled a huff and pushed me aside. "Sorry, I forgot. Let me look."

I blinked my eyes, trying to get them to adjust faster. A shadow seemed to rush across my foot in the dark. I knew that at times as my eyes were adjusting to the dark or the light, they sometimes played tricks on me. Squinting hard, my eyes revealed a few stained white aprons, which hung from hooks on a short wall. It was then I noticed one of their tie strings had wrapped around my ankle. Kicking it free, I heard a soft plastic clicking sounded in the distance, but the kitchen lights refused to come on.

"I think the power's still out," came Sergio's voice from behind one of the huge stoves.

"Do they have gas stoves?" I stepped forward to see. "Maybe we could turn on a burner and light this place up."

"That would light this place up real good. Boom." He emerged from behind the stove. "Do you trust the gas lines in here? You know, after the hurricane." Sergio came and stood next to me.

"It wasn't an earthquake," I reminded him.

"Fine," he said, pulling out his stolen lighter. "You do it." He handed it to me and stepped back.

"Maybe we should just make do with something cold. We have a choice. Should we raid the pantry or see what they have in the walk-in cooler?" As soon as that idea came out of my mouth, images of Duane and Gary's lifeless bodies being stored in there sent shivers over my damp form. Where else would they have put them to keep them fresh? "Maybe we should check out the pantry first?" My eyes darted away from the cooler.

Sergio glanced over to the cooler and understanding registered in his eyes. "Do you think…?" He nodded toward the door.

"I don't even want to think about it."

"Do you think they would still use the food in there? You know if…" His face scrunched up. "I mean." He swallowed hard. "Where else could they have put them?"

Working with the cadavers in grad school had been very interesting, but to think of seeing someone I knew didn't sit well with me. I had seen both of them once already, I didn't need a repeat viewing. "Let's go check the cabinets," I suggested.

Walking to the other side of the kitchen, we found all of the cabinets were chained shut. "I hope your lock picking skills are up to this challenge."

Sergio walked up to one cabinet with a loose chain. "I think I can squeeze my hand into this one." He pulled hard on the door's handle and slipped one of his hands into the narrow opening. He reached up to his elbow and dug around. Cans clicked against each other and tumbled over. "Ouch!" He jerked his arm down, but not out of the cabinet.

"Careful," I cautioned. Leaning forward, I asked, "Can you get anything out?"

"Hang on. I think I got something." Then his smile died on his face. "Correction, I think something has got me."

"What?" I said, stepping closer to help.

"Ah! There's something in here," his voice shrilled. "It tickles. It…"

Then his whole body started to convulse as he tried to pull his arm out.

"It bites!" One of his legs reflexively braced against the lower cabinet, and he began to pull back with all his might. "Help me!" Panic was taking over. He twisted and tried frantically to free his arm. His body was bucking uncontrollably, but neither the cabinet nor whatever held onto his arm released their holds.

I grabbed onto him around his waist and pulled.

"Ow! My arm!" he cried.

I reached up alongside his arm and tried to ease it out of its trap. We pulled harder, and the sound of metal being pulling out of wood cut through the air. The cabinet doors bulged out, the hinges started to snap, and the doors released Sergio's arm. As they pulled out and away, a black wave flowed from between them. The dark mass withered and squirmed as it cascaded over both of us. Several seconds passed before we realized why *La Cucaracha* was a Mexican favorite.

The cockroaches spread out in all directions. Sergio pulled back and slammed his body into mine, thus passing an armload of bugs onto me. The wave hit hard; hissing insects crawled over my skin, digging their sharp feet into me. Both of us waved our arms, trying to flick the roaches off our bodies before they could enter our mouths. Bumping into each other, we tried to escape from the cabinet before more roaches poured out. We continued to back away from the cabinet, trying to avoid the source of this assault.

In our retreat, the wave of bugs continued to follow us across the floor. Our feet crunched bodies with each step. Crack. Crack. Crack. We brushed the creeping insects from our bodies. Suddenly, Sergio stopped. A horrified expression crossed his face, and he started to spasm violently.

"What's wrong?"

"A bunch of roaches just slipped underneath my shirt, and I think they're working their way into my under... AHHH!" With that he screamed and lashed out, slamming his body into mine.

The force drove me back into the wall, where all the aprons hung. My breath expelled from my lungs from white pain that blazed through my body. The impact made a sick-cracking sound behind me, but before I knew what was happening, the thin pressboard splintered inward. The wall split open and swallowed us whole.

Darkness descended over us as we fell into oblivion.

Our descent didn't last long. My back slammed into a sheet of metal that sloped downward into the bowels of the resort. My head dangled and bounced against the metal, but my legs remained sticking out of the hole in the kitchen wall. The wave of bugs washed over me, hissing and clicking. Small feelers probed my eyes, ears, nose, and mouth, even more thoroughly than my doctor did.

A hollow thud reverberated in my ears and Sergio landed on top of me. He continued screaming and thrashing around, trying to get rid of the roaches, which only liberated more onto me. I closed my mouth and eyes tightly, willing my ears and nose to close also. My arms were pinned down to my side, so I wasn't able to wipe away the assault.

With the momentum of Sergio's landing and before I could free my arms and sit up, the traction of my damp shirt slowly began to release. We started to slide down the incline. Small bodies crunched underneath my back. My feet struggled to maintain a foothold on the edge of the hole, but with Sergio's added weight and my wet sandals, the blackness sucked us in. Splintered wood dug into my calves, and my hands struggled to hold traction on the metal. My fingers extended, searching for anything to hang onto, but our descent only accelerated.

Sergio's screams intensified as our speed increased. He continued swiping at the insects. How many were there? I opened one eye, and a huge roach straddled my socket. I closed my eye and pursed my lips together even tighter. My body braced for impact. I hunched my shoulders and flexed my neck forward, in an attempt to prevent a spinal cord or head injury when we landed.

If we landed.

My teeth clenched together as something tried to crawl between my lips. Fearing it would, I exhaled sharply, and the exploring antenna disappeared. At the same moment, the metal slide disappeared from beneath me. I inhaled deeply before flopping onto the concrete floor. If that bug had remained, it would've been ingested, and probably would've been the healthiest thing I'd had the chance to eat so far.

The stone floor didn't soften my landing, but my body cushioned Sergio's. His weight touched down for a second and then lifted off.

I blinked my eyes, trying hard to force them to adjust to the darkness. The impact with the floor had knocked most of the roaches off. I could feel them scattering to the corners of the basement. I raised my head to see where we had just landed and what happened to Sergio. I pushed up to a sitting position, crunching things underneath my palm. Slowly, I got to my feet and swiped at the rest of the little things that continued to crawl over me.

Something flew over my head, and I ducked. Now what? Bats in the basement? I thought they only lived in the belfry. "Why are you still screaming?" I called.

"They're crawling into my…" and then he spat a wet wad onto the floor.

"Then keep your mouth shut, and they can't get in."

With that, his screams stopped, but his moans and groans echoed throughout the dark. I could hear hands slapping skin and the flapping of clothing in front of me, but saw nothing. The blackness swallowed the fading echoes as the cool air settled down on me. A musty smell rose, and the sound of water dripping in the distance welcomed us.

Too bad we hadn't found a flashlight in the kitchen. My hand brushed against my shorts pocket, and I smiled. The stolen lighter was still there. Pulling it out, I called, "Sergio? Are you there?"

He didn't respond, but the rustling of fabric told me he was nearby.

My finger flicked the dial, a spark flashed, and a small blue and yellow flame burst from my hand. I adjusted the dial and the flame shot up and illuminated a small area around me.

Sergio's shirtless form appeared pulling up his shorts a few feet away. "Hey, no peeking." He ran his fingers through his hair and shook his head. His whole body shuddered. With the addition of the light, he was able to examine his body and saw that the roaches were finally off. They were busy, scattering across the floor and away from us and the light.

As I watched them scurry away, I scanned the floor and found Sergio's discarded shirt. That must have been the thing that flew over my head. It was still covered with bugs. I stepped forward and raised my foot to stomp on them.

Sergio shouted, "Wait!" He rushed past me and held up his hands to stop me. "Don't squish them. I don't want their guts mashed into my shirt." Tentatively, he bent over and picked it up by the hem. He shook it violently, spraying the insects in all directions. After a few more shakes, he opened the shirt and looked inside.

I held the lighter higher to shine more light on his examination.

After his close inspection and one extra shake to insure that all the bugs were gone, Sergio finally slipped the shirt over his head. When his face emerged from the opening he asked, "Where are we?"

"I don't know."

As if responding to his question, one of the aprons fluttered and fell from its hook, opening a jagged square of light at the top of the ramp. My eyes gained a wider view of our surroundings.

We stood in the middle of a square area that led off into two hallways, which ran at a ninety-degree angle from each other.

Canvas bags lined the right hallway, and a white arrow was painted halfway up the wall. "What do you think is down there?" I asked.

"Let's find out." Sergio took the lighter from my hand, and the flame went out. He flicked the striker dial, and a new flame shot up. "Come on."

"What about finding something to eat? I thought you were hungry," I asked, but followed his lead. My damp clothing stuck to my skin. I could still feel things crawling on me. I pulled my wet clothes away from my body so I could move around freely and the creepy crawlies were gone.

I can't believe I'm paying for this vacation, I mused.

"It doesn't look like this tunnel goes too far. See?" He held the lighter higher up above his head and the shadows ran along its length. A doorway stood at the end of the corridor. Further down the hallway, the smell of bleach and fabric softeners overpowered the musty stale air. "Maybe we could dry our clothes," Sergio suggested.

"The power's still out," I reminded him.

"Thanks for bursting my bubble." He pulled his clinging shorts away from his backside. "Damp underwear really sucks."

"I know. Good thing I'm not wearing any."

Sergio stopped in his tracks, spun around, and stared at me, open-mouthed. The lighter flame flickered in his eyes. He smiled and shook his head. "Good one. You almost had me with that." He clapped me on the back. "Come on. Let's check this place out, and then get the hell out of here. I want some food."

Inside the laundry, industrial size washers and dryers lined the walls. Bins of sheets and towels were waiting to be washed on one side of the room, while neatly stacked piles of linens were stocked on carts, ready to be used.

"Maybe we should take our clean towels now. I doubt the maids will bring them to us." Sergio walked over to the carts and took one off. He toweled his hair and then draped it around his shoulders. Taking another one, he wrapped it around his waist.

"We still have to find a way out of here," I reminded him.

"I'll wait," he said and threw me a towel. "Come on, let's go check out the other tunnel and then get out of here."

"Sounds good to me. Lead on." I motioned him to continue.

We walked down the short hallway and turned to our right.

Water dripped and echoed as we entered. A red painted arrow pointed into the dark. A trail of lettuce leaves and onionskins dotted the walkway. The smell of overripe fruit and an underlying hint of rot and decay hung in the air, intensifying as we ventured deeper. Small things squeaked and ran from the light. More bugs clicked and crunched underfoot.

"What is that smell?" Sergio pinched his nose with his free hand.

"This must be the garbage tunnel."

"So why are we going down here?" Sergio turned to face me. He pressed the towel to his face and breathed through it.

"You're the one who suggested it," I countered.

"Shouldn't we turn around?" Sergio paused in his tracks.

"We've come this far. We might as well see what's at the end. Right?"

He gave me a doubtful look, but continued. Patches of mold grew on the bricked walls. This place was going to do wonders for my allergies, but something told me to continue forward.

The hallway slanted upward and the sound of dripping water grew louder. A small room appeared off to the left. Various plastic bottles and rusted metal cans were scattered against the far wall. Labels with red skulls and crossbones gazed at us with eyeless sockets. Red and orange flames warned of the flammability of the fluids they contained.

My arm blocked Sergio's approach. "Don't go in there with an open flame." I pointed to the bottles. "We may find the fastest way out of here yet."

He stepped back and walked to the opposite side of the hallway as I continued my search. The only other thing in the room was a push broom that leaned against the wall just inside the entryway. It didn't look like it had been used in a while. Did they use it to push the garbage into the water? Then what? Let it get washed out to sea. So much for giving a hoot, and not polluting. Too bad Woodsy Owl didn't get this far south.

Just past the doorway of the alcove, the floor slopped down toward a pool of water at the end of the tunnel. The water rose and fell rhythmically, lapping like the tide. The back wall had watermarks and lines of crusted salt above the water's surface.

Steps led down into the brackish water. Sergio stepped to the edge and held the lighter up. The flame reflected off the water and the wet walls, making the small space glow yellow. Pieces of lettuce and paper floated at the surface of the pool.

My eyes caught something rocking with the waves just below the surface. "Bring the lighter over here." I pointed to the object.

Sergio knelt down and asked, "Where?"

"Over there. See it?"

He stretched his arm over the water and balanced on the brink.

"I'll get it. I don't want you to fall in." I lay down on my stomach and pulled myself to the edge. Dipping my hands into the water, I fished it out.

A black leather boot with a silver strap wrapped over its bridge rose to the surface. I turned it over in my hands, showing it to Sergio.

"Don't look up my towel." He pressed one hand down to hold the flap close to his legs. Seeing I wasn't amused, he asked, "How did that get there?"

"Better yet, whose is it?" I countered, but I thought I already knew the answer.

Sergio brought the lighter closer, the flame reflecting off the wet black surface. "Do you think?" he whispered.

Before I could answer, a spotlight flashed into our faces and a voice commanded. "Freeze!"

"Mike, is that you?" Sergio asked, raising his arm to shade the light from his eyes.

The wet boot slipped out of my hands. The heel struck the floor, sending echoes down the hallway.

"What are you two doing down here?" Mike demanded, bouncing the beam back and forth between us.

"Nothing," we said in unison.

"I saw the doors ripped off their hinges in the kitchen, along with a huge hole in the wall…" Mike started.

I bent over, quickly picking up the boot and hiding it behind my back.

Mike's beam shifted to me, following my sudden movement. "What do you have there?" He extended his flashlight like a fencing sword and tried to parry out an answer as he approached.

"It's a boot," I said simply, bringing it out from behind my back. I offered it so he could see.

"Where was that?" He lowered the beam from my eyes and trained it on the boot.

"It was in the water." I motioned to the end of the hall. "It looks like they're using this pool as a garbage disposal."

"So, whose boot is it?" Mike cocked his head to the side.

"We don't know." Sergio stepped forward. "It's not like it has a name in it or anything." He turned to me and whispered, "Does it?"

Mike moved closer and played the light across the boot's surface. Nothing was visible externally. He motioned with the flashlight for me to rotate it. I tipped the boot so the opening was facing him, and he pointed the light in. A piece of lettuce clung to the side, but nothing else.

"Do you have any ideas?" His eyes narrowed at me.

Did he suspect the same thing we did? Or had he overheard our conversation? He didn't appear to be too surprised to see a boot down here.

He reached over and took it from my grasp. "I think I'll give it to Geoff and see what he has to say about it. Maybe he'll be able to come up with something. But I'll let him know," he winked at us, "that you two were the ones who found it."

Maybe it was the tone of his voice or the dampness of the basement that sent shivers across my body.

"Good," I took a step forward. "Maybe, now, we can have breakfast. Has the staff arrived yet?"

"We tried to find something to eat and ended up down here," Sergio continued for me. "They need to call an exterminator for this place. It's really starting to fall apart around here, if you ask me." He raised his eyebrows. "And if they're not careful, they'll lose their five-star rating."

I poked him in the back, trying to get him to shut up.

"Well, they could," Sergio said over his shoulder in protest.

"Since you guys are so ambitious, maybe you can help me get breakfast started. You two can cook, can't you?" Mike asked.

Sergio held up his hands. "You wouldn't want me in the kitchen unless you have a smoke detector and a fire extinguisher. I use them both at home to let me know when my food is done."

"I know my way around a kitchen, but I've never had to cook for so many."

Mike rolled his eyes, turned around, and led us down the hallway. With his flashlight, he motioned to something behind the garbage chute, which we had ridden down. A small spiral staircase came into view. I hadn't noticed it before. He motioned with his hand and directed the beam up the stairs.

Sergio made a dash for the bottom step. "We should hurry. I'm sure there's a mob forming for food out there, and I want to be first in line." As his foot touched it, he stopped and turned to Mike. "We'll get a discount for helping, won't we? I mean, like a refund or something. It's not like I mind helping, but…" He extended his fingers and looked at the backs of his hands.

"I'll see what I can do." Mike motioned up the staircase with the flashlight again.

"We're going, we're going. Don't rush the slave labor." Sergio grabbed onto the railing with both hands, but didn't move.

I gently pushed him up the stairs and followed close behind. The narrow metal steps cut into the soles of my sandals as we ascended the stairs. A small door opened at the top, and we stepped out from behind the walk-in cooler, which we gave a wide berth.

Mike set the boot and flashlight down on the floor next to the cooler. He clapped his hands together. "So, what do you think we can whip up for the crowd?"

"Corn flakes and milk, if it's still good since the power went off," Sergio offered.

"If you can find it, you can serve it." Mike smiled.

Sergio rubbed his hands together, remembering what he had found earlier. "Maybe that wasn't such a good idea. All the cabinets are locked." He pointed to the chains on the handles.

Mike reached into his pocket and pulled out a ring of keys and tossed them to Sergio. "This should help."

"Thanks," he said, catching them. He looked at me and offered the keys.

I held up my hands and shook my head.

"If you unlock that door," Mike pointed to the one behind the huge stove, "and go to your left, you'll find the storeroom with cases of breakfast cereal. See if they have any corn flakes."

Sergio tossed the keys up in the air and caught them. "I'm outta here." His index finger gave me a salute, and he headed for the door.

"What can you help with?" Mike asked. He went to the walk-in cooler and grabbed the door handle.

My eyes stared at the door. I wanted to see what was really inside, but yet, part of me didn't. I swallowed hard. "I can fry eggs or bacon, I think."

"Go turn on the stove and get the gas griddle fired up. I'll bring you the eggs and whatever else I find." He pulled the silver handle, and the door opened.

Two large mounds lay on the floor of the cooler. Mike walked up to them and stepped over. Were they big enough to be…? My eyes tried to size them up or pick up on a telling detail. All the while, a force seemed to draw me toward the cooler. As my foot took a step, I resisted and raced to the stove. Scanning the panel of knobs, I found an icon that looked like the grill. I turned that dial on the panel, closed my eyes, and clenched my fists, not knowing what to expect.

Nothing happened.

Sergio returned with a case of corn flakes.

"Do you still have that lighter?" I asked.

Sergio set the box down and reached into his pocket.

I motioned him over. Turning the knob again, a hiss of gas escaped, and Sergio clicked the lighter. The gas ignited with a whoosh into a blue flame.

"Here," Mike said next to me, making me jump. "Sorry to startle you, but I found these." He set a case of what looked like smoky links on the side table. "And I'll be right back with the eggs."

Dawn's light filtered down onto the countertop from the windows above the stove. Sergio and I took a few deep breaths and opened the box. Nothing crawled out, so I looked in and found rows of neatly piled sausages. Grabbing handfuls of them, I covered the griddle in a few minutes. A large spatula hung from a hook above the butcher block and soon the grill was sizzling.

Mike found a large bowl and broke eggs into it. He grabbed an industrial size whisk and started whipping like crazy.

Sergio walked over to his discarded box and asked, "Where do you want the corn flakes?"

Mike set the whisk down and wiped his hands on his shorts. "I'll get the milk and you can set them out in the dining room to get some of the people started."

John walked in a few minutes later. After twisting his long hair into a hairnet, he helped Sergio carry the food out to the dining room. As soon as one left the kitchen, the other returned with an empty pan, ready to be refilled.

The next few hours passed in a blur of eggs, sausages, bacon, toast, and dry cereal.

We did have the chance to grab a bite of this and a bite of that as we cooked, and I was even able to finally eat something, since I was sure it was safe.

After the rush was over, we sat in the kitchen and looked at the piles of dirty dishes and utensils, not quite sure where to start cleaning up the mess. The lights flickered on and off a few times and then remained on.

A chorus of "Yeahs" echoed from the dining hall.

"Finally," Mike said.

"I'm not washing dishes, if that's what you're thinking," Sergio said, as if reading my mind.

As I stood up to start filling the sink with hot water, five plump Mexican women walked into the kitchen. Each one grabbed an apron off the hooks on the wall, at least what was left of it, and started cleaning up our mess.

"We're saved! Help has arrived!" Sergio pulled off his apron and threw it on the countertop. "I'm outta here." He turned to me. "Are you coming Taylor?"

Before I could answer, Geoff walked in. "I hear you've been busy."

"If you only knew," Mike huffed. "By the way, where have you been? We could've used your help a while ago."

Geoff's expression was blank. "I've been checking the damage, mon."

"I think feeding the guests is more important, don't you? I doubt they've had anything to eat since breakfast yesterday."

Geoff's head ticked slightly to the left, but he said nothing.

"Oh, I almost forgot," Mike said. "We found a boot in the basement. I think you should check it out."

"A boot?" Geoff asked.

Mike pointed to Sergio and me. "They found it in that water hole at the end of the tunnel. Do you know anything about that?"

Geoff pressed his lips tightly together and shook his head. Finally, he asked, "Where's this boot?"

Mike sat up straight in his chair, but before he could rise, I walked to the stove. "I'm up. I'll go get it," I said to Mike.

He tried to protest, but I didn't give him a chance. I walked through the new kitchen crew, rounded the stove, and ignored the walk-in cooler's door, which still beckoned to me. As I entered the small entryway to the basement door, I stopped dead in my tracks.

The boot was gone.

The flashlight was still in the same place Mike left it, but the boot was gone. A faint outline of the boot's tread was barely visible. Our only proof had evaporated, as if it hadn't been there at all.

I walked back to Geoff. Shrugging my shoulders and turning my hands palm up, I said, "It's gone."

"What?" Mike and Geoff said at the same time. Both men pushed up from their chairs and rushed through the kitchen and behind the cooler.

"What's gone?" Tom asked, walking through the kitchen's swinging door. He stopped Geoff and Mike raced from their seats. He motioned to Sergio and me to come out into the dining area. "They told me you two were in here, cooking of all things." A questioning smile played across his mouth as he tried to read our expressions. "I had to see that one for myself."

An unsettled feeling descended over me. Why did Tom always seem to show up just after something like this happened? Poor timing? Or had he taken the boot? Destroying evidence? Just a coincidence? Feeling suspicious about the people around me was really starting to drain all my energy. Or was it the heat from the kitchen?

Sergio walked up to me and rested his hand on my shoulder. "Come on. You need a break."

"But…" I started to protest, but Tom stepped to my other side and helped Sergio drag me from the kitchen.

"If they need you, they know where to look. It'll probably be weeks later, and we'll be home by then. At least I hope," Sergio said, running his hand through his spiked hair. "Besides, I'm sure they can finish without you. You've done more than your share, and so have I for that matter." He peeled his shirt away from his skin and crinkled up his face. "Mike had better come up with something great for us after all our blood, sweat, and tears."

Tom's eyes passed from me to Sergio. "How did he rope you two into helping in the kitchen? I can't say that you're the domestic types."

Sergio pursed his lips together tightly and let out a huff of air.

"Just kidding," Tom held up his hands in surrender. "I see you as more the…the cosmopolitan type."

"I don't read *Cosmo*." Sergio lowered his eyelashes. "We have it at the salon, but I just look at the pictures."

"Yeah. That's what they all say." I smiled weakly.

Sergio huffed at me this time.

"So what did I just miss?" Tom pressed. "I feel like I walked in on the middle of something." He led us to a vacant table in a back corner of the dining room. The breakfast crowd had thinned. Outside, a steady downpour of rain obscured the view of the beach.

"I could use a drink," I said.

Tom popped up from his chair. "Since you guys made breakfast, allow me to get you something to drink." He held his arm cocked like a butler on PBS. "What would you like?"

"Coffee for me," Sergio said.

"A Pepsi would taste great about now." I settled into the chair and doubted I would be able to get up again.

"Be back in a few." Tom bowed curtly, clicked his heels together, and was gone.

"Are you going to tell him?" Sergio leaned across the table toward me.

"I don't know. We've told him everything else so far, why stop now? If we don't, he might get suspicious and think that we're hiding something."

"So? It's not like we've done anything wrong." He paused for a moment. "Except breaking and entering, stealing evidence, losing evidence, withholding evidence, looting, pillaging. All we have to do now is add armed robbery, rape, and murder, and we'll have all the bases covered."

"You make me feel so proud of myself and my accomplishments, you know that?"

"I do what I can," Sergio said and looked over his shoulder. "He's coming back."

Tom set our drinks down in front of us and placed one in front of himself. "Are you going to tell me what happened?"

Sergio took a long sip of his coffee and stood up. He pulled the shoulder of his shirt under his nose and sniffed. "Whew! I smell like a French fry after working in there." His face scrunched up. "I have to go. Besides, I really want to take a shower, you know," he motioned to the kitchen with his head, "after the…" He clawed his hands and made them crawl all over his chest. Leaning forward, he whispered to me, "Do you think we violated any health codes in there? You know, with… Las Cucarachas?"

Tom's tan complexion took on a pale, greenish hue, but he said nothing.

"I wouldn't worry about it. I'm sure the Club Fred staff have broken more health codes than we have."

"Oh, goodie." Sergio said and rubbed his hands together, heading off to our room.

I took a long drag on my pop. The cold, sweet flavor never tasted so good.

"Hey, go easy on that stuff so early in the morning." When he didn't see me smile, he tried another way. "I heard a lot of compliments about the food. Do you know who cooked? They said it was the best meal they've eaten since they had gotten to this resort."

"It was probably just the munchies after the all-day drinking binge they had yesterday, followed by no food for over twenty-four hours."

"No. It was good. I even had seconds, and I never have seconds." He patted his stomach. "I have to watch my figure, or no one else will."

A smiled played across my mouth. "I bet you had the fruit and corn flakes."

"Nope. Sausage and eggs. Did you cook them?"

I nodded.

"So what was missing from the kitchen?"

"It's a long story." I took another drink from my pop.

"Isn't it always?" He motioned around the room, "Besides, it's not like there's anything better to do, right?"

As if in response to his question, the sky opened up, and torrential rains beat against the windows and ground.

I took a deep breath. "Sergio and I were hungry. In our search for food, Sergio got his arm stuck in a cupboard, but instead of finding food, we found cockroaches, millions of them. In his panic to get them off, Sergio slammed into me and we fell down the garbage chute."

Tom laughed and stuck out his tongue. "I'm sorry I asked."

"Oh, it gets better. While we were in the basement, we found a boot. A man's black leather boot."

"So?" Confusion showed on his face.

"I think it was Duane's," I said.

"Duane who?"

"Duane." I motioned with my hand to hurry his memory along. "The guy I tripped over on the beach the first night we got here?" I put my hands down after I realized he didn't know any of this. "His feet were bare when he washed up on shore, and if my memory serves me right, Duane wore a pair of boots just like the one we found."

"So you knew him from before?" Tom asked.

"No." I shook my head. "He tried to pick Sergio and me up when we were checking in and looking for a roommate."

"So, the boot you found in the basement is missing from the

kitchen?''

I nodded.

"Did you see who took…" His voice trailed off as his eyes narrowed on mine. "Sorry, stupid question. That's why you looked so surprised when you were coming back from the cooler."

"I was so busy cooking. I didn't pay any attention to who or what was going on around me. I was just frying sausages and eggs."

"A lot of people are happy you did. I know I was starving when I came down for breakfast this morning."

"Tom, can I ask you something?"

"Sure."

"What did you mean earlier, when you said we didn't look domestic?"

His face flushed red. "You strike me more as a man of action and adventure, not a homebound bookworm."

"What?" I said.

Tom smiled. "You know, you look more like the blue Speedo type, than the boxer swim trunks."

My heart stopped in my chest. Now what did he mean by that? Could he have planted the snake in our room and been the one who took my blue Speedo? Maybe the snake hadn't eaten it after all. Why was Tom asking me about them now? Was he trying to pump me for more information? Was he warning me to back off? Or was he telling me that I was next?

CHAPTER 43 - RAINY DAY GAMES

"Remember, it's almost five and we have Bingo starting in ten minutes, and at six there'll be a tea dance, which will go on until supper is served. The staff is back and working, and, I'm sure, you'll all be happy to hear that I'm not cooking," Mike said into the microphone.

Cheers came from those listening to Mike's announcement.

"Like he did any of the cooking anyway. You did most of it." Sergio poked me with his finger.

I swatted him away. After breakfast, we ran to our room to shower and get clean clothes, but the rain soaked us again on the way back to the dining hall. I was damp again, and my underwear was sticking.

John stepped up to the small stage, where they were setting up the mixer boards, CD players, and turntables. He took the mike. "We've searched the whole resort for umbrellas and slickers, but we've come up empty. Who would've thought that they wouldn't stock these items in a tropical paradise."

He motioned outside. "It doesn't look like it'll be letting up anytime soon. So," he waved for Mike to bring something over, "we have these for those of you who want to keep dry."

Mike carried a cardboard box up to John and bowed to him. John reached in and pulled out a large, white plastic garbage bag and unfolded it. "Now, we're going to see how many ways we can design," he paused for effect, "Weather gear." He waved the plastic bag at the crowd.

"He's got to be kidding," Sergio scoffed. "Is this the level we have sunk to, rainy day crafts from summer camp? Just what this crowd needs. Next thing you know, they'll be staging a drag show."

"Don't give them any ideas. At least, we're not singing *Kum ba yah*, yet. Hopefully, no one will put one of those plastic bags over their head," I replied.

John walked past us, unfolding his bag. He stopped at the door and put it over his head. He looked out into the rain and glanced at his watch. He shook his head, took a deep breath, and dashed out into the storm.

Despite spending all afternoon in the dining hall, my morning clothes never really dried. "I want to go back to our room and change again into some clean and dry clothes," I said to Sergio. I grabbed my plastic bag and stood up.

"It's not like that's going to do any good," he said, nodding toward my hand. "As soon as you step outside again, your clothes are going to be soaked."

"I don't care. I just need to get out of these damp things and try to get dry. Maybe hit the shower to warm up." I saw his expression. "I can go by myself."

"I'd feel better if I went with you."

"Afraid to be alone, or concerned about me? I just want to go and change." I looked outside. "It looks like the rain has stopped."

"Each time we try to get across the resort, the rain pours harder. It seems to know as soon as we leave the building. So, are we going to argue about this or go?" Sergio grabbed my bag and threw both of them into the garbage can by the door. "Let's go."

We stepped out into the evening air. The cloud cover from the tropical storm made it seem darker than it should have been for the time of the day. The walkway lights and most of the emergency lights were still off, making the resort appear darker than at night.

We walked briskly by the first building, rounded the corner, and a drop of water hit my arm. It must have fallen from the eaves.

Before I could say anything, Sergio asked, "Was that a dr…?" But he didn't have a chance to finish. The sky opened up.

Sergio nodded to me, and we took a few jogging steps. Not halfway across the resort, the torrential rain returned. "Maybe we should've taken the garbage bags…" Sergio shouted at me through the downpour. The wall of water drenched us.

"We have dry clothes in our room," I reminded him. "We'll be fine."

"But how'll we get back for supper? Run back naked?"

"We can try to bring a change of clothes with us or wear our swimming trunks," I suggested.

As if the storm heard our plans, the rain stopped, and I slowed back down to a walk. Sergio turned, jogging in place. "Coming?" He urged me to hurry up.

"I'm not running back. I'm already soaked, I can't get any wetter."

"Well, I'm not waiting for it to start up again." He laughed. "Besides, I'm going to get the shower first and use up all the hot water." With that, he turned, sprinted around the corner of the next building, and disappeared.

Once he was gone, I noticed how dark it really was. I strained to see. Nothing. My footsteps echoed along the corridor between buildings, but the little light from the rooms didn't illuminate the pathway very well.

The darkness seemed to be closing in on me. Was I getting claustrophobic from all of the darkness and the rain? Or was it the cold and dampness of the day settling into my bones? Too many strange things had happened to me in the dark at this place, and I wasn't going to wait and see what happened next.

Quickening my pace, I called. "Sergio, stop being an idiot and wait for me." I listened for his footfalls. Faintly, up ahead, I heard an echo of running feet at a fast clip, and then suddenly, I heard a wet *thud*.

Rounding the next twist in the sidewalk, I searched the darkness. Something lay up ahead in the center of the walkway. As I drew near, the shape turned into a complaining Sergio, sprawled across the concrete.

"I told you not to go running around in the dark." Extending my hand, I asked, "Did you hurt…?" I stopped in mid-sentence.

Sergio pushed himself up and wiped his hands together. "What the hell?" He shook his head, trying to clear it, and slowly rose to his knees. "I landed on something."

He stood up on shaky legs, and an object emerged from underneath.

My eyes started to focus on what he had tripped over.

A large plastic bag?

It swam into sharp focus. Two bare legs protruded from the bottom of the bag.

Sergio scrambled over to the opposite side of the body and helped me rip the garbage bag open. As I tore through the plastic, I noticed the T-shirt and shorts. They looked just like the ones I had on. My mind raced back to CPR class.

Once the bag split open, we carefully rolled the still form over on his back. His skin was warm but clammy to the touch. His body showed no signs of life.

"Who…?" Sergio started, as the long hair fell back, revealing John's pale face, beaded with fine raindrops.

"Is he breathing?" Sergio asked. "Is he?" His words came out quick and breathy, his hands fidgeted.

"If you'd be quiet, I could…" I held my hand up and dropped my ear down to John's mouth. I strained to detect any rise or fall from his chest.

There wasn't any.

"He's not breathing. Start CPR, and I'll go for help." I pushed myself up to my feet.

Sergio grabbed onto my ankle. "Wait! I don't know CPR." He released my leg and bounded to his feet. "You do it." He pointed to John. "I'll go get help," he said, and was gone.

"Oh great." Crouching down, I tipped his head back, opened his airway, pinched his nostrils, and blew into his mouth. Giving one more breath, I tasted alcohol and orange juice. I sat back and watched his chest fall as the air escaped his lungs. Nothing was obstructing his throat. His airway was open. As my finger traced down his chest to find his sternal notch, my hands interlaced over his breastbone, my elbows locked, and I pressed my arms down and started chest compressions.

What was the ratio? One to five? Two to fifteen? They seemed to change it each year. Who cared? *Just do it*. One, two, three, four, five. I tilted his head back. I gave him a quick breath, and returned to chest compressions. Fifteen would be better. One, two, all the way to fifteen. Breathe. After all my years in the hospital and annual re-certification in CPR, I'd never had to perform it on anyone, until now.

The strong smell of alcohol hung around John. Alcohol poisoning. I needed to induce vomiting. Yeah right. Get his heart and breathing started first. Was that compression three or four? I couldn't concentrate, my mind kept screaming, "Breathe. Breathe."

Nothing.

John wasn't breathing, and his heart hadn't started up again.

My eyes scanned the dark horizon. *Sergio. Hurry.*

I continued CPR, and tried to distance myself from what I was doing. This wasn't the John I knew. This wasn't the "live" John from the beach or from the towel. This was the mannequin we practiced CPR on at the hospital.

But John's face was right there. How could I forget about that?

His heart and lungs had stopped. He was dead.

No. Don't think that. I can't hurt him with the CPR. He's dead. I can't hurt him anymore than he already is. So, the CPR wasn't hurting him, it was the only thing that could bring him back and save his life. Breathe. One, two, three, four, five.

Footsteps echoed through the dark, and they seemed to be running in our direction. *Please be coming toward us.* My ears strained to figure out if they were coming to help or just passing by. The rain had started falling again, and with the footsteps, I lost my place in the CPR cycle.

"Keep going. Stop worrying about what's going on around you. Focus on what you need to be doing to save John."

"He's over here." Sergio's voice directed.

"Thank you, Sergio," I said.

Mike and another man followed close behind him, but I stayed focused on John, completing the compressions and breathing.

The man approached and tapped me on the shoulder. "I'm a doctor. I know CPR." He moved around to the opposite side of John's body so he could face me.

"He'll take over after the cycle," Mike informed me.

I pumped the chest and said out loud, "…fourteen, fifteen." I gave John one last breath and looked across his still form.

The doctor was in position and ready. Mike checked for a pulse as the doctor found the proper place on John's sternum, placed his locked arms over his chest, and tensed, readying himself to start CPR.

Mike, not feeling a pulse, shook his head and said, "Nothing," and motioned to start chest compressions.

The doctor started, counting each one out loud, "One, and two, and three, and four, and five…"

Mike waited for the fifteenth compression and then breathed into John's mouth.

Sergio and I stood back and watched the two men work. After a few cycles, my heart had slowed a little and I asked, "Is there something you want us to do?"

"…five, and six, and seven…"

Mike turned to us. "Go find Geoff, and see if he has the stretcher and the portable defibrillator unit."

"I'll do that," Sergio offered and was off again before I responded.

As Mike and the doctor worked on John, I scanned his body. In the shadows, I didn't detect any bruising around his neck. No telltale red fingerprints appeared on his throat.

I looked further down his body and stopped at his fingertips. Something dark was caked underneath his nails. Moving closer, I noticed scratch marks along the side of his leg. I walked around to the other side, hugging myself for warmth. My damp shirt clung to my trembling body. The marks and his hand were the same. The wounds were oozing thick, dark blood at the edge of his shorts, right where John's hands would have been hanging.

John had dug his nails into his own skin. Why?

The rain increased into a full downpour. Dripping wet, they continued to work on John as I searched for Sergio's return with Geoff.

Then as suddenly as it had intensified, the rain slowed to a gentle shower and Sergio returned. Out of breath, he said, "I found Geoff. He's still looking for the defibrillator pack, but it's not where it's supposed to be."

"What?" Mike shouted.

"It's gone," Sergio said.

"But who would have taken it?" I asked. "And there should be several."

John still hadn't responded from the chest compressions. I couldn't remember how much of a head start John had on us. How long ago had he stopped breathing? A few minutes? Seconds? Longer?

If John's breathing had stopped for over five minutes, it didn't look good for him. And there wasn't a medical facility close by, even if we could get him there under the current road conditions.

Geoff ran to our group, empty-handed. Shaking his head, "I tried the phone, mon. There's nothing there."

"Who would've taken the kit?" Mike asked as he continued checking the pulse.

The doctor stopped compressions and gently touched Mike on the arm. "Anything?"

Mike shook his head slowly.

"I think we've done everything we can. I don't think he's coming back," the doctor said quietly.

I wasn't sure if tears blurred my vision or if it was the rain dripping from my hair. I stood up, wiped my runny nose with the back of my hand, and quickly stuck both hands into my pockets, trying to rid of them of that cold feeling of death, but their warmth wasn't coming back.

Suddenly, my whole body went cold. It was the first time I noticed the chill that was quickly settling over me.

"I'll take care of..." Geoff said, stepping forward. He removed his jacket and placed it over John's still body.

Sergio came over to my shivering form. "We need to get into some dry clothes." He guided me in the direction of our room. "Do you need us?" he asked over his shoulder.

No one responded. Sergio pushed me toward our room before anyone could change their mind.

Sergio guided me across the threshold of our room. "Get those wet clothes off and jump into the shower."

I stood, dripping and shivering in the entryway, numb from the rain and the quickly fading adrenaline rush. My mind still wasn't able to comprehend what had just happened.

"Here, let me help you." Sergio stepped forward, pointed me to the bathroom, and pulled my wet T-shirt over my head. It peeled it away from my skin, and the room's air chilled me further.

He wrung out my shirt and made a small puddle on the already damp floor. He tossed my T-shirt into the bathroom. It landed with a splat. He pointed to it, like I do with Regan's toys. Did he expect me to follow it? Fetch it?

My gaze held the crumpled shirt in the center of the darkened bathroom, but my feet refused. I turned back to face him, but my eyes followed his hand movements instead.

Sergio reached forward and made as if he was going to help me unbutton my pants. "If you don't do it," his eyes met mine, "I will." A huge smile spread across his face. "And you don't want that," his eyebrows rose, "do you?"

But he didn't wait for my response. He moved past me, flipped on the bathroom light, and stepped over my shirt. Reaching around the closed shower curtain, he turned on the hot water and then rifled through a pile of laundry on the floor. He pulled a towel out and felt it, trying to determine if it was the driest one in the heap. He brought it to his nose and sniffed. Satisfied, he folded it and placed it on the stool. "There. Do you need anything else?"

I continued to stand there, shivering, willing my body to move, but my feet were rooted to the floor. That's when Sergio really surprised me.

He stepped forward and gave me a hug.

I just stood there, arms hanging down at my side, my body stiff and quaking, but his body's warmth and his unexpected show of concern calmed me.

He released me as suddenly as he had hugged me, and asked, "Are you going to be all right?" One of his hands rested on my shoulder. "I don't know how you stayed so cool out there. You knew exactly what to do. You didn't panic like I did."

"But he didn't make it," I said.

He shook me gently. "And it's not because you didn't try. He was gone, long before we found him. Hell. At least you tried to save him, that's more than I did." His arms released me. "What did I do? Scream? Run away?" He took a deep breath and exhaled. "Actually, I tripped over and landed on him for God's sake. Like that did him any good."

His humor didn't get a smile out of me.

"You didn't panic. You knew what to do. I was the one who ran away." Disgust echoed in his voice. "I bet I screamed all the way." He held up his arms in the air like the damsels in distress in the silent movies.

"But you ran for help, as quickly as you could. You know I wouldn't have been able to find anyone in the dark."

"Yeah, yeah," he said. He stepped behind me, aimed my head toward the running shower, and gently pushed me forward. "Your shower is waiting. Besides, you're dripping all over the floor." His sandaled foot rose up and tapped me in the butt.

The impetus was all I needed to get moving.

He called after me, "And I doubt housekeeping will provide service today."

I closed the door and kicked off my shoes. Steam swirled around the room and fogged the mirror.

Sergio shouted from the outer room. "And no dilly-dallying in there. I'm hungry, and I want a shower, too. So don't use all the hot water."

My shorts and underwear hit the floor with a splat, joining

my T-shirt. I gratefully stepped into the hot water. It massaged my cold, tight skin, and my blood began to circulate through my arms and legs again.

My shivering stopped as my muscles warmed. I wanted the shower to rinse the taint of death off my body and down the drain.

Sergio banged on the bathroom door, causing my breath to expel sharply. "Hurry up in there. I'm freezing." He paused for a moment, "And if you don't hurry, I may have to join you."

Supper consisted of mashed potatoes and hard rolls, again, along with some other inedible things. Obviously, the recipe book didn't get blown away with the hurricane.

The tea dance was over, and soft Caribbean music played for the dining crowd. Sergio and I waited for Tom and Logan, but neither appeared for supper, so we ate alone.

As the resort guests ate and drank, Mike circled through the dining room. He spoke with a few of them, checking for any concerns. I doubted he'd come by our table and ask us if we had any complaints. With our list, he would never leave. Once he had exhausted his options, and our table was the only one left, he walked over and asked, "Mind if I join you?"

Sergio motioned to an empty seat. "Be our guest."

Cradling a hot cup of tea in my hands, I nodded in agreement.

Mike pulled the chair out and sat down next to me. Leaning in, he said in a hushed tone, "Thanks for all the help out there." He motioned with his head and then sat back in his chair and closed his eyes.

I looked over at Sergio, who shrugged his shoulders. I opened my mouth to say something, but couldn't think of how to begin.

Seeing my hesitation, Sergio pulled his chair closer to the table and asked. "So, what did you find out? You know…about John?"

Mike's eyes shot open and darted around the room. After

seeing no one was paying any attention to us, he started. "It appears that John had been drinking too much. He must've had the garbage bag over his head and stumbled on his way to his room. With all the booze in his system, he passed out and suffocated."

"But why would he put a bag over his head?" Sergio asked.

"He was pretty vain. All models are. I suppose he was trying to keep his hair dry," Mike answered. "I doubt anyone thought to bring an umbrella on vacation. Who would have known that we would've needed one?"

"But that's silly, John wasn't afraid of getting wet," Sergio argued.

Mike folded his arms across his chest, but he didn't look convinced.

"His picture," Sergio retorted.

"What picture?" Mike unfolded his arm, sat forward, and narrowed his eyes on Sergio.

"The one on the Club Fred towel. He's soaking wet there." Sergio shook his head as if to say, "Duh."

Mike's face relaxed a little. "Oh that. I'm sure he got paid very well for that photo, don't you?" He pointed to his chest. "I wouldn't mind getting wet for what he was paid for that photo, not even in this weather." He motioned out the window with his head.

The night was black, and the steady downpour continued to beat against the glass.

Sergio shook his head. "John may have been vain, but I'm sure he was smart enough to know better than to put a plastic bag over his head. They teach that in grade school, and most bags have it written them. Well, maybe he wanted to keep the rain off, but he was strong enough to rip the bag."

"See. That shows you how dumb people can be," Mike countered. "If they have to write it on every bag, it must be a concern."

Mike didn't understand what Sergio was saying and probably never would. So I tried something different. "What about the scratches on John's legs?"

Confusion clouded Mike's face, but he answered quickly. "There weren't any scratches on his legs."

This time it was our turn to react. Both Sergio's and my eyebrows shot up.

"Whoa! Wait a minute." Mike held up his hands in surrender. "What I mean is, that I didn't notice any scratches, not that there weren't any there."

Sergio turned to me. "What kind of scratches were they? Did they look like claws? Did someone or something grab onto his leg? Or was it road rash from the sidewalk?"

"I'm sure when he fell…" Mike started.

Why was Mike trying to explain these scratches? He never saw them. What had he seen? Instead I said, "It appeared to me that he scratched himself with his own hands."

"He scratched himself?" Sergio screwed up his face. "Like in an allergic reaction? Could he have been exposed to poison ivy? Or was it alcohol poisoning? But would that have caused him to scratch himself to death?"

"I have allergies, and I've had some nasty reactions, but I've never scratched myself that bad." I shook my head.

Mike pushed his chair away from the table. "I should go mingle a little more, and see if anyone needs anything. This weather isn't what the guests have paid for, so I need to do some damage control." He stood up, bowed to us, and fell into his scripted Club Fred dialogue. He raised his voice so those nearby could hear. "Let me know if I can do anything else for you two, to make your stay better," and with that, he was gone.

We watched him leave, but he didn't speak to any more guests along his way. He walked through the dining room and out into the night.

"So, what do you make of that? Was he a little defensive or

what?" Sergio asked.

"He wouldn't admit anything about those scratches, and then he even tried to make up excuses for them."

"What do you really think?" Sergio pressed.

I took a deep breath. "If I had to make a guess, I think someone snuck up behind John, pulled the plastic bag over his head, and suffocated him."

"But wouldn't there have been marks around his neck?"

"There would be if they grabbed him around the neck. But don't you remember about those scratches? They were down on his legs, not at his throat. When we ripped the garbage bag off of him, his arms were down at his sides. He didn't try to get the bag off his head, or couldn't, so he dug into his legs."

"Isn't that strange?" Sergio asked.

"I bet when the bag was pulled down, John's arms were held down by his sides, so he couldn't take it off or rip the plastic bag open."

"That's where the scratches came from." Understanding glowed in Sergio's eyes.

"Exactly. John tried to get the bag off of him, but as he struggled, his hands were only able to dig into his legs."

"John was pretty strong and healthy." Sergio's doubt shaded his voice.

"But he'd had a lot to drink. You even commented on how much, and when I did CPR, there wasn't any doubt. Besides, he wasn't expecting to be attacked."

"So anyone could've been strong enough to do that? Tom? Logan?"

"Anyone could have. With the element of surprise and with all of that alcohol, I don't think they would've needed a lot of strength. All they would have had to do was knock him down, lay on him, and hold him on the ground with the bag over his head. It wouldn't have taken long."

"You don't mean…" he began.

I nodded. "John left ten minutes before we did."

"We just missed the killer?" Sergio swallowed hard.

"Not us, you. When you ran ahead and tripped over John, the killer could have still been close by. He could've been hiding in the bushes or around the side of the building."

Sergio's face paled, looking around the room. "If you hadn't been behind me…"

"Let's not think about that." I followed his gaze as we wondered who was turning Club Fred into Club Dead.

Sergio and I sat in silence. I never thought he could be quiet for that long. With my track record, those around me hadn't been faring very well; I double-checked to see if he was still breathing.

He was and his eyes darted from person to person in the dining area. I read the question in his eyes: Which one of these guests was capable of murder?

I wondered the same thing. My eyes followed his gaze around the room. Who was paying more attention to us than they should? Was there anyone here we could trust? In this room, at this whole resort? Looking back at Sergio, I wondered. Could I trust him?

Men strutted around the tables, cruising each other, but they seemed to be avoiding our table. I laughed to myself. Had our reputation spread throughout the resort already?

"What's so funny?" Sergio asked, his attention returning to me.

"Did you notice how many guys are checking each other out, but they're all giving us a wide berth?"

"Disappointed?" Sergio cocked his head and looked over at the next table. The two men quickly avoided his stare. "I see what you mean," he said and then started to smirk. "Maybe we should make a lunge at someone and see if we could clear this place out." He made his hands into claws and snarled at me.

We both burst into laughter, enjoying the relaxed moment, but it didn't last long. Just as we settled down, a guy clad in a black plastic bag with only his head and arms sticking out entered the dining room in a flurry. His hair slicked back against his scalp as water dripped down his face. He shook himself like a Labrador emerging from a lake. He looked familiar, but I couldn't place him.

Sergio noticed the man and my gaze. "Do you know him too? You seem to know everyone at this resort. Are you sure you haven't been here before?" He turned to face me. "You sure get around for a straight boy. Are you sure you're not gay?" His head rotated to inspect the new arrival. "He's not too bad looking, if you like them that...intense."

From across the room, the man's eyes found me and I felt them lock on. He ripped the bag from his body and tossed it to the floor.

"He's coming our way." Sergio leaned forward. "Who is he?"

I shrugged my shoulders and racked my memory, trying to figure out who he was, but nothing would come. Maybe all of the rain was drowning my mind.

The man scowled as he crossed the room. His lips curled back into a sneer, and I flashed on a memory of him on the beach. That face was yelling, yelling at...Tom. Then the name popped into my mind, Sean. Tom's agent, and his mood hadn't improved from our first meeting. "That's..."

Sergio gave me a questioning look as we watched him slither between the tables.

Before I could finish, Sean was within hearing distance.

His footsteps pounded across the tiled floor. Then clicked to a stop at our table. "So where is he?" Sean spat at me.

"Nice to see you again too," I replied, evenly. My humor was wasted on him.

"I don't have time for pleasantries. I need to know where Tom is, and I need to know, now." He stamped his right foot to punctuate his point.

"He..." Sergio began, but I cut him off with a look.

I took over. "We don't know."

Sean glared at me and turned his eyes to bore into Sergio.

Sergio tossed his head to the side. "I have him tied up right now, and once he submits..."

"Enough." Sean slammed his fist down on our table and made us jump. "Good. Now that I have your attention, we'll begin again. Where is Tom?" A vein pulsated in his temple, threatening to explode.

I shook my head. "I haven't seen him since the hurricane hit. We were waiting for him at supper, but he didn't show."

"The phones don't work around here. He won't answer his door. The maids are nowhere to be found, so I can't get into his room," Sean complained.

"What do you need him for?" I asked.

Sean's mouth pinched closed.

I glared back at him. He thought he was intimidating me. I couldn't tell him something I didn't know, no matter how much he yelled. "I don't owe you anything," I began, "besides, I don't particularly like you."

Sean pointed his index finger at me. "If you see him, you tell him that I need to talk to him, A-S-A-P." He frowned at Sergio. "And that goes for you too." He curled his lip like a demonic Elvis and turned on his heel and stalked off.

"We'll hurry right out into the storm and find him for you," Sergio stood and called after him.

Sean stopped, his body visibly tensed. He clenched his hands, and then raced off into the stormy night.

I saluted his departing form.

"You sure have interesting friends." Sergio smiled at me as he sat down. "After that encounter, I could use a beer. Do you want one?"

"Sure, why not? The way this day has been going…" I pushed my chair back and stood.

Sergio held his hands up to stop me. "I'll get it, and it's my treat."

"I thought the drinks were included in the price."

"They are. That's why it's my treat."

As Sergio set our bottles down, Tom stuck his head through the swinging doors of the kitchen. He scanned the room and slowly eased through. Approaching our table, he asked, "What have you guys been doing? Anything fun?" He forced a nervous smile.

"You wouldn't believe us if we told you," Sergio said.

"You owe us big time," I said. "For running interference with your good buddy, Sean."

Tom's brow creased, but he said nothing.

"Aren't you going to ask what he wanted?" Sergio probed.

"No. I think I know," he said, with a flat tone.

"Would you mind telling us?" I said. "After all, we covered for you."

Tom took a deep breath and exhaled. "All right. I'll admit it. I've been hiding from him all week. So far, I've been lucky, but he's persistent." He paused for a moment, and finally he said, "Sean's been trying to get me to sign a new contract."

"Isn't that a good thing?" Sergio asked.

"It is, but I don't want to make any more movies," Tom said.

"Right now or ever again?" I asked.

"I don't know. Right now, I want to move on and try something else." Tom sat back.

"What else can you do?" Sergio asked.

I kicked him under the table.

"Ouch," he said, sitting up.

Tom ignored Sergio. "Not a whole heck of a lot, but I'm willing to try something, learn a new trade."

"Modeling? Hollywood movies?" I asked.

"It's really hard to switch into something like that after you've...exposed yourself the way I have." Tom's face flushed.

"What about your...other plans?" I asked.

"What other plans?" Tom's eyes darted between us and he

swallowed hard.

"Your recent wedding?" I prompted.

Tom's face fell. "Oh, that."

"Is it true?" I continued.

"How did you find out?" He lowered his voice.

"Let's just say I found some information that suggested that you were married ." I made full eye contact.

"So, what do you want?" Resignation settled into Tom's voice.

"I don't want anything."

"What?" He sat up straight in his chair.

I smiled. "I don't want anything. I don't care what you do…"

"Or who you did," Sergio added.

I shook my head. "I'm not trying to extort money from you, if that's what you think. It doesn't matter to me."

"It matters to me," Sergio whined.

I kicked him under the table again.

"Ouch." He leaned forward and rubbed his shin. "Would you knock it off?"

Tom and I turned to stare at him.

His brows shot up. "Well, it matters to me. I may want to see one of your movies, you know, like in the future."

I smiled to myself. "I thought you said…"

"I've never seen one," Sergio blurted out. "Honest." His face glowed pink.

Tom rubbed his hands together. "I wouldn't say that I'm proud of what I've done, but I've made a lot of money making those movies. It was my job, but it isn't what I want to do now. I'm moving on, and the adult industry will have to get by without me. Someone new will come along and take my place."

"No way. They could never fill…" Sergio started. "Did I say that out loud?"

"Quit while you're ahead," I said.

Tom shook his head. "Sean thinks he's going to lose a lot of money if I don't sign the new contract, but he'll find a new star. I'm sure if he stopped chasing me and looked around this resort, he would find my replacement." He motioned around the room. "He could find several stars here and double his return, maybe more, if he worked at it, but he doesn't want to work that hard. He wants to stay with the same old thing, never try to improve his options."

"You can't improve upon perfection," Sergio mumbled.

Tom laughed. "Porn stars are a dime a dozen. My departure won't even be noticed. I've saved my money and have invested it well, so I'm set for a while." He smiled. "I'm happy with my choice. I can't wait for this trip to be over, so I can get home and start my new life with my wife."

"So, is that why you've been hanging around us?" I asked.

"In a way, but you guys were the only ones who actually talked to me," Tom said.

"But I didn't know who you were," I said.

"That's why I knew you were safe to hang around with. I needed to be seen with a good looking guy, and…" Tom said.

"Oh, please," Sergio said.

"…someone that wouldn't be hitting on me…" Tom said.

"So you used me?" I said.

Tom's face flushed red. "I did at first, but I like you. You're a great guy." He pointed toward Sergio. "I figured if you haven't killed him by now, you must be a saint."

"Hey!" Sergio sat up in his seat.

"I didn't mean to offend you, Sergio. I think you're fun too. Taylor maintains a level head. He thinks under pressure and doesn't panic when things get crazy. You should count yourself lucky to have a friend like that. I wish I did."

I felt my face burn and quickly took a drink from my beer.

Sergio did the same.

"Taylor," Tom said. "If I didn't know you were straight, I'd swear you and Sergio were the perfect couple."

Sergio and I spat out the mouthfuls of beer that we had just started to swallow.

"What is this? Synchronized spitting?" Logan said, from behind me.

Wiping the beer from my mouth, I turned to see his smiling face.

"What do you mean a 'perfect couple'?" Sergio stood up and demanded. "Do you think that I would go for him?" He pointed at me.

My eyes opened wide in surprise. "What's wrong with me?"

"You're not my type."

"What is your type?"

"Did I miss something here?" Logan asked. Confusion crossed his face as he looked around our little group. When he didn't get any response, he pulled out a chair and sat down.

I wasn't going to explain all that had happened to us since we last saw him. Sergio could. Instead I said, "We've been running interference for Tom. His agent Sean has been a royal pain."

Logan's face blanched.

"Is something wrong?" I asked.

Logan's eyes darted from me and remained on Tom. Finally, he asked, "Sean Harris is here?"

Now it was Tom's turn to look surprised. "You know Sean Harris?"

Logan nodded slightly, and he appeared to pale even further in spite of his weathered complexion.

Tom nodded along with him. "I see." A wry smile played across his lips.

"Are we missing something here?" Sergio asked. "I think you both know something that you aren't sharing with us."

I had my suspicions, but I waited for Tom or Logan to

confirm them. It didn't take long.

"I thought Sean only represented…" Tom left the sentence unfinished.

That prickling sensation in my neck returned, and I scanned the room.

"What kind of an agent is Sean?" Sergio still expected answers.

"I'll let Logan tell you. It's not my place to say." Tom stopped.

Logan squirmed in his seat and swallowed hard. He cleared his throat and looked around the table. He leaned forward and began in a hushed tone. "Tom is being polite."

"Polite about what?" Sergio demanded.

Logan looked around the room and shrugged his shoulders. "If I can't say this here, I guess I'll never be able to say it." He took a deep breath. "I'm not only doing research here, I'm actually on vacation."

"Yeah, so? We all are," Sergio said, and then he scratched his chin. "Oh, ho. I see."

Logan nodded. "Yes, I am."

Sergio turned to Tom, confused. "You mean Sean only represents gay clients?"

"He does," Tom said.

"But you just told us that you weren't…" Sergio scratched his head.

Logan pointed to Tom. "You're not?"

"No. He's my cover," Tom explained. "Sean's representation only makes me legitimate, or as legit as you get in this business."

"I thought dealing with insurance companies was difficult, but the entertainment industry has more ins and outs than I can keep track of," I said.

"Try swimming in this sea of sharks, where image is everything," Logan said.

"And Sean is the worst," Tom added.

"You said it. I'm so glad I haven't run into him. He didn't say he was going to be here. Not that I told him where I was going. Where has he been?" Logan asked.

Tom shrugged. "Taylor met him on the beach our first day here, but I haven't seen him since our argument."

"He said he's been looking for you," I said to Tom.

"He obviously hasn't been looking very hard, now has he? I've been hanging around, right?" Tom asked.

"What were you two arguing about when I interrupted?" I asked.

"Sean wanted me to be a visible presence here at the resort."

"I thought you were on vacation," Sergio said.

"I thought so too, but Sean didn't mention that when he booked me here. He said that since this was the last week of my contract, he was sending me on a trip to relax, after all the hard work I've done. Ha. He forgot to tell me that Club Fred is paying *him* for me to be here. I get a free trip, but *he* gets paid."

"What are you supposed to be doing?" I asked.

"Sean only told me that I needed to participate in most of the events here at the resort. Play volleyball, snorkel, swim, go horseback riding, whatever comes up at the resort. Be seen. I'm a celebrity, so the guests need to feel that Club Fred attracts stars, just as much as the general public."

"So they can go home and tell their friends that they vacationed with…"

Tom nodded.

"Molly was thrilled," Sergio said. "She was wishing she could be here, but I think after the hurricane, she'd change her mind. When she found out we were hanging around with Tom and Logan, she was green with envy. Wait until she hears about Logan."

Logan's face took on a horrified expression.

"Sergio, I don't think Logan wants us to be talking about his little secret once we get back home. Do you?" I turned to Logan.

"My sales haven't been what they should be. Sean keeps telling me not to worry, but I've seen a lot of great mid-list authors get dropped by their publishers, and some of these are award-winning writers and have very successful and popular series, more so than mine."

"But…" Sergio whined.

"But nothing. We have to respect Logan's right to privacy. If he doesn't want us to talk about this, I think we should honor that. He can out himself, if he wants to, *when* he wants to. That isn't our decision to make." I could still feel like someone lurked behind me. Maybe my damp clothes were irritating my nerves.

"But…" he tried again.

"No. You came out on your own terms. Logan should be able to do the same. Right?" My skin tingled like stinging ants crawling down my spine.

"I guess, but Molly would love to know," he pleaded.

"Then Logan can tell her himself, when he's ready and not before." I looked at Logan, whose expression had relaxed significantly.

Sergio turned to Tom. "Does Sean know about you?"

"He's never asked," Tom said. "And I'm not going to tell."

Sergio smiled at him. "Can I at least tell Molly about you?"

"Sure, why not?" He waved his hand in the air. "I doubt that'll impact my career at this point."

"Thanks," Sergio said. He turned to Logan and gave him the same look.

Logan smiled and shook his head.

With some secrets exposed, our table relaxed. We forgot about everything for a few minutes and enjoyed each other's company. No pretenses, no attitudes. Just four people, trying to be friends in a strange and hostile place. But was someone still watching?

The next morning dawned with…rain. So much for Mike's promise for the best weather and the bluest skies after a hurricane. This black cloud's silver lining was taking its time to shine. Or was it just hanging over the resort?

After finding John's body, Sergio and I decided to stick close to each other for the rest of our time at Club Fred. Our inability to trust anyone made us inseparable. The only chance we had for a few moments of privacy was in the bathroom, and even then, Sergio clung to the bathroom doorknob.

The morning's gloom cast shadows everywhere in the resort. Even the dining room was quiet for the first time. No animated conversations echoed throughout the room. Silverware clicked on plates. Glasses and cups clumped on the tables. The weather had ruined many vacationers' plans, and I overheard many guests praying for a sunny day or a quick trip home.

After finishing breakfast, Sergio fidgeted across the table. He was working up to something, but I didn't want to know. I could feel that this was going to be a bad idea from all the nervous energy he emitted. My flesh started to crawl when he opened his mouth.

"Would you be willing to do me one favor?" Sergio began.

Oh God, here it comes. I closed my eyes and shook my head. I really wasn't going to like this. I just knew it.

"Come on. It won't take hardly any time."

My eyes opened, and Sergio's smile tightened on his lips. There was no way this was going to happen to me. No way. I folded my arms across my chest.

"Just hear me out," he said, and unfolded a sheet of paper and spread it out on the table. "I think we should do this."

I averted my eyes. "I'm not going on another jungle cruise or snorkeling trip. All I want is to go home."

He waved his hands to dissipate my anxiety. "It's not anything like that." He narrowed his eyes and shook his head, pointing to the sheet. "I've always wanted to do something like this and I've never had the chance, so here it is." He pushed the hot pink piece of paper closer to me.

"Club Fred presents: Talent Night!" screamed across the top half of the page.

"No way." I pushed the sheet back to him.

"Just hear me out."

"There is no way in hell that I'm dressing in drag, so get that idea right out of your head." I folded my arms across my chest and sat back in my chair.

Sergio's face fell. "There goes my chance to play Diana Ross."

I covered my ears with my hands.

He leaned across the table and pulled my hands down. "You could be a Supreme. Whichever one you wanted to be."

"What are my choices?"

"Like anyone knows who they were. Mary Wells, Florence Ballard, and Cindy Songbird."

I didn't respond. I turned my head to the side. I tried to avoid his gaze, but my parents' brainwashing forced my eyes to meet his.

When I didn't respond, he changed tactics. "All right, you can be Diana if you really want to." His voice matched the pout on his face.

"Listen to me. I don't want to be Diana…"

Sergio's face shone.

"…Or a Supreme. I won't dress up as a woman. Period. No way. No how."

"If I came up with something else…" A glint flashed in his eye, just for a second.

My mind raced through all the gay icons that I could come

up with. Well, actually, only one came into mind, and I doubted just the two of us could pull it off. So I began slowly, so he couldn't misinterpret my words. "If you could come up with a male group…"

Sergio glowed. He clenched his fists to hold back his excitement.

"And…" I raised my index finger, "I don't have to wear a stupid costume. I would consider it. But just consider it."

Why did those words send shivers down my spine? As soon as they exited my mouth, a lump thumped in my stomach. What did he have in mind? There was no way that he could have tricked me. There was no way.

Right?

Geoff walked by with his camera. He scanned the dining room crowd and spotted us. I waved him over. He looked torn, as if he was searching for someone.

"I'm curious, are you a photographer?" I asked.

Geoff looked down at his camera. "No, mon, I be takin' pictures for the new brochure."

"On such a rainy day?" Sergio asked.

"We need to show we have fun all the time, rain or shine." His eyes widened and he grabbed his camera, ready for his next shot. "I gotta run, enjoy." He hustled off after someone I didn't recognize.

"That was strange." I watched as he wound his way through the tables.

"Like that should surprise you here?" Sergio said. A faint smile played across his lips, and he cast his eyes down, avoiding mine, and suggested, "What about…the Village People? Would you be willing to do them?"

It was scary how our minds worked on the same wavelength, but I had to smile to myself. It was the same one I had thought of, and there was no way the two of us could play six men. No way. Whew. I was safe.

"They could have been fun to do," I agreed, trying to play along with him, "but I doubt two of us could play six roles." I tried to look disappointed.

Sergio scratched his chin, thinking. "I know," he nodded in slow agreement.

"Too bad, it could've been fun." There. I tried. I played along. He should be happy that I even considered it. I smiled ruefully. "Too bad we don't know four other guys…"

Crap.

As soon as those words exited my mouth, a strange feeling overtook me. I swallowed hard. I had been played.

"Yeah, too bad," he pursed his lips and pouted. After a long pause, he started again. "So, if I found four other guys…"

No.

My mind counted. How many guys did we know here at the resort? Logan and Tom. But they would never be willing to do such a dumb thing as this. Or could Sergio convince them?

No way.

But why was I getting worried? Besides, they were only two, we were still two short.

Weren't we?

"I figured that you wouldn't want to dress up as a woman," Sergio admitted, "and I doubted that you'd dress up in any wild costumes. You seem to be more the Levi and white T-shirt kind of guy. Right?"

I nodded. "Yes."

"Maybe the construction worker kind of guy?"

I had been played like a fiddle.

Swallowing hard, I smiled. "You're just kidding, right?"

Sergio's eyes told me "No." He smiled. "Tom and Logan said that they'd like to help."

"When did you ask them?"

"Last night when you went to the restroom. I told them to keep it a secret until I could talk to you about it."

"But we're still missing two." I tried, but I knew what was coming next.

"I bet Skinny and Chubby David would love to help us."

Damn! I'd been had!

"You tricked me." I pointed my index finger at him, as the laughter that he had been suppressing finally burst forth. "I won't do it." I re-folded my arms across my chest, and I refused to look at him.

"Oh, come on, be a good sport. It'll only take five minutes."

"To make a fool out of myself. No. I won't do it."

"The other guys are excited. You don't want to disappoint them, do you?"

"Yes."

"You don't mean that."

Silence stood between us.

Sergio finally said, "This will give you and me the chance to get the whole crew together and see if we can figure out who has been doing all of these things at the resort. We'll have access behind the scenes of this resort to spy on all the suspects and see if we stumble across any more clues."

I remained silent.

"We could interview people, and they'll never know it isn't for the talent show. We'll be able to keep track of everyone and see if someone slips up."

I wasn't going to respond to the carrot he was dangling in front of me.

"Don't you want to figure out who killed John and Gary? Don't you think we owe them that much?" He took a deep breath. "Geoff and Mike haven't done jack to solve these crimes."

I could see why he was such a good friend of Molly's. They

thought exactly alike.

"I'll even let you pick the song," he offered. "The shortest one they have."

"No," I said.

"You can be the construction worker. He wears mirrored sunglasses that will cover your face, and a hard hat to cover your head. No one will even recognize you, not as if anyone here knows who you are anyway, right?"

Why was I going to regret agreeing with Sergio? I didn't stand a chance to win this argument. He had everything planned. I wasn't a dancer. I didn't know the words to any of their songs. I couldn't do this. I didn't want to do this.

But five other guys were counting on me.

Counting on me to make a complete fool of myself.

At least it was in front of a group of strangers.

Gay strangers.

Ones that I'd never see again.

What had gone right on this vacation so far? Nothing. So, why should this?

The more I fought against things, the worse they got.

Go with the flow, my mind soothed.

It's not like I could stop Sergio.

I doubted anyone could. He was a force of nature.

"I'm agreeing to do this only to keep an eye on everyone behind the scenes, to see if we can find out who's been stalking us, to find out who is killing everyone, and if we figure it out before showtime…"

"We won't have to go on stage," Sergio agreed.

Why didn't I believe him?

CHAPTER 50 - DUELING DIVAS

Sergio took charge of organizing our entire act, and the five of us followed his directions, every last one of them. Anytime someone offered a suggestion, they were quickly put in their place, and the dictator, I mean Sergio, took full control, total control.

"Can't we do this one?" I pointed to the back of the CD case. "It's only three minutes and thirty-six seconds."

Sergio snatched the case from my hand and looked at it. "No one knows *Can't Stop the Music*. They may have used it for the title of their movie, but it wasn't one of their hits."

Flipping the plastic case around in my hand, I motioned to the title. "It's on their 'Best of' album. I think that…"

"Don't think. Trust me on this one," he said, "it won't work."

The hair on the back of my neck stood up. I could see it now, we were going to end up doing the extended Thunderpuss re-mix version of their longest song. I just knew it.

"I know it's stereotypical, but '*YMCA*' is their classic song." Sergio looked up to see my reaction. "It's been overdone and is used in just about every known sporting event in the world, but the true essence, the true beauty of that song can only come to light," he spread his arms wide, "here."

"At Club Fred?" I asked.

Reading his expression, I knew I had to drop it.

Two hours later, the rain hadn't let up and neither had Sergio. That song played over and over again as he yelled out stage directions.

I'm sure a full-scale Broadway musical didn't have this much stage direction.

Our two rows of average looking men appeared more like the cast from *The Full Monty* than a disco group. At least the Village People didn't employ the wild dance steps that the boy bands used. Thank goodness.

I decided it was time to confront Sergio. Pulling him aside, I said, "I agreed to this charade, so we could keep an eye on everyone, and all I see is you working us to death over this act. When are we going to find something out? When are we going to start asking questions? When…"

"It's… It's…our cover."

"Well. What have we found out so far? Nothing."

"That's not true."

"I think you're using this just so you could enter the talent show. I doubt…"

"No," he said, with his hands on his narrow hips.

"We need to be focusing on who's stalking us, not whether the dance steps are in time with the music."

A tongue clicking sounded behind me.

"Tut, tut, tut. A lover's quarrel?" Cha-Cha purred.

"We're not…" I began, but Cha-Cha pushed past me and headed straight for Sergio.

A long, sculpted nail extended from her index finger and poked into his chest. "Just remember who's the real diva around here, sweetheart." Each word was punctuated with her nail.

Sergio grabbed her wrist. "When I see one, I'll make way, but until then, we'll just deal with…" he blinked his eyes, "… the falsies. Oops, I mean the false ones." He looked down at her bosom. "Not everyone can wear Nerf, but you pull it off. Lime green or orange?" He turned to me.

Cha-Cha glared into Sergio's eyes. "I'll be the winner of the talent show. You just wait and see. Don't waste any more of your time practicing. I'm a shoo-in. Count on that." They held each other's stare; neither one blinked.

A fruity scent played in the air, and a tickle started in my nose. My tongue rolled across the roof of my mouth, trying to prevent a sneeze from forming, but I was too late. It exploded from me, and was quickly followed by another.

Cha-Cha's eyes darted toward me from the sudden noise.

I felt daggers from her gaze as it bore into me. "Excuse me."

Cha-Cha stamped her foot and turned on her high heels. "You haven't seen the last of me." She stormed past me. A wave of watermelon assaulted my nostrils, and I sneezed again, but as I wiped my nose, I wondered—why did that scent mean something to me?

CHAPTER 51 - BEHIND THE SCENES

"That woman is psychotic," Sergio said.

"Did I miss something? What did you do to piss her off?" I asked.

Before he could respond, Mike's raised voice cut through the backstage curtain. "I could kill you…"

Sergio and I raced over to the curtain. I pressed my ear against the crushed red velvet. The damp fabric stuck to my skin. "Gross," I said, and pulled my head away.

Sergio slapped me. "Shhh."

"What did I do?" an unfamiliar man's voice asked.

Sergio mouthed, "Who's that?"

I shrugged my shoulders and struggled to hear more.

"Haven't you done enough?" Mike huffed. "You're the one who recommended this resort, and this place is falling apart around us."

"It's Mexico. What did you expect? A five-star hotel?"

"There are many five-star places in Mexico."

"This isn't one of them. At the price you're paying for this place for a week, you should be thanking me for all the money you're making."

Mike scoffed. "With this weather? Everyone's wishing they never came, and all they want to do is go home, myself included. I'm sure the next thing will be the guests demanding their money back."

"So?" the man asked.

"Do you think I can afford to refund any of that money? I'd be ruined. Club Fred's barely breaking even. I may have to file for Chapter 11."

"I doubt that anyone is going to ask for their money back. It's not *your* fault that the hurricane hit. It's that time of the year. The guests knew that this could happen. Right?"

"I guess so," Mike said.

"What do you mean, you guess so? Don't you have a rain or shine clause in the contract that you have each guest sign?"

"Well, yes, but…" Mike said.

"But nothing. As long as they've signed it, they can't sue you or expect to get any of their money back. You're covered."

Mike didn't respond.

The man continued, "You've provided them with three squares a day, a roof over their heads, and entertainment."

"If you can call this entertainment," Mike said.

"If you feel so badly for your guests, then offer them a discount for booking their next Club Fred vacation before they go home. That way, you ensure their return, and it makes you look like you care about them."

Anger burned in Mike's voice. "I do care."

"Whatever. All week you've been complaining about a few of your guests that were causing problems. Have you gotten rid of them yet?"

Sergio and I looked at each other in shock. I swallowed hard. Was he referring to us?

Sergio's eyes widened, and he cupped his hand around his ear. He shifted his weight to the other foot, and the wooden stage floor squeaked in protest.

My heart pounded in my ears, drowning out Mike's response.

"You're rid of Gary and John, aren't you?" the man asked.

My breath caught in my throat.

"And you don't seem too heartbroken about losing them. Hopefully, you didn't pay them before they got here. At least that's a few extra bucks in your pocket. Maybe you'll end in the black after all."

"That's cold, even for you," Mike said.

"Like John was such a loss, and you were going to fire Gary when you got back to Los Angeles anyway. After his little stunt, he…"

A finger tapped me on the shoulder, and a stifled shriek escaped from between my lips. Sergio sprang away from the curtain and assumed a defensive kung fu stance.

"How do we look?" Skinny David asked, smiling, clueless that he had interrupted our eavesdropping.

Sergio and I tried to reclaim our dignity when we saw him standing at attention in a white sailor suit. He saluted us and then motioned toward leather clad Chubby David, who looked like he had just stepped off a Harley. Both men looked at us, impatiently waiting for our feedback.

When we didn't respond right away, Skinny David's face fell. "Do I look fat?" he asked, turning from one side to the other, showing us both views. "From the expressions on your faces, I don't think we look right. What did we do wrong? Did we pick the wrong outfits? Are these yours? Did we take Tom and Logan's?"

"No, no, no. You look great," Sergio said quickly.

"What were you doing? Did we interrupt something?" Skinny David asked loudly. "Is there something going on behind the curtain?"

Sergio waved his hands to shut him up.

Not anymore, I thought, with your big mouth. But instead, "You just caught us by surprise. I thought the 'real' Village People were standing there," I said lamely.

"Really?" Skinny David's face glowed. He clapped his hands together and turned to Chubby David. "Did you hear that? We look just like them." He glanced down at his clothes and obviously remembered what Chubby David was holding. "Check this out. We brought you a hard hat and mirrored sunglasses."

"Thanks," I said, accepting them cautiously, expecting them to burn my fingers as soon as I touched them.

"We didn't figure out who you were going to be until we got back," Skinny David said to Sergio, "otherwise, we'd have brought something back for you, too." He bowed in apology. "I guess we should've known you'd be the cop, since he was the leader of the group, and you're our leader..." He motioned toward the dressing rooms where they had returned. "I'm sure I saw a policeman's uniform over there." He scratched his head as he tried to remember.

I poked him. "Yeah, don't you think we should go get your costume?"

Sergio looked at the stage curtain and then back to me. "I..."

"We'll let you get your outfit and relax. We're going to go take a few pictures of ourselves." Skinny David turned to his partner. "We could use these get-ups as Halloween costumes. No. Wait." He held up his hands. "Better yet, we could use these photos as Christmas cards. They'll be so great. What could we write underneath?" He paused only a second. "Don we now our gay apparel. It'll be perfect. I can't wait."

David and David rushed off to find their camera.

"Man, can he talk," Sergio said, and then pointed back to the curtain.

Tentatively, we peeked through the red velvet.

Mike and his unidentified guest were gone. Had they heard David's tirade? And did they know we had been listening to their conversation?

"Who was that with Mike?" I asked.

"I didn't recognize his voice. Did you?" Sergio asked. "If David and David hadn't interrupted…"

"I know." I bit my lip. "Do you think Mike overheard us?" I lowered my voice. "Maybe he knows we were listening to him."

Sergio scratched his head. "If he's the one who has been stalking us, I doubt it could get any worse than it already is. Right?"

"We'll just have to be on guard."

"What else is new?" he said.

"I know. So much for my relaxing vacation. All I wanted to do was lie in the sun, read, work on a tan, and listen to the ocean lap on the beach, but *no*."

"Instead, you get torrential rains, howling, gale-force winds, a hurricane, three dead bodies, and an obnoxious drag queen."

And you, I thought. But I said, "Molly's going to hear about this when I get home. I promise."

"*If* we get home," Sergio exhaled. "Damn. I forgot to ask Mike if the roads were passable, yet. It's not like the backlog of flights is going to get us out of here any sooner, but I'm willing to bet our flights are going to get bumped back a day or two."

"What?"

"It happens. We both took special chartered flights here."

"So?" I said.

"That means we're low priority. Actually, the lowest."

"You've got to be kidding."

"I wish I was. But the commercial flights have priority." A wistful look played across his face. "Maybe the sun'll come out tomorrow."

"Listen Little Orphan Annie, I'll be happy when I get on the plane. No matter when it gets here or how long we have to sit on the runway."

"All this happy talk isn't getting much done, now is it?" Sergio said. "Besides, I need to go and pick out my policeman's uniform for tonight. Did you want to come with me?"

"And watch you try on your costume? No way. I need to go back to the room and find my jeans. Hopefully, they're dry. We didn't jam them against the patio door to help stop the rain from blowing in, did we?"

"I don't think so, but you'll find your jeans," Sergio said. "I shouldn't be too long." He turned to go.

"Wait. Maybe I should go with you?" I offered.

"Nah, don't be silly. I'll be fine. It's broad daylight, what could possibly go wrong?"

A chill passed through my body. "Do you have to ask? You know how things have been going on around here." I took a deep breath and exhaled. "Well, that settles it. You have me convinced. I'm coming with you."

Sergio touched my shoulder and pushed me toward our room. "I'll be fine. I think I can pick out a cop uniform all by myself."

"Molly would kill me if anything happened to you," I warned.

"I'll be fine. Trust me. Go find your jeans. Shoo." He waved me away.

Now, I was worried. *Trust me*, he said, ha. But I headed back to our room. I didn't have the energy to fight with Sergio, not after the workout he'd just given us. I called over my shoulder. "Fine. I'll meet you back in the room in ten minutes. Ten minutes. And if you're not back by then, I'm coming to look for you, and I'll drag you back, kicking and screaming all the way."

"Promises, promises," Sergio shot back.

I opened our door, and a musty smell hung in the air. Images of a locker room made my nose wrinkle and twitch. The maids still hadn't been in to clean, but a pile of dry towels was stacked in the bathroom. Couldn't they have run the mop over the floor, just once, if only to wipe up the rainwater that had seeped in?

I knelt down on the slimy floor and dug through the pile of laundry in our closet. All my dirty clothes lay in a heap, waiting to be jammed into my suitcase and washed at home.

A small gecko scurried out from under a pair of shorts. Jumping back, I got out of his way and spotted a patch of blue denim. After the little lizard ran up the wall to the ceiling, I reached in and pulled out my jeans before our new pet fell on my head. Although my Levis felt damp to the touch, they were drier than the shorts I had on.

Walking over to my bed, I pulled them right side out and tried to smooth the material with my hands. But after the legs were flattened, a few wrinkles hung around the knees. Still, they appeared wearable for our performance. That was, if Sergio approved, and if he didn't, he could iron them himself.

Inserting my hand into the front pockets, I quickly had them in their proper position. I hoped I hadn't added another wrinkle. I flipped them over to inspect the backside, and a faint crackle sounded.

Did I leave something in the back pocket? Money?

My fingers explored. A wadded-up piece of paper crunched between my fingers.

I hadn't left anything in my jeans.

The scrap of paper, wrinkled and torn, emerged from my jeans. As I unfolded it, frantic letters leapt from the page at me: *"Help! They're following me. They're trying to kill me. Gary and..."* The writing stopped.

I swallowed hard. Duane had slipped this into my pocket when he said he was looking for a roommate. Then I realized what his advances had really meant.

He hadn't been trying to hit on me. He was running for his

life, and this was his final plea for help.

The door to our room burst open and slammed into the wall. My head jerked up and my body tensed for the attack.

The gecko fell to the floor as Sergio entered. As he rushed across the room, he didn't see it and stepped on it when he crossed the floor. He slipped a little as it squished underneath his foot, looked at the mess, wiped his sole on the floor, and continued on his way. "What do you think?" He extended his arms out to the side, giving me the whole view. He was clad in a policeman's uniform, brown leather boots, mirrored sunglasses, and a tight policeman's helmet. A billy club dangled from his belt, as did a pair of handcuffs.

When I didn't answer, he noticed the shocked look on my face. His glance moved to the piece of paper in my hand. "What do you have there?" he asked. "Did you find some money in your pocket?" He tossed his wet, sweaty clothes onto his bed. "I love it when I forget that I have money in my pocket and…"

When I didn't smile, he hurried over. "What's wrong?"

"Check this out," I said softly, and handed him the note.

He read it. "Yeah, so? It's a joke, right?" He looked at me, waiting for me to laugh.

I didn't. I just shook my head and swallowed.

"Was this shoved under our door?"

"I found it in my jeans."

"Who put it there?"

"I think Duane did."

"Duane?" he asked, but as soon as he said it, he understood. "He slipped that into your pocket when we were checking in." His eyes opened wide. "He wasn't grabbing your…" his voice trailed off.

"I don't want to think about that right now."

"Oh, my God," Sergio gasped. "Duane was being followed and came to us for help. He must have hoped we'd take him with us and protect him."

"But we thought he was hitting on us. And we ran away. Actually, we drove him away," I added.

"He was acting pretty desperate, going after you and all," Sergio said. "We just didn't know how desperate he really was."

"After we left our room for supper, he must have tried to run back to his room, but entered ours by mistake. Since all the doors open with any key, he got into ours and thought he was safe."

"And someone killed him and threw him in our shower when he heard you returning."

There was a chance I had been in the room with the killer. Good thing Sergio came along when he did, otherwise I could be… I didn't finish that thought. Instead, I ran over to the dresser, opened a drawer, and rifled through my underwear. Pulling out Gary's black notebook, I flipped to the page with our arrival date and pointed to what was written there. "What did Gary mean by 'Meet T & S'? Do you think he meant us?"

"Who else could he have meant? I don't understand why he was going to meet with us. Neither one of us knew him, right?" Sergio looked at me, waiting for my response.

"How would I have known him?" I asked.

"I just asked." Then Sergio's eyes glowed. "Could T & S stand for Tom and Sean?" He paused for a moment and then said, "Probably not."

"Why not?" I asked.

"They're not a couple," Sergio said and shook his head.

"Like we are?" I retorted.

"Excuse me. All I meant was that the way it's written, it would appear that he was meeting with a couple, instead of two separate people. Mike did hire Tom through Sean."

"Sorry I snapped. It just makes me sick that we could've helped Duane, maybe even saved his life if we had only known."

"But we didn't know," Sergio said. "He went about it all

wrong. What did he expect us to think? Oh baby, here's a hairy teddy bear, please come back to our room?"

"I doubt he was thinking rationally at that point." I knew we hadn't been.

Sergio held out his hand. "Let me see that note again."

I gave it to him, and he squinted hard at the piece of paper. "What letter do you think he was trying to write here?" He held the note up to the light and pointed to a small line that looked like a part of a letter. "Does that look like an 'M' to you? Like in Mike?"

I looked over his shoulder. "It looks like there's kind of curve there." I pointed to the arc. "It looks more like a 'C.' Right?"

We both said, "Cha-Cha?" at the same time.

"That could explain why she's been such a bitch," Sergio said.

"She hasn't been hostile to me."

"Just wait, she'll turn on you. She takes pride in being a bitch."

"This isn't the time for the battle of the sexes," I responded.

"When did Cha-Cha arrive at the resort?"

"Like I'd know?"

"Did you notice her on your flight or on the shuttle to the resort? I know she wasn't on mine. Could she have taken an earlier one?"

"Why is that important?" I asked.

"Because, Sherlock, whoever was stalking Duane had to have been at the resort before you arrived, right?" He pointed to the note.

"You're right," I said. "Why didn't I think about that? Whoever was stalking Duane was already here."

"So, who was here before you arrived?" Sergio pressed.

"Everyone. Tom, Logan, David, and David. Everyone. Even you." My eyes narrowed at him.

"Get serious."

"I am. My flight was full, but I can't remember who was on it. I think I was still in too much shock over where Molly was sending me to pay any attention to anything."

"Didn't anyone look familiar?"

"You were the first and the only person I recognized here."

"So what about Cha-Cha?" he asked. "When did you meet her?" he asked, from between clenched teeth.

"In the bathroom," I said.

"Do you know how that sounds?"

"I know, but that's where I ran into her."

"You make it sound so seamy, so sordid," Sergio answered, with a Sandra Bernhard mouth, lips pulled back in an open kiss.

"You're the one who keeps putting a sexual edge on everything that I say."

"Maybe you're just talking sexy."

"Whatever." I gave him an irritated glare. "I think we need to give Cha-Cha a wide berth from here on out."

"You won't be hearing any arguments from me. But remember, she thinks she's the star of the talent show."

"Oh, great."

CHAPTER 53 - TALENT NIGHT

"Why do you think Cha-Cha's the one blackmailing these guys?" I asked. I was still having trouble coming up with a motive other than the money. Was there a connection between the victims? And why did all of these clues keep pointing toward us? Pointing to me? Maybe I was being paranoid, but because of what had happened over the last few days, it felt like I was the target.

"She's crazy. That's why she's doing it. Her wig's on too tight." He ran his fingers through his hair. "Or her nylons are digging in, cutting off the circulation to her brain."

I looked at him, confused.

"Think about it." He pointed from his head to his groin.

My hands instinctively covered myself, my legs crossed in a protective stance. "Oh," I said.

"You know what I mean." Sergio smiled and nodded. "Do you think we should tell Mike? Maybe he'll kick her out of the show."

I started to ask why, but he quickly added. "That is the *only* reason I want her kicked out of the show. *Really*. It's not like she's any competition to us, anyway. I was just thinking more about our safety than anything else." His face flushed. "Honest."

He hadn't convinced me, and Sergio knew it.

Making the excuse, "I need to check myself in the mirror, and see if this uniform looks okay," Sergio quietly retreated to the bathroom. "But I really think we should tell Mike about her." He continued talking to me through the closed door.

I sat down on my bed. Maybe he was right. If Cha-Cha was crazy, she could just be killing people at random. There didn't seem to be any connections between Duane, John, and Gary. Was there a pattern? Whoever crossed Cha-Cha's path? But that didn't make any sense, Sergio and I had crossed her path many times, and we were still standing. But for how long?

I felt like Sergio and I were at the center of the problem. Maybe because these attacks had become so personal—a snake dropped in my seat in the jungle cruise, and another one placed under my bed. And where the heck was my Speedo? Sergio's machete? The thrown rock? The missing boot? Or were all of them a big coincidence? John had left the dining room just before we headed back to our room. All of these events added up to something, but my mind wasn't able to see what.

But if it wasn't Cha-Cha, then who? Tom? He wanted to start a new married life outside of the porn business. Would he kill to escape? If he wanted to stay in the business, he'd want to hide his secret about not being gay, but if he was moving on, why bother?

Sean was in the position to lose a lot when Tom quit. If he lost his biggest star, he would lose a lot of his revenue, and Sean didn't seem willing to work that hard to find a replacement. Sean didn't seem to work very hard on anything, so I bet Tom fell into his lap, and when Tom's popularity skyrocketed, Sean made big bucks without any advice or work on his part.

What was really strange was how Sean was able to represent both Tom and Logan. Wasn't that like playing both ends of the spectrum? I couldn't believe that Sean had the brains to diversify in his representation for both literature and male erotica. Would he be able to kill someone?

But Logan could come up with something. I had read all of his books, and he had killed a lot of people in some very ingenious ways in them. He could be pretty desperate at this point. If his publisher was threatening to drop him from their line-up, and his "secret" was made public, he could be pushed to kill. We'd seen the letter from Sean, his agent—he needed to do something to boost his sales, and staging a murder at Club Fred that resembled the ones in his book could give him the publicity he needed. And it could have the added advantage of killing the person who could drag him out of the closet.

My head was beginning to hurt. Were my nerves starting to act up from this stupid talent show or were we really in danger? I rubbed my eyes and forehead. Who else was there?

David and David? What did we really know about them? They kept to themselves. But was that by choice or did people run away from their presence? Chubby David seemed nice, but Skinny David, whoa. He was a head case. Pushy, loud, rude, opinionated, and he never shut up. How could someone go on and on about nothing at all? How could Skinny David find out anything to blackmail someone with if he never stopped talking?

Sergio's voice continued to echo from the bathroom. "You do have the routine down, don't you? I know, I ran through all those steps pretty fast, but if you get lost, just follow me. I'm sure…"

I shook my head.

Their file had said that they were having financial hardships, so why would they come on vacation? Could they even afford it? Unless they were making money here, but doing what? Taking things in or out of the country? Ancient artifacts? Drugs? Could Skinny David's annoying personality be a cover for a smuggling ring through their store? Was that reason enough to kill?

And speaking about money, Mike's Club Fred wasn't operating in the black. This week had been plagued with one problem after another. Could Mike be sabotaging his business—planning for bankruptcy—with this trip and killing off a few problems along the way?

And I couldn't forget about Gary. He was a letch. He could have been bleeding Mike dry. Maybe that's why Club Fred was going bankrupt. And what about John? He was a pretty boy model and the Club Fred icon. Could he have been thinking of moving on? Asking for a cut of the profits? But they were dead, so they couldn't be the villains. Mike didn't seem too broken up about their deaths, but he sure seemed friendly with Cha-Cha, allowing her to MC the talent show.

And that brought us full circle.

"Earth to Taylor. Earth to Taylor." Sergio said, tapping my arm.

I started and looked at him.

"Welcome back. I see what I've been saying has been *so important* to you." He rested his hands on his hips. "I think we should get to the stage and round everyone up for one last pep talk before the talent show," Sergio said. "I'm glad it's before we eat, because if I ate anything before the show, I'd probably throw up on stage. I'm sure that would win us first prize. Are you listening to me?" He stamped his foot on the floor. "Taylor, I'm talking to you."

"What?" I said, jarred out of the thoughts that had been racing around and around in my head.

Mike's voice boomed through the speakers. "Let me introduce our next act. She flew all the way to Club Fred from Minneapolis, Minnesota."

"On her broom, no doubt," Sergio said, as he turned around and smiled at us.

"The amazing, the talented, the one and the only…"

"Thank goodness there's only one," Sergio said.

"Cha-Cha!" Mike announced.

The driving beat of the opening bars of Tina Turner's "The Best" floated through the air. Cha-Cha stepped out onto the stage in her full glory, with a blond highlighted Tina Turner wig. Her hair stood up in all directions. A slinky black dress draped across her body. The silky fabric shone and reflected black, blue, and silver in the spotlight with every move she made. Her long, tan legs clad in black stiletto heels emerged from the front slits of her dress.

"In her wildest dreams," Sergio said under his breath as he rolled his eyes. He adjusted the holster and gun that rode low on his narrow hips.

I leaned forward, inspecting Sergio's costume. It looked a little loose on him, but it appeared to be a real uniform. I wondered if he had found it in the costume closet, and I hoped the gun was just a toy. The thought of a weapon in Sergio's hands made me cringe. At least it wasn't the machete.

"I'll call to you, when I need you…" Tina's sultry voice began to sing as Cha-Cha removed the microphone from the stand and started her performance.

I had seen the real Tina Turner in concert at the Fargodome, and Cha-Cha copied her every move to perfection.

Sergio turned his back to the stage and said in his commando voice. "Line up men."

Everyone rushed and stood at attention in full costume. We watched Cha-Cha dance as Sergio walked up and down our line. He adjusted here and primped there, making sure real life matched the vision for our act in his mind.

"Remember, keep in time with the music and make sure your arm movements are sharp and crisp. No wimpy, wispy, weak-wristed movements. We're men, right?" he instructed over the blaring music.

A weak round of yeahs greeted him.

"What was that?" he demanded.

"Yes, drill sergeant, sir," I said, loud and firmly.

Sergio nodded. "Good." He turned around and looked on stage. "Live your dream now honey, because you don't stand a chance, not even on *RuPaul's Drag Race*."

"At least she didn't do Diana Ross," I said.

"She can't do Tina Turner either," Sergio replied. "Maybe she should've picked *The Acid Queen*. That's more her style. Simply the best. Ha."

Skinny David said, "At least it wasn't *Proud Mary*." He paused for a second and started to laugh. "Do you get it? Proud Mary?" He continued to laugh as the others chuckled nervously with him.

"No one calls anyone 'Mary' anymore," Sergio whispered to me and rolled his eyes.

I looked around the back stage area. A full-length mirror stood off to the side. My reflection stared back at me, but I didn't recognize myself. The yellow hard hat rode low on my head, while the mirrored sunglasses covered my eyes and most of my face. The white T-shirt clung to my body, even more tightly after Sergio had folded and tucked it into my underwear, before I could protest.

A hammer, a screwdriver, and a tape measure hung from my utility belt, which rode low on my hips. No wonder carpenters always revealed butt crack with all this weight pulling their pants down. I tugged my loose jeans up, higher on my hips. Quickly, I looked around to make sure Sergio still had his back to me. If I had left them where he had adjusted them, they'd have fallen off in the middle of our act. Maybe that was Sergio's plan.

"You're the best…" Tina's voice faded as Cha-Cha bowed forward, leaning over her high heels and spreading her arms out to the side. Whoops and hollers rose from the crowd as thunderous applause reverberated through the night air.

Mike reached over and retrieved the microphone. He stepped back and waited as Cha-Cha took her final bow. He clapped his hands together, around the microphone, and slowly made his way to the center of the stage. "How was that?" he asked.

Cha-Cha stepped back and disappeared behind the back curtain.

The main curtain fell, and Mike remained out in front to work the crowd.

"Places," Sergio said, and pushed Cha-Cha out of the way. Frantically, he pointed to our starting positions.

"All the way from Greenwich Village," Mike shouted into the microphone. "Help me give them a Club Fred welcome… The Village People."

"Break a leg," Cha-Cha sneered.

"Break your neck," Sergio replied.

Cha-Cha stomped her foot down, hard. Her slender heel skidded across the rain slicked stage floor. The impact propelled her shoe off of her foot. Her bare toes emerged as the pump sailed across the back stage and disappeared into a darkened corner. As she stepped forward, she revealed her tan foot to me. Then the same image flashed in my mind, reminding me of something I had seen before. But when? Where?

But before I could recall it, the curtain started to rise. The spotlights swept the floor and the stage lights dimmed, shrouding us in shadows.

Cha-Cha shrieked in rage and raced after her shoe.

The hair on the back of my neck stood on end as a cold shiver ran down my spine. Instead of trying to remember the image, my mind screamed, "What the hell did you get yourself into this time?"

My heart throbbed in time with the intro as *YMCA* started to play.

The curtain rose as the spotlights circled the stage. The backlights slowly intensified, their heat burning the chilling effect of my nerves off my spine. The horns blasted their song and the spotlights stopped. One spotlight trained directly on me and focused its beam into my face. I was blinded. I stood there, frozen, as the music continued to grow and swell.

"On three," Sergio hissed. He swiveled his right leg out to the side as he snapped his fingers in time with each blast of the horns. "One… two… three."

"Young man…" burst out of the speakers, and the six of us stepped forward, following Sergio's lead. Each time "young man" was sung, we took another step forward and swung our hips back and forth.

Despite the hard hat being pulled down low on my head, the mirrored sunglasses did little to decrease the intensity of the blinding light. I shifted slightly to the left, using Sergio to block the glare and enabling me to better follow his lead. I stayed one beat behind each of his movements.

Quickly, the first chorus started, and our arms flew into action, spelling out the letters in the air. My eyes strained to see the crowd through the blinding lights. I thought I saw a wave of arms from the audience, flailing around in time with ours. My heart throbbed louder than the backbeat of the song.

The utility belt and tools slapped my hips with each gyration of my pelvis. I couldn't believe I was doing this. Disco of all things. Was it fear or was my body really able to complete these motions? Maybe I was fooling myself and this wasn't going as well as I thought, and maybe I was making a complete ass out of myself.

But, what else was new?

I didn't have time to worry about it. The next stanza of the song started, and we were off again.

Time fused with light and sound. The stage vibrated with energy and the thunderous disco beat.

As the final chorus repeated, the six of us split into two groups. Our arms were still flapping in time, spelling out letters, as we backed away from the audience and away from each other. Logan, Sergio, and I headed to the left, while Tom and the two Davids veered right. The sides of the stage loomed closer. We were almost done. The crowd roared with applause as the curtain hit the floor.

I exhaled.

We were done. It was over. We survived.

Or so I thought.

Sergio turned to face Logan and me, a huge smile forming on his face. "You guys did it." Then his smile died, and he stopped.

Logan and I turned to see what had happened.

Cha-Cha stood behind us, rocking her foot on a stiletto heel, tapping her toe on the stage.

Mike's voice boomed from the speakers. "Was that something or what? Here at Club Fred, we spare no expense to bring you the best in live entertainment."

I was torn. I wanted to correct Mike and tell him he wasn't paying me anything at all, but Cha-Cha's stance meant business.

Mike continued, "For our next act, put your hands together to welcome The Bondage Boys!"

The crowd screamed and clapped as "Ahhhhhhh, Love to love you, baby…" moaned from the speakers in Donna Summer's sultry voice. The curtain rose, and the back of the stage moved forward, blocking our view of stage right. The floor moved forward. Two shrouded shapes stood center stage as the spotlights blazed to life. They pulled back their monk hoods, and the pierced guys from our Club Fred check-in emerged, standing face to face, staring at each other.

The magnetic boys' shrouds slowly dropped to the floor with a zip of silky fabric across their skin. Underneath were bands of black leather crisscrossing their bodies, strategically covering private parts, but exposing almost everything else. Pierced flesh with rings, loops, and bar bells protruded from everywhere and everything. And I mean everything. Form-fitting leather jockstraps revealed silver rings protruding from slits in the pouches.

I didn't want to know where those rings were attached.

The scent of watermelon assaulted my nose again. I pulled my gaze from the horrific sight on stage, and turned my attention to Sergio and Cha-Cha.

"What is your problem?" Sergio demanded.

"Whatever do you mean?" Cha-Cha batted her long eyelashes.

"You know damn well what I mean. You've been a royal bitch ever since I met you."

Another wave of watermelon hit me, followed by the image of that long, tan leg and foot. This time, it was sitting next to mine.

"I saw him first, and you took him away from me," she shrieked at Sergio, but her eyes bore into me.

Logan backed away from us, trying to avoid the tirade.

Sergio looked at her confused. "What? Who are you talking about? Him?" He pointed at me. "Are you talking about Taylor?"

Her sculpted nail pointed toward Sergio. "Everywhere I go, you're right behind me. I've tried to get to know him," she motioned toward me, "but you're stalking and blocking me, preventing me from talking to him." She reached for the purse slung over her shoulder. "But I'm going to put a stop to it," she flipped the clasp open, "once and for all."

Sergio watched her every move.

Cha-Cha flipped the lid open on her purse and slid her hand inside. "You'll be sorry," is all she said.

Then, my memory flashed and played before me. That tan

foot sitting next to me on the plane here, and the watermelon lotion applied to maintain the tan. Cha-Cha couldn't have killed Duane. She was on the plane next to me. "Wait!" I held up my hand, stepping forward to stop Sergio and Cha-Cha, but I was too late.

Sergio rushed her at full speed, just as her hand emerged from the purse. His weight hit her, full force, propelling both of them backward. Their bodies slammed into the railing at the back of the stage. Both of their breaths were expelled from the impact as the great force threw them over the top bar, where they dangled, each one struggling to right himself. The small of Cha-Cha's back hugged the railing; her head flung back with an unearthly shriek.

Sergio straddled her, clinging to the bar with both of his hands. They teetered back and forth, threatening to fall off into empty space.

"Sergio! She's not the one!" I yelled, rushing forward and trying to pull him off.

But Sergio's feet caught his balance, dropped from the bar, and landed on the stage like a cat. In one fluid motion, he reached down and grabbed hold of one of Cha-Cha's ankles and pulled it up.

With her center of gravity and weight upset, Cha-Cha wasn't able to maintain her balance on the railing any longer. She started to topple over backward, her arms and legs kicking and clawing for a hold. The cigarette she had pulled from her purse flipped out of her hand as she struggled to find a grasp.

Sergio did nothing to stop her fall.

I pushed past him, trying to catch her leg, but in her attempts to right herself, she kicked me, full force in the chest as I approached. The blow drove the breath out of me. My hand, which had caught hold of her ankle, released, and Cha-Cha tumbled over the railing with a shriek.

"What are you doing?" Sergio asked. "Have you gone nuts? She tried to kill us."

"She wasn't trying to kill us," I said.

"Correction, she was trying to kill me."

I looked over the railing. Cha-Cha lay on a pile of palm fronds and discarded costumes. Her chest rose and fell, but otherwise, she wasn't moving.

I turned to face Sergio. "She, I mean he, sat next to me on the plane ride here. I remember her, I mean, his lotion and how tan he was. I never spoke to him or her, or whatever. At least, I don't remember. I think I was still in shock over the trip and upset about coming to this resort. It must've been denial about where Molly had sent me."

"What?" Sergio asked, confusion covering his face.

"Cha-Cha's not the killer. She couldn't be. She arrived here when I did. There's no way she could've been stalking Duane. She wasn't even here yet."

"But the note…?" Sergio paused and turned to stare at a stunned Logan. "So, who does that leave?"

Logan tried to smile at Sergio, but all he did was shrug his shoulders. He turned around to something that moved behind him.

"I know! I know who did it!" Sergio exclaimed.

But before he could say another word, a shadow rose from behind Sergio and swung something down toward his head.

Logan saw the movement and reacted. He jumped behind Sergio, trying to shield him. The shadow arced down. A sickening hollow splat sounded. Logan's face took on a startled expression as his body crumbled to the stage floor.

My legs started to bend in an attempt to kneel down to help him, but Sergio belatedly reacted to the attack and recoiled, driving me back into an upright position.

As Sergio and I backed up, we watched as the dark form moved forward. It stepped over Logan's prone body. A spotlight from the stage swung in our direction and illuminated Geoff's face. His gun, which he had just used to pistol whip Logan, pointed at us.

"You two, stay where you are," he commanded and aimed the gun's barrel at Sergio's heart.

But before we could move, "Bastard!" erupted in an ear-splitting shriek from underneath the stage. Cha-Cha popped up and threw one leg over the lower railing.

All three of us turned to stare at her disheveled state. She ripped the Tina Turner wig off her head and tossed it behind her. She reached below the stage and brought up one of her pumps. She cocked her arm back and hurtled it at Sergio with all of her might.

Sergio dodged and pushed me to the side. We both ducked as the shoe flew overhead. It sailed through the air and struck Geoff on the forearm. The pointed heel hit his hand, knocking the gun from his grasp.

Sergio lunged forward and pushed Geoff backward.

With the suddenness of the assault, Geoff lost his balance and skidded across the wet stage.

In her struggle to pull herself up, Cha-Cha lost her grip on the railing, and she dropped behind the stage with another scream.

In all the commotion, Sergio grabbed my arm and pulled. "*Run!*"

He didn't have to tell me twice.

Sergio pulled me down the side stairs of the stage. My hard hat flew off and tumbled down behind us. I reached up and whipped off my sunglasses, throwing them to the side. In this darkness, I needed all the help I could get.

The rain had finally stopped, and everything appeared black from the wetness. A cement path wound its way between the stage and a row of chaise lounges. It ascended and circled toward the back of the resort. As we raced along the walkway, puddles of water splashed under each step.

"Where are we going?" I called to him.

"I don't know. We have to get the hell out of here."

The path rounded a palm tree and ended at a staircase. The steps traversed the slope and headed to the far side of the resort. Water cascaded down the steps as we sloshed up.

"This must be a service passage," Sergio said, but didn't look back.

"I don't think they'll mind." I followed close at his heels.

A shot rang out behind us, exploding chips of concrete from the stair we had just stepped off. Fine bits of debris cut through my jeans, burying themselves into the back of my legs.

Sergio dashed off the side of the staircase. "Come on!" he shouted, running behind a palm tree.

I followed. My legs sunk into the sodden earth as the ground slanted sharply down. I struggled for traction across an incline covered with plants and grass, adding to the treachery of the slope.

I ran behind a palm tree just as another bullet burrowed into the wood. The trunk splintered, but the bullet didn't exit. "Holy shit!"

Our path veered upward and diagonally, away from the stairs.

Our feet slipped with each step. The mucky ground sucked at our feet, slowing our progress.

"We need to find cover," Sergio shouted.

A laundry cart lay on its side halfway down the incline. As we ran above it, the earth suddenly gave way. The whole rain-soaked slope pulled away and started to slide down.

We lunged forward and grabbed onto the nearest shrubs. The mud pulled down the cart and the ground where we had been standing. My feet slipped out from under me, and I slammed into the ground, knocking the breath from my lungs. If I hadn't been hanging on to the bush, I would've followed.

Sergio reached over, grabbed my belt, and stabilized me. Our knees dug into the ground as we struggled to find a hold. We crawled several feet over the terrain. Finally, the earth leveled out and formed a narrow shelf that led to the nearest building. The cement foundation jutted out from the ground and formed the outside walkway between buildings and into the bowels of the resort. We used it as our runway inside. Just as we passed through the archway, a bullet ricocheted along the walls.

Which building were we in? In the dark and in our panic, I couldn't remember the layout of the resort. As our footfalls echoed along the cement floor, I asked, "Where are we going? We can't go back to our room. It'll be the first place he'd look."

Sergio slowed slightly, so I could run alongside. "I don't know."

"We need to be where people are. We should never have left the talent show."

"I guess I panicked." Sergio exhaled loudly. "My only thought was to get the hell out of there."

"Maybe we should try to make our way back to the stage."

"I don't know if we can," Sergio said, breathlessly.

"At least at the talent show, we had witnesses."

Footsteps echoed down the hallway behind us, just as we turned the corner at a ninety-degree angle. Another shot echoed through the dark passageway.

I pushed Sergio forward. "He's getting closer."

"Over there." He pointed to a door with "Laundry" printed on it. We headed toward it, and he pulled it open. Shoving the brooms and mops out of the way, he motioned to the laundry chute. "There," was all he said.

I didn't question him. I dove through the flapping door and landed on the aluminum slide. My body hit and immediately began to pick up speed as I descended down the ramp. Behind me, another bang resounded as Sergio dove in after. Our bodies bumped and banged along the chute. The noise thundered and intensified in the narrow space.

The slide quickly disappeared from underneath me, and I slammed into the concrete floor. The force of the descent propelled me across the cement, scraping the skin off my forearms.

Sergio landed on top of me, his weight and momentum shoving me further along.

In the dim light, we struggled to our feet, our sore bodies protesting as we limped to the end of the tunnel. Trying to catch our breath, we watched and waited to see if Geoff followed us down the slide.

"Maybe he didn't hear us sliding down," Sergio whispered, hopefully.

But we both knew how loud it had been, and I doubted that Geoff had missed it. "We need to keep moving, so we don't get trapped down here."

Sergio pointed to the rows of washers and dryers. "Should we hide in here?"

"It's a dead end," I said, and pushed him through the door and into the tunnel. I motioned toward the stairs. "We need to get out of here. Head to the kitchen."

Small light bulbs glowed along the tunnel's walls this time. Even with the lights back on, they did little to illuminate the gloom. We pressed our bodies against the wall as we headed to the stairs. Just as my foot hit the bottom step, the kitchen door was flung open, and a shadow blocked the light coming down.

Before Geoff could see us, I stopped and backed up. Sergio ran into me, but I spun him around and covered his mouth with my hand. I pointed down the garbage tunnel, and gently pushed him in that direction. Maybe we could find another way out down there.

Sergio nodded. As we silently ran down the tunnel, he tossed me the gun from his holster. "I have a plan."

The gun was metal and heavy—it appeared to be real. Fumbling, I almost dropped it but managed to slip it into my belt.

As we neared the end of the corridor, Sergio whispered, "I'll search in there for something we can use to hold him off. You see if you can find another way out of here." And then he disappeared into the small utility room.

I scanned the tunnel for a trapdoor. As I looked around, I heard Sergio rummaging in the small room. Plastic bottles clunked and rattled against each other. Something scraped along a wall as it slid down and hit the floor with a resounding tap.

My heart stopped. Nothing like letting Geoff know where we were.

I continued on to the end of the tunnel, frantically looking to see if there was another way to escape.

The water at the end was slapping against the walls and spilling over the lip of the garbage pit. The tide must have been coming in or going out. A thunderous beating throbbed along the tunnel. Or was that my heartbeat?

I looked at the water. Maybe we could dive in and swim out of here. But how long would that take? Could Sergio and I hold our breath that long? Duane's body had made it out of here, but he was dead. Could Sergio and I do the same? Or would we end up like Duane? We'd have to try something. Our options were running out.

As I turned to go back and get Sergio, the thought struck me—could he even swim?

He had gotten seasick on the boat and didn't go snorkeling. I paused, turning back to the water. Maybe I should just go for help. But that would leave him down here, alone with Geoff. I didn't think there was enough time to take that chance. I had to ask Sergio if he knew how to swim.

As I neared the utility room, Geoff's voice echoed down the tunnel. "Freeze! Put your hands where I can see them." The light blinked out and Geoff's rapidly approaching footsteps echoed down the tunnel.

I stood frozen, trying to decide what to do. Should I turn around and dive into the water, race into the side room, or wait for Sergio to emerge? But if I went in after him, I could tip off Geoff to his hiding place.

Before I could decide anything, the lights came back on, and Geoff filled the tunnel. He pointed the gun at me.

My mind reeled. How many bullets were left? How many shots had he taken? It wasn't as if I knew how many bullets his gun held. Wait. I remembered. Sergio had given me a gun. Was it real or only a prop? I stood still, quietly pulled it out of my belt, and aimed it at him.

Geoff came to a stop when he saw my gun. He took one more step forward. Mocking me, he asked, "Where's your friend? Did he abandon you?" He leveled his gun and trained it on my chest.

"He's getting help as we speak," my voice croaked. The gun trembled in my hand.

"I didn't see him go up the stairs to the kitchen. I've been working here ever since I left Miami, and I haven't found another way out." He motioned around the tunnel with his gun and then he swung it back at me.

"He never came down here."

Geoff's smile flattened. He cocked his head to the side and

tried to look behind me. "I bet that isn't a real gun." He took another step forward.

I swallowed hard, but stood firm, trying hard to think.

Out of the corner of my eye, I saw a shadow in the utility room doorway. I forced my eyes back to Geoff and his gun.

Maybe he sensed it, or maybe he noticed that my gaze had flickered to the side, because Geoff suddenly turned to stare into the room.

Sergio burst out. As he flew through the air, he tossed the contents of the bucket he carried at Geoff. The wave washed over Geoff's gun arm, while the rest of the fluid hit him square in the chest. It soaked his shirt and ran into his pants, before splashing in a pool around his feet. The smell of something like paint thinner or gasoline hung in the air.

"Ha. Now, you can't shoot anyone, or you'll ignite yourself," Sergio said, as he landed in front of me.

"Oh, you think so?" Geoff asked. He swung his gun away from me and pointed it at Sergio. A sneer crossed his mouth as he pulled the trigger.

A white flash exploded from the end of the gun. Sergio clutched his chest and crumpled to the ground.

I fell to my knees. "Sergio!" croaked out of my mouth. I dropped the gun and landed hard on the concrete floor. My fingers searched Sergio's neck for a pulse, but as soon as they made contact, Geoff pressed the gun's hot barrel against my forehead. I flinched from the heat.

"Stand up," he commanded, pressing the gun harder against my head.

The hot metal burned my skin. My hands went up as I slowly rose to my feet.

"Don't make any sudden moves. You know I'll use this." He waved the gun in my face.

I looked down at Sergio. My mind screamed at me to run for help, now. Then my eyes darted to Sergio's discarded gun on the floor.

Geoff shook his head. "You're going to take a little swim, just like your buddy did." He motioned behind me.

My eyes glanced down to Sergio.

"Not him, the other guy. The one you found on the beach, but this one will follow." A cold smile crossed his lips.

I swallowed hard. "Duane wasn't my buddy. I didn't even know him."

"Liar!" Geoff spat. "I saw him slip you that note when you arrived."

"I just found that. He was pleading for his life with that note, but I thought he was hitting on me."

"What? You're not…" Geoff gasped and almost lowered his gun. Confusion played across his face. "Why did you come to this resort?" he demanded.

I took a step backward. "A friend of mine booked me here. I didn't know anything about this place before I got here."

"What? You're not a cop?" He took a step forward.

"No," I said, and took another step back. My eyes fell on Sergio's still form at Geoff's feet. He hadn't moved, and from this angle, I couldn't tell if he was breathing.

"You're not working undercover?" Geoff cocked his head to the side. "And he's not either?" Geoff stepped over Sergio's body.

"No. I'm an occupational therapist, and he's a hair dresser."

"Like I believe that one." Geoff tossed his head back and laughed. "He's got a real uniform. If you're not cops, why do you have all of those files in your room?"

"I found those files in Duane's room, when I searched it. They were in his briefcase. I wanted to find out something about him, but I found those files and saw one with my name on it, so I took it, and the other ones with familiar names."

"But your file was empty," he stopped, and tapped the side of his head with the gun. "I thought you were working undercover with Duane, that's why it was empty."

"You're the cop, I'm not."

"Internal Affairs was investigating me. I ended up getting suspended before they found out…" he took another step forward.

"What?" I asked.

He smiled. "Our scheme."

"Yours and Gary's?"

"You got it. Gary was my informant while I worked for the Miami police force. When I was suspended, I took this security job, but he followed me here with an idea. He would sign onto different tour groups that brought their guests here. During their week, he would find out things about them. Who had a fat wallet, who liked a little slap and tickle on the side, who liked a little blow for their noses. We'd find them what they wanted…" A gleam shimmered in Geoff's eyes.

"That's why you were taking pictures all week!"

"Exactly."

"Embarrassing photos from a vacation would net some nice money." I said.

Geoff smiled. "You got it, but Gary got greedy. He kept demanding more and more money, and when I refused, he threatened to expose me." He sneered. "So I gave him a little extra to shut him up. The whole time I was plotting to get rid of him on this trip, but then you showed up. Everywhere I looked, you were hanging around and following him, so I figured you were trying to get him to turn evidence against me, to lighten his sentence."

"You were the one who followed me on the jungle cruise," I accused.

He nodded. "I watched you get on that boat. I should've stayed just a little bit longer. I never figured you would've moved." He shook his head, "I waited forever to throw that damn snake on you, but you had switched seats. I was hoping it would scare you out of here."

"But it landed on someone else." I looked behind him and saw Sergio still hadn't moved.

Geoff nodded slowly.

"What about Duane?" I asked, wishing I could stop Sergio's bleeding and get him medical help.

"He was a private investigator, working undercover, but he was getting too close to discovering our scheme. I heard he had files on all of the guests, and that he was using bank records to identify who our new targets were going to be. When I found those files in your room I thought you were working with him. He had been following Gary for months, and he was trying to find out who was working with him."

"And you killed him?" I asked.

"No, Gary did that."

"But you killed Gary."

"He was getting sloppy. Besides, I didn't need him anymore," he shrugged his shoulders. "Thanks for your help."

"What?"

"You and your friend knocked him out for me. You couldn't have made it any easier for me if you tried."

"What about John?" I asked, but didn't want to know.

"The model? That was my mistake," he smiled. "I thought he was you. He looked just like you. He even had on the same clothes, but with that plastic bag over his head, I didn't recognize him until it was too late. I heard you calling to your friend to wait for you, and then I looked down and couldn't believe I had the wrong guy. So I got the hell out of there."

I took another step back. My foot hit the lip of the water pool, and my shoes slipped. My arms reached down to stabilize my legs. My hands brushed my hips and hit the tool belt that hung there. My fingers brushed against the hammer on the right and circled around the screwdriver on my left.

My right hand curled around the head of the hammer.

"Geoff? Are you down there?" Mike's voice echoed down the tunnel.

Geoff turned slightly to look over his shoulder.

That was all I needed. I pulled the hammer out of my belt and swung it at Geoff. My aim was off. The hammer struck the side of his arm, but the blow knocked him off balance.

In his attempt to remain upright, his gun arm swung to the side and his finger pulled the trigger. The gun went off with a blinding explosion, and the bullet ricocheted off the tunnel's wall. Suddenly, the lights went out and flashed back on. Sparks shot across the ceiling as the lights started to strobe on and off. The crackle of electricity filled the small space.

Geoff flinched away from the shower of sparks and threw himself even further off balance. His feet slipped on the wet floor, and he fell hard, landing on his hands and knees. As he hit the floor, the gun flew from his hand and skidded across the cement toward Sergio.

I ducked and veered away from the water and Geoff. As I moved to the right, I ripped the screwdriver from my belt and held it out in front of me. My right hand joined my left and clamped around it.

Mike shouted down the tunnel, "What's going on down there?"

Geoff crawled into the puddle of lighter fluid and paint thinner as he searched for his lost firearm.

In one of the strobing flashes, he spotted the gun lying in front of Sergio. Geoff turned to see where I was before scrambling after it.

As I stepped forward with the screwdriver poised in front of me, a spark ignited into a flame just behind where the gun lay. The spark came from Sergio's lighter, the one he had stolen from the dining room. He hunched forward, one arm pressed tightly against his chest while the other one held the flame.

"Hey, asshole," he croaked, just as Geoff dove for his gun in the center of the puddle. Sergio brought the lighter down to the pool of flammable liquids. "Go to Hell," he growled, and threw his body back as hard as he could.

The flame ignited the fumes with a whoosh, and fire shot across the puddle. The whoosh echoed down the tunnel like a shot from a cannon.

Stumbling back, I watched as the flames rolled along the floor, shot straight up to the ceiling, and surrounded Geoff. The fire licked and rolled across his clothing, which burst into flames. I watched in horror as Geoff lit up like a human torch.

Sergio hugged his chest with both arms and rolled away from the inferno, disappearing into the utility room.

In the center of the blazing puddle, Geoff screamed as his hand found the gun. Blindly, he pulled the trigger. Shots rang out in all directions against the roar of the fire.

Geoff continued to shoot his gun at every shadow as the flames engulfed him. The fire's roar was deafening, mixed with his screams. He frantically patted at his body, trying to extinguish the fire as he turned to face me. The skin on his face was starting to blister and peel from the heat, and his clothes melted to his body. Inhuman, guttural sounds emanated from his throat. He pointed the gun at me and pulled the trigger again.

The hammer clicked. This time the gun was empty. He looked down at the useless gun in his burning hand and hurtled it at me.

The small area was hot. The smell of burning gas and flesh hung in the air. Smoke filled the space, making it hard to breath. My eyes watered from the fumes and smoke, and I ducked to the side as the gun and a ball of fire sailed over my head. It splashed into the water behind.

Geoff screamed and rushed me, completely ablaze.

In my attempt to get out of his way, my foot slipped on the wet floor, and I landed on my butt.

Geoff's flaming body roared with the added oxygen as he ran at me.

My arms rose up, defensively, in an attempt to protect me from the heat, the fire, and his assault. Both hands wrapped around the screwdriver, and I braced for the fiery impact.

Geoff dove at me, blindly. Ignoring what I held.

My back flattened on the concrete floor, as my feet rose up for extra protection.

Geoff's flaming body hit me. A wall of heat engulfed me, taking away my breath. The fire scorched my hands and knuckles, and the hair on them ignited. I felt the screwdriver slide into his chest. A warm wet wave washed over my hands. My feet connected with his abdomen. As the heat and his weight pressed down against me, I pushed back against his momentum with all of my might. My feet kicked, my arms pushed, and Geoff's body was propelled over me into the garbage pit. My hands let go of the screwdriver and he hurtled overhead. The wave of fire disappeared as fast as it arrived. I rolled over onto my stomach trying to put out the fire. I gasped in a deep breath of black, smoky air and coughed.

Seconds later, the water hissed as the flames extinguished around Geoff's body. The force of his dive sent a wave of cool brine back, washing over me. I sprang to my feet, patting out the flames, and crouched low, ready for Geoff's return.

I waited, choking in the smoke. My burning eyes squinted in the haze and sudden darkness. Tears rolled down my cheeks. A fire still burned behind me, but the one that had flown overhead was gone. I fisted my scorched hands, ready for the next attack. None came.

Stepping forward, I saw Geoff's body floating face down in the water. His whole back smoldered. One small flame flickered out on his shirt. The water beneath him turned darker. The tide rocked him back and forth. His body slowly sank deeper, below the water's surface.

A hand grabbed my shoulder. I yelled and spun around. Was Mike involved in all of this too?

My arm shot forward, but I stopped it in mid-air as Sergio's smudged face materialized from the black smoke.

"Whoa!" He held up one of his arms in protection, his face screwed up in pain.

"Are you all right?" I asked. My hands ran over his chest and searched for a bleeding wound. His policeman's shirt was dark and damp, but I didn't feel anything warm or sticky.

Sergio's legs crumpled beneath him, and he dropped to the floor.

I hovered over him and tried to assess how badly he was hurt.

"You look just like Jamie Lee Curtis in *Halloween*," he said, motioning to my blood-splattered clothing. "Too bad we didn't find the machete. It would've completed your outfit." He winced once, which made him cough hard. He grimaced and clutched his chest in pain.

"He shot you," I said, and ripped his shirt open to see where to apply pressure to stop the bleeding. I looked down at his chest, and said, "I don't understand."

Sergio's chest was covered with a Kevlar bulletproof vest. A single bullet was nestled in a small depression in the center of the vest.

"What the hell are you wearing that thing for?" I demanded.

"Are you complaining?" he moaned.

"No. I just don't understand. Did you think someone was going to shoot at us in the talent show?" I resisted the urge to smack him. "And why didn't you warn me?"

He coughed once and then grabbed his chest and rolled over onto his side. As the pain subsided, he rolled onto his back, and his eyes met mine. "I wanted to look buff on stage, fill out my uniform, and my chest looked so...pathetic..." He paused. "I thought if I wore this," he touched the vest, "it would make my chest look bigger."

"Well, I'm glad you're so vain. It just saved your life and mine."

"Thanks," he rubbed the spot where the bullet had hit, "but let's just keep that little secret between us, okay?"

"It's not like anyone is going to believe me about this trip anyway."

I picked the bullet out of the vest and handed it to him. "You may want to keep this as a souvenir of our trip."

He held his hand over his chest. "I think I already have one, if this pain is any indication."

Mike raced down the tunnel with a fire extinguisher in hand. He quickly put out the fire and pointed the nozzle at us. "What are you guys doing down here?" he demanded. "Trying to burn the place down?"

We both pointed to the pool of water behind us.

Mike walked to the edge and looked down. "What am I supposed to see?" I helped Sergio to his feet, and he leaned against me for support. We joined Mike at the edge and peered into the water.

Geoff's body was gone.

The next morning, *Never Can Say Goodbye* blended into *Don't Leave Me This Way* as Sergio and I worked our way across the lobby to check out. Men milled around with suitcases, while others waited in lines for the buses. The sun blazed down on the damp guests as I kicked my American Tourister bag forward. Sergio pulled his sunglasses down on his face.

Despite the hurricane, the majority of vacationers looked happy and rested, completely unaware of what had happened behind the scenes. Smiles and animated conversations resounded as the lines moved slowly forward.

"It looks like everything is finally over." Sergio looked around the lobby. "Hey, wait a minute!" He paused. "We never did figure out who took your Speedo."

"I haven't checked your bag yet," I teased.

Sergio placed his hands on his hips and rolled his eyes. "Speedos don't do anything for me."

"It sure made an impression on you when we were unpacking," I reminded him.

"I was just surprised that you owned one," he said.

"Sure," I said, eyeing him suspiciously.

"All I can say is that I'm glad it's yours and not mine."

"And what do you mean by that?" I asked.

"Can you just imagine what someone is doing with your Speedo?" A shiver racked his body, and he grabbed his tiny chest and winced.

"That's what you get for being such a jerk," I said. The same thought had crossed my mind, but I wasn't ever going to see it again, let alone wear it for that matter. "Thanks for that wonderful image."

As the first bus left, a white van with a red cross painted on the side pulled up in front of the resort. Mike emerged from the front office and held the door open. Two staff members carried out a stretcher with Cha-Cha lying in the center. She was propped up on a pile of pillows, giving orders the whole way into the van.

As the men loaded her in, her Tina Turner wig slipped off her head.

"My wig. I need…" and one of the ambulance doors bumped her head. "Ouch! You stupid…"

Mike picked up her wig and tossed it in.

"Be careful with that. That's a Tina…" and the other door slammed shut, muting her.

"I thought she'd be flying out of here, "Sergio said.

"She didn't look like she needed to be air lifted, now did she?"

"I didn't mean by air ambulance, I meant on a broom," he said with a smirk.

Before I could respond, Sean pushed and waved his arms as he chased the Magnetic Boys through the crowd. "Wait. Wait you guys. I have the perfect job for you."

The men in the lobby parted as the three made their way through. The Magnetic Boys paused and turned to hear what Sean had to say. "Picture this if you will." He spread his arms wide to the side. "You guys dressed in those leather outfits, the ones that you wore on stage in the talent show, and the title above you will read *Sons of Edward Scissorhands.*"

The Magnetic Boys turned, looked at each other, and walked away from Sean without a word.

He stood there for a second. "What about *The Pirates of the Piercings?*" he called after them and broke into a trot, trying to catch up.

"I guess Tom told him the news," Sergio said. He glanced over my shoulder and pointed. "Speak of the devil."

Turning around, we watched as Tom approach. He held up his camera when he saw us.

We waved him over. When he neared, Sergio smiled. "I see Sean's scouting out new talent."

"I pity them if they're foolish enough to sign with him," Tom said.

"What about you? Do you have any plans?" I asked.

"I think I'm going to take it slow and see what I can afford. After checking with my financial planner, I'll see what business I can get into."

"Maybe you could move to Sioux Falls," Sergio suggested.

Tom looked at me, and I held up my hands. "It's the Midwest," I warned.

Tom smiled and nodded. "The villagers would run me out of town with burning torches, right?"

I nodded. "You got the picture."

"But you could come and visit, anytime," Sergio offered.

"My wife and I would love to meet this Molly you guys have been talking about," he said.

"I'm sure you would," I said. "But seriously, if you ever want to get away from sunny California and see the flat plains and prairie, you're more than welcome to come and visit. You can stay at my house or his," I pointed to Sergio.

"He has a dog," Sergio said, screwing up his face.

"I love dogs," Tom said.

"I could get a dog," Sergio added, quickly, "that is if my landlord would allow pets in the apartment complex."

Tom laughed. "Don't make me an offer that you guys don't mean. I just may surprise you one day and take you up on it. Now, how would you explain that to your neighbors?"

"I doubt your movies are playing in Sioux Falls. They may be playing at his home." I glanced at Sergio. "But I know we can't get them to play a foreign film there, let alone…"

"Say no more," Tom smiled.

"I saw…" Sergio stopped and flushed. "I mean I think I may have seen one of your movies when it was playing…"

I looked at Sergio and his pale complexion took on a shade of red.

"Never mind," he squeaked out.

"I've got to run," Tom said, pointing to one of the buses. He reached into his pocket and pulled out a card. "Here's my address, phone number, and e-mail, if you want to keep in touch." He offered it to me.

Sergio drooled.

Tom turned to look at him. "I have one for you too." He reached into his pocket and handed it to him. He held up his camera. "A quick picture?"

"Sure," we said in unison.

Tom grabbed a guy walking by and asked him to snap a few shots of us. The man did, and Tom shook my hand and gave Sergio a quick hug and was gone.

A stunned Sergio walked in a daze we handed in our room keys and signed the check out forms. As we turned to leave, Logan made his way through the crowd, his head wrapped in gauze. "I was hoping I'd catch you before you left."

"Aren't you going?" I asked.

Logan pulled us out of the crowd to get some privacy. "I'm staying here an extra week. I haven't completed as much of my book as I had originally hoped, because of you two. Thanks for helping me find out that it was Geoff and Gary that had been blackmailing me. I hired Duane months ago to find out who was doing it. He was the one who suggested I come here to help flush out the blackmailer. He had been following similar cases and thought we could solve it here."

Logan looked around at the departing guests. "When I didn't see Duane at the resort, I figured he didn't come. I never thought he had been murdered. Anyway, thanks for figuring it out." Logan handed me a sheet of paper. "I thought you'd like to see this. It's my dedication page for *Kill Me! Kill Me! Kill Me! (A Man After Midnight)*."

It read:

> *This book is dedicated to*
> *Hurricane Brian, Club Fred,*
> *and all the men at the Mexican resort.*
> *But a special thanks goes out to*
> *Taylor, Sergio, Tom,*
> *Cha-Cha, David, and David,*
> *who made a natural disaster,*
> *worse!*
> *Thanks guys!*

I smiled as I read it, and then handed it to Sergio.

"I wrote my phone number and address on there. I hope we'll keep in touch. I'd like to stop off in Sioux Falls and do a book signing on my tour for this one." He held up the bag with his laptop. "I feel obliged, if you know what I mean."

"Cool, I hope you do, Logan. We need more authors to come and sign their books in our town. We'll even take you out to dinner," Sergio said, "Taylor's treat."

"You're on." Logan clapped me on the shoulder. "See you soon." He left.

"Take care," I called after him.

"I'll have to get busy and start reading his books," Sergio said.

"I'm sure you'll like them," I said.

Don't Leave Me This Way mixed and turned into *Please Don't Go.* I frowned when I caught sight of Mike making his way over to us. "Don't look now."

"What's up?" Sergio asked as he turned. "Oh great, just what we need." He stiffly bent over and grabbed his suitcase. "Let's get out of here."

"Hi, guys. I was hoping I'd catch you before you left. I wanted to let you know that we found Geoff this morning. He washed up on the beach, just like Duane."

"Well." Sergio pushed me toward the buses. "We should be going."

"Oh, wait. That wasn't why I was looking for you." He slowly brought his arm, which he had been holding behind his back, in front of him. In his hand, he held an anatomically correct golden statue of a man. "With all the excitement at the talent show and after, you left before they announced the winner."

Sergio's eyes bulged out of his head. He swallowed hard. "We won?"

Mike nodded. "First place." He handed him the trophy.

Sergio tentatively reached for the award.

Mike smiled. "The rest of the guys wanted you two to have it. Congratulations."

"I don't know what to say." Sergio looked at me. "We can share it, if you want... Six months with you and..."

I looked at the figure. "No thanks. I think you earned that one all by yourself. Besides, it won't fit on my mantle."

Mike turned to me. "I wish I had one for you, too."

"No, that's okay." I held up my hands, warding off the thought. "I think I've had enough of Club Fred for a while."

Mike smiled. "Is there anything else I can do to thank you?"

Seeing the expression on Sergio's face, I motioned to the statue. "I think you've already done it."

"Has your vacation been everything you hoped for?" Mike asked.

"I won't go that far," I said, throwing my bag's strap over my shoulder.

"What can I do to make your trip everything you wanted it to be?" he asked.

Molly's voice echoed in my mind, and her words came out of my mouth, "Give me my money back." I smiled.

"Sorry, I can't do that, but I can do this." He handed me a white business envelope with the Club Fred logo on it. "I would like to invite your whole act back to perform again next year."

"I'll think about it," I said.

"Not very hard, I'll bet," he teased.

"You got it."

"Well, let me know, if you change your mind," Mike said, and left.

A tear rolled down Sergio's cheek.

"What's wrong?" I asked.

"It's like saying goodbye at the end of summer camp," he said.

"You went to camp?"

He put his hands on his hips. "No. But I could have. I've seen this scene in a movie once or twice before."

"Was Tom starring in it?" I teased.

Sergio ignored my comment and nudged me. "Open up your envelope. I want to see what Mike gave us."

My finger slid under the glued tab and revealed a piece of parchment, tri-folded inside. I removed the sheet and opened it: "This entitles the bearer and a guest to a complimentary week of fun at any of the Club Fred locations."

"Whaa-whoo! We're going back to Club Fred again next year," Sergio yelled, jumping around, waving his trophy. "It'll be so much fun." He stopped and grabbed my arm. "A reunion! Picture it. We could get the whole gang back together. Maybe we could do ABBA next year or Diana Ross and the Supremes!"

I picked up my other bag and started walking toward the bus.

"Wait up," Sergio said, as he bent over and tried to grab his bag. "Hey. Wait a minute." He stopped. "I have a great idea. We could bring Molly with us next year!"

And with those words, I ran.

ABOUT THE AUTHOR

LANCE ZARIMBA is an occupational therapist working in Minneapolis, MN. His mystery, *Vacation Therapy*, is the first book in his "Therapy" series which involves an occupational therapist who solves crimes with the help, but more likely the hindrances of his friends. He also has two children's books: *Oh No, Our Best Friend is a Zombie,* and *Oh No, Our Best Friend is a Vampire.* His short stories are in: *Mayhem in the Midlands,* Pat Dennis' *Who Died in Here? 25 mystery stories of crimes and bathrooms,* Anne Frasier's *Deadly Treats* anthology, Jay Hartmann's *The Killer Wore Cranberry* and several other short stories for Untreed Reads, and eshort stories on Echelon Press. He can be reached at LanceZarimba@yahoo.com.

LaVergne, TN USA
16 March 2011
220362LV00001B/1/P